destination unknown

destination unknown	edited by peter crowther
book design & layout	larry s. friedman
cover illustration	douglas winter

WHITE WOLF
PUBLISHING

White Wolf Publishing
780 Park North Boulevard, Suite 100
Clarkston, GA 30021
World Wide Web Page: www.white-wolf.com

BOREALIS

Table of Contents

destination unknown
MAY THE AURA BE WITH YOU
by Anne McCaffrey

When I was a little girl, we had radio. We also had a grandmother in the house so we couldn't play the radio loudly.

The radio was set in a large desk, raised off the ground by claw feet, and I would wiggle my way underneath—there was just enough room—with one ear right under the speaker so that I could hear the muted sound.

I had my special programmer: *Bobby Benson*, *The Green Hornet*, the plum-voiced *Lone Ranger* (I fell in love with that voice at 10 years old), and I always knew what the Silver Star Ranch, the Green Hornet's home and Cato, and Tonto and Silver and the Lone Ranger himself, all actually *looked* like.

It has often been said that radio made you see better, but it's true. And you were never wrong about the scenery. It was, ineffably, *yours*. Since then, I have seen many new sceneries, creating them easily enough because I *could* see them so clearly: my apprenticeship as a radio listener having primed that pump.

Mind you, some of the worlds we science fiction and fantasy writers create are pretty bizarre. The critical (who evidently know little of the human internal combustion system called 'inspiration') suggest these worlds/ideas/premises are the products of very bad dreams or, perish forbid, the results of experimentation with 'forbidden substances'. But I have had occasional dreams more bizarre than anything I would *dare* to write about.

During those dreams, though the other 'me' knew everything was crazy, the 'me' who was experiencing the dream accepted the oddities as part of that other reality. And while the rational light of day can dispel some dream auras, others lurk in the hearts of the dreamer. Myself, I have only once used a dream as story material but other writers have said that they frequently use such 'scopes' and describe them (pause for a shudder).

5

The writer of fantasy and science fiction tries to evoke that sense of the suspension of reality, at least for the duration of the story and its purpose in being told. I have—and I'm certain you have from time to time—been so taken in by that story-scape that it lingers in the mind, hauntingly, irritatingly, tenaciously... sometimes even frighteningly. Frankly, I take that as the mark of a well-told tale. I have read so many stories that just faded away when I raised my eyes from the printed page that to have a story stay with me and for me to be able to recall its enchantments is a considerable bonus. That story-scape was *real!*

Back in 1967 I wrote a short story about dragons as the good guys, and I have lived in that world for the past twenty-eight years. (That's rather good mileage for an imaginary trip!)

Pern's landscape is as real to me as the Silver Star Ranch, the Texas plains of the Lone Ranger or the metropolis where evil lurks in the hearts of men. Maybe that's the child in me, yearning for the vivid mindscapes evoked by those old radio programmer... a simpler, kinder world, for I'm talking about the late '30s. I do believe that my radio listening was good training for writing my other-world tales.

Whatever! If the reader becomes as addicted to that story as I was during its writing, then I have justified my existence and performance as a writer. Let me assure you that, while I'm writing Pern, you may totally believe that I am genuinely there... experiencing even more details than I have ever been able to include in over 2,000,000 words currently written about the world that circles the Rukbat star.

There are more fabulous worlds to be had here in this book... locations rich and strange and bizarre, and all yours for the taking.

Here are haunted rooms, elevators and mazes, and towns where strange insect life holds sway or ancient powers return to wreak havoc. Here, too, are off-beat worlds which exist beneath the risers of a staircase or deep down in the bowels of the earth, and alien landscapes where one might invoke the power of the angels, discover long-lost musicians or simply commune with deceased relatives.

destination unknown
MAY THE AURA BE WITH YOU

So, take a trip into the domains of other realities. Suspend your everyday cares and concerns, and travel to 16 different story-scapes where, at least for the duration of the story, your stay may be as real and as vivid as the writer intended. Believe what you read... while you read it. And may the aura of that story stay with you as all good stories always do.

At the end, you may be glad that it *was* only a story... but then that's just part of the deal.

Anne McCaffrey
Dragonhold-Underhill

destination unknown
THE CHINA COTTAGE
by Ian Watson

When Adrian Hollowell's mother Joan died suddenly at the age of eighty, black farce wrote a postscript to a life which had hitherto been quiet, self-contained, respectable, and decent.

Adrian and Hazel could hardly be accused, even by themselves, of having neglected Adrian's mother during her last years. Why, just the previous month they had driven the three hundred tedious miles to the north of England to spend a long weekend taking his mother to some of her favorite places in the countryside. And hadn't there been all those Sunday morning phone calls to her, once a week regular as clockwork?

Rather, Joan had isolated herself.

Ever since her husband Ken died a decade earlier, Joan had grieved in a brave and quiet way. She had been waiting to rejoin Ken for ten long years. Hers wasn't the type of grief which leads speedily to one partner following the other. It was a staunch and cloistered grief. Nun-like, Joan might have taken a vow to do nothing special ever again in the absence of Ken. During preceding years of retirement Ken and Joan had taken a dozen long-deferred holidays abroad—to see the Alps, and Italy, and Greece, and even Canada, fulfilling the dreams of a lifetime. They must have also taken at least a couple of thousand photographs, for memory. But now, no more. Although her widowed friend Mary, quite the globetrotter, tried to prevail on Joan to accompany her on a package tour, Adrian's mother refused to leave home; nor would she ever again set up the slide projector and view the color transparencies alone.

Exceptionally, Joan would visit Adrian and Hazel once a year by bus for a long weekend—until a burglar visited her during one such absence. Home, the shrine, had been violated. Joan wouldn't go away again.

Mary continued to call, yet there had never been many friends to speak of. Joan and Ken had been private people. This reticence extended within the home too. Adrian had grown up with only the scantiest notion of what went on at the building society where his father worked, or even, really, what a building society was. His mother and father rarely attended any staff social event. Later, Adrian discovered that his father had dreamed of becoming a branch manager in some county town away from the urban riverside sprawl. However, Joan had refused to leave the little dream home which had been custom-built for her and Ken in the Nineteen-Thirties—at a time when the view was of cornfields and of the sea a couple of miles beyond. Latterly, the view was entirely of a public housing estate and tarmac.

Farce began shortly after a policeman came to the Hollowells' door in their village of thatched cottages, autumn dahlias and chrysanthemums all in bloom. It was just four weeks since they had taken Adrian's mother to one beauty spot which she had never thought she would see again, so she said. Earlier that evening, Adrian and Hazel had just come back from France, which was why the police up north hadn't been able to get through on the phone, and thus had contacted the local station.

Adrian's mother had been found dead. The officer commiserated. He'd been told no other details. Would Adrian phone the coroner's office up north in the morning?

Next morning Adrian learned how neighbors had noted that his mother's curtains remained closed at the front for several days. Perhaps Joan was away—but they recalled her burglary, when only a couple of pieces of costume jewelry had actually been stolen in lieu of any real gems or video recorders.

A policeman climbed the back fence. The kitchen door wasn't locked. Joan lay dead inside. The obvious cause was coronary thrombosis, to be confirmed by post mortem. There had been some vomit on the floor. Nausea often heralded a heart attack, but basically she wouldn't have suspected anything at all. Joan must have just got out of bed, felt sick, and unlocked the kitchen door for a breath of fresh air. Returning inside, she had died instantly. She wouldn't even have known she was dying.

She must have been lying there for several days, dead. Joan's body was removed to the mortuary, then the policeman had secured the property.

Atkinsons: that was the name of the funeral directors. Adrian must have walked past their premises a few thousand times when he'd been a schoolboy. With a post mortem due, was Adrian able to make arrangements with the undertaker by phone before traveling north?

Oh yes, said the lady coroner. *You can cremate before death.*

He was flabbergasted. Had he heard aright? Whatever did she mean by this?

What she *meant* was that he could set a date for the funeral before the death certificate was issued because there wouldn't be any inquest. *He must think they had some funny customs up north!*

Another dire thought came to Adrian. His mother never let anyone else have a key to her house. So his next call was to the police in the north to make sure that they had removed Joan's keys.

Oh no. The officer—whose name sounded remarkably like Genius—had faithfully locked the back door, put the keys on the table, then left by the front door, latching it shut. He'd done his duty of securing the property all right.

On a very windy night Adrian and Hazel arrived outside his one-time home after three hundred miles on the road, to rendezvous with a locksmith.

The double door was a solid 1930s specimen, stained glass at the top, giant bolts within to secure the side which rarely opened. Its fifty-year-old Yale lock defeated whatever slim flexible instruments the locksmith tried to slide between the abutting halves of the door—Adrian wasn't privileged to watch this operation since the locksmith, who was somewhat paranoid, refused to reveal tricks of his trade to a spectator. The lock then thwarted what seemed from a distance like fifty skeleton keys.

Adrian waited in the fierce wind and Hazel sat in the car during the full hour it took the man to drill through the lock. At half-time, another car pulled up. A man in an anorak, resembling a welterweight boxer, jumped out.

He proved to be a plain clothes policeman. The police station had had a report of some funny business outside this property. They'd told the caller they knew what was going on, but the boxer had come just to make sure.

Was he the genius who had locked the keys in the house?

Oh no, not him. But he couldn't wait to get back to the station to tell the lads.

The next morning a neighbor from over the road would confide to Adrian how she was so busy watching at the curtains that her Jack's supper was an hour late. When that front door finally opened a cry had gone up: *"They've got in!"*

A local Vicar would preside at the cremation. Adrian's mother only ever attended church once a year for the Christmas Eve carol service. Adrian and Hazel did not even condone organized religions, yet a Vicar's presence at the funeral was de rigueur. When the scrawny, broody Vicar called at the house to make some notes, he evinced such a passionate intensity as regards resurrection to eternal life. His knees creaked as he sat and talked, as if his knees were wooden and the joints needed oiling. The next day, the same neighbor confided how everyone local was sure that the bachelor Vicar had AIDS and wasn't long for this world.

Death roosted in the bungalow in another guise too. Whilst growing up, Adrian had always felt so safe—even frustratingly so!—in this ideal home of the 1930s. The bungalow had undergone little change except for some new carpets and new furniture and appliances now and then. It had the same cast iron radiators, of advanced design for 1934, to warm the rooms, same deep stone sink in the kitchen, same wooden ceiling pulley to dry washing, which could be wound down and up by rope, same original Art Deco light fittings, too. By the time his mother died such items as deep sinks had come back into fashion and were eagerly sought in junk shops. When he and Hazel had visited, the house seemed secure and comfortable to the casual eye.

Closer inspection revealed a death trap. Behind ingenious clusters of adapter sockets fitted by his father, and modern plastic switch plates, was Nineteen Thirties wiring, old and brittle. Bumping into the cooker caused an immediate gush of gas. The emergency engineer switched off the house at the mains and slapped on a red prohibition notice pending the digging up of the kitchen floor to fit a new gas pipe. The cooker, also condemned, was an antique such as he hadn't seen in the last forty years.

Joan's larder was so bare. She must have been eating like a sparrow. Every paper bag had been saved for possible re-use. Yet what she had assured her son only the year before was perfectly true. She wasn't at all in need of money. His mother had two very robust savings accounts. She had inherited Ken's pension, linked to inflation. For ten years she'd been accumulating assets.

"Oh she died a good death," exclaimed Hazel, amazed. "Never ill. Able to stay in her home till the last, then out like a light."

For his mother to have become ill or senile had hardly borne contemplating. Their own cottage simply wasn't large enough to accept her. For Joan to go into a nursing home, losing her privacy, would have been horrible for her—besides bleeding away whatever she owned till she was reduced to a paltry residue.

A good death, indeed.

And now her effects must be sorted out: Some fox furs from the 1930s— obscene, in the 1990s. No charity shop would accept such donations.

Boxes and boxes of color slides of Canadian and Swiss scenery, unviewed these last ten years, and of no conceivable interest except to the person who had wielded the camera. These must go to an incinerator.

Ornaments: toby jugs of recent vintage, a lustre vase with a smashed lip, decorative plates...

13

It was whilst surveying the ornaments that Hazel picked up a round china marmalade pot in the shape of a cottage. The walls were of a creamy sort of basket-work. The green roof (which lifted off) was a cone of thick branches. A dormer window receded. A chimney of orange bricks jutted up, whereby to lift off the lid. A few oversized pink or yellow blooms clung near the door and beneath a double window.

The piece wasn't sophisticated in design or detail. Hardly a Meissen marmalade pot! It verged on naive, though it avoided vulgarity. For as long as Adrian remembered, that pot had stood on the mantelpiece—until now.

"Actually," said Hazel, "I think this is the best thing here. The most charming, anyway. It has integrity."

The china cottage was an emblem of rural dreams—a dream which Adrian and Hazel had pretty much fulfilled, though not his parents, except by way of Sunday trips into the countryside....

In the 1930s, Joan and Ken had traveled for their honeymoon on a motorbike, with camping gear, to Stratford-upon-Avon and the Cotswolds. They had been enchanted by cottages such as this. Maybe they had brought back the pot as a souvenir of that honeymoon almost ten years before Adrian was born.

Wary of the lid falling off and shattering, Hazel turned the pot over.

"It says... What's this? *Marutomo Ware.* There's a string of Japanese characters too..." she said. Hazel noticed a maker's mark: a capital T within a circle.

"Why would the Japanese have been making English cottages as jam pots in the 1930s?" mused Adrian.

He had paid scant attention to this green-roofed cottage during all the years he had lived in this house. Yet all of a sudden it seemed to incarnate so much of his dead parents' life and dreams.

Memories washed over him—of sitting by the hearth as a child, that hearth with its false-log electric fire, of spooning up chicken soup while listening to the big old brown pre-war radio, no longer here. There were so many names on the long dial, Hilversum and Hamburg and Helsinki. At Christmas, they had a tree in the corner with all the colored glass balls dangling from the branches. He remembered curling up in an old armchair with a Hotspur comic containing a story of a giant homicidal cactus growing suddenly in London in Hyde Park, firing its spines as deadly spears at passers-by till foiled by the nimble bare-foot runner....

Throughout his adolescence he'd been much more interested in escaping from the north of England, so barren and bleak and downbeat. Anybody with an overactive imagination might bring about the downfall of nations: such was the local wisdom. Native sons traveled to London but soon fled home proclaiming, "It's treacherous down south." Others never returned, or only for fleeting visits. In this category was Adrian.

He'd become a journalist, which Hazel had also been until Alan was born. Alan was at a university now. Had they broken the news of his grandmother's death to Alan a little too brusquely over the phone? All of a sudden they had so much to arrange, and it was impractical for Alan to attend the funeral. Adrian's life was so busy now that he was a freelance. He specialized in economic journalism, a fast-track business.

The absurd aspects of his mother's death, especially the need to drill their way into the bungalow, were like the activities of some clown capering along a precipice of grief.

"I bet they bought that pot in Stratford on their honeymoon," he said to Hazel. "You know, Stratford isn't too much of a detour on the way back."

"But," she pointed out, "that was sixty years ago...."

Almost sixty years of life in the same house, now to be cleared and sold as though erasing a whole directory irretrievably from a computer disc.

Arriving in Stratford was emblematic of having finally quit the north and the past forever—though the psychological barrier between Adrian and his own death (cause yet unknown) had also disappeared.

Stratford of the present was decidedly different from the simpler town where his mother and father had honeymooned. Why, there wouldn't have been a hundred Harley Davidsons and Honda bikes parked along Waterside, nor a fire-eater performing on the greensward, nor a great glittering butterfly beckoning one to cross the Avon for an exotic lepidoptera safari, nor a host of Japanese tourists disembarking from a tour bus.

The world had ramped up into overdrive. Hiroshima had been incinerated, but Japan had risen again triumphantly—yet was already being eclipsed by Taiwan and Korea and Singapore. Should Adrian accost one of the Japanese tourists and ask what they knew about *Marutomo Ware*, about English cottages made in Japan as marmalade pots when the tourists' grandparents were young?

He and Hazel headed for bookshops to check all the collectors' guides they could find.

A volume on pottery marks, containing thirty densely illustrated pages devoted to Japan, listed no letter T within a circle. Books on modern collectibles, on treasures in your attic, on last year's auction prices—none mentioned such a thing as Marutomo Ware. In a world where every trivial object, even quite recent, even blatantly awful, seemed rapaciously collectible and investible-in, the marmalade pot was a non-object. Why should old bakelite telephones and seaside souvenirs and comics and a hundred other ephemeral things be eagerly sought, and not pre-war Japanese pastiches of rural England?

Was this anonymity not, in a sense, the quintessence of his mother's life? Yet wasn't it also disconcerting?

Presently the Hollowells wandered into an antiques mini-market crowded with booths of bric-a-brac and objects of greater virtu, all optimistically priced. And it was there, upon a table in a nook, that they spied three gaudy little china pagodas upon a green tray: salt, pepper, and mustard.

Almost as soon as Adrian and Hazel began examining these cruets a middle-aged woman was by their side, murmuring hopefully, "Do you collect Marutomo Ware?" She was plump and pleasant. Little glasses were perched on her nose. She looked like a genial granny.

And soon she was enlightening them....

Japanese export cottage-ware was the name for these things. Few people were collecting them yet. Nevertheless, the vogue was definitely beginning! Take her word for it. Oh yes, they were a bit crude, but that was the charm, wasn't it?

Now, the vital element was *the magic mark*. The proprietress intoned this phrase in the accent of the wise raven warning that boy in the tale of the Snow Queen that a *splin-ter from the maaag-ic mirror* had entered his sister's eye, alienating her from her brother and from her home—thus, at least, on the story record which Alan had listened to interminably when he was a toddler until he could parrot every nuance perfectly.

The maaagic mark, the maaagic mark.

Either a T in a circle for Marutomo, or a K in a circle for Maruhon Ware. Actually "Made in Japan" was acceptable, even just "Foreign," though the maaagic mark was admirable.

Sharing that table was a little blue donkey-cart led by a fellow in old world peasant costume—blue knickerbockers, green frock coat, blue tricorne hat. This salt and pepper set was "Made in Japan," though more carefully painted and glazed than the pagodas.

Also there was a black candle-holder ornamented with big crude maroon blooms which might be chrysanthemums. This bore the maaagic K mark.

Oh the cottage could never have been *bought* by Joan. During the 1930s cottage ware was given away if you collected enough coupons from packets of tea, tea from Ceylon, ornament from Tokyo or Yokohama. In English homes people would drink tea for a year to acquire a donkey-cart or a marmalade-pot cottage.

How complicated, how bizarre! Imagine Japanese artisans in some back-street family workshop or sweat-shop—arty-Sans who had never been near Europe—receiving commissions from a British tea factory out of Colombo to supply a hundred English cottages and a hundred donkey-carts to be packed in straw and shipped to Liverpool or Bristol.

As the decade slid towards the Second World War, the proud maaagic marks were replaced by a brusque "Made in Japan," then simply by an anonymous "Foreign." Anti-Japanese sentiment was building up among Anglo-Saxons, though a consequence of this would be the fall of Singapore, the surrender of Hong Kong, the bombing of Pearl Harbor.

After a bit of bargaining, the Hollowells acquired all three pieces. They could easily afford to; now they could. Now Joan's cottage wouldn't be alone, as she had been alone.

Over the next few years the quest for Maru' Ware was to take Adrian and Hazel to many junk shops and curio shops and flea markets in many towns. Before long they developed rituals and superstitions for finding their quarry. Humming the old Japanese anthem to the Emperor often seemed to do the trick. Tum-tumti-TUM, tumti-TUM, tumtitum... May the Son of Heaven triumph ten thousand-fold. *Tenno heika banzai yo!*

A whole unknown fabric and population of Maru' artifacts and people lurked, waiting to be reunited at some celestial breakfast or tea party. The Japanese arty-Sans had worked prodigiously if rather crudely on behalf of the tea companies. Not only were there jam-pots of a hundred designs and candle-holders and cruets, but egg cups too and china toast-racks. And tea-pots and tea-strainers and butter dishes and lemon squeezers and ashtrays and sugar shakers. You could recognize a genuine piece instantly from twenty yards away.

Personages included cruet girl-guides with Asian faces, and kneeling cherubs holding bowls aloft, and Beefeaters from the Tower of London. Camels squatted with china hooks for salt and pepper baskets, mus-

tard panniers on their backs. A whole peculiar population existed, and a bestiary too, and an environment of cottages and towers and old curiosity shoppes! An unacknowledged Maru' World!

The makers' distant perception of their market caused some peculiarities. Who was this figure in a costume of tight horizontal blue hoops? He often peered around the edge of a cottage. He almost merged with it. He frequently dwarfed the doorway. The figure seemed like a deep-sea diver in a kind of samurai armor diving suit and helmet.

A Beefeater might well have lost his Tower and his companion (or vice versa), and a girl guide her jamboree tent, or a yellow camel its mustard pot—or a cottage pot its tam-o'-shanter lid. Pieces had been scattered or had suffered casualties. Often there'd be a crack or a chip. Amazing, really, that so much had survived intact. Adrian and Hazel once arrived at a market stall just after an idle browser had picked up a windmill pot and knocked the lid off so that it smashed on the cobbles. One of the sails had already been snapped. The stallholder actually gave the piece away to them as an alternative to tossing it in a bin; a golden day.

You had to be subtle in the search. You had to deny any special interest in cruets or teapots, and only blandly glance at the maaagic marks, even if the pulse beat fast. You mustn't ignite a firestorm of collecting by people who were blind to the spiritual dimension of the hunt.

Spring was a good time to harvest Maru' ware, because old ladies died off in January and February and their homes were cleared. But really the harvest remained reasonable all year long, apart from occasional patches of dearth. Ah, the secret harvest...

Naturally they returned to Stratford, but that middle-aged woman was no longer there. Obviously she'd given up trying to convince tourists of the collectibility of pieces which were becoming rarer and rarer. Yes, she'd gone, like a gypsy with her curse.

Alan had graduated. He did a string of temporary jobs in pubs and clubs in London, pending his breakthrough as an actor. By now their son viewed his erstwhile home as an insane and alienated place, full as it was of cottages and cruets and lemon squeezers and ashtrays and camels and donkeys and windmills. Strangers and acquaintances alike were hardly ever admitted in case they coveted the secret collection, into which—to a fair degree, if travel were included—his mother's money had been transmuted. Alternatively, visitors might fail to perceive the value and regard the Hollowells as potty.

Adrian began to suffer from blood pressure. He relied on an array of blockers and diaretics—and his memory was fraying too, a poor prognosis for a journalist, possibly an early indicator of Alzheimer's. Hazel had lost a breast and lymph glands because of a tumor, and was worried about recurrence. It was hardly likely that either of them would reach Joan's ripe old age!

Yet the quest continued. Their cottage *must* be filled to the seams with that quintessence of cottage, Maru' ware with maaagic marks which arty-Sans had crafted over half a century earlier back when the world was much less full of people and when Joan and Ken had embarked on their honeymoon upon a motorbike from their ideal home, seven years saved for, to pretty Stratford. The trip might only have cost them five pounds in total, or maybe ten. When they had arrived at Anne Hathaway's cottage—of which there were various Maru' copies—they may have shared their tour with just a couple of other visitors rather than with a queue of Japanese and Americans and Koreans and Spaniards.

Adrian and Hazel realized that they themselves were growing old and that Alan was alienated from them, though they did their best to phone him once a week or once a fortnight.

What of Alan's inheritance? Not one marmalade pot, but hundreds of them! Along with a multitude of sugar shakers and candle-holders and butter dishes and all else.

In every room glass cabinets displayed the wares and guarded them from dust. Wares which lacked the maaagic mark thronged tables and almost every shelf including book shelves—the books had had to go, except for some economics literature piled under Adrian's desk.

Alan could virtually open their home as a museum. Though would anyone wish to visit it? What if Adrian and Hazel had effectively, and in secret, cornered almost the entire market in Maru' ware? What if no more Maru' ware remained in circulation and thus could have no meaningful, collectible value assigned? Exchanged for tea coupons, such pieces had never had actual monetary value. In the Hollowells' total success, might there be debacle and futility? Could one envisage a cottage museum devoted to objects to which everyone else was oblivious? The realm of Maru' ware must never be equated with some daft bugger's museum of drawing pins or paperclips.

And of course it wouldn't be! Maru' territory was truly inhabited—if not always by figures then at least implicitly behind the painted glazed windows and doors. Tea-strainers and lemon-squeezers likewise implied a whole virtual existence.

Commissions became fewer for Adrian, though this didn't matter too much so long as the aging car could take him and Hazel to distant marketplaces. When they returned home, if the setting sun dazzled him, sometimes it seemed that their cottage was becoming simpler and rounder, the roof more of a cone, the chimney taller, the flowers in the garden larger and brasher.

One Autumn day after a scary dearth they arrived back triumphantly. They had found a green and mauve pot-pourri vase with slots in the lid to release the scent of dried lavender. Adrian spied a figure in blue disappearing around to the back of their cottage.

"Hazel, there's someone—" His heart thumped. He felt tight and hot. "Someone—"

"What sort of someone?" she demanded. "For God's sake! Is it Alan?"

They hurried from the car, up the brick path, and around.

Adrian almost collided with the policeman, who was returning from the padlocked back gate. Surely it was the same man who had once knocked on their door of an evening. He was older now and seemed to have forgotten that earlier encounter. There'd been a report of a prowler. The officer had parked his car in a side lane, hoping to apprehend by surprise. Glass sparkled on the path. But this window, which was out of sight of the road, boasted two steel bars, fixed inside.

Someone had been trying to unscrew the bars. One was loose. Traces of blood. Someone had cut his hand.

Adrian clung to both bars like a prisoner excluded from his cell, desperate to be readmitted.

Inside, nothing was smashed. Shelves and cabinets and tables of Maru' ware were all intact. Heart thudding, Adrian dashed quickly up and down, and from front to back to ensure that all locks and bars were secure—apart from the wobbly one—while Hazel detained the officer at the door so that he wouldn't intrude, and see. Upstairs, the fax was safe, and his computer, which would have been a bit heavy to lug and was long out of date. The Hollowells thanked the man warmly, saw him on his way, then Hazel too could fully reassure herself.

If the prowler had gained entry, in rage at not finding silver or money he might have vandalized the collection, sweeping dozens of pieces off shelves and tables, shattering them.

"From now on," Hazel said firmly, "one of us will always need to be here."

"I can't hunt on my own...."

"Maybe the hunt's over. Maybe the pot-pourri pot is the last piece ever. We have to safeguard them now."

Adrian needed to sit down and take a pill. "I thought," he told her, "when I saw him round the side—I thought that policeman was the time-diver."

The name had come to him recently, of the lurker in blue, like a samurai warrior, like a deep-sea diver. What had Adrian and Hazel been doing ever since his mother's death but time-diving, picking up sub-

merged treasure and broken shards of the past just as genuine divers had recovered a hold-full of precious Chinese porcelain from some sunken Dutch sailing ship.

Or had the Hollowells been trawling for trash?

"You'd best fetch our pot-pourri pot before some kid thieves it from the car—"

Of course.

Adrian shut the front door as he went out so that no passers-by such as inquisitive Mrs. *Thing* from the Old Parsonage could stare in.

As he returned up the path, cradling the pot double-wrapped in newspaper, the rug of healthy moss upon the roof glowed green in the declining sunshine. Slanting shadows made the texture of the magnolia rendering look like basketwork. The upstairs dormer window seemed to lean away from him. What a huge yellow chrysanth.

Dazed by the shock of the attempted burglary, Adrian stepped inside, into cool shade.

The woman awaiting him seemed so much shorter and slighter—as if she'd been existing on a sparrow's rations for years.

Quivering, she opened her arms to hug him. His heart ached for her.

destination unknown
THE EMPEROR'S SHOESTRINGS
by R.A. Lafferty

Not a bad place as places go,
But Oh the ceilings are so low!
Book of Jasher.

The maiden who chamber-rooms clean'th,
The gum-shoe who evidence glean'th,
Proclaim "Guys, it's swell!
It's a gorgeous hotel,
If it weren't for the tacky thirteenth."
Limerick County Limericks, Clement Goldbeater.

Justin Saldeen was afraid to look under the table. It gave him the stac-cato shivers. He felt impelled, like one in a dream, to point with hand and voice to what was under the table, to call the attention of his com-panions to it. But, as in a dream, his voice would not work and his hand would not.

And Justin's table companions did not seem to notice that there were any strange things going on under the table at all. Would one of them not look and see! But would they be able to see it (staccato shiver-ing again, and consuming doubt) even if they did look under the table? Do you realize just how seldom people do look under a table? Ah flam-ing fudlucks, somebody look!

"We have all received the 'Little Vision'," Marjory Kiljoy was saying. "It is for that that we belong to the NRBWA Peoplehood. Now we can see in the 'little' and in the 'big'. We can see without and within. Do you believe that in all the world else there are as many true visionaries as at our convention here? Yauk, yauk!"

Their table was at pool-side, and Marjory had been sunning herself all morning on the tawny sand beside the pool. And she was tanned or burned into matching pattern to that sand, tawny and grainy and rippled. Persons of sensitive skin always are sun-printed thus to the pattern of their background. Marjory was attractive and wide-eyed from her felted rabbit-fur birds'-nest hat to the lavender and chestnut speckled pinkish nuthatch egg in her navel.

"We are the trained gazers," said Sulky Sullivan. "We see what others cannot see. Only ourselves in all the worlds have true multiplex vision. Nuthatch-watching does that to one. Yauk, yauk!"

Sulky had a pleasant storminess to her sleek skin. She also had been sunning herself through the bright morning, and her skin was now sun-printed with the pattern of the cork walkways on which she had been lying. Her own hat was made of leaves and grass, and the nuthatch egg in her navel was white with just a flush of pink, and it had no more than three lavender specks in it.

"There is no vision that we do not dare!" Gladys Gamaliel challenged with her small voice. "We are the new adventurers and explorers. The true interior vision has a very small exterior aperture, and with us it is the nuthatch egg and the nuthatch world. We are surrounded by kingdoms and realms without number. We have but to open our trained and illuminated eyes to see all things large and small. Yauk, yauk!"

Gladys had an unpainted evocation to her textured skin. She had been sunning herself that morning on the authentic wooden raft in the pool, and she was burned to the unpainted, wet-wood pattern of the raft's old boards. Her hat was made of feathers and horse-hair, and the nuthatch egg in her navel was the chestnut-spotted heavy pink of the Carolina Nuthatch. "We dare to look!" Gladys pronounced in benediction. "Yauk, yauk!"

"Then in the name of the Devil Downhead Nuthatch himself, look under the table!" Justin shrilled, rising suddenly to his feet, toppling his chair, dropping the nuthatch egg from his left nostril. "Dare to look!"

They looked, but they looked at him, in amazement. And he shriveled under their look.

"Oh, pardon my vehemence," he apologized, "but do look under the table." He replaced the nuthatch egg (fortunately unbroken) in his nostril with the prayer that his awkwardness might be overlooked. "Yauk, yauk!" he finished dutifully and ritually.

"Oh sit down, Justin," Rolf Mesange said crossly. "Sometimes I feel that your conduct and bearing are not quite those of a NRBWA Peoplehood member. Sit down. They're bringing the drinks now. Yauk, yauk!"

Justin Saldeen, with a certain nervousness of eye and rump, sat down at the table once more. His five table-mates had glanced briefly under the table and they seemed not to have seen anything unusual there. Why, with their daring vision, had they not seen anything unusual, or anything at all? To Justin's now trepidatious vision, there was something unusual under the table.

There were six people under the table, that's what. They were small people, yes or they wouldn't have fit so easily under the table. They were sitting at a small table of their own down there; and they didn't appear (except for their small scale) much different from the other people at the convention.

A girl brought the drinks to Justin and his table-mates. That was all right. In the brightness of the noon-time, in the super-clarity of the vision, a drink will come in mighty handy sometimes. But a disturbing thing was that (You don't have to look down, you don't have to look under the table if you don't want to) a smaller girl was bringing smaller drinks to those six undersized people at their own undersized table under Justin's table. Once more Justin felt impelled, like one in a dream, to point with hand and voice: and once more his hand and voice failed him.

This was at the NRBWA (Nuthatches and Related Birds Watchers of America) Convention, probably the greatest yearly gathering of the truly open-eyed people. Justin Saldeen, Rolf Mesange, Berthold Chairmender, Marjory Kiljoy, Sulky Sullivan, and Gladys Gamaliel had been sitting together at the table at poolside on the fourteenth floor. The men wore nuthatch eggs in their left nostrils, and the ladies wore them in their navels. All of them must end every speech with the nasal 'yauk, yauk' that is the note of the Common Nuthatch. These six outstanding and intelligent young people, and the entire six thousand at the convention, shared nuthatchery, and the 'Little Vision' as the key to the 'Great Vision' as a way of life.

Justin was a square and spare young man with a robust healthiness that left him nothing to blame his new nervousness on. Rolf was a proud and suspicious man who preached 'Pride in Vision' and the 'Little-See as Portal to the Big-See'. Berthold was an integrating man who spread peace like vegetable oil on the warring waters. He preached the 'Nuthatch Door to Dynamic Peace'.

In some ways, Marjory Kiljoy, in fulfilling her own name, fell below the nuthatch ethic. She sometimes showed strong carnal inclinations. And what quicker than carnal notions and behaviors will kill the joy of an illuminated and intellectual congress?

(Conversations, small-stature conversations, under-the-table conversations that used a different sound-track from regular conversations, Oh, they were uncanny! It was even more startling to hear the under-the-table things than to see them. Really, the talk sparkled more below than above, and there was some pretty good ankle-high wisdom and wit.)

Su lky Sullivan was more serious than sulky. She preached the 'Cosmic Egg' and the 'Ultimate Consciousness', and she did not doubt that the cosmic egg was a nuthatch egg. Gladys Gamaliel, she was the sly and shy one. Like the totem nuthatch, she was small and noticed only by the elite. But she had inner qualities. Everyone said so, and she said so herself.

These were six among six thousand persons of common and incandescent interest (the 'Little Vision of the Nuthatches' as key to the 'Great Vision that encompasses the Worlds') who were met here in convention, in congress, in constellation of personalities for the furtherance of their only-thing-that-matters. So their talk had to be the powerful and rich vehicle of their views.

THE EMPEROR'S SHOESTRINGS

Then why was the chatter of the six little people under the table (whom only Justin seemed able to hear) so much more interesting than that of the big people at the big tables? They were having fun down under.

"Ditch these big guys when the session starts and go to the thirteenth floor with us," one of the under-the-table ladies gave the pleasant invitation to Justin.

"Justin, why do you fidget and look under the table?" Rolf Mesange demanded suspiciously. "Truly illuminated people don't fidget."

"I keep seeing and hearing things that aren't there," Justin mumbled nervously.

"Nuthatches?" Rolf asked sharply.

"No, not nuthatches," Justin said. "Just things, people, comings and goings on the wrong scale, situations. I keep seeing things that just can't be there and nobody else sees them."

"Just so it isn't nuthatches," said Rolf. "There's an unpleasant word for people who see nuthatches that aren't there. Faking is an offence against the 'Little Vision' itself. False reporting is always reprehensible, and proof of it can cost one his credentials."

"Justin, ditch that guy especially," said the friendly small lady under the table, "and c'mon join us on the thirteenth floor."

"Has this hotel a thirteenth floor?" Justin asked his table-mates.

"Of course it hasn't!" Rolf sputtered. "Thirteen floors are something out of the superstitious dark ages. How would there be thirteen floors in a rational area?"

Sudden and loud over the speaker system came the 'yauk, yauk' sound. This was a greatly amplified recording of the genuine nathatch call, and it was used as a signal at the convention. It meant that the first session of the day was due to begin. So the six at the table, and many others from pool-side, left the fourteenth floor roof garden to go down the quick stairways to the twelfth floor sessions theaters.

Between the floors there were little soffit cubicles or cubby-holes about a foot high. "I wonder what those are for?" Justin asked. Nobody else had wondered what they were for. "Yauk, yauk!" Justin added. He'd nearly forgotten it.

"I don't know," said Marjory Kiljoy. "Come along. Yauk, yauk!"

Sessions never begin quite on time. On the twelfth floor, the illuminated people sat and waited.

"Those little cubicles with the little doors on them, that space between the floors where we come down the stairways, it reminded me of other little cubicles on a train when I was a little boy," Justin said.

"Illuminated persons are never reminded of trivial or meaningless things from the past," Rolf Mesange cautioned.

"Well, I was riding on a train with my mother very late at night," Justin stumbled on regardless. "She was tired. There were little cubicles with doors on them along the walls of our railway coach. 'What's in that little room?' I asked, and I tried to open one of the doors. 'Oh, that's where the trainman keeps his lantern,' my mother said, but she hadn't even looked. 'What's this place for?' I asked about another one of them. 'Oh, that's where they keep the extra lantern,' my mother said. And to every one of those little places, my mother said that it was where the trainman kept his lantern. I felt then and I felt now that there was something more wonderful than lanterns (if there is anything more wonderful than lanterns) inside those little places. But my mother was tired and so was I, and a four year old doesn't pursue things out to the ultimate. I was never on another coach that had such little cubicles. They were about the size of the little cubby-holes between the twelfth and fourteenth floors here."

"Well?" Rolf Mesange asked with rising suspicion.

"Nothing," said Justin. "That's all of it. It's just something that I remembered."

"Illuminated persons never remember such trivial and meaningless things," Rolf said severely. But the first speaker of the session now began to talk, so Justin did not have (at that time) to give further account of his childhood memory.

THE EMPEROR'S SHOESTRINGS

"Just as in re-entrant space (that type of space in which we live) any point may be taken as the exact center of the universe," the speaker was saying, "so in re-entrant society (that type of society in which we all live) every valid interest may be taken as a center or pivot for the total meaningful involvement or envelopment of the world. Our own interest in the nuthatch bird, 'the bird of the little way', has proved central to a very important movement, the only important movement really, in the world. Yauk, yauk!"

There were eight scheduled speakers seated at the sessions table or podium table, and the present speaker was a striking medium of their type. As a fact, any of them would have been a good medium type, for they were a re-entrant group, each one a central, and all very similar. And under the speakers' table was another and smaller table with ten (Justin had already divined that there was not a rigid numerical correspondence between the large and the small people) smaller speakers or possible speakers. One of these was now holding forth in an interesting but rowdydow sort of talk. None of the big people seemed to hear this smaller speaker at all. None of them seemed to notice any of the little people.

"Our movement is quite simply the rejuvenation of our tired world," the convention speaker was saying. The world, for lack of the 'big vision', is threatened with a too-early senility. We'll cure that. This present Forty-Fourth NRBWA Convention is a mighty kilometer-stone in the rejuvenation of the world. Yauk, yauk!"

Something was pulling on Justin's trousers cuff. It was a little lady, possibly the same little lady who had talked so friendly to him before. She had her arms folded and was leaning on his cuff as though it were a back fence, and she was looking up at him.

"Ditch these guys, Justin," she said. "They don't know anything at all about the 'little ways' that lead to the 'big way'. Hey, things are starting to open up upstairs now. C'mon, let's go up to the thirteenth floor."

"Justin, why do you keep looking down at the floor?" Gladys Gamaliel asked him. "What's down there anyhow? Yauk, yauk!"

"Look and see for yourself," Justin mumbled dubiously.

"My aren't you snippy today," Gladys said. "Illuminated people are never snippy to other illuminated people. Yauk, yauk!"

"Our great movement began with the nuthatch bird, and with the high hobby of nuthatch-watching," the big speaker was continuing. "The nuthatch is a small, blue-gray-black bird that is almost invisible in the mixed blue-gray-black woodlands and sedgelands and meadowlands. Our own eyes, the opening eyes of the rejuvenated world, learned their minute vision in spotting the small nuthatch on its spotted background. The faint, nasal 'yauk, yauk' note of the nuthatch is almost inaudible against the animated clatter of the woodlands and the canebrakes. Our own fine ears, the opened ears of the rejuvenated world, learned their minute hearing in picking up the nuthatch notes out of the larger noise. We learned to hear the sounds of all the small worlds, of the gateway worlds, by mastering this one crucial small sound. Yauk, yauk!"

"By my grandfather's ears, your own ears are closed," Justin Saldeen interrupted in a loud voice. "You can not hear the sound of the small worlds. You would not recognize a gateway world if it were under your very feet. Tell me, can you hear the minute rowdydow from the small world under your own table right now? Let your ears repent! Let them learn to listen!"

The small people at the little speakers' table under the big speakers' table cheered Justin as their new advocate. But the big speaker at the big table over their heads did not hear their cheering. He did not hear the sounds of the small world at all.

"Who is this person's gauleiter? Yauk, yauk!" the big speaker asked gently.

"I am. Yauk, yauk," Rolf Mesange admitted in a frustrated voice.

"Your subject is perhaps not fully illuminated," the big speaker said. "Very likely he is here in error, as lacking in qualifications. Well, do what you can with him. and be gentle with him. Yauk, yauk!"

THE EMPEROR'S SHOESTRINGS

"I'd like to be gentle to you with a meat-cleaver, Justin," Rolf whispered furiously. "Sit down and be quiet, dammit. Yauk, yauk."

"C'mon, Justin. Forget the big guys. They're weird," the ankle-high girl-friend was saying. "Let's go up to the thirteenth. C'mon."

"Do you know what was in those little cubicles on that railway car when I was a little boy?" Justin asked softly.

"Maybe it was a made-over club car," the shoestring-high lady said. "We used always to have a few clubs going in the club cars. Let's go up to the thirteenth. C'mon."

"Our vision is a generating function," the big speaker was saying again. "Things are seen in such a way; and then they become that way. You know, of course, that the Emperor really was wearing adequate and even splendid clothes until a hostile psychology was brought to bear on him. A child saw through him. And then everybody saw through him. Wherever he is now, he is probably still wearing adequate clothes: but I would guess that he is still being seen through also. The essential emperor could not be seen while his clothes were a barrier. A child broke through the barrier, as we ourselves break through so many barriers. As we see a thing, so that thing becomes. As we see the Emperor, so shall the Emperor be. Yauk, yauk!"

"How about the Emperor's shoestrings?" Justin Saldeen howled out. "Can't you ever look down? What do you see around and about the Emperor's shoestrings? What would a child see?"

"Is that the same unfortunate person as before?" the speaker asked. "Is he even half illuminated? He asks questions, but does anybody know what the questions mean? Yauk, yauk!"

"Bring a child!" Justin spoke with a rowdydow touch of his own. "Let us see what a child can see in the area of the Emperor's shoestrings."

"The unfortunate person deserves some kind of an answer," the big speaker spoke compassionately. "Unfortunate man, a child's vision looks essentially up and not down. A child's vision could see through an emperor's clothes, but I do not believe that a child's vision could settle any question at shoestring level. Only a very tall man could see the Emperor's shoestrings in meaningful perspective. Yauk, yauk!"

"Aw knock-kneed nuthatches, bring on a tall man then! Yauk, yauk!" Justin corrected it.

"The gauleiter of this man will have this man here at this same hour tomorrow," the big speaker said in a voice like illuminated ice. "We will hold judgement on him then. Yauk, yauk!"

"C'mon, Justin," the small lady under Justin's seat said. "Let's take the thirteenth. C'mon!" She had a red line, thin as a thread, around her throat, the fairy mark, the un-nested bird mark, the mark sometimes affected by those who have been murdered.

Five of them, Rolf Mesange, Berthold Chairmender, Marjory Kiljoy, Sulky Sullivan, Gladys Gamaliel, were telling thirteenth-floor stories at one of the pool-side tables that evening.

"Have you yourself ever seen a ghost? Have you yourself ever seen a UFO? Have you yourself ever seen a thirteenth floor? Even we of the 'nuthatch vision' must consider whether such questions are completely obsolete," Berthold Chairmender was saying. "We will see and integrate as many things as we can. It is for this that we are chosen; it is for this that we are special. But we will always miss something. There are things that we, with our channeled vision, must always give up. But if we can pick up one bright thing without dropping another brighter thing, I say Pick it up. Right at this moment I feel a liveliness very near to us, but I don't know how to take a share of it. I wonder where Justin Saldeen is? Yauk, yauk!"

"As gauleiter for this bunch, I had better find out where he is before judgment hour tomorrow," Rolf Mesange grumbled. "And I had better not lose another one of you. Justin was riding some such notion as yours, Berthold, and then he rode it clear out of the corral. But he was always close underfoot, and I believe he still is. I can feel him very near right now. I believe that I can hear him also, but not on an ordinary sound-track. Be careful that you do not wander onto strange tracks, Berthold. Yauk, yauk!"

THE EMPEROR'S SHOESTRINGS

"I myself have seen a thirteenth floor," Berthold said, disregarding Rolf's strait advice. "Oh, don't grumble, Rolf. Thirteenth-floor accounts were considered a legitimate field of investigation before our 'nuthatch vision' movement channeled and contained the 'small kingdom' studies into rational areas. And I know what I saw, even if I only saw it subjectively. I saw, in a tall building in a tall town not very distant from here, rows of windows at the thirteenth floor level. These could not have been fourteenth floor windows. They were too different from the other floors of the building. They were the old-style, openable windows that people might look out of; and people were looking out of them.

"I called to several persons there in the street and asked if they could see the so-different windows and the people looking out of them. Some of the persons in the street denied it outright. A shisk-a-bob peddler hedged and said 'They'd call anybody crazy that admits seeing such things. Sure, I see them. I'm crazy enough to see them. But I'm not crazy enough to admit that I saw them if I'm driven into a corner over it.' 'Sure, I see them,' an old lady said. 'Everyone here can see them now. We can see them about half the days, and some of us have become acquainted with the people who look out the windows. They look happy, but they look crowded too. You can see that there isn't much room there. The ceilings in their part would have to be mighty low. Sometimes people go up there when the window-people call to them to come up. But them that goes up doesn't come down again. And some days we can't see them at all. When the windows are closed, then they seem to disappear, and the place where they were disappears too. There isn't any room for there to be windows there when they're not opened.' That's what the old lady said.

"So I went inside the building: I looked, and I asked. They told me in the building that of course they did not have a thirteenth floor, or any old-style windows that opened out and that people could look out of. I explored the building completely; and there wasn't any thirteenth floor, and there wasn't any space that a thirteenth floor could have occupied.

There weren't any windows that opened out, or that people could look out of. I went down into the street again. Well, I had gone up to where it should have been: and I, at least, came down again. I looked up at the building as I had looked up previously. There were no openable windows of the old sort and there were no people looking out of them. There was no level that was different from any other level. 'Where is the old lady that was here?' I asked the shisk-a-bob peddler. 'You can't see her all the time,' he said. 'And people are likely to call you crazy if you admit seeing that old lady at all.' This is a true, though possibly subjective, account of what I saw one day. Yauk, yauk!"

"Yes, I can feel a liveliness in my feet too," Sulky Sullivan said. "There's magic right under our feet, as it were, and we're missing it. There's always a magic corner right around the corner, or under the floor. We've been looking for magic corners since we were taily apes. I believe that the magic corners that we looked for then were special trees or special branches (probably the thirteenth branch) that we could never quite reach, or could not recognize if we did reach. Have we been missing magic all our lives? Well, need we miss it forever? The magic may be in anything, in a box or a house or a small cubicle. Justin thought that it was in a little cubby-hole where the trainman kept his lantern. Say, Justin's having fun now, isn't he? I can feel it through the soles of my feet. There's a mighty low ceiling there, but he's having fun and magic. Yauk, yauk!"

"I don't know what he sees in that little nit-weight female with the nit's egg in her navel," Marjory Kiljoy groused. "Yauk, yauk!"

"Do you girls know where Justin is?" Rolf demanded. "If you do, then you are bound to tell me. That's a simple case of nuthatch loyalty. Yauk, yauk!"

"They don't know," Gladys told gauleiter Rolf Mesange. "Neither do I. But all of us do have the nuthatch intuition. We know that the place is near, that it is low, that it's of the 'small kingdom' category, and that it's gateway magic. We know that Justin's having fun in it, but not as much fun as he'd be having if he hadn't left his feet outside. In the Nuthatches' Guidebook there's a lament about having feet too big to enter a 'small kingdom'. I think that's symbolic. Yauk, yauk!"

"Not with Justin it isn't," Berthold said. "He really does have big feet. But he still has roots outside in our nuthatchery that he hasn't torn out. This business of crawling into a small cubicle is tricky. You've just got to leave something outside. A spelunker may crawl deeper and into a tighter place, but not much. There sure is a low roof where he is. I'm jealous of the good time that he's having, but I know that he can't get all the way in there in one trip. It's a lucky trick to find the way in even once. And then, with the amnesia of the place a price to pay for bucking out of the place and going back to get the rest of one's self, it would be an exponentially lucky trick to find such a place the second time. But he seems to be enjoying it. Yauk, yauk!"

"You're sure that he'll forget where he's been and what he's done if he's dragged out of his place?" Gladys asked.

"Gladys, why didn't you say 'yauk, yauk' at the end of your statement?" Rolf cut in sternly. "Yauk, yauk."

"I just spelunker-dunker didn't feel like it!" Gladys said, and that is when Rolf felt his power over the group slipping.

"How do all of you know so much about Justin's situation?" the buffeted Rolf asked. "If you don't know where he is or what he's doing, what do you know? Yauk, yauk!"

"Oh, I guess we know pretty much the rest of it," said Marjory. "Everyone to his own taste in magic and everything else. But if the ceiling's so low that you have to lie down and raise on one elbow just to drink that mountain dew of theirs (Mountain dew! Why do they call that thirteenth floor cubby-hole a mountain anyhow?) then I say that things are too cramped for even a small kingdom. But we sense pretty well what Justin senses, and we catch most of the effects that are between the senses. After all, we do belong to the same nuthatchery. We do all have empathy with each other. Don't you feel everything that Justin feels, Rolf? Yauk, yauk!"

"No, I don't," Rolf Mesange said. "Yauk, yauk!'

The sound system mumbled a greatly amplified 'yauk, yauk' then, and the five persons left their table to go down to a late evening session of the convention, left the fourteenth floor roof garden to go down the quick stairways to the twelfth floor sessions theater.

Between the floors there were little soffit cubicles or cubby-holes about a foot high. There was a pair of big shoes sticking out of one of them, and there were feet in the shoes.

"We all know those shoes, if we could just remember whose they were," Berthold said.

Sessions never begin quite on time. On the twelfth floor, the illuminated people sat and waited and talked.

"It's a little bit Brush Arbor music," Sulky Sullivan said, "and a little bit Blue Grass, and little bit Flint Creek. But it's all on a different sound-track, and other things are all on other kinds of tracks. I know that Justin is enjoying, and I enjoy with him. I wish he'd be able to remember it, when he comes back for the rest of himself. Yauk, yauk!"

"No, he won't be able to remember it," Berthold said. "Or it may be that he will remember only one tune out of it, and that will be a tune that we all know. There used to be ten thousand Irish pipers who went yearly into a rabbit hole in the Knockmealdown Mountains. They'd pipe for three days. Each one would be blessed with a new-born tune which he would play like a piping angel. And all ten thousand pipers would learn all ten thousand tunes. But when they came out again, each would remember and play only the one tune 'Over the Hills and Far Away', and each would believe that it was the new-born tune that had been given to them in the mountain. And when the pipers were cleared out, it would be seen that the rabbit hole wouldn't rationally hold ten thousand pipers, or even one. I understand that the custom is dying out in Ireland. There were only a few more than eight thousand pipers last year. That's the way it will be with Justin when he comes out. He'll have forgotten all the music and dancing and topering, all the wining and dining and shining, all the loving and cozening and cousining and carousing, the hunting and bunting, the walking and talking. Or he will remember only one piece of each, a common piece that we already know. I wonder if he'll find his way back there the second time, and if he'll stay there if he does? Yauk, yauk!"

"You all seem to know a very lot about Justin, for not knowing where he is or why," Rolf complained. "I only hope that you can help me find him tomorrow. If I can't produce him, then I can be a gauleiter no longer. Yauk, yauk."

The evening session was excellent, perhaps: a superior expression of nuthatchery and of the 'little way' as gateway to the 'big way'. It was superb, of course.

"Even the dogs are superb where we come from," some small person down under the chairs was saying. "Even the fleas on the dogs are superb."

"Go away, nit-weight," Marjory said crossly. "I have something else on my subdominal mind."

What Marjory Kiljoy had on her lower mind, as became clear when the session ended, was the old carnal jag. She was on one again. Such things are sometimes contagious. People left the group: the group, its joy in illumination and bright discussion and group companionship killed for the while, was a group no more that night.

Group Gauleiter Rolf Mesange was very nervous the next morning. He had to produce Justin Saldeen by the time of the judgment session, and he didn't know where that bemused man had gone to. Rolf and his remaining four group-members were by pool-side up on the fourteenth floor roof garden. But those other members were of no help in the search.

"The little people got him, that's what. Yauk, yauk!" Marjory Kiljoy said.

"When we rediscover what our forefathers meant by 'magic-lantern' then we may find what Justin rediscovered," Berthold said mysteriously. "He likes lanterns. Yauk, yauk."

"It's a little bit like Green Country music, it's a little bit like Whang Whang, it's a little bit like Apple Orchard, it's a little bit like String Chords for Six Thumbs, it's a little bit like Vehicular Tunnel in B Flat, that's the sound of it," Gladys said. "It's a little bit like Dooley's Mountain, it's a little bit like Big Mike's Diamond Mine, it's a little bit like Cloudhopper's Ritz Bar (only with a lower ceiling), that's part of the look of it. And do you want to know what it smells like where he is? Well, the Fleshy Delight Steak House will give you a start of a start on the smell of it. And—"

"No, I only want to know where Justin Saldeen is," Rolf said patiently. "Yauk, yauk."

"When we find what out forefathers really meant when they spoke of the 'Little People" then we might find out what Justin is," Berthold said cryptically.

After a bit, they went down from the fourteenth floor to the twelfth for a morning session (but not yet the judgment session). As they went down the sweeping stairs, they saw again the big pair of shoes sticking out of the cubby-hole between the floors.

"We ought to remember whose shoes and feet those are," Marjory said. "Just because he has amnesia, should we be amnestic of him? It has to be someone we know well. Yauk, yauk."

"Could we take his footprints and send them to a laboratory somewhere?" Rolf asked uneasily. "Well, I don't see how that would help, but something's got to help. Yauk, yauk."

The session was soon shining with intuition and fulfillment and realization. It was a Life-With-A-Glow Instruction Kit, it was a Controlled-Explosion-For-Any-Number-of-Hands actfest, it was a Love-Is-a-Peri-gynous-Type-Flower presentation. But then it became strident, like honey strained too fine.

"Wherever he is, Justin is having more fun there than we are here," Berthold Chairmender gave the free opinion to the five-group. "He's asleep, and his neck is cramped from the low ceiling. It isn't even a foot high: it's about ten inches. And he's forgotten what he went for and what he will have to come back for. But, even asleep, he's having more fun than we are. Yauk, yauk."

There was a short interlude to allow the fevered session to cool off a bit. The first session was over with, and after the interlude there would come the judgment session. And the short interlude was all too short.

A warner came to Rolf Mesange. "You have just one minute to present the deficient man for judgment," the warner said. "Somebody will be judged, you or he, in one minute. Yauk, yauk!'

"Oh, what to do, what to do!" Rolf moaned. "Gang, go get that pair of shoes and feet that are sticking out of the cubby-hole overhead. We can start with them, and maybe we can make the rest of Justin out of something else."

It was very much less than a second to go that they dragged Justin Saldeen in by the heels. The shoes and feet had been his, and with them came the rest of him entire and attached. He still slept the sleep of the imperfectly enchanted, but now he began to wake up, section by section, like a jack-ruler unfolding. He was grinning with loose happiness, and he blew the amnesia off himself like yellow dust.

And the judge was already talking:

"Ah, it is the deficient man," he said, "he who is concerned about the Emperor's shoestrings, and who may never be able to look higher. Are you ready to abjure your deviations and deficiencies? Yauk, yauk!" He was more than judge; he was judge-advocate, and he would have full powers.

"In as much as they are deviations and deficiencies, I will abjure them, as much as I am able to, yes," Justin Saldeen said with that smile-grin on his face.

"Why do you not say 'yauk, yauk' at the end of a statement, false nuthatcher?" the judge-advocate asked. "Yauk, yauk."

"My throat is constricted today. Those words won't come out," Justin smiled.

"Has anyone evidence against this man beyond his obvious unfitness?" the judge-advocate inquired of the session. "Yauk, yauk."

"He runs around with an undersized girl with the red-thread line on her throat and with a nit's egg in her navel," Marjory Kiljoy charged. "Yauk, yauk."

"No. It isn't a nit's egg. It's a Jewel-Bird egg," Justin defended.

"If only that were possible," the judge-advocate commented, "but there haven't been Jewel-Birds in the world for a long time. Why have you abandoned the nuthatchers' quest, deficient man? Yauk, yauk."

"I haven't abandoned it," Justin maintained. "Part of the nuthatchers' quest is the discovery and recollection of small kingdoms. I believe that I am discovering and recollecting one of them now-a-times."

"A small kingdom must not be an end in itself," the judge-advocate reminded. "It has to lead into the large kingdom, or it must be sealed off. Yauk, yauk."

"But can you say by which door it will lead?" Justin argued. "It may be a very small and unregarded back door."

"Tell me, deficient man, what have you discovered about the Emperor's shoestrings? Or what has the hypothetical child discovered?" the judge-advocate asked with near derision. "Yauk, yauk."

"That most important child has discovered that the Emperor has loosened the strings and taken off his shoes," Justin said simply. "The Emperor (actually he is only a local margrave or count of a county) learned that he was walking on holy ground, the ground of the invisible kingdoms. Only those who walk barefoot can walk on magic ground without crushing small kingdoms."

The judge-advocate flushed and was angry. "I have no patience with invisible kingdoms that do not become visible," he yammered. "Every small kingdom must be visibly integrated with our large kingdom or it remains misborn and misbegotten forever. Yauk, yauk."

"C'mon, Justin," came an ankle-high voice from a small lady, with the red-thread or fairy mark on her throat and with a Jewel-Bird egg in her navel. "These illuminated people get mighty murderous if you don't use their brand of light. They'll kill you. Let's go to the thirteenth. C'mon."

"Well then, maybe we are unborn and misbegotten," Justin said, "but it might not be as forever as you believe. What souls do you think we are anyhow?"

"You've the untracked smell on you," the judge-advocate bayed. "You've been in an illicit place. Gauleiter, where was this prisoner captured. Yauk, yauk!"

"C'mon, Justin," the small lady said. Justin went with her.

"I'd rather not say where I found him," Gauleiter Rolf Mesange said uncertainly. "We found him in a ridiculous place. Yauk, yauk."

"Say where it is!' the furious judge-advocate ordered. "Yauk, yauk."

"Oh, he was in a little cubby-hole between the floors," said Rolf with plain embarrassment, "and his feet and shoes were sticking out of it."

"There isn't any cubicle. There isn't any between-the-floors," the judge-advocate barked like a fox. "What cubicle was it? Yauk, yauk."

"It was the little cubby-hole where the night-watchman keeps his lantern. Yauk, yauk." Rolf Mesange spoke, and his cheeks were flaming red with the improbability of it.

Scrub-grubbing fury! Had another one gone deficient, and he a gauleiter?

"There aren't any lanterns. There aren't any cubicles or caves or cavities. This is an illuminated era. You have named an impossible place. Where did you really bring him from? And—what, what, what? He's gone you say—and where has he gone now?"

"He's gone back to that same impossible place, I think," Gladys said. "You forgot to say 'yauk, yauk', judge-advocate."

Well, six thousand members of the NRBWA weren't able to find that impossible place. There are no finer eyes anywhere than those looked out of by the adepts of the Nuthatch Vision, by those experts of the Little

Look, by the elites of the Small Vision as Gateway to the Big Vision; and they couldn't find that cubicle or whatever.

"You people say that there was a row of cubicles here between the floors?" the judge-advocate kept asking the members of the deficient man's group. "But there is nothing here between the floors. There is not room for cubicles or cubby-holes. And what did you say that the place was like? Yauk, yauk!"

"It's a little bit like the "Jewel-Bird Song" with the steel-string background," Sulky Sullivan was saying. "It's a little bit like "Little Red Mark Around My Throat" with git-fiddle. It's something like "Cave in the Cliffs Rag" with wood-winds. There's a lot of that old song "My Blood on Your Hands" with pedal harpsichord in the sound of the place. And "Little Dead Birds" with Swiss bells, that's real soundy for what you're looking for. Yauk, yauk."

"Whatever are you talking about?" the judge-advocate asked testily. "The place where the deficient man hides, the place that we can't find, what is it like? Yauk, yauk!"

"Justin is too big to be with them in their place now. Yauk, yauk," Rolf said quietly.

"No, he was never very big. He faked that part all his life. Yauk, yauk," Berthold Chairmender answered.

"The place is a little bit like red fish," Marjory Kiljoy told the scurrying judge-advocate. "And it's even more like gold fish. It's quite a bit like a fountain that gushes inward, that's if you want to know what the place looks like. It's quite a bit like a lantern with a little light still burning in it. But it isn't easy to describe its appearance. You have to be inside it, I think, to see what it does look like. I've never been more than partly inside it. Yauk, yauk."

The judge-advocate strode up and down the area in exasperation with his hands locked behind him. A much smaller man strode behind him exactly taking off his motions and attitudes. There were several of the other small persons japing about, but nobody looked at them much.

And, really, they were not much to look at: they were all quite small; they all had that thread-thin red line around their throats; and they all had funny faces.

"It is hard to describe the place for the reason that is a movement and drama and not a place," Rolf told the judge-advocate. "It should be right here between the floors though. And, since it is what it is, it can only be described in terms of dramatic kinesis. Yauk, yauk."

"Then for the love of the Great Northern Nuthatch describe it to me as dramatic kinesis!" the judge-advocate roared like an unhappy lion. "Yauk, yauk!"

"Could we pick Justin out from the rest of them if we finally found him now?" Rolf said secretly. "Yauk, yauk."

"No, I don't believe that we could," Gladys Gamaliel doubted it. "He's always been one of them, but he blew himself up like a grown-up person, those big feet and all. He always had the line on his throat too, but we didn't know that he'd been murdered. He has a funny face, of course, but all of them have funny faces."

There were quite a few of the little funny-faced folks larking around but nobody paid them heed. They were on a different sound-track and sight-track.

"The dramatic kinesis we're looking for is very contemporary," said Berthold Chairmender, "like the current murder comedies and haunt skits. It resembles many of the play-bills of recent times. It's a little bit like *Thirteen at the Table*, or *Pumpkin Head*, or *Bright Red Windows in My House*. Its movement will remind one of *Boat That Never Sailed*, or *Tumble-Down Nest*, or *Old Salty Sea*, or *Lightning-Bolt of Blood*. It comes through strong like *Mist and Weeping Rain*, or *Cut by Such Sword*, or *Die Before I Wake*, or *Poor Oriflame*."

One of the little funny-faced folks (he somehow looked like Justin Saldeen) kicked the judge-advocate at shoestring height (it was as high as he could kick).

"Ouch!" cried the judge-advocate. "Yauk, yauk!" But he didn't look down.

"The scene that we are looking for reminds me very much of that murder comedy *Funny Face*," Berthold Chairmender said.

"I don't go to the theater often," the judge-advocate admitted. "An illuminated person hasn't much time for such things. What we need for our search 'yauk, yauk', is a working description of —"

"The thing reminds me quite a lot of *That Real Funny Kind of Love*," Berthold Chairmender said.

destination unknown
WAGE SLAVES

by Christopher Fowler

The office block blotted out the night sky above Canary Wharf. Walls of polished black glass absorbed all reflections, turning the building into a black hole, inhuman and infinite. The surrounding streets were deserted now. At this time of night a single window was still illuminated, on the 35th floor.

Leonard Clarke was in his office studying a document. He was a lifer, heavy, balding, gym-fit, a workaholic whose calculated responses and unflinching stares made others nervous. His office was clinically corporate. The only touches of humanity were a framed photograph of a lost-looking wife and a signed cricket bat—a quota-achievement trophy—mounted on the wall.

Matthew Felix, another executive, but one with an attitude as yet unhardened by the vicissitudes of business life, knocked and entered.

"Ah, Mr. Felix. I've just finished checking your report. Take a pew."

The younger man seated himself and awaited Clark's verdict. "The style is sharp, succinct," noted his boss. "It's very impressive. *Very* impressive." He paced about, studying the document while Felix fidgeted, unnerved by the rare praise.

"Thorough, that's the word. And not afraid to be critical. That's good. It shows integrity." Felix grew increasingly uncomfortable as Clark paced behind him. "How long did this take you?"

"Three days. Well, days and nights."

"It's paid off. It really has. There's just one thing that bothers me. A silly thing. It's this, here." He held the document close to Felix's face. Too close. "Receipt. I before E except after C. But you get it wrong every time. Every single time. Look. Receipt. Receipt. Receipt. *Receipt.*"

Clark carefully removed his prized cricket bat from the wall, giving it a few test swings. "A foolish, tiny, minuscule mistake. Ruining *everything.'"

He took a sudden high swing with the bat. The massive connecting *crack* against the back of Felix's skull knocked him clean out of his swivel chair, sprawling him face down on the carpet-tiles. Clark examined his unconscious subordinate, then dragged him out of the office by the lapels of his suit. "There's simply no excuse for shoddy workmanship these days," he reflected.

Imagine an incredibly complex computer program, a physical structure, skeletal at first, then gaining a dense musculature of electronic cabling, pipework and floors and finally, an exterior skin. A monolithic mirrored cathedral, towering over the city horizon. Below the post-modern fripperies of its entrance, down in the railway station at its base, a train discharged its next batch of commuters. They marched along the platform in regiments, financial warriors heading into fresh battle.

Ben Harper's tie was knotted too tightly. He tried to loosen the knot as he marched with the crowd. Feeling something sticking in his neck, he pulled a pin from the collar of his brand-new shirt. He had yet to notice the price sticker still on his briefcase. He checked his watch and glanced up at the sombre building, its windows darkening as clouds passed.

Ben had the hopelessly innocent face of a young man on his first day in a new job. He watched the other commuters for his cues, swallowed nervously and wondered why he had ever lied in the first place. Then he crossed the half-finished road to the Symax building and entered its pristine foyer.

The Olympian marble hall appeared to have been designed by Albert Speer. A cleaner shuffled behind Ben, carefully wiping away his wet footprints. To access the elevator he had to collect an electronic tag from the commissionaire, who punched in its encoded number. The guards looked like American police officers. Video monitors checked his progress as the lift arrived and he entered.

"Hold the doors!" An attractive young woman slipped into the elevator and smiled at Ben. She stood on one leg and removed her shoe, then belted the base of the door with the heel. The door juddered and shut. "There's something weird with the electrics," she explained. "I should keep a hammer in my handbag." She put the shoe back on.

Ben watched her, fascinated, until the doors opened on the 35th floor.

The reception area was a gleaming shrine to the work ethic, part space station, part rain forest. A large chromium sign read: **SYMAX. The Future Is Now**. Beyond that a bank of TV screens showed corporate videos; images of wheatfields, dolphins and sunsets. The blonde robot behind the desk noted Ben's color-coded badge. "Oh, new boy. I'll call someone."

He watched one of the corporate videos. An avuncular voice intoned something about the first generation of environments that work for you. "A Symax building is an infinitely adaptable stress-free workspace. Light, heat and climate are monitored by sensors that control your staff's constantly changing needs. One day all offices will be this way, because at Symax the future is here to stay."

"Mr. Harper." A corporate-looking woman in her early thirties held out her hand. "Diana Carter. We met briefly at your interview. If you'd care to follow me."

She led Ben through the swing doors, past rows of extreme-technology workstations. The sky dominated, framed in the floor-to-ceiling windows. It gave the area a feeling of peace, as though they were on the deck of a liner coasting its way through the clouds. Staffers had customized their work spaces in odd ways, as if trying to make them cozier and less efficient-looking. All sounds seemed to be absorbed except for the clicking of keyboards.

"There's been a personnel change since we spoke," explained Carter. "Mr. Felix left us rather suddenly. The PR department isn't fully functional yet. Things are a little crazy." She handed him a manual. "Company bible. Read and believe. This desk was supposed to have been cleared. Mr. Temple wanted to welcome you but he's not himself today. None of us are." She gave a brief bleak smile and whizzed off, leaving Ben at his workstation.

49

The girl from the lift was at the next desk. She looked over and smiled, appraising him. Feeling spied upon, Ben attempted to look efficient. Unfortunately, he couldn't find the switch to activate his terminal. Perhaps it needed a key or something. He checked the desk drawers. The first one contained a pair of wet socks, a bottle of painkillers and a hunting knife.

His watch had stopped. His chair-back appeared to be broken. He tried to fire up the computer again, to no avail. He studied other people for tips and got none.

Amused, the girl finally came over. "Try the button at the front."

Ben sheepishly pressed it. The screen came on, but nothing else did. "You've never used one of these before, have you?"

"I'm not familiar with this, uh, make," said Ben.

She reached over and booted up the system for him. 'What are you doing here?" He shifted awkwardly. "I'm the new PR assistant to Mr. Clark—"

"I don't see how. You obviously have no experience."

"I've had dozens of corporate jobs."

"Then go ahead and set your voicemail." She sat back, amused. "You can fool them but not me. You've never worked in a place like this before, have you?"

Ben was flustered. "I thought I'd get a bit further before being found out. It's only ten past nine."

"I won't tell anyone." She held out her hand. "Marie Vine. Let's cut a deal. Tell me what you're doing here, and I'll get you through. Nobody has to know."

There was no point in continuing to lie. "I needed the work," he admitted. "So I faked my CV. I was a teacher, do you know what that pays? I'm twenty-six and sick of never having any money. I can handle this. I know about people."

"If you know so much about people," asked Marie, "why did you stop teaching?"

"I got fired for organizing a student picket. I get too involved. This will be better for me, more—impersonal. It's just press releases. How hard can it be?"

She brought her lips close to his ear. "Here's something for you to think about. This is the most advanced work environment in the world. Yet it gives a job to a little red schoolteacher with a faked CV. What does that tell you?"

At noon, Carter reappeared to take Ben on a tour of the floor. "Over there," she pointed to a thin man in a tight gray suit, "that's Mr. Swan." Swan's posture was birdlike and vaguely irritating. He slowly craned forward. "If there's anything in the company manual that doesn't leap out at you, feel free to give me a tinkle."

"Over there, Mr. Carmichael." Ben nodded to each of the staff in turn, but people were too busy to take much notice. "Lucy, your shared PA. Paula, word processing." They passed another office. The huge shape of an arguing man could be seen through the glass. "Mr. Clark, the new department head."

Marie passed with a sheaf of papers and interrupted in a manner that seemed to annoy Carter. "Mr. Felix was in line for the position but he's gone," she explained. "Vanished like a summer rain."

"Mr. Temple is the managing director, as you know, but he's not often here," said Carter. "He lives on the floor above—"

"—but seeing him is like getting an appointment with the Wizard of Oz," Marie cut in. "Oh well, better get back to work. We're all on Candid Camera, you know. They record everything, and they're everywhere. Even in the toilets."

"I suppose Symax needs good security if it's developing systems no-one else has," Ben replied.

"Exactly so; Mr. Harper," agreed Carter. Marie was disappointed that Ben had chosen to side with the management. Ahead, a crowd was gathering around one of the refreshment stations.

"It's happening again!" called one of the office boys. People were watching a half-filled water cooler that was emitting an ominous rumbling sound. The water inside swirled around in an impossible whirlpool, climbing the sides of the plastic jar. It whirled faster and faster, and suddenly the jar ruptured, spraying water everywhere. The secretaries squealed and jumped back. Ben turned to Carter but found her place taken by Marie. "A bug in the system," she explained. "Look, my little bogus friend, I know it's your first day but I'd like to talk to you. You confided in me. Not here, though. The walls have ears and eyes. You have to be careful who you talk to. Over lunch."

They crossed an acre of gray marble floor to the restaurant, passing a pair of security guards with vicious-looking guns in their belts. "Private security firm," noted Marie, "Those things on their belts are tasors."

"Is that legal?"

"This place is beyond the jurisdiction of the police," she explained. In the restaurant there were fresh salads, roasting chickens, trays of ham and beef. They shared a quiet table away from the chatter-filled main section.

"Three weeks ago Matthew Felix walked out of here and never even came back to collect his belongings," she explained, talking through a mouthful of chicken. "His car's still in its usual parking space under the building, but he's gone. He was my friend. And your predecessor."

"What can I do?" Ben shrugged helplessly. "I just got here."

"The secretaries are always off sick. They say there's something in the air that makes you ill. At this height the windows can't be opened because of the winds. Then there are the phone lines. They randomly switch themselves around, like they've got poltergeists or something."

"It's my first day," he pleaded.

"The staff can sense that there's something wrong even if the management can't, but no one—NO ONE—is willing to talk about it."

"This suit is brand new, Marie. And the tie."

"I'm trying to find someone who's not just a management sheep."

WAGE SLAVES

"I'm not a sheep!' Ben protested. 'I've been in the business world for four hours! Management must be able to do something. Temple, he's the boss-man."

Marie speared a piece of asparagus. "He won't see me. I've already had two official cautions from Clark. One more and I'll lose my job. They all think I like to stir things up."

Ben grew more exasperated. "I should stay away from you. I fought hard for this job and I'd really like to keep it."

"It's not like I'm asking you to do anything illegal, just keep your eyes and ears open, and tell me if you notice anything strange. Do it before the place gets to you and you become like the rest of them."

Ben lowered his fork. "Which is what?"

"You know. Corporate."

"What's wrong with that?"

"You're an individual."

He thought for a moment. "Maybe I don't want to be."

Marie rose to leave. She was frustrated by Ben's attitude. "Maybe you don't. But I think Matthew Felix is dead. The police found his cat half-starved. Maybe he had a heart attack and it was stress-related so they quietly took him away. Somebody here knows more than they're telling. Look at them!"

"Why would they hide something like that?"

"This is a new company. Maybe they're scared of bad publicity. Look, forget it. Just forget I said anything." Ben watched helplessly as she rose from the table and left. He looked out of the windows at the power lines which passed close to the glass. He could hear their eerie hum beneath the moaning wind. There were dead pigeons all along the window ledge, neatly aligned in a row. He thought; *I'm in the Twilight Zone.*

Aided by a bank of video monitors running interactive graphic devices, Clark was giving a talk to a group of potential Symax investors. Ben found a chair and watched his new boss in action.

"This is the first fully operational CAD smart building in the United Kingdom. Created by computer to minimize employee error and maximize profit potential." On the screens behind, Ben could see diagrams of the building's nerve center, the sensor room filled with gauges and cylinders. "A Symax building is designed for every temperature, atmosphere and movement change. In a non-smart building, company staff have to find a way of fitting around the architecture. Climax systems learn from staff habits and adapt to create a unique environment for each company." As the meeting ended, Clark walked with the leader of the group, Ben following alongside, listening in.

"I want New York to see this," said the client. "I'll need a full presentation on Friday. Can you handle it?"

"I have no problem with that at all," Clark replied, seeing him into the lift. After the doors had shut, he eyed Ben suspiciously. "You heard him. Four days to the biggest presentation we've ever had. This place is going to be jumping, and you with it."

Dusk brought a lurid red glow to the windows, which automatically darkened. Ben attempted to set up a stack of books on his desk, which appeared to be perfectly level, but each time he balanced them they shifted and fell over. He took a marble from his drawer and set it on the white melamine desktop. The little glass ball rolled first one way, then abruptly another. He tapped his teeth with a pencil and looked back at Marie, thinking that nothing made sense here. Was that normal in the world of big business? He knew he shouldn't get involved, that it would only lead to trouble, but he decided to talk to Swan anyway.

"My predecessor seems to have left very suddenly," he prompted.

"Mr. Clark fired him," Swan explained. "They had a terrible row."

"What about?"

"I don't know. Work, I suppose. They didn't get on."

"I thought everyone 'got on' here. Isn't that the point?"

"In theory, yes. Did you ever hear of a theory that fully worked in practice? Thought you might like a copy of this. More useful than the office bible."

Ben accepted the proferred pamphlet and turned it over in his hands. It bore the title: GOD IN THE WORKPLACE.

"Er, thanks."

Swan pointed to the small gold crucifix he wore over his tie. "The devil and his works are all around us, Mr. Harper. Better safe than sorry."

That night, as everyone worked late, a secretary swept into the office of her supervisor, Mr. Meadows, and dumped a stack of papers onto his overflowing desk. The executive argued into his headset while signing papers and returning them. "I know it was late because I checked with security, and if it doesn't reach me in time my client won't pay so we all get shafted. Well, fuck-you-very-much but an apology isn't recognizable in fiscal terms—you're hovering, what is it?"

"Accounts on 2," said the secretary. "Wife on 3 and Mr. Clark on the internal."

"I'll call them all back. Close the door, Norma—close it."

She reluctantly left, pulling the door shut behind her. Meadows kicked back, yanking off the headset and thumbing the remote on his stereo unit. Classical music began playing, Smetana's *Libuse*, the volume increased. He stared at the phone, still trilling, and suddenly yanked it out of the wall. Then he shook the buzz from his ears, locked the door and returned to his desk, slipped off his jacket, removed his tie, kicked off his shoes and unbuckled his trouser belt.

Outside the office, two secretaries noticed him through the glass and started to giggle. Meadows continued to strip until he was completely naked. A crowd gathered as he stood at the picture window behind his desk. Everyone yelled when he raised his chair and hurled it through the glass. They hammered at the locked door as Meadows climbed over the broken shards onto the ledge.

He raised his arms high. It was a hell of a drop. Balancing on the balls of his feet, he executed a graceful swan dive out over the glittering city. The office door caved in seconds too late. The secretary screamed. Buoyed by the crosswinds, Meadows fell slowly through the starry sky— fell and fell—and laughed, until he smashed thunderously through the glass canopy of the station roof amid hoards of homegoing commuters.

Ben pulled open the glass doors. Far above him in the sensor room, electronic dials registered the change in temperature and compensated for the sudden fall with a boost. In the reception area, the screens continued to run endless plugs for Symax. Already the words sounded repetitive and hollow. The receptionist was holding her head in her hands. It looked like a bad start to Tuesday.

"You okay ?" asked Ben as he passed.

"The monitors give me a headache," the receptionist replied.

As Ben reached his workstation he could see staff members discussing something, very intently. The broken glass in front of Meadows office was being swept up, the area sealed off.

"What happened here?"

"Just after you left last night Mr. Meadows went for a walk outside the building and missed his train, by about three feet," Marie explained. "Thirty five floors. They scraped him off the tarmac like a dab of strawberry jam. The police are still looking for his teeth."

"He must have been—really stressed out."

"That's an understatement. They're sending people to counselors. Perhaps now you'll believe me. I have to talk to you."

"Not again."

"Remember, I know your little secret." Reluctantly, Ben followed her away from the steady gaze of the cameras to the stairwell, and then up four flights of stairs to one of the deserted floors. Heat dials and movement recorders flickered as they crossed the gray carpet tiles. 'They haven't sold this floor yet. No-one can hear or see us."

destination unknown
WAGE SLAVES

Ben felt guilty. "We shouldn't even be here." He paused and looked down at his shoes. Dozens of tiny dead insects were arranged in neat curving rows across the floor.

"I need to trust someone," said Marie. "I don't want to spoil your chances with the company. I mean look at you. All freshly scrubbed and innocent."

"Matthew Felix didn't go missing, he got fired."

"Nobody knows that for sure. I was due to meet him that night, but he never showed up."

"Did you talk to the police?"

"They said they'd let me know if they heard anything. It's not like I'm a relative. I'm sure something terrible has happened to him. You're new, you could ask around." The big, appealing eyes swayed him. "Please?"

Mr. Carmichael was a fussy timeserver, and today he had an appalling head-cold.

"Of course he was stressed," he told Ben, "he'd just had a terrible argument with Clark. I don't know where he went, nobody knows. I liked him, he was a nice man. I liked Meadows, too. Never thought he'd do something like that. They say it's always the quiet ones, but Meadows... Mind you, everyone hated his guts."

In the ceiling corners, gleaming cameras recorded all movement as the airmixers raised and lowered their pitch. Ben tapped the pencil on his teeth, trying to work it out. Worry often made people overdose on sleeping pills, but what could make you hurl yourself to your death? Ebony clouds rolled past the windows. He looked over at Marie's work-station. She briefly glanced up and gave him an absent, tired smile.

"Want to go for a drink tonight?"

"By the time I'm through there won't be anywhere open. Besides, we shouldn't be seen together. Office fraternizing is discouraged."

Her changes of mood were unpredictable. The day passed at a crawl. Ben concentrated on drafting the press releases Carter had outlined to him. When he left the building that night, the thousand rain-dark panes that looked down on him seemed far more sinister than they had yesterday morning.

Clark had been summoned to the director's office, an elegant low lit suite that was more like a private apartment. Inside, the graying, debonair Temple was checking his watch impatiently, ready to leave.

"I hear the police were trying to get in again, Leonard. This is getting to be a habit."

"I've told them this is private property," said Clark, "that we have our own security force."

"We're still subject to the laws of the land. Anyone know why Meadows did it?"

"I've asked around. He seemed fine, a little hyper, but so is everyone else with this presentation looming...."

"It's not a wonderful advert for a stress-free environment, is it?"

"An unfortunate coincidence. And now these rumors..."

"You're saying we have—*grumblers*?" Temple made the word sound sinister. "If we do, keep an eye on them, report back to me. New York is the big one, the make or break contract. Nothing must jeopardize that. Do you understand? This is more than war. This is business."

In the reception area of the 35th floor, the monitors were still spewing out their 'Peace And Harmony' sales pitch. Ben passed two managers who were shouting at each other, and another who was dropping papers everywhere and looked like she'd been up all night. Lucy, his PA, startled him. "Can cellular phones give you cancer?" she asked.

"I don't know," Ben answered. Why?"

"I get these headaches all the time. Can you get cancer of the head?"

"Have you seen the company doctor?"

"He thinks I'm faking. Maybe it's these things." She tapped his monitor.

"Tell me something, Lucy. What was Mr. Felix like?"

"Really cute. She soon got her claws into him." She pointed at Marie's chair.

"Before he left, did he seem strange to you in any way?"

"Not strange. Angry. He'd had an argument with Mr. Clark."

"They didn't get along?"

"Mr. Clark hated him. He hates everyone. He already hates you."

Later that morning, Ben attempted to requisition a file from a harassed Human Resources Officer. "I told you," insisted the officer, "you can't see Mr. Felix's medical history without proper authorization."

"What about absenteeism?" asked Ben. "Does Symax have many people off sick?"

"What do you expect? Germs travel through the heating system. There are a few repetitive strain injuries. Always more when we're busy. There's a flu virus decimating the place. All companies get them, but this is particularly bad. We've a bigger health problem, but it doesn't make any sense."

"What do you mean?"

"Hard to explain." The officer pulled a pen from her hair and scrubbed something out on a form. "I don't have any figures. Deadlines produce stress, which increases blood pressure, causes headaches, heartburn, sleep disorders... standard stuff. But there's an instability here. People overreact, flare up, lose their tempers, burst into tears. It's something peculiar to this building. You know the hand dryers in the toilets? They're supposed to be more hygienic. They're not. They incubate bacteria. You can get pneumonia from them. Nobody really knows what's good for you or what's harmful, and my clock's running backwards."

Ben was momentarily thrown. "Sorry?"

"My computer clock. They can't do that, can they? Run backwards?"

"Could you give me a printout of the sickness figures?"

"It's against regulations. Haven't you read your manual? Head office don't like it."

Ben fooled around with his computer, but any management files of importance were sealed with passwords. He tried different keys of his own devising, but nothing worked. He watched Marie at her desk. Knowing she could be seen, she crossed her long legs and gave him a sexy look. He drew a heart on a piece of paper and folded it into an airplane. Throwing it in her direction, he was dismayed to see it sucked into the air-conditioning unit that sat between them. The sun suddenly broke through the clouds, causing the photo-sensitized windows to compensate for the changing light density and darken, while the illuminated ceiling panels above them grew perversely brighter.

Ben despairingly studied his monitor, typing slowly, but his attention drifted to Felix's belongings. Rechecking the desk he felt something, a flat square stuck at the back of the bottom drawer. The computer disk was labeled *Property of Matthew Felix.* He pocketed it just as Clark appeared beside him.

"You never seem to be doing any work, Harper."

"I was—going to ask your advice on the press releases," said Ben. "I take it we gloss over Mr. Meadows' first diving lesson?"

Clark glowered at him. "I don't like you, Harper. Why is that?"

"You haven't tried my cooking yet?"

"Just do your job and I won't have cause to lose my temper."

Marie helped Ben load the disk after Clark had moved on. "You'll need the password," she warned. "Everyone is expected to enter and remember their own five letter code."

"Didn't he tell you what his was?" asked Ben. 'I mean, you were friends."

"I liked him, but I didn't exactly get inside his mind. Besides, we aren't supposed to tell each other things like that."

"Then maybe he kept it written down somewhere. You okay?'

'It's nothing, just a headache. We'll have to keep looking."

He studied Felix's belongings again, trying to make sense of it all. In a travel bag beneath the desk he found a book of horoscopes. "You'd think the police would have taken his belongings away."

"They never came up here. Our security firm wouldn't let them."

"What birth-sign was Felix?" he asked Marie.

"Gemini, I think."

He flicked through the horoscope book to Gemini, and found a drawing of Janus. *The Twin-Faced Guardian of Doorways, Entrances And Beginnings*, read the asterisked caption. He typed in 'Janus' and pressed ENTER. The disk started to open its files, but the contents corrupted. The magnetics in this place...

One newspaper clipping was legible before the screen contents vanished. A photograph of the building captioned *Father of 'smart' architecture commits suicide.* Then the item dispersed into the ether.

"Maybe he realized something was wrong with the building and killed himself," suggested Marie.

"Maybe somebody else realized something was wrong and shut him up." They exchanged alarmed looks.

Swan suddenly appeared beside them, looking pleased with himself. "Want to see something really strange?" Before they could reply, he unclipped the steel biro he kept in his jacket pocket and slapped it against the wall above Ben's desk.

When he removed his hand, the pen stayed there by itself. "Some days the whole blessed place is magnetized."

"We need your help," said Ben. "Who designed this building?"

"That kind of information isn't available anymore," Swan complained. "I'd be breaking company rules. Punishable by instant dismissal."

"Who's going to know?"

"In an environment with total information control? Are you nuts? Look, it's not a good idea to get too involved with the work. You could lose your job, your credit rating, who knows what else. Those cameras up there probably lip-read."

"You're being paranoid."

"You're right," agreed Swan. "That's good. It's healthy to be paranoid."

61

The sun set beyond the vast glass window as Paula, the typist, put down her coffee and slopped some of it onto her desk. Tutting with annoyance, she dug out a paper towel and started mopping up the mess. At her feet, one of the recessed floor plugs emitted sparks. Just beyond her field of vision, a wall circuit was scorching a live path to her computer, tiny white flashes jumping across the keyboard. The spilt coffee reached her mouse just as she mopped it. The resulting electric shock threw her across the room.

Several people saw the burning lines short-circuiting in the walls, passing from one computer to the next, rendering each one live. "Where's the main switch?" someone shouted, "keep away from the machines!" Others just looked confused. Nobody moved.

But everyone stared at Ben as he stormed into Diana Carter's office. Carter was on the phone, and not pleased by the interruption. "A girl just got electrocuted and everyone's carrying on as if nothing happened!" he shouted, pointing through the glass. "Look at them!" The workforce was busily going about its business. "This is gross negligence. There's something wrong with the electrics. We had to unplug the terminals."

She eyed his dirty knees. "Everyone is working very hard here, Harper. It's bad enough that half of my girls are off sick without you causing trouble. You're not allowed to tamper with the machines. It's against company policy."

"We'll see about that," said Ben, slamming out.

"One of my staff members, Mr. Swan, brought the matter to my attention," said Clark. "He overheard Harper telling someone he'd lied his way into the job."

"Christ, don't you think I have enough to worry about without this?" demanded Temple. "We're taking orders from all over the world and yet our figures are down. How is that possible? The efficiency of our workforce is plunging. *Inside the world's most efficient building.* What the fuck is going wrong? And now you tell me we have some kind of a spy in our midst. Well, you'll have to deal with it. Nothing can screw up this presentation."

The small hardboard door opened in the wall and a troll-like man, around sixty, looked out. Snowy bristles sprouted from his eyebrows, nose and ears.

"I haven't seen you before," said Hegarty, the caretaker. "What are you?"

"Who am I?" asked Ben.

"No," said Hegarty laboriously. "*What* are you? Are you a drone or an executive?"

"Well, I've only just started."

"Unsullied, eh? You'd better come in, then. Name?"

"Ben Harper."

"Oh, the troublemaker. I've read the e-mail on you. How did you find me?"

"Oddly enough," said Ben, "I thought of the Wizard of Oz. The man behind the curtain operating the levers. Why would this building need a caretaker?"

"Well of course it doesn't, but they couldn't think of another job title for me." Hegarty's hut was as cluttered as an allotment shed. The caretaker boiled tea. "All buildings will be like this soon," he said. "Self-regulating. Auto-balanced. Remote-logic. If you fart it'll spray Atar Of Roses over you. Sugar?"

"One please. You sound as if you don't approve."

"You hear anybody say what a great place this is to work? I thought not. Know why? It's no good."

Ben accepted a cracked, murky brown mug, eyeing it dubiously. "There are bound to be teething problems."

"Listen to me. *It's no good.* The wind changes, the building shifts, the compensation mechanism causes leaks. For every action, a reaction. They haven't allowed for that. Old buildings are lived in, cherished. This one changes people. Causes breakdowns. Action, reaction; people break down—what happens to buildings?"

"You think it's already started happenings."

"You tell me. People are jumping out of windows. Did you know there are live spots all over the building? Come over here." He pointed it a narrow air-shaft, cocking his head to one side. Voices carried from somewhere far above. "You can hear them quite clearly, yet there must be thirty floors between us. Odd, isn't it? There's a gap in the center courtyard where tiny magnetic tornadoes form. Why? Buildings are like women. Each one has a special mystique."

"Why did the architect kill himself?"

"Ah, you know about that. Fair enough. Carrington Rogers was my partner. This building wasn't really his, of course. Computers designed it for Symax. Optimized his sketches. Wasn't much left of the original plans. He knew it would go wrong, even warned them, but there was nothing he could do to stop it. By that time he'd taken the money, you see. There was no other way out for him. His suicide, my breakdown, the end of all our dreams. I came to work here so I could keep an eye on the place, keep the bosses' secrets safe for them."

"Do you still have the plans?"

"Yes, but they're all classified. In case of industrial sabotage." He reached into a battered gray steel filing cabinet and withdrew an amorphous mass of documentation. Maps that consisted of curving dotted lines. Scrawled notes. Clipped articles on the architect and his plans for Symax. He splayed the huge drafting papers across the table. "I shouldn't be showing them to you, but," he smiled, his beady eyes glittering, "into every ordered system prances the imp of chaos. What do you know about electromagnetic fields?" Grinning, the old man set a metal company biro on the concrete floor and watched as it started to spin, faster and faster. Finally it shot across the room and embedded itself into the skirting board. At the same time Ben could feel his hair lifting and prickling. He remembered the insects lined in rows at his feet.

"No wonder my watch stopped."

"It's a vortex, a turbulent area where opposing electromagnetic fields overlap. A modern office building is filled with electrical fields. Every machine you use provides its own forcefield. The only reason why they don't cause havoc is because they're shielded. They have to be. Electromagnetic forces affect brain patterns. In moments of stress they can cause someone's least stable traits to surface violently. Nobody knows the full effects of unshielded mag-force. Symptoms are everything from stress-related stuff like headaches, to terminal disease. Cancer patients have been suing cellular phone companies lately. It's now thought that overhead cables may cause leukemia."

"But if these machines are all shielded, how can they cause any harm?"

"I think something must have upset the system's balance."

"Surely they'll have to evacuate the building until the problem's located?"

"That won't be enough,' said Hegarty. "Look at this." He dug out a dusty diskette and pushed it into an ancient terminal hidden behind tea towels. The screen quickly filled with typewritten newspaper files.

"'People's Architect' to initiate designs for 'ultimate human environment."

"Architect warns of hidden dangers in computer-assisted designs."

"Unshielded electrical fields cause massive electro-turbulence, says top architect."

"The board of directors know there's a problem, but they have no answers. All they can do is bury their heads in the sand and act like nothing's wrong. These systems are on the verge of being sold across the world. Rogers was concerned that the use of so much electronic equipment might have an effect on human occupants. When the computers 'enhanced' his designs, he was worried that they would allow for human error, but not human nature. People are perverse. You try to streamline them and they develop odd behavioral quirks. The computers made improvements which were, by themselves, acceptable. Except that they completely changed the building's electro-radiation levels."

"Surely someone checked for this sort of thing?"

"Computers checked. Their programs change the pressure, the temperature, the chemical composition of the air, calming when the atmosphere is charged, energizing when things are too relaxed. But you can't program people. Every time the computer reacts, they react back and the whole thing escalates. That result is a potential madhouse. And the more electronic equipment that's turned on, the more devastating the effect."

"But if the building's so dangerous," asked Ben, "why aren't we all affected?"

"We are," replied Hegarty, tapping the side of his head. "We don't all feel it yet."

On Wednesday the weather worsened. The wet workforce shook out their umbrellas and entered the building ready for their toughest day. Ben wondered how much longer he could get away with not doing his work, but people were too preoccupied to notice. He sat and shuffled papers, trying to look busy.

"Clark's making everyone go through the night," said Marie. Behind her, the wall lights glowed like waxing moons as the sensors adjusted to the displacement and warmth and movement of stressed-out humanity. The recycled air smelled musty and bitter. By mid-morning everyone was operating at the double. Phones rang, screens flashed, staff swept past in a frenzy of hyperactivity. The sense of collective unease was palpable.

He had been aware of the humming for some time now, a dull rumble that vibrated in his bones. The very air was shimmering. A maelstrom of electromagnetic activity, caused by every damned machine in the place operating at full capacity. Marie had gone missing. He'd only left his desk for a moment. He checked all the workstations calling her name, and missed her as she passed him heading toward the elevator banks.

Marie stepped into the lift and pressed a lower floor button just as Ben spotted her. The doors shut and the lift started off smoothly, but suddenly stopped. Inside, the lights began to flicker and fail. The lift walls snapped and sparkled with cobalt streaks of electromagnetic energy. Ben watched the overhead panel to see where Marie would alight. The panel indicator illuminated 34, but when he took the stairs there he found the doors shut. He held his breath and listened. Something weird was happening in the shaft. He tried to wedge the doors open, but they wouldn't budge. The entire lift shaft was filled with electrical fire. There was a sudden crack as it shorted out, and the lift started moving again. Ben pulled Marie clear as the doors slammed open before him with a vicious, deafening bang.

"Where were you going?" he asked.

"I don't know." Marie rubbed her eyes. "I had some kind of panic attack."

Through the open swing doors they caught sight of Clark, whose efforts to concentrate and compose himself were undermined by his left eye, which twitched uncontrollably. "Harper," he called, "My office, right now."

"Go and get your coat," said Ben, "Wait for me in reception. We're getting out."

Clark ushered Ben into his office and closed the door. My staff are falling apart," he complained. "Half of them have barricaded themselves in the toilets. The rest have gone mad. It's all coming true, everything Carrington and Hegarty warned the board about." Then, as if suddenly jabbed with a pin, he started shouting. "Stress doesn't touch you, though, does it? Because you're not corporate material. You lied to get the job! A teacher, fired for breeding insurrection" He reached for the nearest telephone and punched out a number. "Why did you come here?"

"I wanted something with potential."

"But you've just destroyed your chances. Why would you do that?" Ben thought for a moment. "Human nature."

A huge security guard filled the doorway. "Escort this man off the premises."

67

Ben was pulled from the room. Wary of the tasor strapped to the guard, he went quietly. As they reached the lift he broke into a run, the guard following close on his heels. Suddenly they were confronted by a demented-looking Swan, who forced his way between Ben and the guard. "Been up to see the boss, have we? Reporting back on the workers? Everything was all right 'til you got here."

"I've no quarrel with you."

"So innocent. How do you know what it's like to keep having your quotas raised, to still be working long after your children are in bed?" He furiously poked Ben in the chest. Ben pushed him onto the guard, who immediately grabbed Swan by the tie. As this happened, Ben pulled the tasor from the guard's pocket and fired it, dropping him to his knees like a felled bull. Swan's eyes widened in surprise. He smoothed his tie into place. "That's more like it," he said. "A little respect for a decent Christian. *All hail the Lord.*"

The guard's jacket was smoking. "Christ," said Ben, dropping the tasor. Swan turned on him. "Blasphemer!"

This is not going to look good on my CV, thought Ben as he kneed Swan in the balls and pushed him down the stairs.

The 35th floor was devoid of life. Somewhere in the distance were screams, moaning, the sound of breaking glass. The monitors droned on in the reception area, but the tape of sunsets and dolphins was slurred and distorted. The receptionist was sitting on the floor with her legs straight out, nursing her head like a character from a Laurel and Hardy film. Marie ran to her workstation and collected her coat. She tried to telephone the police, but watched on her display unit as the call was diverted to a dead line. She punched out a 9, then 100. "Hello, operator, I'm trying to get connected to the police. Why can't you? I know we're not under police jurisdiction, that's because the company has its own security services, but surely a 999 call is still—well, yes, it is an emergency." She cradled the receiver under her ear, looking around.

WAGE SLAVES

Lucy had set fire to a wastepaper bin and was standing on a chair holding it near the ceiling, trying to set off the sprinkler system. One of the
other typists was seated at her keyboard printing out hundreds of pages
of O's. Carmichael had over a dozen biros protruding from his back,
and lay sprawled on the floor beneath his desk. Everyone else had fled
to darker corners.

Clark wandered into his office clutching his face. The muffled cries
and scuffles emanating from the floor outside made him look up in a
state of dementia.

"You killed him, didn't you?" said Marie as he hove into her eyeline.

"Felix's report suggested delaying everything while we investigated
the problem," Clark moaned. "The shares would have plummeted. I
didn't mean to kill him. But I—get—these—headaches."

Marie slowly replaced the receiver. "What did you do with his body?"

"Put him in a cool place, somewhere off limits" he replied dully.
"The sensor room."

"My god, that's supposed to be a sterile area. You left a corpse in
there with the building's sensor units?"

"I wasn't thinking too clearly. I'm better now." The heavy executive
suddenly lunged at her, and they fell back onto her desk as Marie desperately cast about for something to hit him with. Grabbing wildly behind her, she smashed a "You Don't Have To Be Mad To Work Here But
It Helps" breakfast mug over his head, which briefly dazed him.

Clark scrambled after Marie as she fought to get away. She rammed
her chair at him, and while he was tipped back against the desk rubbing
his head she pulled the plastic bottle from the seater cooler beside her
and flung it at him. From the way he suddenly grew rigid and began
grinding his teeth she could only assume that her keyboard, too, was now
electrified, and that he was sitting on it in wet trousers.

Marie and Ben stumbled into the building's deserted atrium and
made for the main doors. They had been forced to use the stairs down,
as people were making love in the lifts. Fights had broken out on every

floor. "I'm sorry I took so long to find you," wheezed Ben, "but a gang of bookkeepers ambushed me in Accounts."

"The system won't let us out," said Marie. "These things are locked."

"What do you mean, locked?" he said stupidly, staring at the steel deadbolts that had slid across the inch-thick tinted glass. He hurled himself against the door but it did not even vibrate under his weight.

"We'll never get out now."

"What are you talking about? The police, fire, ambulance, emergency teams, they'll all turn up here any minute."

"No, they won't," shouted the elderly caretaker. Hegarty was hobbling toward them using a desk-leg as a stick. There was a thick smear of blood on one side of his head. "The phone lines are all diverted. The entrances and exits are all sealed. The building will deal with the crisis without enlisting outside help. That's what it's designed to do."

"So what happens now?"

"In an emergency situation—a Code Purple—the system can attempt to restore balance in the building by starting all over again."

"And how will it do that?" asked Ben, dreading the answer.

"By sucking out all of the air, purifying the structure with scalding antiseptic spray, flash-freezing it and then slowly restoring the normal temperature. The process won't harm office hardware. Of course, it's never been used on humans."

Ben looked up at the flashing purple square on the atrium wall and listened as the warning sirens began to whine. "I guess now would be a bad time to ask for a salary increase," he said as the great ceiling ventilators slowly opened.

destination unknown
THE MAZE
by Jeremy Dyson

When Carver thought about the maze he could picture it very clearly. The thick green walls of leaves, the scuffed brown pathway that may once have been lawn, the iron trellis that was pulled across the entrance at six o' clock each evening. But apart from the fact that it had been somewhere in Roundhay Park, he could never recall it's exact location. He wasn't one for remembering anyway. "The past is a closed book," he'd thought to himself, as if it were something that he'd decided. The truth was, the more he tried to open the pages the tighter they clung together.

"Do you remember going to the park on Sundays—when we were kids?" he asked his sister one evening. He was baby-sitting, yet again, but had arrived earlier than usual. He leaned against the doorpost of her immaculate bedroom, watching her reflection applying lipstick.

"Once or twice. I don't think they were Sundays. You make it sound like a regular thing."

"Maybe it was before you were born." There were five years between them but increasingly Carver caught himself thinking he was the younger of the two. It dated back to Cathy's marriage. She had developed an independent life and grown in stature. It wasn't just the acquisition of a husband and children. Having them had brought it about. "What was your favorite thing? What did you like the most?" he persisted.

"I don't remember liking it very much at all. I think I fell in the boating lake once and it put me off going—Caroline Foody pushed me in."

"What about the Children's Fair?" For some reason Carver didn't want to prompt a recollection. He wanted to hear his sister recall the maze spontaneously. He was pleased to see her smiling as she spoke.

"The helter-skelter. Now I did like that. That scary thrill when you got to the top and you had to force yourself to slide down."

"Anything else? He inquired, a little too eagerly.

"No... What's the sudden interest anyway?" she broke off suspiciously.

"Nothing. No reason." Carver found himself feeling stupid and childish, as if there were something to be ashamed of in his questions.

"I've got to finish getting ready. Go speak to Alistair."

He sloped from the room sheepishly. Watching Cathy from behind, hunched over her dressing table surface, covered with its confusion of tubes, brushes and pots, he realized how much she looked like Mum—and how similar she sounded. He could have been nine years old again, the way he felt dismissed.

"Aye, we used to go quite a lot. It was either there or once round Eccup Reservoir." Alistair dribbled the last of the foam out of the Guinness can before passing it to Carver. "I loved the outdoor swimming pool. It's closed now though. Do you remember it? Right down the bottom end."

"Yes. With the artificial waterfall in the woods behind." Carver sat down with his drink and watched Alistair polish his shoes.

"We'd sneak behind the cubicles and peek at the girls. There were loads of holes and gaps in the wood. The lasses would plug 'em up with toilet paper but it was easy enough to poke out. That was only in summer though." He smiled as he spat at the leather.

"What about the rest of the year?" Carver continued trying to make his interest sound as natural as possible.

"We used to hang around the bandstands—smoking, drinking cider..." Carver felt deflated. Alistair's reminiscences were dismayingly adolescent, and worse, they reminded him of an adolescence he never had. He wanted to encourage earlier memories.

"What about the Children's Fair. Did you ever spend time there?"

"Och, yes. Too much time."

Carver smiled. This was more encouraging. "Richard Frost had a weekend job running the mini-octopus. We thought that if we sat with him showing off, the girls would come flocking." Carver sighed inwardly. Alistair wouldn't stray further back than fourteen. "They did of course,

but only the wee ones. Nine and ten." He winked at Carver. And that's no good to man nor beast." Perhaps the best thing was to be open. It might be the only way he'd hear what he wanted.

"Do you remember the hedge maze?" Carver asked.

"Hedge maze?"

"Yes. Before they got rid of it?"

There was a pause before Alistair's face shifted into a smile of understanding. "That'll have been before my time. We only moved down from Dumfries in '79."

"Come on Mr. Chatterbox. Get those shoes on. We won't be able to park." Cathy had appeared, fussing around the kitchen door. She turned to Carver. "And make sure Anne stays in bed tonight. I'd rather not come back to find her watching videos at half past eleven thank you." He winced a little at her rebuke and tried to smile as Alistair squeezed past him, winking again.

That night, at home in bed, the duvet rolled tightly around him, Carver closed his eyes and attempted to place himself back in the park. Not as it was now—faded, smaller in size—but as he remembered it: huge, ever-changing, packed with surprise, with key points of delight whose presence guaranteed pleasure every time. He could see the black-watered boating lake with its moss-legged pavilion hovering above one end. The water lapped gently in his head and he found himself in the little train carriage that circled perpetually in the Children's Fair. He could see Mum through the cut-out window, waving each time he passed her, Dad at her side with his hands in his pockets, rocking on his heels. Now he was at the cream and green bandstand that smelt of wee and wet tobacco, and then he was running through the maze, trailing his hand against the spiky twigged hedge to his left. Try as he might, he could not connect these locations together. He would flip from one to the other with no journey in-between. The hedge maze could have been anywhere and that was what infuriated him most. If it was anywhere, as opposed to somewhere, then it could also be nowhere.

A fragment of an imagined past as opposed to a remnant of a real one. Tomorrow he'd work a little harder at finding his way back.

The home wasn't that bad. The nurses cared. The floors were clean. There was a bright sun lounge they'd opened last year where everyone could sit and sip watery tea from the vending machine. Carver always thought Dad was too young to be here and really he was, but two strokes had left him needing constant nursing. Mum had managed with the first one but the second came with her death and the home had been the only real option. Some of the fees were covered by an insurance policy Dad had taken out through the company he'd worked for most of his life and Cathy and Alistair made up the rest. Carver would have liked to have contributed but he was in no position to do so.

Dad, slumped to the left, made for one of the biscuits on the tray in front of him.

"I was remembering the park, Dad. When we used to go on Sundays." Dad nodded, munching his digestive. Carver waited anxiously for a smile. It didn't come. "I was talking to Cathy. She doesn't really recall it, but it was before she was born I suppose." He felt a little embarrassed at this naked reminiscing. He'd never talked to his father this directly about anything. But he needed to know.

"It was always cold. That place. The wind whipping around the trees." He remembered it. That was a start.

"I was thinking about where we used to go. The boating lake. The Children's Fair. The helter-skelter..."

"Aye..." his father nodded again, releasing a few crumbs down his sweater.

"I wondered what you could recall." There was a pause and some more munching.

"Cold. It was always cold." Carver sat back in his seat and reached for the thin plastic cup of tea which was also cold. Dad slumped a little

more and released a roaring yawn. For a moment Carver contemplated reaching for his hand but he suppressed the urge. It would be an impossible thing to actually do. Instead he spoke again.

"The maze, Dad. Do you remember the maze?"

"The maze..." His father looked at the floor and the edges of his mouth twitched. Was he smiling? Carver, his teeth tightly clenched, willed him to speak some more. Very slowly Dad's eyes closed. His breathing increased in depth as he drifted into sleep. Carver waited for a moment.

"Dad?" The only response came in drowsy respiration.

On an impulse walking to the bus-stop, Carver crossed the road. He'd decided to take the bus into town instead of back home. Then he could get another up to Roundhay. It seemed the obvious thing to do. A walk round the park might jog his own memory. Why seek the help of others when surely somewhere inside he had an answer himself?

He took the number 10 from outside Lewis's that ran all the way to the park gates. It was funny to be on a bus journey that he hadn't traveled for nearly twenty years. He had been to the park since, but usually by car. To do it this way was like riding back to his childhood. Much had changed but the topography remained the same. The Clock Cinema was now an electrical showroom, Texas Homecare had sprouted from what he remembered as open ground but then, as Carver approached the park things became increasingly familiar. High metal railings flicked past on the right, first black, then bright green. Huge Victorian homes, veiled by poplars and oaks, lay to his left, although many of them were now announced as hotels or nursing homes by conspicuous signs.

The terminus came at one of the parks entrances. With a faint feeling of excitement Carver dismounted and made his way in. It was a fine autumn afternoon. It was strange to be so cold under a bright blue sky but very pleasant all the same. The frosty air was sharp with the dull tang of mud. The cries of children mingled with the calls of birds over the lake. The occasional skateboard roared across the car park. Carver trod discarded lollipop sticks underfoot, the remnants of a summer now distant.

It wasn't that the place looked different, it also felt different. This was partly because he knew its geography now—how one entrance linked with another, how the park fitted into the rest of the city. It was still huge, but now in adulthood, Carver could conceive its size. When he was a child it had been boundless.

He passed the crumpled metal nets of bins and wandered off the concrete into the park, to begin his search for clues. Sure enough there was the Children's Fair up ahead. He paused at the miniature dodgems cowled for the winter and the little merry-go-round, its chair-swings trussed up like game in a butcher's shop. The train wasn't here but there was a line of slot-machine rides: two faded clowns on a see-saw; an angular Bambi with an extended neck, staring ahead with an expression of permanent surprise; a little Noah's Ark sporting, absurdly, a racing car's steering wheel.

Carver closed his eyes and tried to imagine walking from here to the maze. He saw nothing. Then he wondered if he might look suspicious, skulking around the children's rides in his overcoat with his eyes pressed closed. Frustrated and embarrassed he opened them and moved on.

There was another car park, visible behind the fair. It must serve as an overflow during the summer. Perhaps the maze had been there, its roots buried forever beneath heavy gray concrete. If this were the case there was nothing to mark it. It was just an empty guess—Carver felt no confirmation within.

THE MAZE

Although there were other people about, the scale of the park made it feel quite empty. People stood out as spikes on distant hills... or moved quickly past, trailing dogs and children. Carver wondered about a woman he saw squatting in the middle of a patch of grass until he came closer and saw it was in fact a long-haired man, searching for magic mushrooms.

The lake lay up ahead, introduced by a rolling incline. There was the pavilion, which had recently been converted into a waterside cafe. The new wood around the walls smelled like freshly sharpened pencils. As he moved round the side, Carver tried to force another memory. Could the maze have been up here, an added attraction after taking a boat? Ducks pulled rippling V's across the brackish water. He knew it wasn't at this end. He felt like stamping his feet. How could he be so sure about where it wasn't and not know where it was?

On his way back to the bus-stop, Carver fought off despair. The maze had been here. He knew it had been here. Perhaps what dismayed him was the fact that he had so few people to ask if they too remembered. He shook off the feeling and tried to focus his mind. There must be other options. Official channels. Public records. He looked at his watch. He had time to get to the library before it closed.

The bus ride back to town touched Carver with sadness. He had traveled here in expectation of reaching something, only to discover that there was no entrance available. The late afternoon gloom and the percussive rain didn't help. He thought of the present and shivered a little. Outside slipped past, wet and unreal. He remembered the front of the maze the last time he had seen it, the dark iron of the padlocked gate, strange against the rich green of the leaves which encircled it. He'd asked Mum why it was closed in the middle of the day. She'd mumbled something about a boy being hurt. How could you be hurt in the maze? He'd wanted her to take him round, lead him to the park bench in the middle, lift him up to drink from the water-fountain that stood at its side. But she didn't. Not ever again. He couldn't remember when they went to park after that.

There were other mazes. Hampton Court on a school trip. Its seedy replica in the Blackpool Pleasure Beach. A mirror maze at a visiting fair. But although they all promised it, none of them actually delivered the same feeling. They were available to too many people. Just another attraction.

The maze in Roundhay Park had been made for Carver.

Hurrying down the Headrow, his collar up to keep off the rain, Carver glanced at his watch. It was almost five twenty-five. He wasn't sure what time it closed. Passing the squat blocks of the Art Gallery, he ran towards the ornate shelter of the library buildings.

Not unlike the park, the library offered a sense of Victorian comfort— a suggestion of a simpler, more ordered past. Perhaps there was something sterner here, a building of learning, not pleasure, but the general air was the same—a steady municipal calm. Breathless from his sprint through the rain, Carver had to take the steps slowly. They doubled back on themselves making little landings as they rose and at each corner a chunky stone griffin was carved, clinging fiercely to the banister. They looked strangely out of place against the mosaic tiling and polished brass rails.

The reference library was right at the top, softly lit behind heavy swinging doors. Carver passed inside and made his way to the inquiries desk. His heart was still thumping at speed, no longer from exertion, but rather fueled by nervousness and a touch of excitement. The roomy silence only added to the difficulty of speaking to the untidy young librarian

intent on his computer screen. Forcing himself, Carver managed to form his question.

"I'm trying to find out about Roundhay Park, about its history...?" Without looking up the man directed him through a passage that ran behind his desk and told him to walk right to its end.

It felt like he was doing something he shouldn't be allowed to do. The narrow corridor seemed out of the public domain. But then, unexpectedly, it opened out into shelves and shelves of books, an extension of the library that Carver never knew existed. Someone old looked up as he passed, before coughing and returning their gaze to the page.

The passage continued amongst the bookcases ending at another room without a door.

LOCAL HISTORY, read the sign over the entrance. It was brighter inside than the main library. The shelves stretched higher, holding a greater variety of books. A large woman in a pink cardigan smiled at him as he entered. He wandered towards her desk.

"I'm trying to find out about the history of Roundhay Park, particularly the maze?" The woman smiled and gestured to him to sit down. As she did so, Carver noticed, with an unpleasant little jolt, that three fingers were missing from her left hand.

He found himself terribly excited. The prospect that he might have his memories confirmed so directly promised a feeling of great satisfaction, as if the hole he had observed growing within him might be about to be filled. The woman returned with a small number of items. She looked at her watch as she spread them out before him. Carver tried to avoid glancing at the shiny, pinkish stumps between her index and little fingers.

"If there's anything more you want just come and ask."

The first book he picked up was a tatty pamphlet, produced in the 1970s. It looked older than the others even though it was the most recent thing there. Carver flicked through its thin pages, eagerly scanning the pale gray photographs and text for a hint of the maze. There was none. He ran backward through the leaves just to be sure. Nothing. A little desperately he picked up another book.

This one was mustier, bound in heavy green leather. ROUNDHAY PARK: A COMPLETE RECORD. It was dated 1897 in faded gold type on its spine. There was a set of engravings, clustered in the center. The waterfall, the folly, the old mansion house. No maze. Carver felt panic tugging in his stomach. He reached for a larger book, an A3 size laminated folder containing a pull-out supplement from the *Evening Post* dated 1981. ROUNDHAY PARK CENTENARY. Pictures of the Canal Gardens in faded color, a panoramic photograph of the lake. He scoured each page for the merest hint of hedge and trellis, but found none.

Fighting tears, he pulled across the last item—a cardboard mounted section of an an ordnance survey map. Resigned to finding nothing, Carver still traced his finger carefully across its dirty white surface. He could make out various landmarks from their shapes: the bandstand; the cricket pitch; the old refreshment rooms... His eyes jerked back to the edge of the cricket pitch. There was an oblong shape at its edge that he didn't recognize. It had a little block protruding from one corner. Could that be it? Frantically he examined it more closely. It was terribly nondescript. There was nothing around it or in it to indicate its nature. This was maddening. What he really needed was an aerial photograph—or any collection of photographs. He was sure they kept them somewhere in the library—maybe away from the public section.

The large woman was tidying things on her desk. Carver hoped that he wasn't too late.

"I was really hoping to find out what the maze looked like, and where it was located. Would there be any photographs, anything that might show that?" He was aware of the tremor in his voice. She picked up her glasses with her crippled hand and went round a corner. After a moment she returned with a card.

"We haven't much time. Come on," she said a little conspiratorially.

Carver had difficulty keeping pace as the woman walked ahead, briskly taking a twisting path through the warren of book-lined shelves that made up the local history department. He hadn't realized it extended this far back, or that Leeds's history was so thoroughly archived.

They passed down a small flight of steps into a lower-ceilinged room. The light was dimmer here, the air stale. The woman paused by some shelves. As she reached down, Carver realized they disguised a door. The bookcase swung inwards and they walked through.

They were in a small, stone-floored corridor with a spiral staircase just visible at the end. The woman handed Carver the yellowed card reference. "Down the stairs love, but you haven't got long." She turned and walked back through the door.

Carver gripped the elaborate iron banister tightly as he descended. He'd never liked stairs you could see through as you walked down them. The clang of his feet on the metal echoed softly off the stone. He looked at the reference on the card: 720.6.2

The staircase was surprisingly long, so Carver was relieved when he reached the dim and musty-smelling corridor that lay at its bottom. The corridor curved round slightly as it progressed, so he was unable to see where it ended. Iron doors were visible on both sides. He hoped they had a photocopier down here. The doors had white numbers painted on them, in a rather fussy italic script. 720.5.9, read the first; 720.6.0, the next; then 720.6.1, 720.6.2... Carver realized with a little shock that this was his card reference. Tentatively, he pushed open the door.

It was dark inside, but not dark enough to prevent him from seeing. His legs went suddenly weak and he almost slipped down the three small steps that led into the chamber. It wasn't the smell that so disturbed him, unusual and specific though it was—dry yet earthy, like a pile of autumn leaves brushed into a garage and left to molder until spring. No, it was the thing that faced him, so impossibly, that sent his heart thumping and brought a jagged taste of metal into his mouth. He leaned against the wall staring and breathing heavily, feeling the fusty air in his nostril.

It was brown now—a light, almost sepia shade—not a hint of green anywhere. The leaves had thinned out revealing a skeleton of iron-railings beneath. There was no doubt this was the maze—imperfectly preserved but here all the same. Carver must be facing the back, or one of the sides, since there was no sign of the entrance. For a terrible moment he worried that it might have been sealed up, that he would have no access to the interior, because he knew, even now as he gazed, that he must walk within.

Very slowly, he stood upright and edged towards the desiccated hedge. The fence rails that were visible were brown too, rusted darker than the leaves. The hedge still had its height—it nearly reached the low ceiling—and its shape. In fact the corners were sharper now, where the foliage had thinned and stubby little twigs poked out like knuckles. He wanted to touch the branches but restrained himself. He would wait a little longer.

There was a gap between the hedge and the room's wall, just wide enough to walk down. As Carver did, he thought how peculiar it was to see the shrubbery, even in its dried-out state, against the shiny tiles. He held his

breath when he saw the entrance; the trellis less rusty than the railings, folded open around the darkness within. The hedge formed a little arch over it which Carver found himself remembering perfectly. As he came level with the opening he couldn't help but wonder whether the bench would be there, still the goal to aim for at the maze's heart. Breathing again he passed inside.

Almost without thinking, Carver found his hand reaching out to touch the hedge to his left. The leaves felt surprisingly resilient. He had thought they might crumple if he pressed too hard but they were stiff and tough, making a noise like a pack of cards being riffled as his fingers ran along. He turned the first corner not caring if his route were correct; he was just happy to be back there. In fact it was hard to remember when he had last felt joy like this.

Another junction came, the hedge opposite him almost naked, the rails clear with branches twined around them. He looked down for the first time and noticed the thick tarpaulin on the floor, in place of the scuffed pathway that he remembered. Of course not everything could be perfect he thought as he turned another corner, and passed through a further gap. He was almost enjoying the idea of getting lost when he was startled by a noise some distance away.

Someone else was there.

Carver stopped moving and listened anxiously. The footsteps made it clear they were outside the maze. That was a relief. He wanted to be alone in it. In fact, when the trellis hinges groaned and squeaked as they were closed behind him, Carver felt himself moving deeper inside once again. Somewhere, far, far above, the Town Hall clock struck six while nearer, much nearer, a key twisted solidly in its lock.

destination unknown
THE BOY WHO WAS A SEA
by Alan Dean Foster

"I think I've found the trouble. Your boy has salt water in his veins."

George Warren turned uncertainly to his wife. Eleanor Warren put a protective arm around their son Daniel, who continued to toy content-edly with his transformer robot while ignoring the adult conversation.

"He's always liked the ocean, but I don't see how that explains what's wrong with him."

"You don't understand. I don't mean that he's attracted to the sea. I mean that he really has salt water in his veins. And not just plain, ordi-nary salt water. Sea water. See?" Taking a thumb-sized vial from a pocket of his white coat the doctor passed it to George Warren, who held it close to his face and up to the light.

After a moment he passed it to his wife. "There are things moving around in it."

Kindly Dr. Lowenstein nodded sagely. "Very unusual things. Ex-ceptional things. One might even go so far as to say extraordinary things. Things without precedent. Tell me; when was the last time Daniel suf-fered a severe cut?"

Mr. and Mrs. Warren looked at one another. "Daniel never had a bad cut, Doctor," his mother replied. "Is there something wrong with his blood?'

"Wrong? Dear me, no, Mrs. Warren. There can't be anything wrong with your son's blood because he hasn't any. Not in the conventionally accepted sense, anyway. His circulatory system is full of seawater and fur-thermore, it is inhabited..."

George Warren was a hard worker and a devoted husband and fa-ther, but he was not an especially imaginative man. He was having some trouble following the doctor's explanation.

"You mean Daniel is full of ocean water instead of blood?"

Lowenstein nodded again, solemnly this time.

"Then how can he live?" an understandably concerned Mrs. Warren inquired.

"Deuced if I know." The doctor rubbed the little patch of white whisker that clung like a paralyzed moth to his lower lip. In his spare time, infrequent as it was, Dr. Mark Lowenstein liked to play the trumpet. This in no way inhibited his work or made him less kindly. He was quite a very good pediatrician.

"Along with other minerals, there's a lot of iron in seawater. In the case of your son there seems to be enough to supply adequate oxygen to his system with the aid of some as yet undetermined hemoglobin substitute. It's all really quite fascinating. I don't know whether to call in a biochemist or a marine biologist..

"But will he be all right?" Mrs. Warren asked earnestly.

Dr. Lowenstein shrugged elaborately. "So far he behaves like any other ordinary, healthy boy of six. I don't see why he shouldn't continue to mature normally."

"But the chills," George Warren wondered, alluding to the reason for the office visit in the first place.

"It's not unusual for a child to have chills. Not in Chicago in January. What is unusual is the way your son's, uh, blood, seems to be responding to the change in climate. There are what appear to be tiny ice floes forming in his bloodstream. Seastream."

Mr. and Mrs. Warren exchanged another glance.

"As you might expect, they're most prevalent at the extremities. I suspect that's why his feet are always cold and he has these headaches when it snows. There are also definite signs of a small glacier forming in the upper region of the superior vena cave. Many of these ice floes are the result of the berg calving which is taking place in the chest cavity." At the alarmed look on Mrs. Warren's face he added, "I don't foresee any danger at this time."

"What can we do?" a worried George Warren asked.

Lowenstein scratched his lower lip. "Your blood, Eleanor, is normal

Type A, and you, George, are AB. Daniel appears to be TS."

"TS ? " George Warren echoed.

"Tropical Sea. I would suggest a move to a warmer climate. His specialized internal biota seem more closely related to the kinds of organisms one would be likely to encounter in the vicinity of the equator. There is evidence of coral-like building from the aortic arch on downward as well as throughout the jugular. As soon as this, um, reef building reaches maturity, growth appears to cease, thus posing no danger to the boy's general circulation. It's calcification of the arteries to be sure, but not the sort that results from an excess of cholesterol. The rest of his internal biota seems quite healthy."

"What sort of 'internal biota', doctor?" Mrs. Warren was still concerned, but less anxious.

"Most remarkable. I've observed evidence of schooling in more than twenty separate varieties. There is also a healthy population of sedentary forms. Everything seems to thriving. Your son is a most benign host."

"A warmer climate." George Warren looked thoughtful.

"Indeed," murmured Lowenstein. "Somewhere on the ocean. "

"I'm a manager for K-Mart. It may not be easy to get a transfer to a place like that."

"I'll write you a prescription." Dr. Lowenstein smiled encouragingly.

"Remember when he was two?" Mrs. Warren gazed fondly down at her son, cuddling him close. "When we went to Florida and he swallowed all that water and didn't even gag?"

"That wouldn't cause something like this." Her husband hesitated and turned back to the doctor. "Would it?"

"Nothing should cause something like this," Lowenstein replied firmly. "But so long as the boy is healthy, why worry? Marvel, yes; worry, no. "

The K-Marts in Florida were all at full strength and had no need for the services of George Warren. But the family persisted, and kindly Dr. Lowenstein (kindly being an anomaly in these days of munificent malpractice suits and individual medical corporations) was there to help at every turn.

So it was that the family came to settle in Kahului, Maui, the largest town on the second largest island in the placid and agreeable Hawaiian chain. No longer did Daniel suffer from annual shivering. They knew they'd made the right decision the first time he splashed excitedly into the shallows at Makena. His condition had been thoroughly explained to him and he had come, as boys are wont to do, to simply accept it.

"I'm in the sea and the sea's in me!" said he as he threw handfuls of warm water into the air.

A smiling George Warren took his wife's hand in his own and squeezed reassuringly.

Just as Dr. Lowenstein had predicted, Daniel grew into a strong, healthy young man, handsome and with an air of the faraway about him that was very attractive to the ladies. Students at the college did term papers on the singular liquid that ebbed and flowed through his body, competing to see who could be first to identify the next new microspecies. One transfer student even qualified for her thesis by providing evidence of seasonal migration within his veins, showing that at least two Danielian species migrated from his arms to his legs every spring, returning to his arms in the winter.

Displaying an abiding interest in oceanography which understand-ably exceeded that of are but the most avid graduate students, Daniel did his best to assist the professors at the college, willingly volunteering samples of his life-fluid whenever it was requested for study. A serum derived from his veins helped to save the life of an especially beloved Orca at Sea World in San Diego, and another dose did wonders for a sick dolphin in Honolulu's seaquarium.

Doctors decided that his heart forced water across the microscopic reefs in his system in much the same way that daily tides refreshed atolls and reefs in the Pacific and Caribbean. At the college and hospital they came to speak of the tides of Daniel, and tried to determine if his heartbeat was affected by the phases of the moon. When one day he was admitted suffering from dizziness and weak spells it was decided that his system needed the sort of replenishment supplied to normal seas by land-based rivers. Upon further analysis, a weekly dose of specified minerals matching precisely those found in the bathysphere were prescribed, and sure enough the spells soon went away.

It wasn't that he had no aptitude for academics. It was just that he couldn't bear to be long away from the water. So despite his more than adequate grades, college was passed over in favor of vocational studies, and in due course he received his ship captain's license and divemaster's certificate.

Desirous of seeing other seas, he initially spent some time in the merchant marine, always acquitting himself honorably and astonishing seasoned sailors with his ability to pick a course through difficult waters without the aid of GPS or chart. After some years he returned to live permanently on Maui, preferring to work as a divemaster with a state-side concern instead of opening his own business.

"I'd rather not have the responsibility," he told his now-retired parents when they questioned this decision, "and have more time free to dive on my own."

They understood, of course.

Urged on by his mother, he gave serious consideration to marriages but there was some concern as to the physical status of prospective children, and despite his modest fame he had a difficult time with dating. No spray or mint could mask his breath, which smelled now of kelp, now of sargassum, and at its worst, of a weathered planktonic bloom. So he had ample female company, especially out on the water where such things were not as noticeable, but few amours.

There came a day, fine and sunny and not at all in anyway ominous, when he was working in the dive office out on the pier and Fredo came running breathlessly from town to lean exhausted against the open portal.

"Have you heard?"

Everyone, including Daniel, looked up. "Heard what?" John Renssalear inquired on behalf of them all.

A junior divemaster, Fredo hugged the entrance as if reluctant to let loose of it. "Come and see for yourselves!"

Some curious, some concerned, they shuffled out of the building onto the pier. Fredo pointed them not toward the bustle and haste of nearby Lahaina but south toward Kahoolawe. In between Maui and that uninhabited source of constant contention lay the tiny volcanic crescent of Molokini, famous as a dive site and marine sanctuary. There was next to no vegetation on the rocky outcropping, which made the smoke rising from its northeast flank very puzzling.

"It's a tanker!" Fredo informed them breathlessly. "The Comco Sulawesi. She was bound for the refinery at Honolulu with sixty thousand barrels of Indonesian crude aboard when she went aground!" He swallowed, his throat dry. "I was monitoring the coast guard. She's afire and the crew's preparing to abandon ship."

"They can't do that!" Martine Renosa exclaimed.

"What about the tug at Kahului?" Renssalear's voice was calm but tension caused his weathered face to crinkle like brown tinfoil.

Fredo shook his head violently. "There're no ships due into the harbor today so the crew went to Hilo for a break. They're sending three ocean-going tugs from Honolulu."

"They'll never get here in time," someone muttered angrily. "What the hell's a tanker doing in the channel anyway? Especially at this time of year."

"Nobody's sure," Fredo explained. 'They think the Captain wanted to see the islands close up." From the back of the crowd someone groaned.

"Sixty thousand barrels." John Renssalear had been a commercial diver on wells in the North Sea and the Gulf of Mexico, working deep water under potentially lethal conditions. It took a lot to shake him.

"If she breaks up, that much crude could kill all the reefs on this side of the island, all the way from La Perouse Bay up to Kapalua. Not

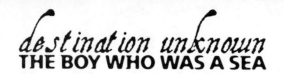

to mention everything around Kahoolawe, Lanai, and maybe even Molokai."

"What about Molokini?" someone asked.

"Molokini?" Renssalear barely had the energy to shrug. "Molokini's as good as dead. That oil will turn the sanctuary into an underwater desert."

"Never mind Molokini," growled Renosa darkly. 'What about the whales?" No one said anything. Everyone knew it was the height of the calving season and that the channel was full of migrating humpbacks and their newborn young.

"Say, John." Renssalear turned to Daniel Warren, who was staring levelly at the burgeoning plume of black smoke. "Can you run me out there?"

The owner of the dive operation cocked his head slightly to one side as he regarded his most valued employee. "What did you have in mind, Dan?"

"Just run me out there. Maybe—maybe I can do something."'

Wide-eyed, Fredo looked from one man to the other. "Are you two crazy?"

"That ship's on fire. She could blow at any minute"

"Or not," Dan Warren whispered.

Renssalear didn't hesitate. "Let me get my gear."

The powerful little boat crashed through the waves, heading south toward the burgeoning pillar of doom. They raced around retreating yachties, dodged the coast guard cutter which had positioned itself to keep back curious tourists, shot past the two big lifeboats that looked like fat waterborne grubs which were carrying the multinational crew of the tanker to safety.

The emergency ladder they'd left behind flupped and banged against the side of the stricken ship. Maneuvering with the skill and experience born of many years at sea, Renssalear put the diveboat close alongside. Still, it took three tries before Dan Warren was able to make the leap to the dangling ladder.

Renssalear backed off, watching tensely as Daniel ascended the dangerously flapping rungs.

Long moments passed. The coast guard frequency was screaming at him. Renssalear ignored it, acknowledging the radio only when it crackled on a prearranged frequency.

"I'm in the pilot house, John."

Renssalear murmured a silent prayer. "Nice going, Dan. What now? "

"I'm going to try and back her off the reef. I know it better than that Indonesian Captain ever could. I know its bumps and ridges, where the hollows are and every twitch of the current. I know where the sand is deep and where the coral grows shallow. I can feel it, John! Its just something I've got in me. Now, give me some space."

Renssalear waited as the immense diesels rumbled to life within the belly of the tanker. Props bigger than his dive boat churned the water, sending bottom dwellers like rays and flounder flying.

At first nothing happened. Then a deeper groaning became audible. Not many people would have recognized that noise, but Renssalear did. It was the sound of a steel keel grinding against coral and stone.

Spewing smoke like a drunken volcano, the mortally wounded Comco Sulawesi slowly backed off the eastern horn of Molokini. Once safely behind the islet, above the dive site known to locals as the Edge of the World, with three hundred and fifty feet of water under the hull, Dan Warren turned the injured vessel south and headed for the open Pacific.

"Put her on autopilot and get off there!" Renssalear shouted into the radio. "I'll pick you up."

"Sorry, John," came the steady reply. "No can do. Autopilot doesn't respond. I'm going to have to find something to lash the wheel."

Time elapsed. Too much time. The Comco Sulawesi cleared the southern tip of Maui and then Kanahou Bay on Kahoolawe, passing through the Alalakeiki channel on its way out to open ocean. Renssalear followed grimly, fighting the rising seas in his small boat.

Finally, a response. "Got 'er!"

"What'd you use?" Renssalear demanded to know.

"Duct tape..." Renssalear could almost see his friend grinning. "Advanced technology can't function without duct tape."

"I'm going to tie you up in duct tape and mail you off on a forced vacation!" Renssalear wiped a tear from one eye. "I'll come around and pull up to the ladder. The seas are pretty high. Find a lifejacket or preserver and jump in if you have to. Don't worry, I'll get to you."

"I know you will, John. I'm on my way!"

Two minutes later the Comco Sulawesi blew up in a spectacular shower of metal, wood, and oil, bringing to mind for a few minutes the far greater but no more terrifying eruption of Mount Saint Helens. A cursing, screaming Renssalear fought the wheel of his dive boat, angling it into the backwash and somehow keeping it afloat. Crude drenched his skin, his boat, his equipment, but he didn't care. He kept wiping it from his eyes as he fought his way to where the bloated tanker had been only moments before.

"Didn't need to worry about the damn autopilot," he muttered to himself as he searched the incredible sheet of debris for signs of life. "Should've got off when he had the chance. The brave, dumb son-of-a-bitch should've got off."

It was counted a minor miracle when they found Dan Warren clinging to a piece of the shattered decking, badly burned and semi-conscious. The coast guard cutter which had been following threatened to burn out its own engines as it put on speed for Kahului harbor, the medics on board doing their best to subdue the pain and keep their patient alive. But there wasn't much they could do. They had not been trained to treat the likes of Dan Warren.

At the local hospital they knew him better, but despite their best efforts he continued to weaken. While his parents and friends crowded the waiting room and spilled out into the halls and even the street, stricken physicians caucused outside the operating room.

93

"There's nothing we can do," mumbled one. "It's all through him. He just ingested too much of the stuff.'

"His circulatory biomass is dying," declared another sorrowfully. He's suffering from an internal oil spill. All the specialized organisms, the unique coraline structures—the loil is killing them all. He needs a transfusion. Of blood."

"We can't do that." The head of surgery resignedly eyed his colleagues, voicing what they all knew. "You know what his system is like. A normal transfusion would kill him."

"I wonder why the solution didn't work? " muttered another. They had tried replacing Daniel's singular body fluid with a saline solution blended to duplicate that of seawater. Even the pH was correct to a dozen decimal points. But it hadn't worked.

"It doesn't matter." Another doctor was insistent. "We have to try real blood. There's no other way."

"Maybe one." Surprised, they all turned to the head nurse. "Wait for me."

Outside, she dialed the emergency room. Everyone there knew what had happened. Everyone knew how Dan Warren had sacrificed himself in his desperate attempt to save the island's underwater treasures.

"Is Jimmy Wakamao there?" she asked. He was. "Jimmy, this is Gena Pukalani. I want you to go up to Point Waihee. There's a little reef there. Take the ambulance and don't let anybody or anything stop you. I want you to bring back five gallons of water off the reef, where the current is strong and the water is clear. Yes, you heard me right. Five gallons. Take Steve Portugas with you.'

While they waited they did what they could for Dan Warren. They were arguing over whether to proceed with a transfusion of type AB when the ambulance driver and his assistant burst into the conference room. Together they unloaded the precious seawater.

"What's this?" the chief of surgery asked. "We already tried a saline substitute."

"A sterile saline substitute," the head nurse argued. "Dan Warren's body fluid isn't sterile. It's full of life, of living things. It's the sea in miniature. Only the sea can restore him."

"Or kill him," insisted the doctor who was in favor of trying real blood. He indicated the plastic jugs. They smelled of open ocean. "Who knows what kind of micro-organisms are floating around in there?"

The head nurse looked back at him. She was a local, and had more confidence in the sea than the good doctor from Philadelphia.

"Nothing more dangerous than has been living in him for his whole life, I'll bet."

Everyone looked to the head of surgery for a decision. If he decided wrongly, he would be accused of letting a state hero die.

He nodded somberly to his head nurse. "Let's try it."

The clean seawater flushed out the oil. There was damage, but with time and therapy Dan Warren's system gradually rehabilitated itself. The coraline structures that lined his veins and arteries slowly rebuilt themselves, the unique microspecies once more swam and thrived in the inlets and fjords of his legs and arms.

The state gave him a medal, and the locals threw the granddaddy of all luaus in his honor. After awhile all the fuss died down. There were pineapples to be gathered, and protea to harvest, and golden macs to box and ship.

Tourists needed looking after, and gods old and new required propitiation.

Dan Warren is still there, working out of Lahaina. You can go diving with him if you wish. You can't miss him. He carries the aroma of the sea about him like a halo. His eyes are blue, of course.

But like no blue you've ever seen.

destination unknown
A BITE TO EAT IN ABBOTSFORD
by Michael Libling

Payday was in the air.

θ θ θ

Larry Heffer burst into Bert Kobol's Silver Diner, eyes wide, tongue dragging, and nude except for the leather belt which hid nothing. "There must've been a million of 'em," he blubbered, struggling to control the pitch of his voice.

A few heads turned his way, eyes indifferent, then resumed the task at hand—dinner. The evening special was moving fast. Mondays were rump roast days, so Tuesdays were shepherd's pie days (some weeks, Wednesdays were, too). The recipe called for double corn, and Bert cut it fresh from the cob, buttered, salted and sprinkled with parmesan.

Bert hitched up his apron. "If you're planning on staying, there's a trash bag in the john you can borrow. It's free if you wear it here and eat. No food, it'll cost you a buck."

From the kitchen in back of him, two hairy hands pushed a stack of steaming plates onto the aluminum sill. Once, the dishes had been a fairly sincere imitation delft; few alive, however, could recall. Bert hoisted the stack onto the grease-stained overhang. "Got to get some shelving paper," he muttered, neglecting to make a mental note for, perhaps, the thirtieth time that year.

"You don't know what happened out there," Larry protested. "Look at me."

The kitchen door swung open and Pauline barrelled through, three orders of the special on each arm, two with extra peas on the side. "Nice bod'," she grinned.

Larry's hands shot to his crotch. "Are you people nuts? Listen to me!"

Pauline patted a stool at the end of the counter. "Relax, honey.

There's nothing we haven't seen. You'll feel better after a bite to eat. How about a special? And a coffee?"

"Look, my wife's waiting for me in the car. She saw it all happen. I've got to get back to her."

Bert cast a furtive glance towards the window. "Two specials to go, then?" he asked, seemingly intent on the sale.

"Please, you've got to help me. Can't you see? I don't have any money. I don't even have a wallet. Or, for that matter, a pocket to put a wallet in."

Bert shrugged. "You come to Abbotsford, buddy, you got to dress for it. You shouldn't have panicked. I bet your wallet was right at your feet on the sidewalk. They wouldn't have touched that."

"So you know about them, then?" Larry's relief was evident.

"Of course, we live here."

"And we live *with* them," Pauline piped in. "Why the heck you think we dress like this? You know the kind of rash we get from this stuff in the heat?"

It was only then that Larry noticed everyone in the restaurant was wearing plastic or leather or a combination of the two—this, despite the fact that Abbotsford was nowhere near the Sunset Strip.

There were thirteen stools at the counter, all occupied, and four tables with four chairs each, all but three of the seats taken. An air conditioner droned above the entrance, several BTU's too powerful for the size of the restaurant. Appetites were whet by the aroma of frying onions. A less distinctive, underlying scent reminded Larry of citronella.

"Now, what'll it be?" Pauline prodded, snatching the pen from behind her ear. "Two specials?"

"I told you, I don't have any money."

"Sure you do, fella." Bert motioned Larry over to the window. He slid aside the sun-faded *Bush/Quayle '92* poster and pointed to the street. "See, just like I told you, there's your wallet, under the street lamp, next to the hydrant. Say, is that your wife sitting there?"

"That's Nan," Larry nodded.

"Nice car," Bert said. "What is it—an Audi?"

"BMW."

"Great," Bert smiled. "They're very popular. Expensive, too. You got a telephone in there, too?"

"In the car?"

Bert nodded.

Larry shook his head. "Never really needed one."

"Yeah, I guess not," Bert said, with what may have been the slightest trace of disappointment.

At that moment Nan looked up, spotting her husband in the window. She waved. He waved. Bert waved. But much to Larry's horror, she interpreted his gesture as a signal to join him and, without a trace of caution, she emerged from the car. Before she could shut the door, let alone change her mind, they were upon her, obscuring her beneath a flurry of mottled wings.

A moment was all it took and they were gone as suddenly as they had come.

"Damn," Bert said, "they got your car seats, too."

"They were velour." Larry was numb. "Special order. Nan's vegetarian. She hates leather."

Nan Heffer lay naked in the street, her tank top, shorts and sneakers long-digested. All that remained were two diamond earrings, so impoverished of carats that even the full moon failed to play off of them.

A moment passed, enough time to realize that she was on her own, that no one, not even Larry, was coming. She rose slowly, covering herself as best she could with trembling arms and hands, retrieved Larry's wallet, and crossed to the diner. Her presence of mind impressed most everyone watching.

θ θ θ

Both Larry and Nan felt better after the shepherd's pie (Nan eating only the potato topping), although neither was fully at ease in the plastic trash bags.

"Dark green is your color, my dear." Pauline placed a friendly hand on Nan's shoulder.

"Thanks," Nan said, smiling for the first time. She raised the mug to her lips, welcoming the warmth in the air-conditioned chill.

Larry tested the resiliency of his tapioca pudding. It contained raisins. Larry detested raisins; he would have to eat around them.

"It was the bug doctor who started it all," Pauline began.

"But he wasn't a bug doctor then," Bert said.

"Not in the beginning, anyways," a man with whipped cream on his mustache added.

"That's right. He was what you call an etymologist—a guy who knew all about words." Pauline wore her knowledge like a fresh corsage on a hand-me-down prom dress. "He taught up at the state university and used to come down here to get away from it all. We don't get too many tourists, so he sort of stuck out."

"So people—mostly the farmers—started asking him about bugs. Like which pesticides to use and stuff like that."

"I sure did that," a farmer chuckled. His hard-hat bore a fluorescent yellow Newt Weimer-brand fertilizer logo—a yellow not unlike the bulbs that lit the diner.

"Me, too—and more than once," snorted another.

Others tittered in agreement.

"But you said he was into words—an etymologist?" Larry was eager for an explanation. With so many vying for the floor, he feared losing track of the story.

Pauline topped off Larry's coffee. "He was. But most of the folks around here thought that meant bug doctor. More tapioca?"

"You see," Bert cut in, "an etymologist studies words and an entomologist studies bugs. But most of us thought they were the same."

"Carrie Norway was our local spelling-bee champ. I suppose she could've made a difference if we would've asked her, but she moved away years ago."

"Yup, last I heard, she was up in Norway."

"Sounds logical," Larry said, his testiness a shade closer to the surface.

"So however you spell them," Bert grinned, "they still come down to the same thing—bug doctor."

"What is this, a Greek chorus?" Larry quipped, pleased with what he thought was a clever analogy. A copywriter with a 'hot' East Coast ad shop, clever analogies were Larry's stock and trade.

"Greek, Latin—what's the difference? We've had our fill of both," snapped Bert.

It was overdue, but Larry and Nan were beginning to seriously wonder what they had gotten themselves into. Their hands met under the table, in search of mutual comfort. *This was one strange burg.*

"Anyhow," Pauline continued, "this went on for about five summers. He'd come down and as soon as word of his arrival leaked out, folks would start pestering him."

"Well, why didn't he just tell everyone he didn't know about bugs?" It was a question Nan had to ask.

"Yeah," Larry said. "That would've made a lot of sense."

Bert smiled in the way small town people often do when forced to explain the apparent obvious to city people. "Oh, he did in the beginning, but most thought he was just putting them off—being unfriendly. And whenever he tried to explain the difference between entomologist and etymologist, it came off like he was being uppity—Mister University and all. It sounded like he just couldn't be bothered to help."

Bert leaned within a nose-length of the Heffers, breathing his words more than speaking them. The odor of fried onions was not exclusive to the grill. "We've got this reputation for keeping to ourselves—you know, not letting any outsiders in. Now, it's not really true around here—after all, we're talking to you—but most strangers expect it. The fact is, we're so far off the beaten track we hardly get any visitors. In case you hadn't noticed, Abbotsford is what the newspapers call 'an economically depressed area'. The only tourists we get are the lost ones."

"Like us," Nan giggled self-consciously.

"Anyhow," Bert went on, "he rightly decided it wouldn't look too good if he were to make a habit of telling us locals how dumb we were— not knowing the difference between entomologist and etymologist."

"So?"

It was Pauline's turn: "So he stopped trying to explain what he wasn't and answered our questions instead."

"And, by golly, he had some real fine answers." The farmer with the Newt Weimer-brand fertilizer hat shoveled a line of spilled sugar into his mug.

"Not all the time," someone else shot back. "And I told him so."

"Me, too. His advice screwed up my carrots and radishes real bad."

"And, if you ask me, we never had worse black flies around here till he come to town and started tampering. And I told him so."

"You told him? I told him!"

"He cost me plenty! You better believe we told him."

"And if you wouldn't have started nagging him, none of this would have happened," Pauline chided. "He was just trying to be nice. It wasn't his fault his advice stunk. Breaking his windows, knocking down his fence, slashing his tires, that was downright nasty. He didn't come looking to give advice, you went looking for him. He just came to Abbotsford to get away from it all."

The room went silent, eyes downcast in guilt.

Larry seized the opportunity: "Broke his windows? Because his advice was lousy?" He shook his head.

"Well, he shouldn't have pretended he was a bug man," a faceless someone muttered bitterly.

Bert waited a suitably dramatic moment before picking up the thread: "Next thing you know, he sets up a lab in his house and is doing all kinds of things with bugs. Strange things, too, because he won't let anybody in now. Bars on the windows. Alarm system. Stuff like that. Overnight he's acting almost like a hermit, not saying much to any of us anymore."

"Like that *Doctor Frankenstein* guy." Pauline squirted vinegar onto a rag and wiped the spot where Larry's dish of tapioca had been.

"But he was an etymologist," Larry protested. "He knew balls-all about bugs."

"Maybe so, but he must've learned fast. Things started being delivered to him. Lots of books. And white mice. Lots of white mice."

"And don't forget those aquariums or those fish or the doll clothes."

"And remember that funny bucket? I delivered that one. It looked like the kind of thing you used to see in those old Life magazine stories about the A-bomb."

"Doll clothes?" Nan blinked. "A-bomb?"

"Yeah, that's right," Bert acknowledged. "And then at the end of last summer, he didn't leave here at all. His lights were burning night and day as if he was working on something real big."

"Well, to make a long story short, three months ago, this Friday, he shows up one night with a box in one hand and a couple of books in the other and lays them right here on this table." Pauline planted a finger on the spot. Her nail polish, a shameless red called Cleopatra's Revenge, was chipped. "But it wasn't the box or the book that caught our eye. No, not at first."

"He wasn't wearing a stitch," Bert explained. "The guy was standing here nude, right in the middle of my dinner, stark naked—just like you when you walked in, except he didn't have no belt—or earrings like you, Miss. Well, that opened our eyes, that's for sure. I just figured he'd flipped out. Nobody said a word. Nobody moved."

"And then he says real quietly: 'I have a gift for you people.'" Pauline lowered her voice several octaves. "'These books and this,' he says, and he taps the box, turns around and walks out."

"... Last we seen of him—in the flesh, at least. He sure moved fast—like somebody was on his tail."

"Boy, I'd like to have him without a stitch right now. What he did to my turnips... "

"Yeah, but look what he's done for the economy of our town," said the man in the Newt-Weimer hard-hat. "Can't fault him for that, by golly," he chuckled.

"One of the books was a dictionary—Merriam-Webster," Pauline said. "He'd dog-eared two pages and on both those he'd circled a word."

"Let me guess," Larry ventured. "'Etymology' and 'entomology'?"

"Dead on. And the other book was *The 500 Most Misunderstood Words in Modern English*. Did the same thing in there."

"What about the box?" asked Nan.

"I'm the one who opened that," said Bert.

"And... ?"

"I thought it might be a bomb but it seemed too light. So I said 'What the heck,' and took my chances. Just in case, though, I made everyone stand by the door."

"Not me. I stood right next to Bert," declared Pauline, her eyes primed on pride. "That's when I noticed what was written on the box. But Bert didn't wait to figure out what it meant."

"I lifted the lid and that was that. They were all over me—all over everybody. I'm sure the whole attack didn't last more than a minute. We were left nuder than a bunch of newborn babes—every last one of us."

"It wasn't a pretty sight," said a man, cleaning his fingernails with the edge of his place mat. "Except for you, Pauline."

Pauline scribbled quickly on the back of her order pad and slid it across the table to the Heffers. "This is what was written on the box...."

Serrasalmus Nattereri

Lepidoptera Abbotsford

"Serrasalmus Natter—Lepidop—Abbotsford... and what's that supposed to mean?" The punchline was far too long in coming for Larry.

"It's Latin or Greek or something," said Bert. "And according to my nephew—he got straight A's in science—the Abbotsford means us, the Lepidoptera means moth, and the Serrasalmus Nattereri... "

"... That means piranha," said Pauline.

θ θ θ

"Piranha moths?" It was beginning to sound like a grade-B flick from the 50's. "You've got to be kidding."

"If that's the case, fella, who swiped your clothes?"

"Then how come I've never heard of them anywhere else?" Larry countered.

"Because we're the only place that has them."

"Don't give me that. Bugs don't stay in one place."

"They do if the feeding's good and the feeding's good here."

"Maybe so, but this is no way to live."

"We're living better now than we have in years. They don't like daylight, so we got the days to ourselves—to fetch supplies and such. Come nightfall, we stay indoors, getting together like this. It's nice, real family-like."

"You're living better, now, because of the moths?" Larry shook his head. "What's that supposed to mean?"

"Nothing," Bert growled, upset with himself. "It just means life's more exciting around here since all this happened. Cripes! We don't even get cable TV."

"Something's wrong." Nan was confused. "Isn't it only the moth larvae that eat clothes? Besides, Larry's shirt was a cotton and polyester blend and my sneakers were nylon or something. Since when do moths eat synthetics?"

"Since they come to Abbotsford, lady. Now, you tell me: when have you ever heard of a piranha being picky about what it eats?"

"I don't know anything about piranhas, Mr. Kobol, but I do know something about moths."

"Not our moths, Mrs. Heffer. Not our moths."

"I don't care what you people say, somebody should be told about these creatures," Nan insisted. "They could upset the whole ecosystem here. And if they spread to other areas, just imagine the panic. It could be a disaster. You've got to bring the authorities in. You've got to tell somebody."

"Not so aggressive, dear," Larry whispered through clenched teeth, unaware that a kernel of corn lingered between an upper left bicuspid and an incisor.

Nan ignored him. "You people don't seem to realize how serious a problem you've got." She stood abruptly. "If you're not prepared to do anything about it, I am." She marched to the door, her plastic bag rustling.

"And you don't seem to realize how broke most of us have been," Bert shouted.

"What's that got to do with the environment?" Nan shouted back.

Larry opened his wallet. "Uh, how much—uh—do we owe you for lunch?" Larry's smile was a weak attempt to cut through the sudden tension. "It was—uh—really good. Best shepherd's pie I've had in a long time... "

"It's on the house," Bert grunted.

"No, I couldn't let you...," Larry protested.

"I said it's on the house!"

"Well, okay." Larry slid three dollars under his coffee mug and joined Nan at the door.

Nan looked to see if the street was clear.

Pauline opened the door.

Nan tugged her husband by the arm. "Please, Larry, let's get out of here."

"Well—uh—bye," Larry said, stumbling onto the sidewalk. "Have a nice day."

θ θ θ

Bert sidled over to Pauline. He called to the departing couple. "One thing we forgot to tell you... "

Larry turned. "Oh yeah, what's that?"

"We did find our entomologist's bones."

"His bones?" Larry froze. Nan kept walking.

"Yup," Bert winked. "It seems that once they get a taste of your clothes, they come back for the rest of you." Pauline shut the door and bolted it.

Faces pressed against the glass, the patrons of Bert Kobol's Silver Diner took in the show.

0 0 0

"What do you figure the BMW will fetch, Bert?"

"More than the Toyota that come in last week, that's for sure."

"It's payday," the man in the Newt-Weimer hard-hat said, rubbing his palms together.

destination unknown
THE EXTRA HOUR
by Lisa Tuttle

1

An extra hour, that's all I want. One more hour in every day for me, for writing. Then I could finish my book, and—well, that would be a start.

Of course, I could be working on finishing it now, moving it along a little bit more, advancing another page or two or three towards the end. David thinks I'm up here in my corner of our partially converted loft, working on my novel instead of drinking wine and watching a video with him, instead of grading papers, or ironing, or any of the other more useful or sociable things I could be doing, and what am I doing? This isn't writing, it's doodling. I don't deserve an extra hour. I have one—one hour, almost every night, all to myself, my writing time—and look at how I waste it, daydreaming and doodling. If I had another hour, wouldn't I waste that, too?

No I wouldn't. One hour isn't enough to do anything—but two can be. I've had two hours up here, writing like a demon, then going down-stairs feeling spent and satisfied and with something to show for my time. If I had two hours *every* day—

But it's just not possible. There aren't enough hours in the day, or not enough energy in my body. I tried the traditional surviving-on-less sleep routine, but I couldn't sustain it. Somebody, maybe not me, would have died. If I didn't have a job already—but I do, and I'm good at it (which I might not be at writing) and we need the money, and when I'm home I want to be with my family. After all, I wanted this family—nobody forced me to get married and procreate. Trying to carve out another hour for myself, insisting on it, would be unfair to David and the kids, and even, ultimately, to myself, my deepest needs.

But I need to write, too. Or I think I do. These conflicting needs wouldn't be so in conflict if there was just one extra hour in every day, an hour I could have just for myself. I wish

2

I heard a clock strike the hour. I was so absorbed in my own thoughts that I reacted as if it were an alarm. I jumped up without pausing to wonder where the clock was, whose it was, or what strange time it kept until I was on my way downstairs. And then I saw a door where one shouldn't have been.

It was just at the turn of the stairs, in the wall we share with the house next door. If there really was a door there it would open on to the Corkindales' staircase, and my first thought on seeing it was that our neighbors had knocked through to our property, and I was furious.

How dare they—and I put my hand on the knob, and it opened.

I was so astonished by what I saw that I walked straight in. The door swung silently shut behind me. No room like this was in the Corkindales' house, or in any house along our road. This was a room from my dreams.

My daydreams, I should say: if I were a rich and famous author, this was the study I would have.

The walls were paneled wood, lined with books or hung with paintings. Gold, velvet draperies at the far end concealed either a window or another door. On the floor were Oriental rugs in luscious, luxurious shades: apricot, cinnamon, crimson and teal. There was a deep leather armchair with a reading lamp standing behind it, a chaise longue, and an elegant walnut escritoire, but what caught my attention was the plain oak table with everything needed for writing: a jar of sharpened pencils, a stack of notebooks, a dictionary, a directional lamp.

Wherever this had come from, wherever I was, I wasn't looking a gift horse in the mouth. I went straight to the table and sat down on the chair in front of it and picked up the notebooks. They were full of blank pages and smelled delicious. I chose a pencil and took possession of the room in the only way possible: I began to write.

It wasn't my novel. I started a new story. It seemed right.

I didn't manage to finish it, quite, but I wrote pages and pages. I don't know how long I wrote, because I wasn't wearing a watch, and although it was the sound of a clock striking which had brought me there, I didn't see one in the room. I just wrote until I was too tired to go on, until I didn't feel like writing any more. Then I closed the notebook, stood up, and walked through the door and back down my own familiar staircase and into the sitting room where David was still watching his video.

He looked up at me in surprise. "You're down early. Not inspired?"

"What do you mean? I wrote ever such a lot; I thought you'd be in bed by now." Then I saw the time on the videorecorder and did a mental double-take. According to it, I'd been upstairs for half an hour.

It was then that the strangeness struck me full force. I rushed out of the room and back up the stairs where—of course—I could find no mysterious door.

But the story I wrote in that room exists, and it didn't before. I don't have the notebook, but I remember it perfectly well. I know I can write it again, and as a second draft it will be even better.

Where did that story come from? When did I write it? The only possible explanation seems to be that I fell asleep at my desk. I must have nodded off and dreamed the whole thing in about five minutes.

3

I've finished the story—"Wings"—and it's the best thing I've ever written.

I'm ditching the novel. It doesn't interest me any more; there's something static, predetermined about it. For a long time I'd been telling myself I was only tired because I'd been thinking about it for so long, but I've decided that if it bores me it would bore anybody else, too. Liberation!

There'll have to be a new novel, but just now I haven't a clue about it. I'm going to write another story next, semi-fantastic, yet at the same time very ordinary, full of the quotidian, about a woman who loses her place in her own life—as if life were a book one read. About time and memory, fear and desire, the tricks the mind plays—like the way I dreamed myself into "somewhere else" in order to find the time I needed to write. I haven't felt so excited about writing in ten years.

4

It happened again. I went back.

I was working on "Irrevocable Decisions"—which isn't the neat, sweet short story I'd thought it would be, but just keeps growing—as I had been all week. Two nights running I'd been up late with it, well past my usual hour, and lack of sleep was telling on me: I nearly dozed off on my way to school. Luckily, David was driving. He said I must have an early night for once, and when he couldn't talk me into giving up my hour at the desk, he made me take an alarm clock up with me.

Hateful things, they are. I didn't want to be interrupted in mid-flow, I didn't want to be shocked out of my writing dream, so I wrote against time, obsessed by the presence of the clock all the while I struggled to lose myself and forget it.

I did manage to lose myself in the writing, but I was still so keyed-up to expect an interruption that when I heard a clock strike I jumped up without really noticing that this sound was not the irritating electronic buzz of a travel alarm.

Only half-way down the stairs, when I saw the door again, did I remember.

Full of pleasure and anticipation I went through and straight to my table. I picked up notebook and pencil and, set free from time, returned to my story.

I wrote until my vision blurred and my handwriting was a pained and drunken scrawl. I longed to put my head down and close my eyes. Maybe a short nap would help.

As I stumbled across the room to the chaise-longue I thought that when I woke I would be stiff from sleeping at my desk in the corner of the loft. I should go downstairs now—but I was too tired to go any further.

THE EXTRA HOUR

Against my expectations, against what seemed like reason, when I awoke I was still there in that room. It was as if I'd only dreamed I'd lost something, and woke to find it was still mine. I was so happy. I jumped up and went back to the writing table, back to work, as invigorated as if I'd had a full night's sleep.

But although I was eager to get on with my story, I was thirsty. I really fancied a cup of tea. If this was my ideal study, I thought, there must be a kettle, and likely an emergency stash of food. So I got up to have a look.

Maybe the presence of a white china tea-set on top of a low cupboard had struck a subliminal chord. Inside the cupboard I found an electric kettle, two bottles of still water, containers of powdered milk and loose tea, and a tin of digestive biscuits.

"All right!"

I filled the kettle and plugged it in. While I waited for it to boil I investigated the bookshelves. It was pretty amazing I'd managed to resist their lure for this long. Most of the books were duplicates of my own, downstairs, but there were also some volumes I'd always wanted and never managed to afford: the OED, all of Pevsner, the letters of Henry James, lots of big, glossy art books, and just about every useful or interesting reference work I could think of.

In spite of the powdered milk my cup of tea tasted especially delicious, the way it does when it's most welcome—after hiking up a mountain with friends, or after a dismal journey in the rain. It was as good as that first cup of tea after Rachel was born. When I'd finished it I went back to work. The ending was in sight. Many of the sentences I wrote were clumsy, crippled in some way, but I knew it didn't really matter. This was only a draft, a sketch. I would take more care when I rewrote; now, the important thing was to finish.

I didn't linger afterwards. I wrote "The End" in huge letters, and then left the room, clutching the precious notebook to my chest.

But as soon as I was back on the stairs the notebook, like the door, had gone.

6

I began a new novel last night and straight-away—I'd only written a page—I heard the clock strike.

My first reaction was not pleasure but irritation and some dismay. Oh, no, and just as I was getting started! I was tempted to ignore it. I had to remind myself that it wasn't really an interruption—it meant I would have even more time to write. All I had to do was leave one desk and notebook and take up at another. Then I could write for many hours, not just one.

So I went and wrote until my hand ached, and then I stopped and made myself a cup of tea. I couldn't tell which cup I'd used before—both were clean, although there was nowhere to wash up—and the biscuit tin looked as full as the first time I'd opened it.

I prowled my domain. There was no hurry. I could stay as long as I liked. Not since I became a mother had I known the luxury of the time I had now: time to waste, to lazily work up to writing, to get in the mood, or to slowly wind down. Nobody was going to yell at me to come and look, come and help; there was no ironing to do here, no papers to grade, no cooking or washing up. I was tired, yet the hour when I'd have to get up and go to work was drawing no closer. I could stay as long as I liked and still have eight hours in my bed.

After a good browse among the books I wandered over to have a closer look at the pictures hanging on the opposite wall. There were two portraits: they looked like reproductions of oil paintings, but I didn't recognize them. There were few clues to era, but I guessed early twentieth century. One showed a woman, nude, seated, presented in side view but half turned away as if to hide her nakedness. She turned back to stare out of the picture with a bold, somehow malicious stare which made me uneasy. The other portrait was of a man in an old-fashioned military uniform, sitting on a yellow chair. The chair made

Only the story was still there, achieved, finished, in my head—and I knew I would be able to write it again from memory.

It feels so real, what happened to me, but it must be imaginary. No time passes while I am away. I don't actually go anywhere. So what happens? Maybe, just as I come to the turn of the stair, I suffer a sort of brain-wave, fall into an incredibly rich, vivid, real-seeming dream for what feels like hours, only to snap back to consciousness a few seconds later, and continue going down the stairs, under the mistaken impression that in that gap I've written forty pages, had a nap, and consumed one cup of tea and six digestive biscuits....

I have heard of people dreaming epic novels overnight, and supposedly in the second before you die your whole life flashes before your eyes: time doesn't work the same way subjectively as objectively, everybody knows that. I'm surprised Oliver Sacks hasn't written about this phenomenon. God, what if it's the first sign of a tumor or brain lesion or something? I can't see going to a doctor about it, and describing my "symptoms." This symptom's a gift; I don't want to lose it!

5

Going there—should that be 'going there'?—is dependent on a mental state which I can't simply produce at will. I have to be writing, and immersed, utterly concentrated on what I'm writing, which can be anything, this journal, or a story, yet there must also be something in me which holds unhappily apart, frustrated by limits, angry, dissatisfied, waiting for the bell. It doesn't happen when I wait for it or try to will it, and it hasn't happened these past two weeks when I've been using David's lap-top to type the final draft of "Irrevocable Decisions." I wonder if it's because I'm typing—"keying in" I guess it's called now—rather than writing. It doesn't feel natural to me; I hate reading words on a screen. When I have a pen or pencil in my hand and the smoothness of paper racing away beneath, everything is different, my writing room draws closer.

me think of Van Gogh, but the painting was not in his style. At first I thought I preferred this picture, but after a moment I began to suspect there was something wrong with it, or with the subject. He wasn't a man, after all, but a woman in disguise; a deeply unhappy woman, unwillingly disguised.

I turned away to the other paintings, which were water-color landscapes, pleasant, uncomplicated studies of the sea and sky, with no people in them. They made me wonder about what was outside the room, so I went over and opened the drapes and, for the first time, I saw.

It was day—early afternoon, to judge from the autumnal light, and the city that should have been there had completely vanished. Stretching away before me was open countryside: rolling downs dotted here and there with copses of trees. In the distance, shining like a silver coin, I could see a lake. I saw no buildings, no roads, nothing manmade, not even the electricity pylons and telephone poles which have penetrated everywhere in the world I know. Not only the city but civilization itself seemed to have withdrawn, leaving me utterly alone. I looked down, and the house I owned with David had also vanished. I could see no doors or windows below mine. It appeared that I was in a tower built of stone.

I was utterly lost. Where was my family, my home, my world? Panic gripped me, and I ran for the door. The sight of my own familiar stairs when the door opened wasn't enough for me, though—I had to race downstairs and then outside into our tiny back garden where I could see the sodium orange glow of civilization in the night sky, and smell the chilly, polluted air of life as we know it today.

"What's the matter?" asked David, hovering in the kitchen, his hair in little tufts like eyebrows raised in astonishment. I was so pleased to see him. Love for him surged through me, warming me and making me tearful.

"Nothing," I said. "Nothing. Oh, I just suddenly thought how lucky I am to have you!"

He put his arms around me, puzzled but pleased, and I began to kiss him with enthusiasm, so happy and relieved to be safely home again. One thing led to another, and then to bed.

7

It doesn't frighten me now, the view from that window. It's like everything else there—mine, even though I wouldn't consciously have chosen it. But it stands to reason that if I could have a room of my own, furnished exactly to my taste, expense no object, I wouldn't want a view of the backs of houses to go with it. The country outside reminds me a bit of the South Downs, where David and I went for our dirty weekends long ago, and a little bit of that place in Scotland where we went for our first family holiday, just after Phoebe was born—only it's much wilder, obviously much more remote, than anywhere I've ever been. No rising smoke, no flocks of sheep, no footpaths, no signs of any other human habitation. There's only me in my tower.

Spring arrived between one visit and the next. I opened the window and breathed in the pure, fresh country air. I spent about ten minutes just watching the birds and some rabbits hopping about. I'm not so driven now; I know that when I'm there I have plenty of time to think, read, daydream—I don't have to scribble furiously the whole time. I can plan what I'm going to write, and things I won't. I can even daydream about things that are nothing to do with writing, have thoughts just to please myself. The time I have inside is all my own, I don't have to juggle conflicting demands and make sacrifices and feel guilty stealing one little hour to myself. The time I spend in there doesn't take away from the children, or my job, or David, or even the housework. I could spend the whole day writing in my room and emerge less than an hour after going upstairs, enough of the evening left to do some ironing and talk to David about music lessons for the girls.

I wonder... this trick I've stumbled on: could anyone do it? Do we all have this capacity, a secret room hidden away inside us, just waiting to be unlocked? Writing is the key for me, but could it be something else for someone else? Wishing is part of it, I'm sure, but also hard work and a particular kind of concentration.

8

And pride goeth before a fall. Ouch.

I haven't been back into my room for three weeks: not for lack of wishing, not for lack of trying.

It was hard, sometimes, settling down to write out here when I wanted to be writing *in there*, but when I did (because I knew I'd never get anywhere if I didn't) I kept breaking my concentration because I thought (hoped) I'd heard the clock strike. Well, that was the first week.

Finally I managed to stop hoping, to stop expecting anything and just write. I got quite a bit done—I'm well into the novel now and can see my way ahead.

This has made me rethink my theory.

Maybe it's nothing to do with me. Maybe that room actually exists in some other universe, and our house just happens to be built on a bor-der-line, and I just happened to be going down the stairs on a few of the occasions when the door between two worlds manifested itself, and it could just as easily have been David, or a visitor looking for the loo, who went through...

Or maybe it was a gift from God, or a passing good fairy, who kindly granted my wish until I got so unbearably smug about "my" room, at which point He, She or It took it back.

Oh, please, if you're out there—whoever You are—please please please give me another chance.

9

Halfway through the novel and I've hit an intractable hump. Where do I go from here? Maybe I should have stuck with the first novel, which at least had a proper sort of plot. I should have outlined first, the way they tell you in books. I was seduced by the ease of those two short stories into thinking it would just kind of work itself out as I went along.

Are the characters the problem? Maybe she's too much like me and he's too much unlike anybody I've ever met. Or it's the situation. Meant to be difficult, it's become impossible. There's no obvious solution, maybe no unobvious one, either, no way out.

But there must be a way out, if there was a way in. Just not an obvious one. Something unexpected happens, something that changes the way she looks at her life. A door suddenly opens. A clock strikes when there is no clock—

Thank you.

10

Not just weeks, as for me outside, but months passed in there, the turning of the seasons. It was spring before, but when I went in two nights ago I found a dark, winter landscape outside the window. It was early morning. As I sat at my table and struggled to write myself back into my stalled novel the blackness outside began to lighten. The sun came up. There was snow everywhere; looking down I saw what had to be deer tracks in the snow. And as I went on gazing, my eyes roaming, dazzled, across the white expanse, feeling awed by its immense purity, I glimpsed a splash of red. It moved. As I continued to stare I made out a solitary human figure, well-bundled against the weather (the red was a scarf), trudging through the snow.

My heart raced and I felt quite giddy. I wasn't alone! As I watched, it became clear that the figure was coming towards me—hardly surprising, since mine was the only building anywhere in sight. I debated what to do, considering the wisdom of caution—in other words, should I escape back to my own world before I was seen—but was won over by curiosity and the inability to believe that I could be in any real danger in what was my own dream. I opened the window and, when he was close enough to hear, called out a greeting.

He replied, but I couldn't understand a word he said. It was clear that he knew no more of English than I knew of his strange language. He mimed climbing up: would I let him in? He looked so cold, poor thing, and I was cold enough shivering by the open window, so I nodded and beckoned him to come up.

He climbed up the rough stone very nimbly while I thought disjointedly about Rapunzel and other princesses in towers without doors. I felt very strange when he came in. I felt shy. The whole atmosphere of the room was different with someone else in it. I think he felt shy of me, too. He avoided my eye but kept up a stream of incomprehensible talk while he divested himself of backpack and heavier outer garments. He could have been talking about the weather, explaining he was a king's son, or telling me filthy stories for all I knew. I think he said his name was Jack, or Zak, or Jacques, but that's only if he understood what I was asking him.

Jack—I might as well call him that—was a nice-looking if rather grubby and stubbled individual, a few years older than me and a bit shorter. He had shortish, fairish, gray hair and what there was of his beard was nearly white. Blue eyes, long nose, decided chin—quite a pleasant, humorous, intelligent face. He reminded me more than a little of Josh, that long-vanished Canadian, which maybe helps explains why I—but I'm getting ahead of myself.

"Would you like a cup of tea?" I asked, and mimed drinking. His face brightened and he nodded, and dug into his rucksack and brought out food: russet apples, a small, round loaf of brown bread, a chunk of hard yellow cheese, nutty and buttery tasting. Eating together we relaxed. I liked his company (the way he looked at me; the warmth of his eyes; that physical and psychic whiff of Josh, making me feel much younger than I am) and could tell he liked mine, although our attempts to communicate anything more profound or abstract than "this cheese is delicious" were doomed to failure. I have no ear for languages: I'll never forget that time I asked a man in a bar in Scotland if he spoke English, under the misapprehension that the language he'd been regaling me with for the past ten minutes was either Gaelic or Norwegian! I got through French at school only because there was so much less emphasis on conversation than on reading and writing. Looking at words, reading them, I can make some sort of sense. The things I hear, though, slip away. I'm struggling now to recall the words Jack told me for "apple," "bread" and "book."

After eating the warmth of the room made him drowsy; he began to yawn and it was obvious he was having a struggle to keep his eyes open. I gestured him towards the chaise-longue, mimed sleep, then pointed to the door and made him understand I would leave him to it. This won from him a burst of speech, but as I hadn't a clue as to whether he was asking me about toilet facilities or simply thanking me, I could only shrug, smile, and wave bye-bye.

The door was there again last night. As soon as I came in Jack rushed to meet me, wide-eyed and talking a blue streak, desperately trying to explain something to me. All I could make out was that he'd nearly given up hope of ever seeing me again and had been about to leave.

I'd been gone only a day in my world, but that was so much longer in his. He drew me to the window and showed me that the snow was melting. He pointed to the remains of a deer carcass and I understood he'd been living off it—and my tea, made with melted snow—after exhausting the supplies in his rucksack. He'd waited as long as he could.

But why? I didn't understand why he had waited for me until, our eyes meeting, he reached out to touch my face.

He loved me.

We made love.

121

Just writing those words, I feel myself swept away again. I can't justify it. I'm happily married (and how suspicious I've always been of people who use that defensive phrase!) and he was a stranger.

My stranger. My fantasy. I guess that's the only explanation there is. Anything is possible, and everything permissible, in a dream, and the life I lead in that room is a dream.

We spent a whole long day making love. In some ways it was the most natural thing to do—what is there, when you can't communicate in words? There are gestures, there is touch; looks and smiles, caresses, the language of the body.

He wanted me to go out the window and away with him. It was obvious my door did not exist for him, which is just as well, since I could hardly have taken him back here, into my real life! I know he won't be there when I return, which is

11

I must not go back.

So much for my smug, self-serving belief that I could do what I wanted in my own private world without affecting anyone else.

David came upstairs last night, looking a little green around the gills, wanting to talk. Instant guilt attack. If I hadn't still been writing it, I would have imagined he'd just read in my journal about Jack.

So I went down with him and we talked. It was a talk about feelings, a vague but impassioned something's wrong/what's wrong discussion of a kind unusual in our relationship. We had one just before we got married, I remember, and a couple when I was pregnant and paranoid, but in general we've both had a practical, if uninquiring, attitude towards our relationship, as to life in general; a belief in not stirring up trouble. We don't argue very often but when we do it tends to be about something specific, not the "you don't talk to me/I feel we're drifting apart/ what's happening to us" blether of last night.

And the pig of it was, I couldn't shrug off his vague fears any more than I could make them concrete with the truth.

"There isn't someone else, is there, Chris? You're not seeing someone else?"

His name is Jack, and he's not real—I made him up. "When would I have time? No, there isn't anyone else."

"I didn't think so. But if it isn't someone, it's something."

I know he found it painfully difficult to express. He's always been supportive of my writing—for all the good it's ever done him!—and he doesn't want to start being obstructive now, even though he's started to feel that it is taking me away from him; away from him and the girls.

It's true; I had to admit his fears were well-founded. Between my job, his job, looking after the children, doing basic house work and other chores, my writing, and—this is the part he still doesn't know about—my secret fantasy world, there's nothing left over for him, for us—nothing special, that is. We eat together, sleep together, go places as a family, and that's about it. I don't spend any more time away from him, physically, than I have in the past three years, but mentally I do. And mentally makes the difference. There aren't enough hours in the day and never have been, but back when we first got together (both of us with full-time jobs and ongoing, if unsatisfactory, relationships with significant others) we used to focus a lot of energy on making the few hours we did have together something special.

"There aren't enough hours in the day," David said last night. "I know that. We have to work, and Rachel and Phoebe need our time and attention, and there're always other things to be done, but we need time together, just the two of us. I'm not asking you to give up writing—I'd never do that, I know how much it means to you—but something has to change. Even when we are together I don't feel you're really with me. Your mind's somewhere else. It bothers me."

I hadn't meant for it to happen and I didn't want it to be true, but it was. I agreed that I would make an effort to change—we both would. We'd get a sitter and go out together occasionally and, just as important, we would spend more evenings together the way we used to—sharing a bottle of wine over dinner, listening to music, talking, making love.

I won't have to give up writing, but I'll lose my precious "extra hour."

I was a fool to think I could do whatever I wanted without consequences. Everything makes a difference; everything has its cost.

I must not go there again.

I feel as sad and despairing as if this meant giving up writing. Maybe it does. By luck or magic I found a way to make more time in which to write, and now I'll have to do without.

But if I carry on like this I'll destroy my marriage. If it was only my happiness at stake maybe I'd risk it, maybe I'd choose the unknown over present comfort. But there are the children to think of as well, their lives, their happiness. I'm not that selfish. I know, *pace* Charlotte Perkins Gilman and all the other feminist writer-heroines, that writing—especially *my* writing—is simply not that important. People's lives are what's important, my family's happiness, not my own selfish gratification.

Besides—I have to keep reminding myself—it's not writing I'm giving up, just the sneaky, supernatural way I've been doing it lately. I will finish my novel.

Only not tonight. My hour is up, and I haven't done a thing. I'll have to give up this journal, too. Cut back to the basics. We'll survive.

12

Twice I heard the clock strike, twice I ignored it, as I'd promised myself I would, but the third time—

It was nearly four months since I'd heard it, and I'd thought I never would again. This might be my last chance.

Oh, David, I never meant to betray you, or leave you, and I still don't. Maybe, if you read these pages, and can bring yourself to believe them, you'll understand why, if not how, I have gone.

THE EXTRA HOUR

I got up when I heard the clock strike. It was half-conscious impulse, a powerful desire, unreasoning, that drew me. I hesitated when I saw the door at the turn of the stair, hesitated and thought of you. What would happen if I called you? Would the door vanish, or would you be able to enter with me?

I wish now that I'd tried, had given you the chance to see, but I didn't, and it's too late for second-guessing. I did what I did.

As soon as I stepped into the room I was seized, attacked, by over-whelming pain. I staggered forward, doubled over, struggling to cope with whatever was happening to me, and then the pain passed. I could breath again, but I was weak and covered in sweat. And there was something fa-miliar about the pain. I looked down and realized I was pregnant.

The pain wracked me again. This time, the shock and terror were nearly as overwhelming as the physical labor. I was having a baby!

The contractions were very close together and horribly intense, with scarcely any space to rest in between. I didn't really have the time or energy to worry about the fact that I was all alone and wonder how I'd cope—I just had to get on with it. It never occurred to me to try to leave the room; what I was going through so consumed everything that there was no chance of thinking coherently. All my energies were devoted to getting through the next surge of pain, and then the next, and then in pushing the baby out. I managed to get my clothes off, and located some towels. I suppose it was all over rather quickly, although it didn't feel like it.

Then everything happened much too fast, and there was a baby slip-ping between my legs as I struggled to grasp and lift the slippery, bloody little creature. We rested for awhile on the floor and she—yes, she; an-other girl, of course—looked up at me with her dark blue eyes and gave a peeping, mewling cry more like a newborn kitten than a human child. She was so much smaller than Rachel had been, tinier even than Phoebe, but she was just as solid, just as real, and the protective, wondering love I felt welling up in me for her was just as strong as it had been for my other two.

Oh my baby

Those splotches are tears. Well, I'm post-partum, I can't be expected to—I can't help it, I—

But looking at me now, looking at my breasts, you'd never guess that a few minutes ago they were swollen at least two bra-sizes bigger. You'd never know from looking at me that I just gave birth. There's no trace left of the sweat and blood or any of the other fluids—I don't even smell of anything much, as if I'd done nothing more strenuous today than walk up and down the stairs.

We lay there together awhile, first on the floor where she'd been born, then up on to the chaise-longue. All of a sudden I felt hungry, but what I wanted even more than something to eat was to have a good wash, and to wash her, and get some fresh clothes for both of us. Also, I was worrying about the umbilicus, having nothing to cut it. I had a vague notion that something awful could happen if you left it too long, although I couldn't for the life of me remember what. We couldn't just stay there in post-natal coma like that forever. I guess I knew it was a risk: nothing and no one from that world could go out my door with me; I'd never even been able to take out a notebook. But I'd taken ideas, stories, out, and she was as much a part of me as my stories—she was even still attached to me.

I thought it might work, but it didn't. As soon as I stepped through the door she was gone, and I was alone and intact in this world again.

That's why I screamed, and lied so unintelligibly when you called up to me.

Then I ran straight back here, to my desk, to my notebook, to try to write my way back inside to my baby.

She needs me; she can't live without me, and I can't let her die.

Newborns can go several days without food (I keep reminding myself of these comforting facts), but how quickly will several days pass in there while I'm out here? I won't leave my desk, I won't sleep, until I hear the clock strike to let me back in.

You do understand why, don't you, David?

It's not that I value her life more than your happiness, or Phoebe's, or Rachel's, only—only it is her life we're talking about, her actual life weighed against mere comfort. She needs me in the way the rest of you don't. The three of you can survive without me—she can't.

But maybe you can both have me; maybe we can all survive. Time works so differently there. It might be, as I hope, that I can go back there, climb out the window and scale the rough stone wall of my tower with my baby strapped to my front, and carry her across that beautiful, wild emptiness to another house or a village or a castle—Jack came from somewhere, so there must be other people, and habitations, there—find her a foster home and wet-nurse, and then come back. I just want to save her life; I don't have to raise her myself.

If I can do all that in the same sort of no-time in which she was conceived, then I'll be back here before bedtime. You'll never have to read this, never know what I've been through, and I'll pretend—and eventually convince myself—that it all took place inside my head.

But if you don't find me when you come upstairs looking for me, and you read this, I want you to know the truth.

The clock!

Remember, I love you all.

destination unknown
THE MAIDEN DEATH
by Terry Dowling

What to make of Koronai? In the rush and flux of history, in the plundering of memory and time that gave us the Reality Crisis and so the Tribation, it is Samhain and Beltane and Easter, Halloween and Mardi Gras, El Dia De Muerte, the Dionysia, Carnevalle, Saturnalia, so many festivals and holidays crammed and jammed together, one moment something bright and golden, life-affirming festivals of light like Christmas and Channukah—the next, with a hint of menace, an edge of something dark, it shimmers and shivers with a sense of prices to be paid and deeds to be done, glossed with just enough unease to make every smile suspect.

Everyone comes to Twilight Beach for Koronai. In the moody autumnal light that falls between the Deliverance Moon of February and the Mask Moon of April, the crowds of tourists and revellers arrive in the hot dry days and frenzied nights of Keylock Week, and stay on until the wind comes.

Koronai always ends with a larrikin wind, the Kolki, the Collector, the blood and demon wind that blows souls clean, hones and flenses psyches, rubs life between its bloody hands and turns it out again, reprieved and new.

It's bad luck to ask for good luck in the days that follow Keylock Week. It is a time of risks and chances, of dares, jeux d'esprit and braggadocio. Each door gets its red handprint and its sprig of harbinger, bowls of Christi coins are set on window sills and left at intersections, strings of Biste lanterns and bounty lights, streamers and singing wires lace the streets, deliberately left for the Collector, the Kolki, to blow away, something to be visibly lost when the town is stripped clean again, robbed of all but memories, which become stories, the things that keep life eternal.

The stories, yes.

One began like this, this time, here at the coast with a street and a sailor, a sand-ship sailor in from the deserts, no stranger to this town either. His name was Tom, a captain in fact, here on the 24th day of Koronai. He stood at the end of Akaty Street again, a street like so many others except that it wasn't a regular street, not for him.

There are streets you just don't go down, he would tell you. Just don't. At first it's circumstance, merest chance. You've always found other ways to where you were going. Then it's because you haven't, have always taken those ways, which your mind makes the right way, and tells you that you musn't take this street, the unlucky street. You invent stories, fancies, find reasons to forbid and explain, and while you rehearse telling the story, you never do take that street.

Then, working through the pattern, you fall to the other side of your reasoning, as Tom now did. Who gives a damn? And: How dare it! Which brought him here, this time, during the winding down of Koronai, with a wind in the promise, with the singing wires, the bounty lights, the whole town waiting.

Akaty Street. Raggedy Akaty, as a passerby once rhymed it for him when he asked about the name. Six metres wide, overshadowed by the whitewashed, lion-colored, red-brown, old-brick walls of villas, tenements, lofts, who could say?, set with receding colonnades and what may have been countless small shopfronts (certainly how they seemed), dog-legging out to the harbor most likely, since there was no clear line of sight. None of the dazzling blue. Who knew what was down there?

And on the 24th of Koronai, at last, long last, Tom crossed Coronet Avenue and entered Akaty Street, determined, resolved, throwing caution, almost literally, to the wind. He would probably never be able to describe what it meant to take those few steps.

He was rewarded almost immediately. Not far into the laneway he found a curious thing—an old Twilister belltree standing back in a shadowed recess where the side and rear walls of 89 Coronet Avenue gave way to Number 1 Akaty. A Twilister—once one of the greatest AI's the Ab'O life-scientists of Australia had produced. Long ago.

destination unknown
THE MAIDEN DEATH

It was a stripped tree, fourteen feet tall but with no embellishments. Its two remaining sensor arms were high enough to be clear of the reach of vandals and souvenir hunters in the street. One, slightly bent, was possibly the result of those efforts—someone clambering up or, more likely, reaching out from the first of the security-grilled, shuttered windows. The other aimed into the warm blue sky like an arrow.

There was no-one about. Tom crossed to the tree, studied the drab diligent canister above the two arms, wondering if it still lived.

"You're a Twilister," he said. "I wouldn't have expected to find one here."

"You're a sailor," the voice came. "Likewise."

"Pardon me?"

"I wouldn't have expected to find one here."

Tom smiled up at it. "I've been told this street leads out to the sea."

"This street is a dead end."

"There'd be a sign. Others have said where it leads."

"Well, I do admit I've never been down there myself."

Again Tom smiled. "When the life-houses made Twilisters they made cynics and sophists."

"When they made national sandship captains, they made questing romantics and easy targets, ample justification for Twilisters."

Tom laughed, delighted. Koronai was a life festival as much as anything else. Every year, the countless sects and festival societies persisted in bringing out their latest life-experiments to carry or lead through the streets, often tricked up with costuming, prosthetics or heavylight to hide their usually pathetic, invariably malformed shapes (always claiming that what they made was their original intention!). Sometimes there'd be the old-style clones and hanivers done up as clowns or merry-andrews, but nothing, nothing like the occasional tribal cognates you saw, splendid and strange but real AL, real AI, not travesty or mimickry, nothing even like this downgraded, neglected tribal tree which, in its very abandonment and neglect, showed how far the rest of the world's biotects had yet to go.

"You know me?" Tom asked the tree, feeling better about his mission already.

"I tap into the net. Yes. The belltrees speak of you, Tom Rynosseros. And I've watched you. You sometimes come and stand out there in Coronet Avenue and just look. Five years of that. I suspect that today is a big day."

"It's Koronai. I'm hoping for bad luck."

"Break a leg then."

"What's that?"

"An old invocation. From a religion or a Beckett play, I'm not sure. maybe the religious performance of a Beckett play. Or Thomas a'Beckett's performance of his religion. It all amounts to the same thing."

"It does?"

"Of course. Neither of us has been here before. All our lives have brought us to this moment."

"You can say that of any moment. Any encounter."

"Yes."

The simplicity of the answer struck Tom there in that empty street on the 24th of Koronai, what it meant in view of the tree's condition, its sense of irony, its exquisite grasp of life in the instant, its evident determination to survive.

"I know an old poem," it said. "From way back. You might care to hear it."

"Please."

"Good man. Perfect answer. Listen:

"What is in the empty hand but the universe entire,
What is in the eye but all there is.
What is for the heart but the only fire,
And for the soul, the only moment, this."

θ θ θ

"A human poem," Tom said. "Hand. Eye. Heart. Soul."

"Yes. But all life too. Universe. Fire. Moment. All. This."

Like the surprise of a haiku, a note in a bottle or a fortune in a cookie, like the force of a previously bland aphorism suddenly lived and understood, what the old tree said made Tom marvel, left him with nothing to say.

There was silence then, a not-quite-silence, just the distant sounds of life in the adjoining avenues, the barest hint of belltree song from over the rooftops, perhaps the sea far off bringing its waves to the beaches and seawalls of the town, but nothing in Akaty Street, just blank walls and doors, windows with slide-aside shutters behind stout security grilles, the shadowed, receding colonnades, mirror-glassed shopfronts, paving stones, the sense of silence, the aptness of it.

"Why did you tell me the poem?"

"It's Koronai. You finally came down here. On your way to the sea."

"But a dead end you say."

"Not if you're here, of course." Safe sardonicism again.

"You must have a name."

"Nearly five hundred years old, you'd think so. All I have is a number, Tom. You could give me one. A memento. I'd like that. "

"And you could let me snap off a sensor spine. That bent one. As a memento."

"Let me be nameless rather than blind. Give me a name anyway."

"I'll think about it, give it to you on the way out—since it's a dead end."

"Hurry then. You'll have the Kolki on your back."

Tom looked up, saw the distinctive striations of cirrus marring the blue between the deserted roof-gardens, tails hooked into scimitars where the rooflines met the sky.

"You're right. That's larrikin."

"The Collector."

"I'll be back.

"I'll be here."

And Tom was off, feeling exhilaration rather than disquiet now at being in this street. Koronai was closing; everywhere wind-parties would be starting, the revellers desperately seeking a delirium to match the wind's arrival, something appropriate for when they later told their stories of Koronai at Twilight Beach. The Chung Yang kite-fliers would be lofting Kolki Demons and their gorgeously wrought defiance kites for the final bravura display; the Walpurgis torch-women would be afoot, blazing he-taerae, filling the boulevardes with their cry of "Ooroorake! Ooroorake!"

All this as out there, plunging home, the larrikin was on its way, messenger wind, death wind, soul-snatcher, life-bringer, cleanser. Pneuma. Breath of Amphion and Saramaya, Aeolus and Vayu.

Such Romantic notions couldn't last. A further five minutes down Akaty and his irrational fears were there again. Perhaps it was the quiet laneway itself, the countless reflections that came at him from the windows of locked and abandoned shops, the sudden bites of shadow from each colonnade; perhaps it was what was happening to the light.

For the scimitar clouds had gone; the sky overhead, what Tom could see of it, was a harsh striated gray, the larrikin pall touching everything, deepening shadows, softening building lines to the unreality of dream, giving the tree's words 'dead end' a new weight of meaning. And this was just the beginning. Soon there would be the dust and the wrack; soon the Kolki, the Collector, the Red Hand, would truly have the town and Koronai would be done for another year.

Perhaps all this kept him from noticing at first, but suddenly Tom realized that not one of the doors he passed bore a red handprint, not one had a harbinger sprig or even one of the less common festival signs. You could expect one or two such doors, yes, people away or bent on humbuggery, disdaining the month-long round, but every door? Every single one?

He actually hurried to find one then, one marked door, just one, but they were all blank, all of them, which brought back the dread, the air of some preternatural dislocation. It occurred to him too that he must seem a strange, driven creature to any who did watch, head turning this way and that, but the shops were sightless mirrors, the houses too silent, just like—

A corio street, he realized.

It had to be. Not out on the desert's edge near Tomb Street where the old sandsmen inns stood, The Highwayman, The Black Wind and The Cannon, where the sand drifted in, blew against doors forever sealed on their still occupants, but here. Corio *here*. It explained everything.

The authorities had to know, had to have let it happen. Probably some wealthy socialite, some benefactor dying, their request to be interred in their home of so many years honored, delicately, discreetly, because of the Tomb Street tradition out there where Twilight Beach fell away to nothing. One distinguished local, then two. Who would ever know? And one by one the corio houses grew, and Akaty Street, in the midst of so much life, became more and more quiet, cut off from the bustle and excitement, cut off even from the silence.

Tom smiled. Corio here, in a backstreet just off the Byzantine Quarter. Appropriate for Koronai's dark underside, for a town where Black Madonnas were still carried out to the sea and candy skulls were gnawed on by laughing children, where masqueraders followed the Teutonic ship-wagon processions of Fastnacht to ensure the world stayed bountiful, and Passover was reduced to a red handprint on a door.

But a whole street? He ran past the dead, blind houses, wanting to discover where this pocket necropolis ended and the living town, his town, resumed. Imagine it: somewhere close by there were families enjoying windparties, arcane and outrageous rituals, festivities with origins long out of mind, and just a wall away, round a turn in the stairs, on the other side of a shadowed court or quiet square, there was a house, then another and another, where the occupants lay unmoving in silent rooms beside dim corpse-lights, bodies filled with dessicants and retardants, sealed inside the cloudy mummiform comfit shells that remained even when the bodies themselves sank away. Sometimes timers brought up music, fragments of song, voices and images, hologram and heavylight, bits of a forgotten life, just enough of a signature, just enough. And if relatives did visit (an increasingly rare thing - something about the insidious nature of corio discouraged it), it was only to lay wreathes at locked street doors, never to enter.

Twilister humor again: dead end indeed.

Tom hurried along under the thickening, reddening sky, more than ever determined to find one door, just one, that might prove him wrong. The sea was not the right destination now, not with the wind almost on the town, but he was in the street, already committed, already rewarded with a reason why Akaty Street had troubled him all these years.

And there ahead it widened into a small square, barely that, with a dry fountain at its centre like a discarded chess piece, the street ran to either side and continued on at a fifteen degree angle.

That bend would do it, he was certain, would show him the dead pewter ocean, the scoured silver swells, the Pier already closed in the growing, old-blood larrikin light.

He was so intent on reaching it that he was actually startled to see the palm print on the shop door, the sign: Akaty Street Keepsafe, whatever that meant, with: J.D. Ras, Proprietor, and the dim glow of a stormlight showing, other lights within.

An open shop. Living.

Tom laughed from sheer relief, turned the door handle, burst in, forgetting where he was, how it would seem.

It was the elderly man at the counter who cried out in fright, not the dark-haired, much younger woman sitting near him. The color went from her face; her dark eyes widened, her mouth opened, but she did not scream. Her expression might have been of delight, relief, wonder for the complex startlement it showed.

"Sorry!" Tom cried. "I'm so sorry! I wasn't thinking. I'm Tom Tyson, a sandsman, captain of *Rynosseros*. I was taking a short-cut to the sea. The houses weren't marked."

The tableau changed. The young woman stood, came to the counter; the old man sank back in her chair and glared, one hand placed theatrically, alarmingly on his chest. He breathed deeply, regaining composure, but through it all his stare remained. As much as it was a special arrival for the woman, this was clearly as an intrusion for him.

Tom tried again. "These corio houses. I didn't expect anyone."

"Nor did we, " she said. "Not now. Not with the wind." Her face remained oddly animated, filled with elusive emotion. "But we hoped. And now you've caught us red-handed, Captain. I am Katya; this is my grandfather, Jayco Ras. What may we get you? There is tea. Or, if you prefer..."

"Tea, yes. Thank you." First the fear, now hospitality. Koronai still, this side of the wind. He seized on it, seized on the life of it.

The woman gave a nervous, somehow ambivalent smile, as if reluctant to leave, then disappeared into the back of the—shop? Studio? There was precious little furniture, no evident wares, just dark-colored walls, some chairs behind the narrow counter. Akaty Street Keepsafe. What could it be? A security desposit facility? To the side of the curtained door Katya had taken, there was another, of black metal, like a ship's door or airlock, hermetically sealed; perhaps that led to a security vault. Pawn shops, antique stores, were often the last to close in formerly well-established areas, trading off the discarded goods of departing neighbors.

"I'm afraid it's really not a good time," Ras said, with no warmth at all. Perhaps it was the shock he'd been given, or the pending wind, some religious custom here, Tom thought, but he plainly wanted him to be gone before Katya returned. The old man was even standing now, leaning on the counter as if willing his unwanted visitor back out onto the darkening street.

"Mr. Ras, give my apologies to your granddaughter please. I think..."

"No!" Katya cried, pushing back the curtain, hurrying in bearing a tray with cups and a steaming pot. "Red Hand, Jayco! We agreed. Captain Tyson, please sit over here." She tried to give a smile, but it was mostly ruined by the look she gave her grandfather.

More than ever Tom wanted to be gone, but he had not missed the urgency in her gaze, the almost beseeching quality; it was as if a vital private contest were unfolding; the tension of it filled the small dark interior of the shop.

As they sat and Katya poured the tea, the old man looked sullen, dejected, but he feigned courtesy. "You're right, Kat. I did promise. Captain, forgive me. It was your sudden entry. All day we've set tea to boiling, first her pot, then mine. It's the wind, you see, this wretched wind."

Which further convinced Tom that the red hand was Katya's idea, her way of reaching out, of belonging to more than corio.

It was as if she read his mind. "We weren't always corio factors," she said. "This was a neighborhood pharmacy when my grandmother was alive, then a pathology lab and a medical centre as the locals got on in years, finally a holding cell."

"Say what you mean," old Ras interrupted. "A morgue."

"When I was a girl, Jayco became the unofficial undertaker..."

"As corio became the overtaker," Ras said. "Tell it all, Kat. Because they wanted discretion, right? Couldn't have people knowing it was corio, could we, Captain? Think of it. I took an honors degree in bioengineering, but who needed another National bioengineer? For twenty years I did diagnostic mockups, ran bio sims and controls, raised cultures, spent hours in the clean room." He glanced at the sealed black door.

His door, Tom decided. Separate pots. Separate doors. More than ever, he was convinced he had stumbled on some private Koronai ritual and wanted to be away.

But the old man continued. "As close as I ever got: helping police with forensics when the big labs were overcommitted. But did any offer contracts? Tenure? Oh no. I came up with a comfit solvent fifteen years ago, something to penetrate a shell so an autopsy could be done on that Maynar heiress out in Tomb Street."

THE MAIDEN DEATH

"Maynar?"

"The younger Maynars bribed a medic, sapped a records AI, drugged their mother and sealed her up alive. It was my solvent that opened the shell. But what happens? First lobbying from nervous relatives, then tribal outcry. Comfit is a tribal patent, it turns out. So mine was confiscated."

"They paid, Jayco," Katya said, frowning, as if troubled by something.

"Oh yes. They paid. Thank you very much."

Tom heard this exchange with an odd detachment, a deep and growing lassitude, a deadening of the extremities. He realized that he had been drugged, and so easily, that Katya had too. He tried to stand, fell back in the chair, worked his face muscles to keep his vision clear.

Katya was working her jaw muscles too, looking terribly afraid as she fought to stay conscious. "You promised, Jayco! This time, you said. You said—if someone came. You said—"

"Kat, what am I supposed to do? It's a sarcophage, for heaven's sake!" (What it sounded like: sarcophage!)

"Not this time! You—my tea as well. Why? Why?"

"I'm a life-scientist first, Kat. I'm all it has. That has to count for something. Responsibility. Now we can do it."

Tom couldn't move, was finding it hard to concentrate, to follow this crucial exchange, realized that Jayco Ras had crossed to the metal door and was undogging it, pushing it back.

"Please," Katya managed, the word slurred, her eyes half-closed.

Tom's vision, all his senses, were going too. He could smell chemicals and tried desperately to listen to whatever the man told his granddaughter, pretending more drowsiness than he felt, then finding it so easy to go on pretending, to sink away inside the pretence.

"Talk later, little one. It's time we play the Maiden Death."

Katya spoke again, and the old man did, and Katya may have, but the darkness was flowing out from the room beyond the black metal door and there was simply nothing else.

Images. A clutch of remembered words.

You promised. Sarcophage. Life-scientist first. The Maiden Death. Now we can do it.

Tom awoke in the deep gloom of a large chamber, a living-room perhaps, or a master bedroom, lying on a futon or a mattress on the floor against a wall. Fighting stupor and sudden waves of nausea, sorting bits of detail that resolved to strong wind gusting outside, a starving of light, not his headache, not vision impairment, he leaned up, supported on his arms, and confirmed his first conclusions. The hint of light through shutters, two double sets, showed him a living room, yes, or a bedroom. High-ceilinged, two closed doors, but no furniture, just un-certain dark shapes, blocks of darkness, mounded, scattered across the floor. Nothing else.

No, that wasn't true. There was a gaping hole in the far wall, a huge opening, shadow in shadow, the size of double doors, more startling because the last thing seen for what it was. The rubble lay scattered about, the bricks and plaster were the shapes he'd seen, some of it flung across the parquet floor as far as where he lay. Unless…

Tom leant further forward, saw with amazement another large opening just next to him. Another supporting wall had been breached.

Where was this place? The room beyond the metal door?

He tried to stand, head still reeling, nausea surging up, but man-aged to support himself on the wall and stepped off the bed. He then went to the opening near him, peered through into another large, dimly lit chamber, the violated living-room of another house, and beyond that into another, the same dark holes, blackness in blackness, imagined oth-ers, house linked to house.

Corio houses, he was sure of it, though, mercifully, he saw no comfit shells. He'd been lying on a corio bed, proved it by pounding on the shut-ters with a two-brick lump of rubble till they fell aside, letting in light. Then he looked through the glass and the solid security grille out onto the Akaty Street Keepsafe which sat on the opposite side of Akaty Street, still with its red handprint, still with its single storm-light showing.

He saw too what the day had become, for the larrikin was on the town, tyrant and thief, symbol and emblem, universal in this guise: Algerian Sirocco, Turkish Samiel, Arabian Simoom, Egyptian Khamsin, African Harmattan, the Santanas and Tehuantepec winds of the Americas, the dry rattling Meltemi, bright sun-wind of the Aegean. Out there it snatched the Chung Yang kites, stripped them, broke their backs, threw them from the sky, sent the torchfrau blazing home; here it brought a mean haunting blood-light, brought seething funereal darkness to corio rooms broken open, robbed of their silent occupants.

Turning his head aside, Tom raised his heavy, clumsy bricks and shattered the glass, then stood in the roaring, raging edge of the gale, in the stinging sand, and pounded at the grille itself. It was no use; the frame was too sturdy. He would find his way down to a street door, come back to it if necessary.

Since the two interior doors were locked and solid (the handles were removed in keeping with the corio practice of the One-Way Door) Tom went through the breach into the adjoining house, again battered open the shutters to let in what mean light there was, then examined what doors there were for any sign of springing.

They were secure, the interior almost a duplicate of the one he had awakened in. There were no corio shells here either, just the two empty beds where they had been, the overturned remains of bedside tables, the shattered corpselight fixtures.

Looted? Why would anyone—even vandals—batter open walls to steal comfit shells? Sometimes the house-burials did have furniture, personal effects, but rarely anything of value, precisely to discourage such violations as this. The houses out in Tomb Street didn't even have grilles on the windows.

Tom studied the latest wall opening. There was rubble, debris scattered about, yes, but hardly what such a breach would give. These had been done gradually, systematically, the bulk of the detritus had been carried away, probably used to seal up the doorways to ground level, he was certain. The interior doors he had tried all had the same solid feel. There was no echo when he pounded. Again, such systematic planning. But why? Why?

Ras's words: sarcophage. A life-scientist first.

Tom continued through the houses, forcing shutters, trying doors. Floor plans varied: often one room became two or three; sometimes the breaches were off-center or out of alignment, or there were multiple breaches into the same dwelling; sometimes there were openings in the back walls as well: this manifestation of the corio practice extending beyond Akaty Street so it was more a maze than ever.

Tom kept to the Akaty Street axis, breaking locked shutters but no longer shattering glass to try the grilles. The larrikin was howling out there and he needed as much quiet as he could get, sensed that hearing acuity might be vital now. He couldn't be more than six hundred metres from Coronet Avenue. He would explore—learn what he could about the pierced walls, the missing bodies, until he found something, some way out.

What else had old Ras said? The Maiden Death? And her cry: "Not this time!" Other things. Hints of Koronai contests, corio rituals, but the Maiden Death, definitely that.

Was Katya here somewhere too, drugged, silenced, sealed in comfit and already dead? Or, failing that, allowing that the Maiden had already played her part, what took Death's role here? Was it imprisoned by the same grilles and bricked up doors that confined him?

Tom already suspected what it might be, perfect for the underside of Koronai. There were no comfit shells, none of the milky, cloudy mummiforms, not one. Just the empty beds where they had been, the shattered deathwatch lights. Ras—more than a thwarted bioengineer—was a thwarted life-scientist. Yes, he dreaded what played the role of Death.

He was pounding at shutters in the fourteenth or fifteenth house when he heard it, a thumping just slightly out of time with his own, set against the raging of the Kolki. It stopped seconds after he stopped to listen. He hurried then, sharp with the acid rush of fear, busting locks, flinging aside shutters, peering out through shuddering glass at the blood-red day as caught, segmented, rationalized in the makeshift draughtman's frames of the grilles.

The next time he stopped to listen, the thumping continued, irregular, unmistakable, diffused through the architecture so he couldn't be sure from which direction it came, but definitely there in the plundered houses and sundered rooms.

As he ran from one burial house to the next, casement to casement, smashing, breaking, letting in the swathes of demon light, he made himself ponder what Ras could have made in that black-doored chamber and released here. What other tissue and DNA sources did he need than the occasional passer-by and the contents of the corio shells, the man using his solvent to open the dead-white mummies, taking what he needed. No wonder the shells were missing; he had dozens, probably hundreds to work with.

The thumping was nearer, louder, a steady rhythmic pounding now, sliding, rasping, something bludgeoning, pushing through the rooms.

Unable to trust his directional hearing, unwilling to, Tom pressed back in the deepest shadows he could find, huddled low, hauled up a corio mattress to conceal all but his head and eyes as the pounding came closer, whatever made it thundering, slamming, humping along in its deformity.

The shutters were still intact here, thank goodness, but through the nearest breach he could see devil's patches of red in the blacks and deep grays of the room he had left, saw, then, lunging through the breach where he hadn't yet been, something moving in blackness, something gray, pallid white, heaving, ridged, something!

From behind the mattress, Tom saw the strange, elongate shape push from one wall opening to the other, hauling its articulated form behind it, thirteen, fourteen meters, more. The thing was huge.

Only when it had gone completely through did Tom emerge from hiding, slip through the opening into the unvisited rooms, hurrying, finally running, zig-zagging this way and that through holed support walls, through pierced, less substantial interior divisions, using whatever he could find to pound at shutter locks, leaving a trail of footfalls and slamming to draw the creature after him once more, but not daring to stop. He needed light more than anything, light as fraught and starved as it was, anything to drive away the darkness.

He grew used to the pattern of it, the running, the abandoned beds, the pieces of overturned furniture, shattered corpse-light fittings, doors without handles, without echoes, his only consolation the knowledge that he was running above Akaty Street, re-tracing his course. From one dead end to another most likely, but trying.

And behind now, when he paused, straining to listen over wind-race and heart-race, he could hear it again, the slamming, frantic thudding, Ras's creature on its way, blindly, dumbly, possibly with intelligence, probably without, rather a set of tropisms, mindless, aching to fulfil minimal function, yet every bit of that.

Tom ran and ran, lost in the pattern of smashing at shutters, running through deserted rooms, arms aching from the bricks and lathe he carried to bring in the light, came finally to a room with no opening in its far wall, no retreat but the way he had come.

Somewhere back there, out there, was the door Ras had used to carry him into this maze, a door that would echo when pounded on, resonate with emptiness beyond, with stairs down and freedom. Though Ras was cunning. No doubt it would have been muffled too, made to sound like any of the dozens, hundreds Tom had tried.

The thumping, the thudding was louder.

What to do? What? Against a creature he hadn't seen, didn't know the anatomy and weaknesses of. Made from the insides of corio shells. *Of* corio shells! Impervious.

Breathing hard, fighting the panic, Tom leaned against the wall of this newer, different dead end. His mind raced. Sarcophage, Ras had called it, if he'd heard correctly. From sarcophagus: flesh eater. The ancients had believed the sarcophagus actually devoured the contents placed within.

Perhaps that was it. Not discarding the comfit shells at all, *using* them as exoskeleton, placing the creature inside.

Dead end. Here above Akaty Street, his deadly taboo street. With the Kolki on his back; Koronai in ruins. Ruins.

Tom smashed at the shutters, ripped them aside, pounded the glass again and again till it shattered, strained to look out in the running blood of the wind, out and down, saw—yes!—the top of the old Twilister, thrumming, soughing, keening in the blast there below his hand.

Reached down, arm stretched painfully against the grille, found the single singing dagger of the straight sensor spine with his fingers, strained to grip as far down the needle as he could, made an agonising fist, gripped hard, hard, applied what pressure he could, snapped it back, clean through.

He drew it back into the room in his bloody fist in time to see the Ras creature two rooms away, a heaving, milky-white, utterly unhuman yet humaniform construct blundering, lunging through the wall hole— of corio shells, one mounted on the other, stretching back and back!

What it was: shell upon shell like deck-chairs stacked and left to slide, like a tug-of-war team fallen forward in defeat, turned to stone or salt, Lot's wives, impossible Siamese twins: the first almost flat on the floor but supported by a remarkable foot, a striving pad of muscle that let it hop, haul and drag, hop, haul and drag, the second shell mounted atop the first, fused chest to back, head peering intimately over its shoulder, the third joined head and chest to waist, the fourth higher up, chest to shoulders, welded, bonded, on and on. Yes, like deck-chairs spilling, like some heroic tug-of-war captain dragging the team, joined as the houses were and housing what Ras had made.

Tom had anatomy now, sought process, all in moments. Impervious shells, a solvent discharge to pierce and use, feed, some re-bonding capability to fuse new shells to old and so extend the animal. Not Maiden Death, no. Ras had said: Made *in* Death, had fashioned something that circumvented the dessicants and other embalming chemicals. Existed in spite of them. Used them.

Even as it came at him, Tom wondered how it defecated, rid itself of waste. Perhaps there were gases, secretions using the same pink, wet-looking mouth opening on the head of the footed first shell.

Poisons? Gases? He stood in the inrush of wind, glad of the dust, the stinging grains of sand, and gripped the half-meter sensor spine.

The creature was not built to fight, merely maintain. Barely able to turn itself, far too long and cumbersome, it lunged blindly on, almost leapt onto the spike Tom drove deep into its orifice and brain, made no sound, flailed, shuddered, clattered its length, settled finally into death, sent that final message back into all that it was.

Almost leapt? No. Did leap, Tom realized. Wanting death. The absolution of Koronai. As Ras and Katya had intended.

By the time he did force a grille, climbed down into the wind-race of Akaty Street and made his way back to the store, Tom knew what had happened, knew they'd be waiting in the open doorway just as he found them, Ras with his arm round his granddaughter.

"You tricked me," he said, when they were in out of the wind.

Jayco gave his first smile, thin and brief, one filled with the proper weight of sadness and regret. "Yes, Captain, we did. We made a story, Kat and me, figured villainous old man and captive ward would do it."

"The reason?"

"To put it out of its miserable life," Ras said. "Corio drove the life out of this street. No-one ever asked permission of the living. Oh no. So long ago—I—" Tears spilled from the eyes, were fiercely wiped away.

"He devised a solution for all this death," Katya said. "Something to end it once and for all."

Old Ras shook his head. "Which, as usual, did not justify the means. We needed—another solution."

Tom stared blankly at the rush of wind in Akaty Street. "Which I provided. "

"Which we all provided. You and me. Katya with her dream."

"Dream? "

Katya nodded. "That today someone would come. That today would be it. Before Koronai ended. Someone out of the storm. It made us act. Finally."

Tom walked towards the door, towards the racing wind. "I see."

"I hope you do, Captain," Katya said. "Because now our work really begins. Restoring the houses. Bringing back the life."

Tom smiled, then turned and hurried up Akaty Street to where the Twilister thrummed and sang in the howling flow, its remaining sensor arm curving into the storm.

He stood close against the shaft, gripping it, eyes half-shut. "Quite a task," he called up. "Fighting death."

"Even when it goes wrong it's better than just accepting. How did you know?"

Tom felt the question in his hands and cheek as well as heard it. "Your poem before. You love life. Being in a corio street would have been so hard."

Jayco must have come down here one day, spoken with you. I'm sure it seemed a good plan at the time."

"*Our* design. You understand. We couldn't kill it."

"I think it knew."

"I fear it did. But there's triumph here, Tom; the last line of a poem by Swinburne. Here too Death lies dead. Do I get a name?"

"Sinon."

"Ah. The Trojan who persuaded his people to drag the wooden horse into Troy. That means 'deceiver'."

"It does."

"I like it. He changed the course of history. Will you come back and see our street? It leads to the sea. Tom."

"I will, Sinon."

He turned then and blew away into the dying hours of Koronai, determined to remember the kinship in stories, that whatever else happens, we are always part of someone else's story too.

destination unknown
IN THE PINES
by Charles de Lint

Life ain't all a dance.
- attributed to Dolly Parton

It's celebrity night at the Standish and we have us some lineup. There are two Elvises—a young one with the swiveling hips and a perfect sneer, and a white-suited one, circa the Vegas years; a Buddy Holly who sounds right but could've lost fifty pounds if he really wanted to look the part; a Marilyn Monroe who has her boyfriend with her. He'd be wearing a JFK mask for her finale, when she sings "Happy Birthday" to him in a breathless voice. Lonesome George Clark has come out of semi-retirement to reprise his old Hank Williams show and then there's me doing my Dolly Parton tribute for the first time in the three years since I gave it up and tried to make it on my own.

I don't really mind doing it. I've kind of missed Dolly, to tell you the truth, and it's all for a good cause—a benefit to raise money for the Crowsea Home for Battered Women—which is how they convinced me to do that old act of mine one more time.

I do a pretty good version of Dolly. I'm not as pretty as her, and I don't have her hair—hey, who does?—but I've got the figure, while the wig, make-up and rhinestone dress take care of the rest. I can mimic her singing, though my natural voice is lower, and I sure as hell play the guitar better—I don't know who she's kidding with those fingernails of hers.

But in the end, the looks never mattered. It was always the songs. The first time I heard her sing them, I just plain fell in love. "Jolene." "Coat of Many Colors." "My Blue Tears." I planned to do a half hour of those old hits with a couple of mountain songs thrown in for good measure. The only one from my old act that I was dropping was "I Will Always Love You." Thanks to the success Houston had with it, people weren't going to be thinking Tennessee cabins and Dolly anymore when they heard it.

I'm slated to follow the fat Elvis—maybe they wanted to stick all the rhinestones together in one part of the show?—with Lonesome George finishing up after me. Since Lonesome George and I are sharing the same back-up band, we're going to close the show with a duet on "Muleskinner Blues." The thought of it makes me smile and not just because I'll get to do a little bit of yodeling. With everything Dolly's done over the years, even she never got to sing with Hank Williams—senior, of course. Junior parties a little too hearty for my tastes.

So I'm standing there in the wings of the Standish, watching Marilyn slink and grind her way through a song—the girl is good— when I get this feeling that something is going to happen.

I'm kind of partial to premonitions. The last time I felt one this strong was the night John Narraway died. We were working late on my first album at Tommy Norton's High Lonesome Sounds and had finally called it quits some time after midnight when the feeling hit me. It starts with a hum or a buzz, like I've got a fly or a bee caught in my ear, and then everything seems... oh, I don't know, clearer somehow. Precise. Like I could look at Johnny's fiddle bow that night and see every one of those horse hairs, separate and on its own.

The trouble with these feelings is that while I know something's going to happen, I don't know what. I get a big feeling or a little one, but after that I'm on my own. Truth is, I never figure out what it's all about until after the fact, which doesn't make it exactly the most useful talent a girl can have. I don't even know if it's something good or something bad that's coming, just that it's coming. Real helpful, right?

So I'm standing there and Marilyn's brought her boyfriend out for the big finish to her act and I know something's going to happen, but I don't know what. I get real twitchy all through the fat Elvis's act and then it's time for me to go up and the buzzing's just swelling up so big inside me that I feel like I'm fit to burst with anticipation.

We open with "My Tennessee Mountain Home." It goes over pretty well and we kick straight into "Jolene" before the applause dies off. The third song we do is the first song I ever learned, that old mountain song, "In the Pines." I don't play it the same as most people I've heard do—I learned it from my Aunt Hickory, with this lonesome barred F# minor chord coming right in after the D that opens every line. I remember cursing for weeks before I could finally get my fingers around that damn chord and make it sound like it was supposed to.

So we're into the chorus now—

> *In the pines, in the pines,*
> *Where the sun never shines*
> *And the shiverin' cold winds blow.*

—and I'm looking out into the crowd and I can't see much, what with the spotlights in my eyes and all, but damned if I don't see her sitting there in the third row, my Aunt Hickory, big as life, grinning right back up at me, except she's dead. She's been dead fifteen years now, and it's all I can do to get through the chorus and let the band take an instrumental break.

2

The Aunt—that's what everybody in those parts called her, 'cept me, I guess. I don't know if it was because they didn't know her name, or because she made them feel uneasy, but nobody used the name that had been scratched onto her rusty mailbox down on Dirt Creek Road. That just said Hickory Jones.

I loved the sound of her name. It had a ring to it like it was pulled straight out of one of those old mountain songs, like "Shady Groves," or "Tom Dooley."

She lived by her own self in a one-room log cabin, up the hill behind the Piney Woods Trailer Park. She was a tall, big-boned woman with angular features and chestnut hair cropped close to her head. Half the boys in the park had hair longer than hers, slicked back and shiny. She dressed like a man in blue jeans and a flannel shirt, barefoot in the summer, big old workboots on those callused feet when the weather turned mean and the snows came.

She really was my aunt. She and Mama shared the same mother except Hickory had Kickaha blood, you could see it in the deep coppery color of her skin. Mama's father was white trash, same as mine, though that's an opinion I never shared out loud with anyone, not even Hickory. My Daddy never needed much of a reason to give us kids a licking. Lord knows what he'd have done if we'd given him a real excuse.

I never could figure out what it was about Hickory that made people feel so damn twitchy around her. Mama said it was because of the way Hickory dressed.

"I know she's my sister," Mama would say, "but she looks like some no account hobo tramping the rail lines. It's just ain't right. Man looks at her, he can't even tell she's got herself a pair of titties under that shirt."

Breasts were a big topic of conversation in Piney Woods when I was growing up and I remember wishing I had a big old shirt like Hickory's when my own chest began to swell and it seemed like it was never gonna stop. Mama acted like it was a real blessing, but I hated them. "You can't have too much of a good thing," she told me when she heard me complaining. "You just pray they keep growing awhile longer, Darlene, 'cause if they do, you mark my words. You're gonna have your pick of a man."

Yeah, but what kind of a man? I wanted to know. It wasn't just the boys looking at me, or what they'd say; it was the men, too. Everybody staring down at my chest when they were talking to me, 'stead of looking me in the face. I could see them just itching to grab themselves a handful.

"You just shut your mouth, girl," Mama would say if I didn't let it go.

Hickory never told me to shut my mouth. But then I guess she didn't have to put up with me twenty-four hours a day, neither. She just stayed up by her cabin, growing her greens and potatoes in a little plot out back, running trap lines or taking to the hills with her squirrel gun for meat. Maybe once a month she'd head into town to pick up some coffee or flour, whatever the land couldn't provide for her. She'd walk the five miles in, then walk the whole way back, didn't matter how heavy that pack of hers might be or what the weather was like.

I guess that's really what people didn't like about her—just living the way she did, she showed she didn't need nobody, she could do it all on her own, and back then that was frowned upon for a woman. They thought she was queer—and I don't just mean tetched in the head, though they thought that, too. No, they told stories about how she'd sleep with other women, how she could raise the dead and was friends with the devil and just about any other kind of foolish idea they could come up with.

Course I wasn't supposed to go up to her cabin—none of us kids were, especially the girls—but I went anyways. Hickory played the five-string banjo and I'd go up and listen to her sing those old lonesome songs that nobody wanted to hear anymore. There was no polish to Hickory's singing, not like they put on music today, but she could hold a note long and true and she could play that banjo so sweet that it made you want to cry or laugh, depending on the mood of the tune.

See, Hickory's where I got started in music. First I'd go up just to listen and maybe sing along a little, though back then I had less polish in my voice than Hickory did. After a time I got an itching to play an in-strument too and that's when Hickory took down this little old 1919 Martin guitar from where it hung on the rafters and when I'd sneak up to her cabin after that I'd play that guitar until my fingers ached and I'd be crying from how much they hurt, but I never gave up. Didn't get me nowhere, but I can say this much: whatever else's happened to me in this life, I never gave up the music. Not for anything, not for anyone.

And the pain went away.

"That's the thing," Hickory told me. "Doesn't matter how bad it gets, the pain goes away. Sometimes you got to die to stop hurting, but the hurting stops."

I guess the real reason nobody bothered her is that they were scared of

153

her, scared of the big dark-skinned cousins who'd come down from the rez to visit her sometimes, scared of the simples and charms she could make, scared of what they saw in her eyes when she gave them that hard look of hers. Because Hickory didn't back down, not never, not for nobody.

3

I fully expect Hickory to be no more than an apparition. I'd look away, then back, and she'd be gone. I mean what else could happen? She was long dead and I might believe in a lot of things, but ghosts aren't one of them.

But by the time the boys finish their break and it's time for me to step back up to the mike for another verse, there she is, still sitting in the third row, still grinning up at me. I'll tell you, I near' choke right about then, all the words I ever knew to any song just up and flew away. There's a couple of ragged bars in the music where I don't know if I'll be finishing the song or not and I can feel the concern of the boys playing there on stage behind me. But Hickory she just gives me a look with those dark brown eyes of hers, that look she used to give me all those years ago when I'd run up so hard against the wall of a new chord or a particularly tricky line of melody that I just wanted to throw the guitar down and give it all up.

That look had always shamed me into going on and it does the same for me tonight. I shoot the boys an apologetic look, and lean right into the last verse like it never went away on me.

> The longest train that I ever saw
> Was nineteen coaches long,
> And the only girl I ever loved
> She's on that train and gone.

I don't know what anyone else is thinking when I sing those words, but looking at Hickory I know that, just like me, she isn't thinking of trains or girlfriends. Those old songs have a way of connecting you to something deeper than what they seem to be talking about, and that's what's happening for the two of us here. We're thinking of old losses and regrets, of all the things that might have been, but never were. We're thinking of the night lying thick in the pines around her cabin, lying thick under those heavy boughs even in the middle of the day, because just like the night hides in the day's shadows, there's lots of things that never go away. Things you don't ever want to go away. Sometimes when that wind blows through the pines, you shiver, but it's not from the cold.

4

I was fifteen when I left home. I showed up on Hickory's doorstep with a cardboard suitcase in one hand and that guitar she'd given me in the other, not heading for Nashville like I always thought I would, but planning to take the bus to Newford instead. A man who'd heard me sing at the roadhouse just down a-ways from Piney Woods had offered me a job in a honkytonk he owned in the city. I'm pretty sure he knew I was lying about my age, but he didn't seem to care any more than I did.

Hickory was rolling herself a cigarette when I arrived. She finished the job and lit a match on her thumbnail, looking at me in that considering way of hers as she got the cigarette going.

"That time already," she said finally, blowing out a blue-grey wreath of smoke on the heel of her words.

I nodded.

"Didn't think it'd come so soon," she told me. "Thought we had us another couple of years together, easy."

"I can't wait, Aunt Hickory. I got me a singing job in the city—a real singing job, in a honkytonk."

"Uh-huh."

Hickory wasn't agreeing or disagreeing with me, just letting me know that she was listening but that she hadn't heard anything worthwhile hearing yet.

"I'll be making forty dollars a week, plus room and board."

"Where you gonna live?" Hickory asked, taking a drag from her ciga-rette. "In your boss's house?"

I shook my head. "No, ma'am. I'm going to have my own room, right upstairs of the honkytonk."

"He know how old you are?"

"Sure," I said with a grin. "Eighteen."

"Give or take a few years."

I shrugged. "He's got no trouble with it."

"Well, what about your schooling?" Hickory asked. "You've been doing so well. I always thought you'd be the first one in the family to finish high school. I was looking forward to that—you know, to bragging about you and all."

I had to smile. Who was she going to brag to?

"Were you going to come to the graduation ceremony?" I asked instead.

"Was thinking on it."

"I'm going to be a singer, Aunt Hickory. All the schooling I'm ever going to need I learned from you."

Hickory sighed. She took a final drag from her cigarette then stubbed it out on the edge of her stair, storing the butt in her pocket.

"Tell me something," she said. "Are you running from something or running to something?"

"What difference does it make?"

"A big difference. Running away's only a partial solution. Sooner or later, whatever you're running from is going to catch up to you again. Comes a time you're going to have to face it, so it might as well be now. But running to something... well."

"Well, what?" I wanted to know when she didn't go on right away.

She fixed that dark gaze of hers on me. "I guess all I wanted to tell you, Darlene, is if you believe in what you're doing, then go at it and be willing to pay the price you have to pay."

I knew what she was trying to tell me. Playing a honkytonk in Newford was a big deal for a girl from the hills like me, but it wasn't what I was aiming for. It was just the first step and the rest of the road could be long and hard. I never knew just how long and hard. I was young and full of confidence back then at the beginning of the sixties, invulnerable, like we all think we are when we're just on the other side of still being kids.

"But I want you to promise me one thing," Hickory added. "Don't you never do something that'll make you feel ashamed when you look back on it later."

"Why do you think I'm leaving now?" I asked her.

Hickory's eyes went hard. "I'm going to kill that daddy of yours."

"He's never tried to touch me again," I told her. "Not like he tried that one time, not like that. Just to give me a licking."

"Seems to me a man who likes to give out lickings so much ought to have the taste of one himself."

I don't know if Hickory was meaning to do it her own self, or if she was planning to put one of her cousins from the rez up to it, but I knew it'd cause her more trouble than it was worth.

"Leave 'im be," I told her. "I don't want Mama getting any more upset."

Hickory looked like she had words for Mama as well, but she bit them back. "You'll do better shut of the lot of them," was what she finally said. "But don't you forget your Aunt Hickory."

"I could never forget you."

"Yeah, that's what they all say. But then the time always comes when they get up and go and the next you know you never do hear from them again."

"I'll write."

"I'm gonna hold you to that, Darlene Johnston."

"I'm changing my name," I told her. "I'm gonna call myself Darlene Flatt."

I figured she'd like that, seeing how Flatt & Scruggs were pretty well her favorite pickers from the radio, but she just gave my chest a considering look and laughed.

"You hang onto that sense of humor," she told me. "Lord knows you're gonna need it in the city."

I hadn't thought about my new name like that, but I guess it shows you just how stubborn I can be, because I stuck with it.

5

I don't know how I make it through the rest of the set. Greg Timmins who's playing dobro for me that night says except for that one glitch coming into the last verse of "In the Pines," he'd never heard me sing so well, but I don't remember it like that. I don't remember much about it at all except that I change my mind about not doing "I Will Always Love You" and use it to finish off the set. I sing the choruses to my Aunt Hickory, sitting there in the third row of the Standish, fifteen years after she up and died.

I can't leave, because I still have my duet with Lonesome George coming up, and besides, I can't very well go busting down into the theatre itself, chasing after a ghost. So I slip into the washroom and soak some paper towels in cold water before holding them against the back of my neck. After awhile I start to feel... if not better, at least more like myself. I go back to stand in the wings, watching Lonesome George and the boys play, checking the seats in the third row, one by one, but of course she's not there. There's some skinny old guy in a rumpled suit sitting where I saw her.

But the buzz is still there, humming away between my ears, sounding like a hundred flies chasing each other up and down a windowpane, and I wonder what's coming up next?

6

I never did get out of Newford, though it wasn't from want of trying. I just went from playing with housebands in the honkytonks to other kinds of bands, sometimes fronting them with my Dolly show, sometimes being myself, playing guitar and singing back-up. I didn't go back to Piney Woods to see my family, but I wrote Aunt Hickory faithfully, every two weeks, until the last letter came back marked, "Occupant deceased."

I went home then, but I was too late. The funeral was long over. I asked the pastor about it and he said there was just him and some folks from the rez at the service. I had a lot more I wanted to ask, but I soon figured out that the pastor didn't have the answers I was looking for, and they weren't to be found staring at the fresh-turned sod of the church-yard, so I thanked the pastor for his time and drove my rented car down Dirt Creek Road.

Nothing looked the same, but nothing seemed to have changed either. I guess the change was in me, at least that's how it felt until I got to the cabin. Hickory had been squatting on government land, so I suppose I shouldn't have been surprised to find the cabin in the state it was. The door was kicked in, the windows all broke, anything that could be carried away long gone, everything else vandalized.

I stood in there on the those old worn pine floorboards for a long time, looking for some trace of Hickory I could maybe take away with me, waiting for some sign, but nothing happened. There was nothing left of her, not even that long-necked old Gibson banjo of hers. Her ghost didn't come walking up to me out of the pine woods. I guess it was about then that it sunk in she was really gone and I was never going to see her again, never going to get another one of those cranky letters of hers, never going to hear her sing another one of those old mountain songs or listen to her pick "Cotton-Eyed Joe" on the banjo.

I went outside and sat down on the step and I cried, not caring if my make-up ran, not caring who could hear or see me. But nobody was there anyway and nobody came. I looked out at those lonesome pines after awhile, then I got into my rented car again and drove back to the city, pulling off to the side of the road every once in awhile because my eyes got blurry and it was hard to stay on my own side of the dividing line.

7

After I finish my duet with Lonesome George, I just grab my bag and my guitar and I leave the theater. I don't even bother to change out of my stage gear, so it's Dolly stepping out into the snowy alley behind the Standish, Dolly turning up the collar of her coat and feeling the sting of the wind-driven snow on her rouged cheeks, Dolly fighting that winter storm to get back to her little one-bedroom apartment that she shares with a cat named Earle and a goldfish named Maybelle.

I get to my building and unlock the front door. The warm air makes the chill I got walking home feel worse and a shiver goes right up my spine. All I'm thinking is to get upstairs, have myself a shot of Jack Daniels, then crawl into my bed and hope that by the time I wake up the buzzing in my head'll be gone and things'll be back to normal.

I don't lead an exciting life, but I'm partial to a lack of excitement. Gets to a point where excitement's more trouble than it's worth and that includes men. Maybe especially men. I never had any luck with them. Oh they come buzzing around, quick and fast as the bees I got humming in my head right now, but they just want a taste of the honey and then they're gone. I think it's better when they go. The ones that stay make for the kind of excitement that'll eventually have you wearing long sleeves and high collars and pants instead of skirts because you want to hide the bruises.

There's a light out on the stairs going up to my apartment but I can't even find the energy to curse the landlord about it. I just feel my way to the next landing and head on up the last flight of stairs and there's the door to my apartment. I set my guitar down long enough to work the three locks on this door, then shove the case in with my knee and close the door behind me. Home again.

I wait for Earle to come running up and complain that I left him alone all night—that's the nice thing about Maybelle; she just goes round and round in her bowl and doesn't make a sound, doesn't try to make me feel guilty. Only reason she comes to the side of the glass is to see if I'm going to drop some food into the water.

"Hey, Earle," I call. "You playing hidey-cat on me?"

Oh that buzz in my head's rattling around something fierce now. I shuck my coat and let it fall on top of the guitar case and pull off my cowboy boots, one after the other, using my toes for a boot jack. I leave everything in the hall and walk into my living room, reaching behind me for the zipper of my rhinestone dress so that I can shuck it, too.

I guess I shouldn't be surprised to see Hickory sitting there on my sofa. What does surprise me is that she's got Earle up on her lap, lying there content as can be, purring up a storm as she scratches his ears. But Hickory always did have a way with animals; dying didn't seem to have changed that much. I let my hand fall back to my side, zipper still done up.

"That really you, Aunt Hickory?" I say after a long moment of only being able to stand there and stare at her.

"Pretty much," she says. "At least what's left of me." She gives me that considering look of hers, eyes as dark as ever. "You don't seem much surprised to see me."

"I think I wore out being surprised 'round about now," I say.

It's true. You could've blown me over with a sneeze, back there in the Standish when I first saw her, but I find I'm adjusting to it real well. And the buzz is finally upped and gone. I think I'm feeling more relieved about that than anything else.

"You're looking a bit strollopy," she says.

Strollops. That's what they used to call the trashy women back around Piney Woods, strumpets and trollops. I haven't heard that word in years.

"And you're looking pretty healthy for a woman dead fifteen years."

Maybe the surprise of seeing her is gone, but I find I still need to sit me down because my legs are trembling something fierce right about now.

"What're you doing here, Aunt Hickory?" I ask from the other end of the sofa where I've sat me down.

Hickory, she shrugs. "Don't rightly know. I can't seem to move on. I guess I've been waiting for you to settle down first."

"I'm about as settled down as I'm ever going to be."

"Maybe so." She gives Earle some attention, buying time, I figure, because when she finally looks back at me it's to ask, "You remember what I told you back when you first left the hills—about never doing something you'd be ashamed to look back on?"

"Sure I do. And I haven't never done anything like that neither."

"Well, maybe I put it wrong," Hickory says. "Maybe what I should have said was, make sure that you can be proud of what you've done when you look back."

I don't get it and I tell her so.

"Now don't you get me wrong, Darlene. I know you're doing the best you can. But there comes a point, I'm thinking, when you got to take stock of how far your dreams can take you. I'm not saying you made a mistake, doing what you do, but lord, girl, you've been at this singing for twenty years now and where's it got you?"

It was like she was my conscience, coming round and talking like this, because that's something I've had to ask myself a whole pile of times and way too often since I first got here to the city.

"Not too damn far," I say.

"There's nothing wrong with admitting you made a mistake and moving on."

"You think I made a mistake, Aunt Hickory?"

She hesitates. "Not at first. But now... well, I don't rightly know. Seems to me you've put so much into this dream of yours that if it's not pay-back time yet, then maybe it is time to move on."

"And do what?"

"I don't know. Something."

"I don't know anything else—'cept maybe waiting tables and the like."

"I see that could be a problem," Hickory says.

I look at her for a long time. Those dark eyes look back, but she can't hold my gaze for long and she finally turns away. I'm thinking to myself, this looks like my Aunt Hickory, and the voice sounds like my Aunt Hickory, but the words I'm hearing aren't what the Hickory I know would be saying. That Hickory, she'd never back down, not for nobody, never call it quits on somebody else's say-so, and she'd never expect anybody else to be any different.

"I guess the one thing I never asked you," I say, "is why did you live up in that old cabin all on your ownsome for so many years?"

"I loved those pine woods."

"I know you did. But you didn't always live in 'em. You went away a time, didn't you?"

She nods. "That was before you was born."

"Where'd you go?"

"Nowhere special. I was just traveling. I...." She looks up and there's something in those dark eyes of hers that I've never seen before. "I had the same dream you did, Darlene. I wanted to be a singer so bad. I wanted to hear my voice coming back at me from the radio. I wanted to be up on that big stage at the Opry and see the crowd looking back at me, calling my name and loving me. But it never happened. I never got no further than playing the jukejoints and the honkytonks and the road bars where the people are more interested in getting drunk and sticking their hands up your dress than they are in listening to you sing."

She sighed. "I got all used up, Darlene. I got to where I'd be playing on those dinky little stages and I didn't even care what I was singing about anymore. So finally I just took myself home. I was only thirty years old, but I was all used up. I didn't tell nobody where I'd been or what I'd done or how I'd failed. I didn't want to talk to any of them about any of that, didn't want to talk to them at all because I'd look at those Piney

Woods people and I'd see the same damn faces that looked up at me when I was playing out my heart in the honkytonks and they didn't care any more now than they did then.

"So I moved me up into the hills. Built that cabin of mine. Listened to the wind in the pines until I could finally start to sing and play and love the music again."

"You never told me any of this," I say.

"No, I didn't. Why should I? Was it going to make any difference to your dreams?"

I shake my head. "I guess not."

"When you took to that old guitar of mine the way you did, my heart near' broke. I was so happy for you, but I was scared—oh, I was scared bad. But then I thought, maybe it'll be different for her. Maybe when she leaves the hills and starts singing, people are gonna listen. I wanted to spare you the hurt, I'll tell you that, Darlene, but I didn't want to risk stealing your chance at joy neither. But now..."

Her voice trails off.

"But now," I say, finishing what she left unsaid, "here I am anyway and I don't even have those pines to keep my company."

Hickory nods. "It ain't fair. I hear the music they play on the radio now and they don't have half the heart of the old mountain songs you and me sing. Why don't people want to hear them anymore?"

"Well, you know what Dolly says: Life ain't all a dance."

"Isn't that the sorry truth."

"But there's still people who want to hear the old songs," I say. "There's just not so many of them. I get worn out some days, trying like I've done all these years, but then I'll play a gig somewhere and the people are really listening and I think maybe it's not so important to be really big and popular and all. Maybe there's something to be said for pleasing just a few folks, if it means you get to stay true to what you want to do. I don't mean a body should stop aiming high, but maybe we shouldn't feel so bad when things don't work out the way we want 'em to. Maybe we should be grateful for what we got, for what we had."

"Like all those afternoons we spent playing music with only the pines to hear us."

I smile. "Those were the best times I ever had. I wouldn't change 'em for anything."

"Me, neither."

"And you know," I say. "There's people with a whole lot less. I'd like to be doing better than I am, but hell, at least I'm still making a living. Got me an album coming out and everything, even if I did have to pay for it all myself."

Hickory gives me a long look and then just shakes her head. "You're really something, aren't you just?

"Nothing you didn't teach me to be."

"I been a damn fool," Hickory says. She sets Earle aside and stands up. "I can see that now."

"What're you doing?" I ask. But I know and I'm already standing myself.

"Come give your old aunt a hug," Hickory says.

There's a moment when I can feel her in my arms, solid as one of those pines growing up the hills where she first taught me to sing and play. I can smell woodsmoke and cigarette smoke on her, something like apple blossoms and the scent of those pines.

"You do me proud, girl," she whispers in my ear.

And then I'm holding only air. Standing there alone, all strolloped up in my wig and rhinestone dress, holding nothing but air.

8

I know I won't be able to sleep and there's no point in trying. I'm feeling so damn restless and sorry—not for myself, but for all the broken dreams that wear people down until there's nothing left of 'em but ashes and smoke. I'm not going to let that happen to me.

I end up sitting back on the sofa with my guitar on my lap—the same small-bodied Martin guitar my Aunt Hickory gave a dreamy-eyed girl all those years ago. I start to pick a few old tunes. "Over the Waterfall." "The Arkansas Traveler." Then the music drifts into something I never heard before and I realize I'm making up a melody. About as soon as I realize that, the words start slipping and sliding through my head and before I know it, I've got me a new song.

I look out the window of my little apartment. The wind's died down, but the snow's still coming, laying a soft blanket that takes the sharp edge off everything I can see. It's so quiet. Late night quiet. Drifting snow quiet. I get a pencil from the kitchen and I write out the words to that new song, write the chords in. I reread the last lines of the chorus:

> But my Aunt Hickory loved me,
> and nothing else mattered
> nothing else mattered at all.

There's room on the album for one more song. First thing in the morning I'm going to give Tommy Norton a call and book some time at High Lonesome Sounds. That's the nice thing about doing things your own way—you answer to yourself and no one else. If I want to hold off on pressing the CDs for my new album to add another song, I can. I can do any damn thing I want, so long as I keep true to myself and the music.

Maybe I'm never going to be the big star the little girl with the cardboard suitcase and guitar thought she'd be when she left the pine hills all those years ago and came looking for fame and fortune here in the big city. But maybe it doesn't matter. Maybe there's other rewards, smaller ones, but more lasting. Like knowing my Aunt Hickory loves me and she told me I do her proud.

destination unknown
MONTEITH
by Bentley Little

Monteith

Andrew stared at the word, wondering what it meant. It was written in
his wife's hand, on a piece of her personalized stationary, penned with a
calligraphic neatness in what looked to be the precise center of the page.
There was only the one word, and Andrew sat at the kitchen table, paper
in hand, trying to decipher its meaning. Was it the name of a lover? A
lawyer? A friend? A co-worker? Was it a note? A reminder? A wish?

Monteith

He had missed it totally on his first trip through the kitchen, had simply placed his briefcase on the table and hurried to the bathroom.
Coming back to pick up his briefcase afterward, he'd seen the note but
had not given it any thought, his brain automatically categorizing it as
a telephone doodle or something equally meaningless. But the pre-
ciseness of the lettering and the deliberate position of the word on the
page somehow caught his eye, and he found himself sitting down to
examine the note.

Monteith

He stared at the sheet of stationary. The word bothered him, disturbed him in a way he could not quite understand. He had never read it
before, had never heard Barbara utter it in his presence. It set off no
subconscious alarms of recognition, but those two syllables and the aura
of sophisticated superiority that their union generated in his mind made
him uneasy.

Monteith

Did Barbara have a lover? Was she having an affair?

That was the big worry, and for the first time he found himself wishing that he had not gotten sick this afternoon, had not taken off early
from work, had not come home while Barbara was out.

He stood up, hating himself for his suspicions but unable to make them go away, and walked across the kitchen to the telephone nook in the wall next to the door. He picked up the phone, took the address book out from underneath and began scanning the pages. There was no "Monteith" listed under the M's, so he went through the entire alphabet, the entire book to see if "Monteith" was a first rather than last name, but again he had no luck.

Of course not, he reasoned. If Monteith was her lover, she would not write down his name, address and phone number where it might be stumbled across. She'd hide it, put it someplace secret.

Her diary.

He closed the address book and stood there for a moment, unmoving. It was a big step he was contemplating. His jealous imagination and unfounded paranoia was about to lead him into an invasion of his wife's privacy. He was about to break a trust that had existed between them for fifteen years on the basis of... what? Nothing. A single ambiguous word written on a piece of stationary.

Monteith

He looked back at the table, at the sheet of paper on top of it.

Monteith

The word gnawed at him, echoed in his head though he had not yet spoken it aloud. He was still thinking, had not really decided what to do, when his feet carried him into the living room, then through the living room, into the hall, then down the hall, into the bedroom.

The decision had been made, and he strode across the beige carpet, opened the single drawer of the nightstand on Barbara's side of the bed, and took out the small pink diary. He felt only a momentary twinge of conscience, then opened the book to the first page. It was blank. He turned to the next page. Blank. The next. Blank.

He flipped quickly through the pages, saw only blankness, only white. Then something caught his eye. He stopped, turned the pages back.

In the middle of the middle page, written in Barbara's neatest hand, was a single two-syllable word.

Monteith

He slammed the book shut and threw it back in the drawer. He breathed deeply, filled with anger and an undefinable, unreasonable feeling that was not unlike dread.

She was having an affair.

Monteith was her lover.

He thought of confronting her with his suspicions, asking her about Monteith, who he was, where she'd met him, but he could not, after all the discussions, after all the arguments, admit to snooping. After all he had said over the years, he could not afford even the appearance of invading her privacy. He could not admit to knowing anything. On the other hand, maybe she wanted him to learn of her indiscretion, maybe she wanted him to comment on it, maybe she was looking for his response. After all, she had left the stationary on the table where he was certain to find it. Was it not reasonable to assume that she had wanted him to see the note?

No, he had come home early, before he was supposed to. If this had been a usual day, she would have removed it by the time he returned from work, hidden it away somewhere.

Andrew's head hurt and he felt slightly nauseous. The house seemed suddenly hot, the air stifling, and he hurried from the room. He did not want to go through the kitchen again, did not want to see that note on the table, so he turned instead toward the back of the house, went through the rec room into the garage, where he stood just inside the doorway, grateful for the cool dark air. He closed his eyes, breathed deeply, but the air he inhaled was not clean and fresh, as he had expected. Instead, there was a scent of decay, a taste of something rotten. He opened his eyes, reached for the light switch and flipped it on.

A dead woodchuck was hanging from an open beam in the dark far corner of the garage.

Andrew's heart skipped a beat, and he felt the first flutterings of fear in his breast. He wanted to go back into the house, back to the bedroom, back to the kitchen even, but, swallowing hard, he forced himself to move forward. He crossed the open empty expanse of oil-stained concrete and stopped before the far corner. This close, he could see that the woodchuck had been strangled to death by the twine which had been wrapped around its constricted throat and tied to the beam. Hundreds of tiny gnats were crawling on the animal's carcass; their black pinprick bodies and clear minuscule wings moved between the individual hairs of the woodchuck and gave it the illusion of life. The insects trouped in growing black colonies on the white cataracted eyes, swarmed over the undersized teeth and lolling tongue in the open mouth.

Bile rose in Andrew's throat, but he willed himself not to vomit. He stared at the dead animal. There was something strange about the discolored lower half of the carcass, but he could not see what it was because of the angle at which it hung. Holding his breath against the stench of rot, he took another step forward.

A section of the woodchuck's underside had been shaved and an "M" carved into the translucent pinkish white skin.

Monteith

Was this Monteith? Gooseflesh prickled on Andrew's arms. The thought seemed plausible in some crazily irrational way, but he could think of no logical base for such an assumption. A woodchuck named Monteith? Why would Barbara have such an animal? And why would she kill it and mutilate it? Why would she write its name in her diary, on her stationary?

He tried to imagine Barbara tying the twine around the woodchuck's neck in the empty garage, hoisting the squirming, screaming, fighting animal into the air, but he could not do it.

How well did he really know his wife? he wondered. All these years he'd been kissing her good-bye in the morning when he left for work, kissing her hello at night when he returned, but he had never actually known what she did during the times in between. He'd always assumed she'd done housewife-type things—cooking, cleaning, shopping—but he'd never made the effort to find out the specifics of her day, to really learn what she did to occupy her time in the hours they weren't together.

He felt guilty now for this tacit trivialization of her life, for the un-spoken but acted upon assumption that his time was more important than hers. He imagined her putting on a false face for his homecoming each evening, pretending with him that she was happy, that everything was all right, while her lonely daylight hours grew more confining, more depressingly meaningless.

So meaningless that she'd turned to animal sacrifice?

He stared at the hanging insect-infested woodchuck, at the "M" carved on its underside. Something was wrong with this scenario. Something was missing. Something did not jibe.

He spit. The smell was starting to get to him, he could taste it in his mouth, feel it in his lungs, and he hurried out of the garage before he threw up. He opened the big door to let in the outside air. He took a series of deep, cleansing breaths as he stood at the head of the driveway, then walked over to the hose to get a drink. He splashed the cold rubbery water onto his face, let it run over his hair. Finally, he turned off the faucet and shook his head dry.

It was then that he saw the snails.

They were on the cracked section of sidewalk next to the hose, and they were dead. He squatted down. Barbara had obviously poured salt on three snails she'd found in the garden, and she'd placed the three dis-solving creatures at the points of a rough triangle on the sidewalk. Two of the shells were now completely empty and had blown over, their black openings facing sideways, the drying mucous that had once been their bodies puddled on the concrete in amoeba-like patterns, but the third snail had not yet dissolved completely and was a mass of greenish bubbles.

With a safety pin shoved through its center.

Andrew pushed the third shell with a finger, looking more closely. The pink plastic end of the safety pin stood out in sharp relief against the brown shell and green bubbling body. He stood. He'd never had any great love for snails, had even poured salt on them himself as a young-ster, but he had never been so deliberately cruel as to impale one of the creatures on a pin. He could not understand why Barbara would make a special effort to torture one of them, what pleasure or purpose she could hope to gain from such an action.

And why had she placed three of them at the corners of a triangle?

There was emerging here, between the woodchuck and the snails, a sense of ritualism that made Andrew extremely uncomfortable. He wished he'd never seen the stationary on the table. He wished he'd never followed up on it. Always before, he had phoned ahead prior to coming home. Even on those few occasions when he had left work ill, he had telephoned Barbara to let her know he was coming home, believing such advance notice an example of common courtesy. This time, however, he had not phoned home, and he was not sure why he hadn't.

He wished he had.

Monteith

Maybe it wasn't the name of a lover after all. Maybe it was some sort of spell or invocation.

Now he was being crazy.

Where was Barbara? He walked out to the front of the house, looked up and down the street for a sign of her car, saw nothing. He wanted to forget what he had seen, to go inside and turn on the TV and wait for her to come home, but the knot of fear in his stomach was accompanied by a morbid and unhealthy curiosity. He had to know more. He had to know what was really going on here—although he was not sure that this had any sort of reasonable explanation.

The thought occurred to him that he was hallucinating, imagining all of this. He'd left work today because of severe stomach cramps and diarrhea, but perhaps he was sicker than he'd originally believed. Maybe he didn't have a touch of the flu, maybe he was in the throes of a full-fledged nervous breakdown.

No. It would be reassuring to learn that there was something wrong with himself instead of Barbara, would relieve him to know that this insanity was in his mind, but he knew that was not the case. His mental faculties were at full power and functioning correctly. There really was a mutilated woodchuck in the garage, really was a triangle of tortured snails on the sidewalk, really was an empty diary with only one word on one page.

Monteith

Were there other signs he had missed, other clues to Barbara's... instability? He thought that there probably were and that he would be able to find them if he looked hard enough. He walked around the side of the garage to the back yard. Everything looked normal, the way it always did, but he did not trust this first surface impression and he walked past the line of covered plastic garbage cans, across the recently mowed lawn to Barbara's garden. He looked up into the branches of the lemon tree, the fig tree and the avocado tree. He scanned the rows of radishes, the spreading squash plants. His gaze had already moved on to the winter-stacked lawn furniture behind the garage before his brain registered an incongruity in the scene just passed, a symmetrical square of white tan amidst the free-form green.

He backtracked, reversing the direction of his visual scan, and then he saw it.

In the corner of the yard, next to the fence, nearly hidden by the corn, a small crude hut made of popsicle sticks.

He stared at the square structure. There was a small door and a smaller window, a tiny pathway of pebbles leading across the dirt directly in front of the miniature building. The house was approximately the size of a shoe box and was poorly constructed, the globs of glue used to affix the crooked roof visible even from where he stood.

Had this been made by one of the neighbor's kids or by Barbara? Andrew was not sure, and he walked across the grass until he stood in front of the hut. He crouched down. There were pencil markings on the front wall—lightly rendered shutters on either side of the two windows, bushes drawn next to the door.

The word "Monteith" written on a mailbox.

Barbara had made the house.

He squinted one eye and peered through the open door.

Inside, on the dirt floor, was an empty snail shell impaled by a safety pin.

He felt again the fear, frightened more than he would have thought possible by the obsessive consistency of Barbara's irrationality. He stood, and his eye was caught by a streak of purple graffiti on the brick fence in front of him. He blinked. There, above the popsicle stick house, on the brick fence wall, half-hidden by the grape vines and the corn stalks, was a crude crayon drawing. The picture was simple and inexpertly drawn, the lines crooked and wavering, and he would have ascribed its origin to a child had it not been for the subject of the illustration.

Himself.

He pushed aside the grape vines and stepped back to get a better view, to gain perspective. Seen from this angle, it was obvious whom the rendering was supposed to represent. Distance flattened out the jagged veerings of the crayon which occurred at each mortared juncture of brick, lent substance to the rough hesitations of line. He was looking at his own face simplified into caricature and magnified five fold. The receding hairline, the bushy mustache, the thin lips: these were the observations of an adult translated into the artistic language of a child.

Barbara had drawn this picture.

He noticed dirt spots on the brick where mudballs had obviously been thrown at his face.

The question nagged at him: why? Why had she done all of this?

He dropped to his hands and knees, crackling through the garden, fueled now by his own obsession. There was more here. He knew it. And he would find it if he just kept looking.

He didn't have to look long.

He stopped crawling and stared at the cat's paw protruding from the well-worked ground beneath the largest tomato plant. The paw and its connected portion of leg were pointed straight up, deliberately positioned. Dried blackened blood had seeped into the gray fur from between the closed curled toes.

destination unknown
MONTEITH

Maybe Monteith was the name of the cat, Andrew thought. Maybe she had accidentally killed a neighbor's cat and had guiltily buried the animal out here to hide the evidence.

But that wasn't like Barbara. Not the Barbara he knew. If she'd accidentally killed a pet, she would have immediately gone to the owner and explained exactly what happened.

Perhaps, he thought, she had deliberately killed the animal in order to provide nutrients for her soil, for her plants. Or as part of a ritual sacrifice to some witch's earth deity in order to ensure the health of her crop.

He thought of the woodchuck in the garage.

He wondered if there were dead animals hanging in other garages on the street, if pets were buried in other back yards. Perhaps the neighborhood wives took turns meeting at each others' houses while their husbands were gone, performing together dark and unnatural acts. Perhaps that was where Barbara was right now.

Such are the dreams of the everyday housewife.

The tune to the old Glen Campbell song ran through his head, and he suddenly felt like laughing.

An everyday housewife who gave up the good life for me.

The laughter stopped before it reached his mouth. What if Monteith wasn't the name of an animal at all but the name of a child? What if she had killed and sacrificed a child and had buried the body under the dirt of the garden? If he dug down, below the cat's paw, would he find hands and feet, fingers and toes?

He did not want to know more, he decided. He'd already learned enough. He stood up, wiped his hands on his pants and began walking back across the yard toward the house.

What would he do when he saw her? Confront her? Suggest that she seek help? Try to find out about her feelings, about why she was doing what she was doing?

Would she look the same to him, he wondered, or had the woodchuck and the snails and the cat and everything else permanently altered the way in which he viewed her? Would he now see insanity behind what would have been perfectly normal eyes, a madwoman beneath the calm exterior?

He didn't know.

It was partially his fault. Why the hell had he come home early? If he had just come home at the normal time, or if Barbara, damn her, had just been home, he never would have found all this. Life would have just continued on as normal.

The question was: did his newfound knowledge automatically mean that he gave up his right to happiness with Barbara? Part of him said no. So what if she sacrificed animals? She had, in all probability, been doing that for years without his knowledge, and they'd had what he'd always considered a happy life. Unless she was unhappy, unless this was all part of some twisted way she was trying to exorcise her negative feelings about their marriage, couldn't he ignore what he had learned and continue on as normal?

Monteith

It was Monteith he couldn't live with. He could live with the animals, with the fetishes, with the graffiti. If Monteith was some god or demon that she worshipped, he could live with that. But the idea that she was seeing another man behind his back, that Monteith was her lover, *that* he couldn't abide.

Perhaps she was with Monteith now, both of them naked in some sleazy motel room, Barbara screaming wildly, passionately.

But why couldn't he live with that? If she had been doing this for years and it had not affected their relationship until now, why couldn't he just pretend as though he didn't know and continue on as usual? He could do it. It was not out of the question. He would just put it out of his mind, make sure that he did not come home early any more without first checking with Barbara.

He walked into the house through the garage, walked back to the kitchen, sat down at the table.

He stared at the piece of stationary, but did not pick it up.

Ten minutes later, he heard the sound of a key in the latch. He looked up as Barbara walked in.

Her gaze flitted from his face to the paper and quickly back again.

Was that worry he saw on her features?

"I felt sick," he said dully. "I came home early."

She smiled at him, and the smile was genuine, all trace of worry gone—if it had been there at all. She walked over to him, patted his head with one hand, picked up the stationary with the other. She gave him a quick peck on the cheek. "Other than that, how was your day?"

He looked at her, thought for a moment, forced himself to smile back. "Fine," he said slowly. "Everything was fine."

destination unknown
THE HOUSE OF LAZARUS

by James Lovegrove

Visitors were welcome at the House of Lazarus at all times of day and night, but it was cheaper to come at night, when off-peak rates applied. Then, too, the great cathedral-like building was less frequented, and it was possible to have a certain amount of privacy in the company of your dear departed.

Because it was dark out, the receptionist in the cool colonnaded atrium betrayed a flicker of amusement that Joey was wearing sunglasses. Then, recognizing his face, she smiled at him like an old friend, although she didn't actually use his name until after he had asked to see his mother, Mrs. Delgado, and she had called up the relevant file on her terminal.

"It's young Joseph, isn't it?" she said, squinting at the screen. She couldn't have been more than three years Joey's senior. The query was chased by another over-familiar smile. "We haven't seen you for a couple of weeks, have we?"

"I've been busy," Joey said. "Busy" didn't even begin to describe his life, now that he had taken on a second job at a bar on Wiltshire Street, but he didn't think the receptionist wanted to hear about that, and more to the point, he was too tired and irritable to want to enlighten her.

The receptionist folded her hands on the long slab of marble that formed her desktop. "It's not my place to tell you what to do, Joseph," she said, "but you are Mrs. Delgado's only living relative, and we do like our residents to get as much stimulation as possible. As you know, we wake them for an hour of news and information every morning and an hour of light music every evening, but it's not the same as actual verbal interaction. Think of it as mental exercise for minds that don't get out much. Conversation keeps them supple."

"I come whenever I can...."

"Of course you do. Of course you do." That smile again, that smile of old acquaintance, of intimacy that has passed way beyond the need for forgiveness. "I'm not criticizing. I'm merely suggesting."

"Well, thank you for the suggestion," he said, handing her his credit card. The receptionist went through the business of swiping it, then pressed a button on a panel set into the desktop. A man in a white uniform appeared.

"Arlene Delgado," she told the orderly. "Stack 339, Drawer 41."

"This way, sir." The orderly ushered Joey through a pair of large doors on which were depicted, in copper bas-relief, a man and a woman, decorously naked, serenely asleep, with electrodes attached to their temples, chests and arms.

As they entered the next room, a vast vaulted chamber, the ambient temperature dropped abruptly. Cold air fell over Joey's face like a veil freshly dipped in water, and his skin buzzed with gooseflesh. He craned his neck to look up.

No matter how many times he came here, the wall never ceased to amaze him. At least a hundred and fifty feet high and well over a mile long, it consisted of stacks of steel drawers, each about half as large again as an adult's coffin. Each stack began roughly six feet above the floor and rose all the way to the roof, and, with a thousand of these stacks all told, the wall loomed like a sheer unclimbable cliff, lit from above by arc-lights that shot beams of pure white down its face. It was hard to believe sometimes that each drawer contained a human being.

At the foot of the wall plush leather armchairs were arranged in rows six-deep, all facing the same way like pews in a church. About a quarter of them were occupied by people murmuring quietly, as if to themselves. Every so often someone would nod or gesticulate, and silent pauses were frequent. The human sibilance was echoed by the sound of machinery, thousands of cryogenic units all whirring and whispering at once, fans exhaling, tubes pumping liquid nitrogen.

The orderly wandered down the aisle between the chairs and the wall, with Joey in tow. Some acoustical trick carried the clack of Joey's boot-heels up to the iron rafters but kept the squelch of the orderly's crepe soles earthbound.

Arriving at Stack 339, the orderly gestured to Joey to take the nearest seat, then began tapping commands into a portable console the size of a large wallet. Without needing to be asked, Joey picked up the mike-and-earphones headset that was wired into a panel in the arm of the chair and fitted the skeletal black device over his head. He took off his sunglasses and folded them into his breast pocket. The orderly glanced twice at the dark purple rings beneath Joey's eyes. Joey looked as if he had been punched, but the rings were just very heavy bags of exhaustion, packed with long days and late nights.

Realizing he was staring, the orderly returned his gaze to his console. "Right," he said, "I've given her a nudge. Can you hear anything?"

Joey shook his head.

"She may take a moment or two to wake up. Press the red button if you need me and push the blue switch to disconnect when you're done. OK?"

Joey nodded.

"Pleasant chat," said the orderly, and left, squelching along to a door set into the wall. The door was marked "STRICTLY PRIVATE" and could only be opened by tapping a five-digit code-number into the keypad set into its frame. It hissed slowly shut on a pneumatic spring.

Joey sat and waited, his gaze fixed somewhere near the top of the stack of drawers where his mother lay.

The first sounds came as if from deep underwater, where whales wail and the mouths of drowned sailors gape and close with the come and go of the currents. Up they surged in the earphones, these subaquatic groans, bubbling up to the surface in waves. Indistinct syllables, tiny glottal clucks and stutters, the gummy munches of a waking infant, the wet weaning mewls of still-blind kittens—up they came from the darkness, taking form, taking strength, slowly evolving into things that resembled words, white-noise dream-thoughts being tuned down to a signal of speech, babel finding a single voice.

>wuhwhy the—dear? is that—huhhh—nuhnnnno, nothing, no, no, nothing—on the table, you'll find them on the—huhhhello?—she never said that to me—hello? is there someone—hrrrhhh—dear, I'm talking to you, now please—it's these shoes, you know—wuhwwwwell, if you want to buy it, buy it—someone at the door, would you—yes—hahhhhhhello? is someone listening? I know someone's listening. Hello? Hello? Who is that? Who's there, please?<

"Hi, mum," said Joey. "It's me."

>Joey! How nice of you to drop by. It's so good to hear your voice. Been a while, hasn't it?<

"Just three days, mum."

>Three days? It seems an awful lot longer than that. It's so easy to lose track of time, isn't it? Well, anyway... How have you been keeping?<

"I'm well. And you?"

>I must be all right, mustn't I? Nothing much changes in here, so I suppose I must be staying the same. Are you quite sure it's only been three days? I try and keep a count of the number of times they wake me. The news. And that dreadful music. Mantovani, Manilow...<

"OK, maybe not three. A few days."

>You shouldn't feel you have to lie to me, Joey.<

"I've been meaning to get down more often, mum, but what with one thing and another..."

>It's all right, Joey. I do understand. There are plenty of things more important than your old mother. Plenty of things. How's work?<

"Oh, OK. Same as usual."

>It's not a job for a bright boy like you, taking shopping orders, It's a waste of your talents."

"It's all I could get, mum. I'm lucky to have a job at all."

>And have you found yourself a nice girl yet?<

"Not yet."

>Don't make it sound like such a trial, Joey. I'm only asking. This isn't the Spanish Inquisition. I only want to know if you're happy.<

"I'm happy, mum."

>Well, that's good, then. And the apartment? Have you had the cockroach problem sorted out?<

"I rang the Council yesterday. They said they'd already sent a man round to deal with it, but he never turned up. I think he must have been mugged on the way. I read somewhere there's a black market in bugdust. You can sell it to rich kids as cocaine and poor kids as heroin."

>Really, Joey, you ought to have moved out of the wharf district by now. Even with a job like yours, surely you can afford somewhere nicer. There's lots of new property being built. I heard it on the news. Apartment blocks are popping up all over the city like mushrooms. Why do you insist on staying where you are?<

"I like it there."

>That's as maybe, but I don't like the idea of you being there.<

"I can't afford the down-payment on another place."

>Oh, rot! There must be more than enough left over from the money your father left us.<

"Mum, it's not as straightforward as that."

>Seems perfectly straightforward to me.<

"Well, it would, wouldn't it?" He was aware of raising his voice. In that great archetraved ocean of cryogenic susurrus-and-sigh it was the merest drop of noise, but to his mother, in the dark, cramped confines of her mind, it must have sounded like he was bellowing.

>And what's that remark supposed to mean?<

"Nothing, mum," Joey said softly. "Nothing at all. I'm sorry."

>What is it, Joey? What's wrong with you? We always start out chatting so nicely, and then I say *something*, I don't know what, but something, and suddenly you're shouting at me, and I don't know what it is I've done, I don't know what it is I say, but I wish you'd tell me, Joey, I wish you'd tell me what it is I do that makes you so angry.<

"It's nothing, mum. Honest. Look, I've had a long day, that's all. I get a little snappish sometimes." He decided not to tell her about the bar job. She would only worry that he was taking on too much, and if, with her acute sense of what was proper and what was not, she thought working for TeleStore Services was bad, what would she have to say about serving drinks in a glorified pick-up joint?

>Yes, well...< she said. >I'm sorry too, then. But you must understand, it gets very lonely in here. Very, very lonely. It's just me in the dark, and you're my lifeline to the world, Joey. You're all that makes the solitude bearable. If it wasn't for your visits, I don't know what I'd do. Go mad, I expect. If I didn't know that you were coming, if I didn't know that you were going to visit me again soon...<

"I will, mum. I promise. And I won't leave it so long next time."

>That's the best I can hope for, I suppose. Off you go then, Joey. Thanks for dropping by. It was lovely talking. Come back when you can. Ha ha—I'm not going anywhere.<

"All right, mum. Take care."

>Bless you, Joey.<

"Goodnight, mum. Sleep tight."

He removed the headset, pushed the blue switch to Disconnect, and sat there for a while, listening to the hum of the electric tombs of fifty thousand slumbering men, women and children, his skin tingling with the icy chill that radiated from the wall of steel drawers, until the orderly arrived with his portable console to shut down his mother's brain and send her back to sleep.

θ θ θ

The receptionist presented him with a bill to sign.

"I took the liberty of adding the rent for this quarter. Seeing as it's due in a couple of days, I thought it wouldn't hurt."

It did. Joey winced at the figure at the bottom of the slip of paper.

"I'm not sure my credit's up to this," he said. "I can afford the conversation OK. I just wasn't expecting the rest."

Her smile of a lifetime's affinity lost a fortnight, but no more than that.

"That's fine," she said. "I just thought it would be easier this way. You do, of course, have a month to come up with the rent, although I should remind you that failure to settle the account by the end of that period could result in the contract being declared void and your mother being decommissioned."

"I know," he said, returning the bill to her.

"I just thought I should remind you," the receptionist said, and tore the bill up and printed off a new one.

"How was she?" she inquired as Joey signed for the price of the conversation.

"Same," he said. "Same as she always was."

θ θ θ

It had been her last request.

I don't want to die.

Spoken in a small, frail, frightened voice by dry gray lips, while eyes too big for the sockets rolled, trying to find and focus on Joey's face.

Oh Joey, I don't want to die.

On the bus bound for home, Joey pressed his face to the window and watched the city ease by. The black stone walls, the shopfronts behind their protective grilles, the sulfurous tint of neon on the pavements, fast, gleaming cars and drab, slow-moving citizens—all sliding by with a steady, measured grace.

I don't want to die.

She had barely been able to talk. Each sentence had been an effort, gasped out between blocked-drain gurgles. Moving her head had been a Herculean labor, but she had done so, in order to fix those swollen, terrified eyes on him—glassy marbles that were already losing their luster, pale blue pupils swimming in sepia-tinged white.

Her arms, so thin. The veins, strings binding flesh to bone. Brown-paper skin.

The man next to Joey was watching a game-show on the screen set into the headrest of the seat in front. He chuckled and gave a little round of applause whenever a contestant answered a question correctly. He groaned if a contestant was eliminated. He groaned harder if he knew the answer to a question and the contestant didn't. He was very drunk.

There are ways, Joey.

He remembered that her cheeks had been so sunken that she had appeared to have no teeth, no tongue, just a sucking vacuum where her buccal cavity had been. Her skull had loomed beneath her face.

Outside, the city slicked by, silk-lined with artificial light.

In a hard hospital room, where there had been too much brightness, Joey had taken his mother's hand. It was the first time he had touched her in as long as he could recall. She had touched him often enough, held his arm, kissed his cheek—he had never been the one to reach out across the space between them and make contact.

She tried to squeeze his fingers. He felt the creak of her knuckles as they grated together.

We have money, she said. *Your father left us enough.*

A sales rep for the House of Lazarus had been around the hospital the previous week. He had left brochures and leaflets in every ward. There were leaflets by Joey's mother's bedside. They had been well read. One of them contained a form which she had half completed, filling in the blanks with scrawled handwriting like an EEG read-out until the effort had become too great for her.

A girl wandered down the gangway as the bus pulled into a stop. Earlier on she had given Joey a long simmering look. Had he not been so dog-tired, he might have done something about it.

"Next stop Eastport," chimed a disembodied voice. "Change at Eastport for the Satellite Islands and the Coastal Route."

We have money. Were it properly invested...

It had all seemed so simple to her in the last dwindling days of her life, with her body failing organ by organ. It had all seemed so clear, during her moments of painful lucidity, at the ebbing of the drug-dimmed tide. She didn't want to die, and here was her chance not to die.

I just need you to help me complete the form and give your consent.

What choice had he had?

It's what you father would have wanted, she had said.

She had been so sure.

There's plenty of money.

Had she known?

Isn't there?

Perhaps she had known. All along. Perhaps she had known, and had begged him to sign anyway, not caring what it might cost him.

I can't do it without your signature, Joey. They have to have the consent of a close relative.

And why hadn't he told her? Why had he kept his mouth shut? To spare her? Or to spare himself?

The game-show gave way to a commercial break, which included an advertisement for the House of Lazarus. Gordon Lazarus, sleek-haired proprietor, delivered the pitch from a well-appointed office, perched casually, yet in a bent-backed attitude of the utmost sympathy, on the edge of a walnut desk, with a marble bust of some patrician-looking Roman to his left and, to his right, a murky Augustan landscape in an ornate gilt frame. He gazed unwaveringly into the camera.

"There comes a time when each of us has to say good-bye to someone we love," he intoned. "For many, it is the most painful thing they will ever have to do."

The camera glided slowly in.

"But what if you could be spared that pain? What if you were able to remain in touch with your loved ones even after they had been taken from you?"

A slow, snakelike smile. Cut to a moving crane-shot of the wall of fifty thousand steel drawers.

Lazarus, in voice-over: "Here at the House of Lazarus, years of research into cryogenic technology have borne fruit. The result? The actual moment of passing can now be delayed indefinitely."

The camera continued its swoop, finding Gordon Lazarus at the foot of the wall, standing in front of a family who were clustered around a single headset in parody of some long-forgotten pre-television tradition, taking it in turns to talk to grandfather or great aunt or poor little junior who was torn from this world far too soon. For bereaved people they looked remarkably happy.

"Until recently, communication with the departed was the province of mediums and clairvoyants. No more. Here at the House of Lazarus we can keep your loved ones permanently at the threshold of the hereafter. I won't blind you with science. Suffice it to say that by stimulating the neural impulses that remain in the cerebral cortex we can enable your loved ones to talk and interact with you long after the breath has left their bodies. Though departed, they won't be gone. Though lost, they will live on." Another ingratiating smile. "To find out more, simply e-mail me, Gordon Lazarus, care of the House of Lazarus, or call the free phone number below."

A number appeared at the bottom of the screen in gilt-edged Gothic script.

With a spread of his arms, as if to say, *It's that easy*, Lazarus reached his conclusion: "The House of Lazarus. Where nothing is inevitable."

The image froze, and there was a brief burst of jingle—a few bars of the chorus to "Never Can Say Good-bye"—and then a caption appeared:

THE HOUSE OF LAZARUS
KEEPING THE MEMORIES ALIVE

"Poor bashtards," muttered the drunk man beside Joey. "Let 'em resht in peace, thash wha' I shay."

It's for the best, his mother had said as he had signed in the presence of the hospital-haunting sales rep. *You'll see.*

Through blurring tears Joey had appended his name to the form, which the rep had then taken and folded with a satisfied air, slipping his thumb and forefinger along the crease.

"We'll see to it that everything is in place," the rep had said. "For the final moment. It is essential that we are present for the final moment, in order to take possession of the body during the brief window of opportunity between the moments of physical shutdown and actual clinical brain-death. I'll make the arrangements with the hospital to alert one of our stand-by units when the time comes. Before that, we'll have to take tissue-samples and carry out a few tests, including a full psychological profile. And then there's the question of payment…" He had raised his eyebrows meaningfully.

Joey's mother had strained and struggled to turn those eyes on him again, to look at him, to beg.

Had she known? That there had been almost nothing left of the money his father had bequeathed to her? That after the government and the lawyers had taken their bites, there had been just a crust left over to pay for her treatment? That keeping her alive for six months had used up the very last of the capital?

Joey had to believe that she had not, that she had been too ill to make the calculations, that the sickness sucking on her like a spider had cocooned her from practical considerations. Otherwise… But the alternative was too awful to contemplate.

"Eastport," chimed the bus's P.A.

No one except Joey got off.

θ θ θ

He was almost too exhausted to undress. He barely made it down to his underpants before the weight of his tiredness dragged him down onto the bed. With the last ebb of his strength he switched out the bedside light, and then he was rushing down into a darkness like every curtain in the world closing at once.

And at some point during the night he dreamed that he was standing over his mother's grave. It was a traditional grave, dug in traditional ground, with a traditional headstone carved with the name ARLENE DELGADO. Beneath that were the dates that bookended her life, and then the inscription:

A GOOD MOTHER
LOVED BY HER SON

The earth that covered her had not yet been grassed over, and when Joey prodded the side of the shallow mound of soil with one toecap it gave softly and loosely, spilling in a tiny crumbling landslide around his boots. He reasoned—with the unassailable logic of dreams—that his mother could only have been buried within the past twenty-four hours. He even vaguely remembered a funeral service.

It was a large, tomb-crowded cemetery, stark in winter, lit by a bright unclouded sun, and he was alone. In front of him, not two yards beneath his feet, the body of his mother lay. It was almost impossible to believe that she could be so close, and yet seem so distant. (Perhaps this was an alert part of his consciousness gently reminding him that he was dreaming; that his mother really lay elsewhere, halfway across the city.) If not for the earth and the lid of the coffin, he could have leaned down and actually touched her cold, placid face. The idea made him quite angry. What a ludicrous convention this was, to shove the dead under a few feet of soil. It was a kind of masochism, to allow your loved ones to be left so tantalizingly near. The dead ought to be thrown into bottomless pits, where they could disappear for ever and be forgotten. They shouldn't be put where any-one with two hands and sufficient determination could dig them up again....

As he was digging his mother up now.

He had no recollection of falling to his knees and starting to hand-shovel the earth away. The dream had edited that bit out in a jump-cut.

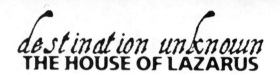
and that he was already scraping the lid of his mother's coffin. Not even the full six feet down! What kind of cheapjack gravediggers did they employ at this cemetery?

The earth cleared easily from the lid, rattling down into the gaps between the sides of the coffin and the walls of the grave. Suddenly, with dream simplicity, the lid was free from dirt, shiny and clean. Its brass fixtures were untarnished and shone in the sun. Six butterfly nuts secured the lid. Feverishly Joey unscrewed them, tossing each over his shoulder as it came free. As the final nut was removed the lid gave a little jump, as though eager to be opened.

Here, the dream allowed Joey to hesitate. Seconds away from seeing his mother's face again, it occurred to him that she might not be a very pretty sight. Already decay and worms might have begun their work. Did he really want to remember her rotten and half-eaten?

But no—he had to see. He had to see her for himself: lifeless, motionless, serenely and securely under death's spell.

He wedged his fingers under the lid and levered it up. It was surprisingly light, as though made of balsa rather than pine. It all but flew off, landing and bouncing on the graveside grass, finally settling upside down to lie rocking gently to and fro.

And now the unknown director of his dream decided to shoot everything in slow-motion, and it took Joey what seemed like an eternity to transfer his gaze from the upturned lid to the open coffin. He was anxious that he might wake up before he had a chance to look. So many of his dreams ended on precisely this kind of anticlimax. And having actually thought about waking up, he became more anxious still, because the thought usually preceded the reality. He forced his gaze towards the coffin, forced himself to stare in....

And even as he surfaced from sleep, to wake the customary three minutes before the alarm-clock went off, he realized that he had known all along that the coffin would be empty. What else had he expected? His mother was lying in cold storage at the House of Lazarus. Of course she mother was lying in cold storage at the House of Lazarus. Of course she wasn't buried in any cemetery. Honestly, he did have the dumbest dreams sometimes.

θ θ θ

But if only it had been that easy to dismiss the dream. All through that day, while he processed the orders that came through on the TeleStore computer and made sure that the correct parcels were dispatched to the correct addresses, Joey couldn't shake the dream's closing image: the gaping box, the lining of flesh-red quilted satin, the absence of any indication that his mother had lain there for even a second. Likewise at his evening job at the bar on Wiltshire Street, there was not a minute, not even during the headlong rush of happy hour, when he did not think of the coffin's mocking emptiness.

During a lull he mentioned the dream to Adrienne, the bar manageress, who was into horoscopes and prediction and what-have-you. She nodded knowledgeably as he described the dream to her. "It's a classic guilt/anxiety manifestation," she explained. "The empty coffin symbolizes the loneliness you feel. The red lining symbolizes your pain and grief, which are still unresolved. The fact that you dug her up means that you're trying to confront your dilemma, bringing your subconscious uncertainties to light." She smiled, glad to be of service. "Does that help?"

"Yes," he said. "It does. Thanks."

But it didn't. Not one bit.

The trouble was, he could no longer remember his mother's face clearly. This had obsessed him all day, the obsession deepening as the day wore on and the work became more and yet more numbingly dull. In vain he racked his brain for an image of his mother that didn't involve her lying in the hospital bed with eyes full of fear and almost no flesh on her body. He tried to recall how she had looked when he was a child, and nothing came. He tried to think of a hairstyle, a shade of lipstick, a favorite item of clothing, anything that might jog his memory. No use.

by the image of the pitiful thing that had pleaded with him in the hospital, clutching a House of Lazarus brochure in one skeletal hand. He could barely even recall what she had looked like then. She had become almost completely associated with an emotion, and that emotion was disgust, and the disgust smeared everything in dark, obscuring hues that buried facial features, expressions, gestures, kindness, love.

At midnight, when the bar closed, Joey mopped the floor, bagged the empties and left them out on the pavement, and then did not take the bus home. Instead, he took the bus across town to the House of Lazarus.

θ θ θ

The receptionist was mildly surprised to see him, but no less displeased for that. This time she remembered his name straight away (it had, after all, been only a day since he had last visited). This made Joey feel uncomfortable. He preferred the formality of anonymity.

"Your mother will be delighted," the receptionist said. She obviously felt that, in successfully persuading Joey to come to the House of Lazarus more often, she had done her job well.

An orderly Joey didn't recognize took him through to the chamber. This one had either worked in a funeral parlor before or else had decided that a sepulchral voice and a funereal pallor were appropriate to the job at hand. He talked with his lips alone. The rest of his face did not move but stayed completely frozen, like a wax death-mask.

"Sir is familiar with the arrangements here?" he inquired as Joey sat himself down.

"Sir is," Joey replied, fitting on the headset.

"Then," said the orderly, tapping a last few instructions into his keypad controller, "have a most enjoyable conversation."

There were perhaps no more than three dozen living souls in the entire chamber (not counting the fifty thousand sealed in their sub-zero halfway-houses) and while Joey waited for his mother's voice to manifest

itself in the earphones, he glanced around until he had located the customer who was sitting closest to the door marked "STRICTLY PRIVATE"
through which the orderlies came and went as required. The customer
was an old lady with whom bereavement clearly agreed. She was talking
animatedly into the headset mic, stopping only to listen briefly and laugh
before continuing her side of the dialogue.

When he heard the first muffled murmurings of his mother's voice,
Joey hit the Mute button on the chair's arm-rest, slid the volume control down to zero, and started to talk quietly.

"I know you can't hear me, mum. If it's any consolation, I can't hear
you either. I'm sorry about this. It must be very confusing for you. You're
probably wondering what's gone wrong. You're probably complaining
bitterly. I'm sorry. This is just something I have to do...."

All the while, as he apologized to thin air, his attention was focused
on the old woman. He was waiting for her to finish her conversation and
hit Disconnect with her gnarled old finger, which would automatically
summon an orderly.

And at last, after about five minutes, the woman began gathering
her belongings together, settling her handbag on her lap in readiness to
leave. One final good-bye, and then her hand went to the arm-rest.

Joey snatched off his headset and got to his feet.

He hadn't had a plan when he had taken the bus here instead of
going home. He had simply been following an instinct, an urge. And
even now, when he was about to take action, he still didn't have a plan.
He was extemporizing, using situation and circumstance to get him to
where he wanted to be: on the other side of the wall. For, he believed, on
the other side lay the means of reaching Drawer 41 in Stack 339, and not
just reaching the drawer but opening the drawer and looking into the
drawer....

It was the dream that had done it. The dream had in fact supplied
the answer to its own question: the coffin had been empty because Joey
could no longer remember how his mother had looked. Adrienne had

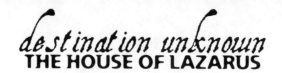

been wrong. The coffin represented his own memory. And so he had to see his mother's face again. It was no longer enough just to hear her voice, to talk to her and listen to the disembodied replies coming from an electric void. He had to fix her features once more in his mind. He had to see her once more in the flesh. This was something that a standard burial did not allow but which the House of Lazarus made possible (or so the dream had seemed to be telling him, if a little obliquely). All he had to do was get to the drawer, pull it open, take a good long look, and he was sure he would never forget her face again.

He was already moving towards the door when an orderly came out to shut down the old woman's relative. The orderly nodded politely to Joey as he passed, no doubt thinking that Joey was simply making his way to the main exit. The door crept shut on a slow sigh of its pneumatic spring, and just as it was about to close Joey stepped nimbly into the gap, holding the door back long enough to slither through.

He found himself in a white corridor that reverberated with the throb of all the hardware above. About ten yards along, set into the left-hand wall, was a door which he presumed led to the place where the orderlies waited when they weren't attending to customers. Opposite it was another door marked "W.C." At the end of the corridor, about thirty yards away, was a lift.

Joey was almost certain that he had not been spotted sneaking in behind the orderly's back, but he couldn't afford to hang around, just in case he had not been as stealthy as he had thought. (Even now the orderly could be tapping in his door-code, alerted by some vigilant customer.) He set off down the corridor at a loping jog-trot, scarcely able to believe that he had had the audacity and the opportunity to get this far. He was on the other side of the wall. The lift surely would provide access to each and every drawer. He was going to see his mother again!

He smacked the button to summon the lift, and the heavy doors trundled back. He was just about to enter when the lavatory door back down the corridor opened on a crescendo of flushing water. Joey froze, down the corridor opened on a crescendo of flushing water. Joey froze, and then, realizing that this was precisely what he shouldn't be doing, skipped smartly across the threshold of the lift. Turning to face the control panel, he caught sight of an orderly in the corridor. It was the same funereal fellow who had dealt with him earlier. Blindly Joey hit the first button his fingers found. At the same moment the orderly turned and caught sight of him. A startled look discomposed his waxy features.

"Hey! What are you—?"

The lift doors closed and cut off the rest of the question.

Joey ascended swiftly. Of the three floor-levels listed on the control panel—Ground, Maintenance and Administration—he had, more by luck than judgment, hit the button for the one he wanted: Maintenance. When the lift hissed to a halt, the doors opened to reveal a gantry that traveled parallel with the wall, running some twenty feet above floor-level. Like almost everything else on this side of the wall, the gantry was painted white.

In front of Joey the drawers rose in their stacks, much as they did on the side he already knew. The stacks stretched in both directions as far as the eye could see, and the mechanical hum was just as prevalent here. The major difference was that on this side the drawers were serviced by hydraulic cranes. In the distance two of them were moving with a slow and stately grace up and down and along the stacks, each carrying a white-suited orderly in its cherry-picker. The cherry-pickers paused at each drawer to allow the orderlies to run diagnostics checks. Watching the two long mechanical arms rising and falling, Joey thought of a pair of long-necked dinosaurs engaged in some elegant, elaborate courting ritual.

Behind him the lift doors suddenly rolled shut and the lift began to descend. It required no great leap of the imagination to assume that the funereal orderly had raised the alarm. Joey realized he must move fast now.

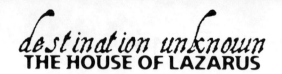

destination unknown
THE HOUSE OF LAZARUS

His eye fell on the nearest crane, which was parked a few yards along from where he was standing, its cherry-picker stationed against the rail of the gantry. A sign on the rail said:

STACKS 300-350

The next thing Joey knew, he was standing in the cherry-picker and examining its control panel. The On switch was easy to find, and once the small display lit up, operating the crane was simply a matter of following the onscreen prompts as they appeared. As instructed, he tapped in the location of his mother's stack and drawer, then pressed Enter, and the crane obediently began to move. First it extended forwards until Joey was within arm's reach of the wall. Then it began to glide horizontally past the drawers, heading for Stack 339. Joey noted that each drawer was fitted with an access panel and a rotating handle that was marked off in a hazard-striped circle. So much more convenient than digging through dirt, he thought. A twist and turn of the handle, the drawer would slide smoothly open, and there she would be…

A shout from the gantry brought his head snapping around.

"You! What the hell do you think you're doing?" It was an orderly with an electronic clipboard. He was standing wide-legged on the gantry with a look of outrage and disbelief on his face. "You're not qualified to operate that!"

"I'm going to see my mother," Joey replied straightforwardly.

Just then the lift arrived to disgorge another three orderlies, including the funereal one.

"There he is!" the funereal one shouted. His pale cheeks were flushed. Two pink circles glowed unhealthily against his pure white pallor.

"Come back here at once," said the orderly with the clipboard, striding along the gantry now, keeping pace with the progress of the cherry-picker.

"I pay to keep her here," Joey replied. "I break my back to make enough money to keep her here. So I'll damned well see her if I damned well want to."

"But you don't understand," said the orderly. "The seal. If you break the cryogenic seal, the shock could kill her."

Joey shook his head calmly. "I just want to take a look at her. It'll only be for a few seconds. She'll be fine." He turned back to face the wall. The crane stopped abruptly, and for a few heart-deadening, hope-dashing seconds Joey thought that it had broken down—or that the orderlies had a means of overriding its controls. Then the cherry-picker began to move again, this time vertically. He had reached Stack 339 and was rising.

"Somebody go and get Mr. Lazarus," the clipboard orderly said, and there was the sound of running feet clanging on metal.

"Mr. Delgado?" said the funereal orderly. He was pleading now. "Please come back down. I don't think you have any idea what you're doing."

Ignoring him, Joey gazed upwards.

"I'm coming, mum," he said softly. "I'm coming to see you."

θ θ θ

Gordon Lazarus was there when they finally managed to bring the crane back down from near the top of Stack 339. And it was Lazarus who first stepped into the cherry-picker, in which Joey was sitting hunched, his legs drawn up to his chest, his knees pressed against his shoulders, his hands fisted beneath his chin, his gaze fixed somewhere on eternity.

"Joseph?"

Recognizing the voice of the founder and proprietor of the House of Lazarus, Joey stirred.

"Come with me."

Meekly Joey stood up and allowed himself to be taken by the hand and led back onto the gantry, through the crowd of a dozen or so order-

lies that had gathered, into the lift and up to Administration. All the
time Lazarus talked soothingly, encouragingly, reassuringly to him. In
the commercial, Lazarus had come across as cold and vaguely insincere,
but in the flesh he seemed genuinely caring. His dark suit stood out
amongst all the eye-watering whiteness. It was strangely restful to look at
his suit, when everything else was so painfully white.

Lazarus sat Joey down in his office—not the office shown on television. This was an altogether more functional place, rather like mission
control for a space mission, fitted out with the very latest in communica-
tions technology. The chairs were comfortable but not extravagantly so.
The desk was broad and spacious, but skeletally constructed from plastic
and steel, not wood. There were no pictures on the walls and no windows.

Lazarus asked Joey if he wanted a drink, and when Joey didn't reply,
poured him one regardless. The chunky tumbler, half full of whisky, sat
heavily in Joey's unfeeling fingers. Lazarus poured himself a drink too,
and then sat on the edge of the desk and began talking. Explaining things.
First he talked about faith. The transfiguring power of faith, the absolute
necessity of faith when all else fails. Then he started talking about the
unfeasibility of cryogenics, how it was impossible for complex organic systems to survive prolonged exposure to sub-zero conditions, and how for
this reason cryogenics would always remain an unrealizable dream. Joey
didn't quite understand what Lazarus was saying. Wasn't that the entire
principle on which the House of Lazarus was based—keeping the dead alive
on ice? So what was the deal here? Then Lazarus began using phrases such
as "connectionist networks" and "subcognitive modules", "rule-based symbol manipulation" and "Gödel's theorems about enclosed formal systems."
None of these would have meant anything to Joey even if he had been
thinking straight, but when Lazarus said the words "artificial intelligence",
Joey remembered what he had found in the drawer that was supposed to
have contained his mother's body, and things began to fall into place.

After he had talked some more, Lazarus fell silent, obviously expecting a reply. When none came, he spoke again: "Well, Joseph, I've

said all I've got to say. I've been as honest as I can. The question now is, what are *you* going to do?"

Joey made several hoarse attempts before finding his voice. "I don't know."

"Are you going to go to the police with this information? The media? I have to know, Joseph. It determines how I... deal with you."

"She was just wires and chip-boards and a hard drive and..."

"But she's *real*, isn't she, Joseph?" Lazarus said with a glint in his eye. "She's *real* to you. That's what counts."

Joey couldn't deny the truth of the statement. "What did you do with the body?" he asked.

"We gave her a proper send-off."

Joey looked at Lazarus doubtfully.

"I swear," said Lazarus. "We employ a multi-denominational priest full-time at our private crematorium. I'm not a monster, Joseph. I have a healthy respect for the dead. After all, one day I'm going to join that club myself. But you still haven't answered my question."

"I don't know what I'm going to do," Joey said finally. "I need some time to think."

"I can't give you time, Joseph," said Lazarus, glancing at his watch as if considering whether it might not actually be conceivable for him to shave off a portion of the universe's relentless tick-tock and hand it to Joey. "Time is the one thing I do not have. If you are prepared to be reasonable with me, I can, however, make you an offer."

"An offer?" said Joey.

"A very generous offer. As I said, I'm no monster."

And Lazarus explained.

θ θ θ

"Mr. Delgado. How good to see you again."

Joey was such a regular these days, perhaps the receptionist's smiling familiarity wasn't feigned after all. And now that he had privileged customer status and was entitled to make all his calls for free, her smile seemed less patronizing, more deferential.

"Go on through."

Into the chamber of gleaming steel drawers. Into the mechanical exhalation of the thousands of fans, chilling the skin, bringing a tincture of winter to the air—a marvelously bogus touch, the confirmation of a mass preconception, like a magician's cape and wand.

Stack 339. Drawer 41.

"Mum?"

And telling her everything he had done that day, everything he was doing tomorrow.

"I'm thinking of moving. I've applied to the Council for a transfer. They say the chances are good."

Building up a life for himself. For her.

"Still looking for a new job, but there's enough left from the money Dad left us to tide me over."

Some of it false, but most of it real, and the real encroaching on the false day by day.

"I've found someone. You'd like her. I'll bring her along some time so you can meet her."

Because all along, without his realizing it, he had needed his mother just as much as he had believed she had needed him.

"I'm happy now, mum."

Because he hadn't wanted her to die any more than she herself had wanted to die.

"Honestly. I am."

And because sometimes an illusion is so enchanting, so alluring, so life-enhancing, it is infinitely preferable to the truth.

"And I'm glad you are too."

Isn't that so?

"Very glad."

Isn't it?

destination unknown
THE LOW ROAD

by Tom Shippey

The dreadful snap.

Would he feel it, or would the dreadful snap itself cut off all feeling?

Iain Mhor MacPharIain, Iain an Toisich, Big Iain MacFarlane the Champion, stared straight in front of him at the steep ladder leading up to the gibbet. Not that it mattered much either way. His business now was to climb the ladder without a shake or a quiver—no easy business with his hands tight-lashed behind him—then turn and face the hostile crowd, the English crowd, his enemies, and wait while the hangman fixed the noose under his ear from its projecting derrick, then step to the edge and jump out. If he jumped high enough, if the hangman had in charity allowed enough slack, then his neck would break and there, at last, would be an end. Better to go that way than twisting at the end of the rope, struggling to free his hands, till some squeamish soul among the English did him the favor of pulling on his legs till he died.

The priest at his right hand had finished his gabble. Iain Mhor stared down at him, hearing a question. Absolution? Confession? What did the wee man want of him?

"Ye're wasting your time, father," called the guard. "The likes of this one will go his own gait on the doorstep of Hell itself. Up with ye, then, ye animal. Ye'll be down soon enough."

Ian Mhor set his foot on the bottom rung, began to climb. Hell, he wondered, I never thought of that. Will there be something the other side of the rope? Fire and devils and endless pain, like the priests say?

Better that than for Iain the son of Domnal to be nothing.

He turned at the top of the ladder and looked out across the crowd. All the time, as he waited, he had been aware of a regular chunk of metal on butcher's block, of muffled cries of pain, and the stench of seared flesh. Now he could see what the good burghers of Carlisle had been at.

They had been just, according to their lights. Every man of the reivers' party that they had caught had had his trial. Those who had merely stolen horse or cattle, or had meant to steal—and if they had not meant to, what were Scotchmen doing with arms south of the Border?—they should lose a hand and take themselves back to the Highlands to beg. But for Iain Mhor there had been other charges, sworn home by fathers and husbands. For him, not the block, but the rope. And too good for him at that, many had added.

Aye, there would be little joy when word of his raid limped back to Glen Fallach, Iain reflected, searching the crowd. And the old carlines would say it was small wonder. Had Auld Meg herself not seen the spectra, the Horse-Toothed Man of Ballintilloch, barring the path of the reivers, and gesturing to them to turn back? Not that they would, or could. It would have been dishonorable for men of the MacFarlanes to turn aside for mere forebodings, or the rant of an old wife—firmly as most of them believed her.

In the line of plaids inching towards the block, the blade and the searing iron, Iain Mhor caught a face turned towards his: Dugald Canmore, his mother's brother's son. He would have liked to call out to him one last time. But there was nothing to be said. If Dugald lived, he would carry word home of how Iain an Toisich had died: thief, warrior, *duniewassal*, great lifter of cattle and of women. The more need for such a man to make a good end.

The noose was round his neck now. Time to step to the edge of the platform, to jump up and out. In an instant the hangman's hands would be on him and he would be hustled forward like a coward.
As he drew in his last breath, Iain Mhor, eyes fixed on Dugald, thought of the old song:

Oh ye'll tak the High Road
And I'll tak the Low Road...

It would be the king's high road back to Scotland for Dugald right enough. And for him the other, the Low Road along which the souls of dead Scots traveled.

A hand on his elbow. Iain Mhor wrenched free, marched forward two paces like a grenadier of the redcoats, the *sidier rod,* and leapt up and out into space.

As his body strained and fell, he waited for...

θ θ θ

Stone under his feet. A paved pathway, overgrown here and there with turf, leading away through low woods. Over his head, a gray sky. For some reason, Iain Mhor did not like to crane his neck, but just by rolling his eyes upwards, he could see there was no sun up there, nor clouds. The sky was just a gray featureless mirk, seemingly only a few yards above his head.

Shuffling his feet and turning his whole body round, he looked behind him. Instead of the woods and the moss and the stone path, there was—nothing. Just a wall of gray fog, immediately at his back. Iain was used to fog and sea-mists and the gray *haar* of the Highland winter, but this was fog he did not care to go into.

He must go along the road, then. As if to confirm his decision, he saw footprints slowly staining the sky above him, each one imprinted as if pressed down, then slowly leaking color, fading as another one came into being. They led on above the stone road. Iain Mhor recognized them for what they were: the bloody footprints of his cousin Dugald, hobbling along the highway in the world above, cradling his stump in his other hand, and begging his bread from those he would once have robbed. Leading him back to Scotland and to Glen Fallach. Deliberately, Iain Mhor set off along the stone road under the low sky. At his back, the fog rolled soundlessly forward.

Iain Mhor had once spoken with a man who had come back from the dead, a Cameron from Mamore. Men of Clan Chattan had caught him, put a rope round his neck, and hauled him up to a tree-branch to throttle for their amusement. But after he had ceased struggling, men of his own clan had appeared, driven the others off, cut him down, and bled him with their dirks till he recovered.

What he had seen, he said, was this. After the agony of dying was over, he had felt a great wave of peace and joy. And a light had appeared, as if at the mouth of some cave in which he had been imprisoned. And as he stepped towards the light, figures had come to meet him, smiling happily. His dead father, and the brother he had lost in a snowstorm, and what might have been his grandfather, who died when he was a babe. And then he had seen beyond them his wife, who had died with their first child. But as he ran with his arms out to reach her, he had come back to life with the blood pouring down his neck where his clansmen had opened a vein.

That was not what he saw here, Iain Mhor reflected. No peace, no light, no joyful meetings. Just the sky, and the trees, and the grass, and the road, and above and before him the bloody footprints spreading and fading.

The path turned between close-set pines and dropped down to a stream. A broad, swift stream, glinting silver-gray, like the Forth they had crossed at Stirling Bridge.

Down it two swans floated: giant swans, their heads as tall as a man's, their black eyes glinting. Iain watched them from the pinewoods, awe-struck. Their white plumage gleamed brighter for the gray around them, as if an invisible sun were on them. Their necks arched proudly and strongly, in graceful-curves.

Something was coming to meet them, humping awkwardly across the water. A strange creature, like a paper tube that looped itself along the surface of the stream. Not a smooth tube, but a crinkled one that stretched and contracted as it moved. It had a wide, flat head.

The looping creature arced up to the nearer swan, still swimming impassively on its way. It reared its head back and struck, at the back of the swan's neck, in the center of its graceful curve. The blow had no force, no fangs showed, but instantly bright blood sprang out on the dazzling plumage. Iain heard a faint 'pock', like the sound of a dandelion stalk breaking. As if the air had been let out of it, the swan-neck drooped, drooped, sank down to the shining water, became a shapeless clot of feathers drifting away.

The other swan floated on, seemingly innocent of what had happened. Awkwardly but unhurriedly, the crinkled creature humped across the water towards it. Iain Mhor felt a cry rising to his lips, restrained it, shrank back. In this strange land any intervention might be bad.

Again the strike, the 'pock,' the spurt of blood, the proud strong neck punctured and deflating, sinking. Another clot of feathers swept down the stream, its murderer writhing ungainly after it.

There was a bridge, Iain Mhor noticed, emerging cautiously from the shadows. And a fortunate thing too. He had no mind to go swimming with the likes of that in the water. From habit, he looked cautiously along and under the bridge where an ambusher might lurk. Nothing there. Stout tree-trunks, with rough-hewn planks laid across. Cautiously, with an eye always on the bloody footprints leading on ahead, Iain Mhor stepped across.

The end of the bridge was oddly dark, and he frowned at it, trying to see why the gray sky's no-light here failed. In his path there was a strand of floating spider-web. He plucked at it impatiently, pulling it aside. As the strand gave it thickened, coiled round his arm, began to bind arm to side. Iain Mhor wrenched free, jerked at it again, to snap the coil and trample it under foot.

The more he struggled, the more came, streaming out of some hole in the darkness. As Iain fought silently to keep the stuff out of his face, a man walked out of the gloom. A small man, with a mild face. Effortlessly he broke the pouring spider-stuff in the air, wrapped two coils of it round Iain Mhor's arms and body, jerked him off his feet and knotted him like a bundle of firewood to the post at the side of the bridge.

"There will be a toll to pay," he said quietly. "A toll for you, Iain Mhor son of Domnal." As he spoke, he stepped round in front to look his captive in the eye.

For a few moments the two looked at each other. A small man, Iain Mhor saw. Meanly dressed, in rough fustian, in the tunic and breeks of a Lowlander, or an Englishman. His face was inoffensive, spiritless even. His slightly bulging eyes dropped in seconds before the hawk's gaze of the son of Domnal.

But there was something else about him. His neck. Too long. Not twisted round backwards, but just the same, it looked as if...

"Aye," said the little man. "Someone raxed my thrapple for me. Would you be remembering who that was, Iain Mhor MacFarlane?"

For long moments Iain Mhor could remember absolutely nothing. Then, the phrase, a faint remembered sensation in the biceps of his left arm...

Iain Mhor had long ceased to count the number of men he had slain. If asked—as often he was—he would laugh and say that a warrior who could count the number had seen little of war. Nor could he honestly be sure, in night raid or sudden clash, who had lived or who had died under his blows or before his fine clawhandled pistols.

But that had not always been so. There had been a time when the difference between having three or four, or four or five souls on his score had been of importance to him. So, that time, coming back from a wasted foray, when they had kicked in the door of a lonely bothy to ease their impatience, to have something to boast of to the women, that time in the dark with the frightened children screaming... Yes, someone had run into him in the confusion, and he had seized him, lifted him off his feet, caught his throat in the crook of one arm, and twisted as you might twist a chicken"s neck between your fingers. There had been no threat, no risk, no profit in it. Yet as they rode off minutes later with the burning bothy behind them, Hector MacFadyean had asked him what he had done, and he had laughed and said—making out that a manes death was to him, Iain Mhor MacFarlane, a mere incident—had said: "I raxed his thrapple for him." And Hector had laughed. And that was what he, Iain MacFarlane, had gained from the night"s work.

"Aye," said the little man again from the gloom, "It was you did that for me."

Iain Mhor found his voice. "And have you been waiting then all this time for your revenge, wee man?"

"That I have. And a long wait I've had of it. But once it was known what I intended, the Lords of this place found a use for me. I have kept this bridge a long while now, and you are not the first of your kind I have caught here. For here I have been granted what my kind do not have in the world above.

"And that is power, Iain Mhor. Power to bind, and to loose, to hold—and to show.

"For I have something to show you."

A hand jerked out, caught Iain Mhor's chin, twisted it sideways. Terrible pain shot down Iain's spine, almost dragging a groan from him. As it faded and his eyes cleared again, he saw an image in front of him, a scene bright-lit as if through a window in the mirk.

Three children lay on rags, thin faces, pale skin, the bright eyes of starvation, though one lay shut-eyed and still, too still. The other two were slowly, listlessly passing something between them, stroking it, talking to it, playing with it as if it were a doll. It was a small black kitten. But as he looked on at the scene, Iain Mhor realized that the kitten too was dead.

"Aye," said the small man a third time. "Bairns will play, no matter what. But all mine had to play with before they died was a kitten, and that was dead too. With no man to till the ground and bring in the sheep, it's a short life for wife or bairn along the Border. Thanks to you, Iain Mhor, you and your like. I have watched that scene through often enough down here, by my bridge, through to the end.

"Now listen." He jerked the head back again, and again the pain ran like fire down the Highlander's spine. "This is the way of it. From me you took, by my count, maybe twenty, thirty years. And from my bairns, maybe fifty each."

"I cannae give ye them back," grunted Iain Mhor.

"Not you. But yours. See again."

Again the window in the mirk, the bright vision. But this time, in front of the leaping fire, two children wrestled cheerfully, shouting, clashing their toy claymores of painted wood. With terror Iain Mhor recognized the red hair, the freckles of his sons.

"Tadg and Murdo," he gasped.

"Aye. Stronger than my poor bairns, are they not? But see on."

As he watched, Iain Mhor saw a cloud grow in the shadows, a cloud with a shape that seemed to reach out a black hand to the small scuffling shapes.

"The plague cloud," said the little man. "The Lords of this place have given me many powers, and that is one. I can bring down the plague on yours. Fifty years each of your sons has on him, maybe more, for they are a sturdy race. Give me them, and I will cry you quits.

"And see you." The small man's voice had grown certain, dominating. "They will not come here. They are innocents yet. A better fate is in store for them. Maybe a better fate than they would have if you left them to grow as they have been reared. You can give their years to me without guilt, for they themselves will never come to me."

"And see you this too." Iain Mhor found himself spun, dangling over the bright water. Below him two of the crumpled-paper creatures looped lazily in the water, the pinhole eyes in their strange flat heads looking up. "If you refuse, it is in me to drop you down to my pets. You have no protection here. They will suck the marrow from you, not once but many times. And when they have left nothing but a husk, still you will not die. I will take the wisp that is left and leave it in the changeless woods. And through eternity you will lie for the spiders and the small beasts of this land to make their nests in you. You will stare at the mirk if I turn you up and at the mold if I turn you down. And never will your strength come back, or you go on to what is appointed for you.

"Choose now, Iain Mhor." Once more he found himself face to face with the bulging eyes, shining now, no longer dropped. "Give back the years you took from me and mine. It's but justice."

Iain stared up. He thought of the swans, the way the strength had gone out of them. He thought of the dying children with their pet. He thought of the plague cloud reaching out, the foul buboes breaking out on the pale flesh of his sons.

"I cannae dae it," he whispered.

Round and round he span, like a whipped top. But not down to the water and the hopeful swimmmers. As the spinning stopped, Iain found himself on the bridge, staggering, but free, the coils stripped away.

"I have no power to take them without you," said the little man resentfully. "Nor you, at this time, for that cause."

"Is there no—punishment, then, for what I did?" asked Iain Thor, half-disbelieving.

"Punishment?" The little man reached out with uncanny speed again, seized the other's chin, flipped his head without force so it lay sideways on the shoulder. "They punished you for your crimes in Carlisle. Down here other things are weighed."

He was walking away into the gloom. Slowly Iain Mhor reached up, set his head straight once more. The dark was clearing from the stone path, showing him the way he had to go. But the bloody footprints in the sky, he realized, they were far ahead now.

Oh He'll tak the High Road
And I'll tak the Low Road
And I'll be in Scotland afore ye...

But he would not be, unless he made haste. He must get on. Carrying his head gingerly on its snapped neck, Iain Mhor broke into the reiver's trot that eats up the mountain miles. He must overtake Dugald, reach Glen Fallach before him.

θ θ θ

Hours later, Iain Mhor checked his pace. He could not be sure how long he had run in this sunless land. He felt no hunger or thirst, was not even out of breath—indeed, he did not seem to be breathing. Nevertheless he was not drifting effortlessly forward like a shadow or a cloud. He had to put one foot in front of another, steep braes slowed him, the hill-burns he splashed through were cold on his feet in their deerskin brogues. He would be glad to rest. Above his head, too, the bloody footprints had ceased their plodding, turned into a stationary stain. Somewhere up there in the world above, the maimed Dugald had stopped for the night; or, it might be, fallen unconscious from pain or fever.

Rest, then. But not on the road. During his run, Iain Mhor had come to realize that he was not alone in this land. Twice his feet had warned him of approaching hoofbeats. Both times he had drawn aside, skulked in the stiff brown bracken. The first time it had been a group of riders going his own way: armored riders, he had seen from his hiding-place, with the marks of war on them: shattered limbs, holed breastplates, the dreadful wounds of roundshot. The riders trailed a light artillery-piece behind them. Dead mercenaries from the wars in Europe, Iain Mhor reflected, on the Low Road like himself, going back to Scotland to... To die? To rest? To turn spectra?

The other group had been more frightening, and had been riding the other way. Seeing them, Iain had remembered the man with the raxed thrapple's remarks about the Lords of this place. They had come down the road on their white horses, men and women in brilliant clothes that shone a luster through the mirk, tall folk with hair that flowed like the manes of their horses, calling and laughing to each other as if this sunless land was theirs, and all others trespassers.

Looking at them, Iain had known them for the *sidh*, the Good People, the People of Peace, whom the unwise might call the fairies. Even the priests, Iain knew, would accept that there was a station between life and death, between Middle-earth and Hell or Heaven. You might live, or die. You could also be Taken.

As the *sidh*-folk came level with his hiding-place, invisible in the bracken, only his wary eye peering through, not over the fronds. Every rider had fallen silent, as one by one they had turned their glowing eyes on him.

Yet they had ridden by. Slowly, Iain felt his spirits beginning to rise. He was off the road, taking no chances, and he would have been glad of a fire or food or whisky. Still, he could rest. And when he had rested he would travel again. The great thing was that Iain son of Domnal had not been condemned to mere black eternity and oblivion.

Even the adventure with the bridgekeeper was cause for hope, seen rightly. He had done wrong to kill that man, Iain recognized. It had been a boy's trick with little credit in it. Still, he had reflected on his past as he covered the miles, and he was sure that for all his other manslayings there had been excuse and reason: they had been enemies with weapons in hand, or if taken by surprise then enemies who would have done the same to him. The bridgekeeper had talked of justice. Well, by justice he, Iain Mhor, had met the worst deed he had committed, and he had been freed of it.

So much showed a kind of fairness in the way things were down here. If that was so, maybe matters might yet improve. After all, he reflected, he had not done wrong all his life. Far from it. Many had been glad of his coming, and sorry of his departure. Maybe they too would have influence with the Good Folk. Surely the Good Folk could recognize a *duniewassal*, a man of honor. Self-satisfaction twitched Iain Mhor's lips.

Down on the road, something was moving. A tartan plaid. No, not a plaid, a shawl, a woman's shawl. It was a woman right enough, moving slowly as if her feet bothered her. As Iain watched, she sank down on a turf-bank by the road, threw her shawl aside and laid back. From where he was, he could see pale skin gleam above her gown.

Iain rose from his hiding-place and strolled down the grassy, rock-strewn slope. A canty lass, he observed with admiration, and she observing him at the same time without moving. No girl, but a fair-fleshed wife. He could see the gold ring on her finger. The sight struck him with caution, and he looked anxiously, searchingly, at her face. But he did not recognize it. And he had always been careful to look at their faces, as he had not with men he had killed. It had been a part of his pleasure.

"Good day to you," he said, sitting down on a stone within reach of her knee. She drew her legs up modestly beneath her skirts, but otherwise did not change her position, lying back, arms spread, in a sleeveless, low-necked, long-skirted gown. "And what is your business on the Low Road, mistress?"

"I doubt it is the same as your own," she answered quietly. "Back to my home."

"There will be a man there for you?"

"Aye. I have a man. And a bairn. I am hoping the Good Folk will let me have a sight of them."

Iain remembered the scene the bridgekeeper had shown him, of Tadg and Murdo in the firelight. "I have bairns myself," he said.

The woman looked at him, and her tongue peeped slyly for a moment between her lips. "A fine big man like yourself maybe has more than he kens of."

Iain smiled, for the first time in the sunless land. "Well, that might be. That might well be."

The woman stirred, reaching forward to lay a hand on his. "I daresay you know already, but I can tell you that in her heart no woman thinks the worse of a man who finds favor with other women." Iain nodded, carefully, still smiling.

"So you can tell me, honestly now, how many other men's wives or daughters might have had cause to carry your child?"

Iain Mhor did not count the men he had killed, looking on that as business and in any case uncertain. But he had no doubt how many women he had seduced or ravished or lain with, never caring for their consent. He hugged the tally to him as a matter of pride and triumph.

"Well, mistress. You know the way of things. When we are out lifting the cattle in the Lowlands or among the English, whiles the men fight us and whiles they are away. And whiles, if they know we are out, they will take themselves into their peel-towers and steek the doors against us. But wherever the menfolk are, the women will stay in their homes. We do them no harm. Maybe a bit of sport, to make them forever discontented with their own puny weaklings. They may cry out and complain at the beginning, but I have known such women greet sair when I left in the dawn."

The woman smiled in complicity. "How many now, big man?"

"Well, since you ask. Twenty-seven other men's women I have taken, and asked no-one's leave. That is all on raid or foray, and not to count women back in my own glen, whom I courted or who courted me. Twenty-seven, and with not one did I stay more than the one night. Or it might be only as long as it took me to do the deed, he added, remembering a girl he had come upon tending her father's cattle. He had taken the cattle and her maidenhood too, and left her greeting. But that was for the cattle, he told himself.

The woman licked her lips again, sat up slowly, her legs stirring beneath the skirts. "Well. Twenty-seven. I doubt there are many to match that. There must be something you have. And my man is far from here and out of sight. Even here, in the land of the Good Folk, it may be you would increase your score."

She eyed the loose plaid which was all that Iain wore, clasped round with belt and sporran. Amazingly, beneath the sporran, he felt his manhood stir and stiffen.

The woman rose to her feet, long skirt trailing, still holding Iain Mhor's hand.

"Come then. Behind this rock will do. We have no need to go far."

She looked up into his face, trying to fix his eyes as she tugged his hand, swaying her hips a pace ahead of him.

Swaying her hips? Iain Mhor wrenched free, jumped back as she too sprang to face him.

He stared at her a moment, reached down, twitched her skirt aside. Long, pale, shapely legs. No feet.

No. The feet were there. But they were turned backward on her ankles.

"You are the token," he gasped. The Ill Woman, the vengeful ghost. The Woman of Temptation, who lures the unwary from their camp-fires and takes them away to torment.

Her lips curled back, showing the pointed teeth. She was circling him, moving easily now she had no need to disguise her gait, circling him as a wolf does a sheep. Iain Mhor turned steadily to face her.

"But why? Why have you come to me? You are not like the bridgekeeper who had cause. You are not one of the women I ravished."

"I am *all* the women you ravished. But two or three in particular. Did you never think, Iain Mhor MacFarlane, after you had shed your seed, and the women were left greeting as you rode away? Did you never think why they grab?

"A woman with seed in her can have a bairn. And a woman who has a bairn, what is her chance of dying with it? One in every four? You take your pleasure for a night, and it may be death to her forever. And no love, no companion even to sweeten the risk.

"Dead women and frightened women, dead bairns and orphans are what send me, Iain Mhor. And to you they were just cuts on a tally-stick."

She was circling still, but Iain Mhor's heart had come back to him. Ill Woman she might be, but only a woman nonetheless. He did not think she would charge home.

"Ye cannae hurt me," he said with sudden confidence. "I gave no consent to the deed."

She stopped in her tracks, looked at him. "I cannot hurt you then. But I will give you something. There is a song has been in your mind. I will give you the next line of it.

Oh He'll tak the High Road
And I'll tak the Low Road
And I'll be in Scotland afore ye..."

Her hand shot out, a long fingernail tapped Iain Mhor over the heart. *"But me and my true love will never meet again."*

Iain Mhor's heart turned to ice. He ignored the triumphant smile on the face of the token, remembering only his true love. Remembering as he did so that he had not thought of her since he had reached this land, and that this was the longest time she had ever been from his thoughts, since they parted.

But till now he had had hope. *Will never meet again.* There was the true pain of death.

The Ill Woman turned and walked away, ignoring him now that she knew her words had struck home. Numbly, Iain saw that the gown was only on her front, only a disguise. As she walked away her back was revealed. From skull to foot, all was hollow, and writhing with maggots.

θ θ θ

Wearily, Iain Mhor hauled himself up the slope. The last slope, he hoped it would be. He had plodded along the Low Road, no longer running, no longer resting, the bloody footprints of Dugald Canmore left far behind. He had not hidden again from the other travelers of the Road. Some he had overtaken: a blind man tapping his way along with a stick, an old woman stepping calmly and peacefully on her way, two ragged children, a boy and a girl, clutching each others' hands and struggling together over the rough places. Others, the riders, had overtaken him, mostly men with the mark of war or murder upon them.

Only when he saw the *sidh* did Iain step aside. The *sidh,* he knew, were the Lords of this place.

All the way the words of the Ill Woman had run round and round in his mind. *But me and my true love;* How had he been able to forget her? Caitlin, the tacksman's daughter of Ardlui. She was not the mother of his sons: that one, poor woman, had gone to her grave some years before, worn out with childbirth and, some said, with being the wife of

Iain Mhor. His heart had lifted as he followed the coffin, thinking himself free to make his gifts to the Maiden of Ardlui.

She had had none of them. He and she had never married, never lain together in one bed. Always she had spurned him. Yet it had been in him that one day her resistance would cease, one day she would know what a fine thing it was to be the wife of Iain Mhor. Till then, no need for him to change his ways. Secretly, he had had no mind to. That would do when he was old. And when he was old, a fine thing it would be to be the husband of a young wife, of Caitlin, the Dark Rose. He had had time. She was there, like the dish of brose at the very end of a great meal.

And so he had left to one side the best of all. *Will never meet again.* It did not occur to him to doubt the Ill Woman's words were true. As when he walked to the gallows, he wanted now to have an end. Above all, to get his head above this endless gray mirk, to see the real world and the sun one last time.

The *sidh*, it had come to him, lived in the fairy mounds, and came out from them from time to time to ride across the human lands. So the mounds must be gateways between the two worlds. Once, not far from the Road, he had seen one swelling upwards, its dark entrance showing. Even in his weariness, it had drawn him from his path, half-hoping to go in, and through, and out into the air.

Just inside the entrance had stood a tall warrior of the *sidh*, pale sword drawn, eyes gleaming. Iain Mhor had studied him for a while, without fear if without confidence. A tall creature, but slightly built. Once upon a time Iain would have walked up to such a one, wheedled, cajoled, bided his time for a sudden spring past the bright sword to the hand that held it.

He knew here that would do no good, and turned away. As he turned, the *sidh* spoke, with a clear music in its voice. "Ballintilloch," it said. "That's the place for you, Iain Mhor MacFarlane."

And now there he was, drawn to it across the leagues, as he came closer recognizing the fords and braes and valleys that matched those of his familiar world above. The Mound of the Brae of Ballintilloch.

Sidh warriors stepped aside as he reached the entrance. For a few paces the gray light held, enough to show him the foot of a narrow stair winding upwards. Then, as he set foot on it, the light faded. He groped his way up and up, left shoulder always brushing the wall, right hand out in front of him—until a new light began to seep into the blackness. Unbelievably, a golden light, a light he had thought he would never see again.

Still inside the mound, Iain Mhor stepped out from the stair on to a platform. He knew feet of earth still lay between him and the world outside, but by some magic the light streamed through. He saw the sun.

It sank weltering across the hills, throwing long blue shadows from every rise and hummock, so that the land looked as if its muscles were rolling beneath a smooth multicolored skin. From where he stood, looking south, he could see almost the whole length of Loch Lomond with its many islands, Ben Lomond rearing up to the east, to the west the gentler slopes, and behind him his own home, Glen Fallach, running its whole length from Inverarnan to Crianlarich. Everywhere he looked, chimneys smoked, the plumes rising peacefully. Farmers called in their cattle, children played outside the Lyres, wives dragged out their stools to take the milk: the end of a summer's day, in a country guarded from war.

"On the bonny bonny banks of Loch Lomond," whispered Iain Mhor, remembering the next line of his song unbidden. He knew that he had the Sight now, to see as he wished, and to see the truth.

Up Glen Fallach he looked, to his own home. News had not waited for Dugald Canmore to limp home. Outside his croft he saw the fine black horse of Colin Roy, second son of the chief himself. He had come to break the news, and the sons of Iain Mhor were brought outside to hear it like men, mere boys that they were.

"And so your daddy won't be coming home," ended Colin Roy, squatted down on his heels before the two small solemn faces.

Tadg, the elder, screwed his face up as if determined not to cry. But Murdo, two years younger, whispered something, whispered again as Colin Roy bent forward to hear.

The words came to Iain Mhor clearly, "He said, our daddy, he said when he came home it would be at him to let us have a shot with his pistols. Will we not be getting a shot now?"

Iain Mhor saw Colin Roy pull free one of the steel-handled tags he carried in his belt, and hold it out. And he saw both boys' faces lighten.

Inside, the Sight showed him his old mother lamenting, her face in her hands, her gray hair torn. "He was a good son, a good son to me," she cried, the *coronach* already in her voice.

Her second son, Iain's brother Finn, patted her shoulder. "He was no', mither," he replied. "Never here, aye on the stramash. Free with his silver when he had any, true enough. But how often was that? And who had to cut the peats and put the broth on the table when he had none? A great lifter of what wasnae his, but all in all, the world is well quit of him."

And though his mother shrieked and tossed her head, the Sight showed Iain Mhor that she felt the truth in what Finn had said.

Lastly, as he had known it would, Iain felt his vision drawn across the miles to Ardlui. There she stood, face pale, hands still in the dough she was kneading, and even in his despair the grace of her body stirred his heart. It was not Colin Roy who brought the news to her, but the chief himself, Black Fergus, Fergus Dhu MacFarlane. And as he spoke, she at least began to weep.

There was an arm round her. Unwillingly, disbelievingly, Iain Mhor saw it was the arm of one of the cottar's sons from the back end of Inverarnan, a youth so untried and lacking in note that he had not even learned his name. Yet he saw how Caitlin leaned towards the boy's arm, instead of shrinking away as she had done with him, with what he had thought—and the thought had excited him—was a mere show of maidenly reluctance.

Behind Iain Mhor, warriors of the *sidh* were filing out on to the platform. They did not wait, they gave him no choice. Their hands were on him, they thrust him out, through the earth, on to the grassy slopes of the mound, beneath the open sky.

It was night already, lit only by the stars and a quartermoon. For an instant, Iain Mhor felt dissociated, a mere wisp to be blown on the breeze. On the Low Road, he had not breathed or slept or eaten, but he had felt as if he had a body. Now, out here, what was he? A ghost? A spectre?

In the moonlight a few feet away, something stirred. Iain Mhor looked carefully at it: an old man, in a plaid like his own, but with a great torque of gold round his neck, and strange shapes on the brooch of his plaid and the bracelets on his wrist. The long sword clipped to his belt had a strange green sheen, like the bronze of ancient guns. Above the full gray beard the mouth had been split by a blow. Two long front teeth jutted out over the lower lip, the one crossed over the other to make a tusk.

"Do you know who I am?" said the shape.

"You are the Horse-toothed Spectre of Ballintilloch. You warn of ill-luck for the reivers. Some say you bring it."

"I bring nothing not there already. Do you know who I was?"

Silently, Iain Mhor shook his head.

"You will know the name when I tell you. For I was one of your ancestors, and they called me Domnal Vrych. Your father was called after me."

"Fire on the headland," said Iain Mhor, remembering an old heroic lay, "Bright swords in the sun. And the head of Domnal Vrych, ravens gnawed it."

"So they did," said the spectra. "Many generations ago, the men of Ireland rowed over in their long galleys, and rode up the loch-side, and I fought them. And I lost. Their chief—I settled my score with him!—cut off my head and hung it from his saddlebow. But as you can see," the specter touched its mouth, "I have a tooth or two longer than ordinary. And as my head swung and swung on his saddlebow the teeth cut into his thigh and made a sore. And the sore festered, and so he died, in his bed, like an old woman and no warrior. So he passed on.

"But I—I stayed. And since you are one of my children's children, I am here to tell you what choice lies before you. Now tell me what you saw inside the Round."

Iain Mhor's lips twisted. "I saw the next two lines of a song that has been haunting me:

Oh the wee birdies sing, and the wild flowers spring,

And the sun on the locheide lies Gleaming.

I saw all that. And I saw that I had no part in it."

"Aye." The specter moved as if to give awkward consolation. "The fact is this, son of my sons—you're no use. You're an evil man. I've watched you all your life. Your heart is rotten—rotten with revenge, and pride, and wrath, and lust. Rotten all through. Mine is as well. I showed that even after my death."

"So what choice lies before me? To be a ghost?"

"Na, na. Ghosts are just folk who haven't realized they're dead. You knew what you were from the start."

Iain nodded, still carefully.

"So: there are some folk who go from here to Judgment Day, to Heaven or Hell or it may be Purgatory. But they have consented to that. In your heart, you never paid any priest any heed.

"So most like you would go to the *sidh,* and the *sidh* would take them, and wipe away their memories, and send them back one day to another body. To try again, and maybe do better.

"But with you they've given up. They've put you out. So there are only two choices left.

"If you walk down the hill to the burn there, you will see a pool, the Black Pool of the Brae of Ballintilloch. That pool has a property, for such as you. If you jump into it as you jumped from the gallows—then the *sidh* will melt you down. Melt you down like a silver button in a casting-ladle, and purge away the dross, and mingle you with others like you, and make a new soul. Not your soul, mind, but there will be something left of you."

"And the other choice?"

"Stay here with me. Be a specter. Don't go on. Stay as you are—as we are. You can watch, think—warn sometimes. But you stay on this hillside. Once in a hundred years someone takes the pool. Once in a thousand, the hillside."

The memory of the raxed thrapple was on Iain Mhor, and of the Ill Woman with her hollow back. But most of all, he remembered his true love leaning back on her lover"s arm. He grinned without mirth and for the last time set his head straight on its shoulders.

"Your choice?"

"I will sing my song out to its end. It is the bonny banks of Loch Lomond for some.

> But my broken heart shall ken nae second spring,
> Though the waeful may cease free their Greeting.

I saw them cease from their greeting for me soon enough. And the only second spring I will ken is the one I will take into the Black Pool, the pool of forgetting. Melt me down, you say? I think that is the best road for me. The one that does not lead back."

As he paused on the edge of the pool, Iain Mhor thought his last thought: how much easier it was to leap from the gallows to death than to leap from death to nothingness.

On the slope above him, the horse-toothed spectre watched fretfully, one of many silent spectators.

"Gey cauld it is on this hillside," it complained. "Gey cauld here all alone."

destination unknown
BETWEEN THE FLOORS

by Ramsey Campbell

Though the view from his window looked like the end of the world, it wasn't the reason why Jack Latimer was anxious to go downstairs. A straight line divided the sea and the sky, slabs of two shades of the grey of a solitary pigeon gliding back and forth against them like a kite left behind on the beach by the departed summer. As he straightened his tie and smoothed the wings of his shirt collar, he spied from the window on a tram eight stories below him, feeling its way along the wire into Blackpool. The pane was as good as a mirror, and showed him his eyes waiting to be amused, his black mustache as sleek as his hair, his features rather too small for the face that even workouts at the gym near his flat couldn't reduce. He picked up the key by its six-inch plastic tag from the dressing-table strewn with glossy brochures and let himself out of the functional room.

To his left, through the window of the exit to the fire escape, was what might as well have been exactly the same view of the sea. To his right, eight doors identical with his and interrupted only by framed prints as subdued as the lighting, led to the first of a series of fire doors beyond which the corridor must eventually find its way to the main bank of lifts. There was a lift opposite Jack's room, however, and he barely hesitated before prodding the askew lozenge-shaped button further into its niche in the wall.

Once again he felt as though the summons hadn't reached its destination. A wind mumbled under the door onto the fire escape; otherwise there was silence, not even the sound of a radio or television in any of the rooms. For a minute or two he contented himself with performing an impromptu tap-dance that rattled the key on its tag, but when he found himself compelled to sing he felt he'd waited long enough. "I'm singing in the rain," he crooned, "just sin—" and was stabbing at the button when he heard beyond the door that was as grey as the seascape a voice not much louder than the wind. "Gubless us, we're coming as quick as we can. What do they want me to do, get out and push?"

Jack was tempted to retreat into his room so as not to be seen to have rung twice. But he wasn't a child, he was nudging fifty, and he was damned if he would let any petty official intimidate him. As the doors inched open, the scratched outer door withdrawing behind the wall before its twin began to sidle in the opposite direction, he tugged the jacket of his suit down and folded his hands, dangling the plastic tag. The door was still creeping into its hiding-place when the attendant greeted him. "It's the feller they stuck at the top," he said in his low Northern groan. "Don't tell me, it's Mr.... Mr. Latitude."

"Latimer."

"Aye, well, are we going to stand here arguing about it till some other bugger starts playing with my ding-dong? Step in, there's a dear, and I'll take you to the rest of the royalty."

Jack had been preparing to apologize for his impatience with the lift, but now he was provoked just to laugh, except he couldn't quite manage that either. He stepped over the threshold into the stuffy box that smelled like the square of dusty carpet no wider than a double bed, and felt outnumbered at once.

Since there must be as many of himself as of the attendant in the mirrors facing each other from halfway up the side walls, he could only assume that his uneasiness was to be blamed on the indirect lighting, which was the color of fog. It and the mirrors displayed the attendant to him, the pouchy globe of a face which Jack had to remind himself wouldn't be as pale in any other light, the uniform which looked as dusty as whatever book was sprawled face down on the folding stool under the handle that controlled the lift, the curly mop of faded red hair that reminded Jack more than ever of the kind of wig which came attached to a seaside hat. "Gubless us," the attendant groaned at the handle, grasping it with both pudgy hands and leaning his weight on it until the doors shut and the lift began to creak downwards, and then he turned to Jack. "That's what I should call you, isn't it? Know why?"

Like his voice, his clump of features—eyes so protruding they made Jack wince, small beaky nose, inverted whitish V of a mouth above a nub of chin—seemed constantly on the point of adopting another expression. Perhaps it was his being half a head shorter than Jack and having to peer up at him from beneath his hairless eyebrows that made him appear sly, but Jack felt like a stooge singled out from an audience. "Why?" he couldn't help asking.

"Isn't that a good word for you folk in the picture palace game?"

It took some seconds for Jack's bewilderment to give way to relief. "Royalty, you mean. That's droll. You ought to be at the end of the pier."

"Gets a bit lonely out there in the cold and the wind, specially after dark."

Though it wasn't as though Jack had wished that on him, he found himself feeling defensive. "The cinemas these days aren't what you'd call palaces," he said, "and we're just managers."

The sixth floor went by with a creaking shudder of the lift, and a bulb guttered behind the number in the line set into the wall above the stool. All of the attendant's heads shook themselves slowly, putting Jack in mind of some fairground sideshow being switched on for the night. Either the attendant resented managers or was unhappy with Jack's self-deprecation, because his mouth drooped even further before he said, "On our own, are we?"

"Depends what you mean."

"Aye, it all depends, that's what they say." The attendant had lowered his gaze to Jack's crotch or rather, Jack hoped, to the plastic tag hanging in front of it. "Remember that old song?"

Jack shoved the key into his breast pocket, where the tag felt as though it was probing for his heart. "Yes, it's from—"

"Hit... owl... deep-ends... hawn... hayouuu." The attendant had abandoned his Lancashire accent and was singing in a hideous parody of

Cockney without raising his gaze; then he stared Jack in the face. "Was it you I heard doing a song and dance?"

If Jack blushed, surely that couldn't be visible in the grey light. "Did you hear someone?"

"Aye, and I've brought no other body to your floor. Happen it's you should be at end of pier."

"I'll stick to the job I've been doing for getting on for thirty years, thanks all the same."

"Happy in our job, are we?"

The number 3 flickered and went out, and Jack felt close enough to quitting the lift to be able to retort, "I don't know about you."

"If truth be told, lad, I'm not so sure about thee either."

This time Jack certainly felt himself redden, though there was no sign of it in the mirror. "What the devil do you mean by that?"

"No need to bring him into it. Just trying to keep us lively while we go down."

The man's face had begun to remind Jack of stage makeup seen closer than it was meant to be seen, so that he wondered if the attendant could have been a seaside comedian before ending up in this job. "When do they let you out?" Jack said.

"Who's that?"

The question was so sharp that Jack almost looked for someone in the mirror. "The manager, I suppose, or whoever comes after you, rather. How long before you get out of here?"

"Depends."

The attendant's gaze had lowered itself again. Jack stared over the mop of red hair, noticing how dusty the light made it look, until the lift stumbled to a halt. When there was no further movement, he said, "Aren't we here?"

"Aye, and soon one of us won't be."

Jack was about to ask how soon when the attendant did something with the handle to release the doors. Beyond them was a nondescript stretch of corridor, and Jack lunged for it, glimpsing the ranks of himself disappear as though they were returning inside him. Before he was over the threshold the attendant seized him by one upper arm, in a grip which felt unexpectedly strong and yet somehow diffuse. "Up you go," he muttered in Jack's ear.

Only when Jack almost tripped did he realize that the floor of the lift had come to rest an inch lower than the corridor. "Thanks," he said and stepping up, glanced back. The attendant had already let go of him and was out of reach of the light from the corridor. As Jack moved away, digging a finger in his ear to get rid of the sensation of its being clogged with a dusty whisper, he heard the attendant start mumbling to his crowd of grey selves before the doors creaked shut.

Though the corridor changed direction several times on its way to the lobby, it didn't present as much of a challenge as it had when he was carrying his suitcase. The receptionist who had directed Jack to the lift was at the desk using one of her silver-tipped fingers to trace a route on a street map for two cinema managers Jack didn't recognize. He gave his tie a last adjustment as he crossed the lobby to the bar, where he saw Lucinda Dodd at once.

She was on the far side of the horseshoe overhung by inverted glasses, her plump bare arms resting on the bar-top. Again he thought she had the biggest smile he'd ever seen—almost as wide as her generous face—but now she was directing it at Rex Smythe beside her. "Here's my rival. We were just talking about someone like you, Jack," Rex said in his infuriatingly penetrating voice.

Jack was almost sure he saw Lucinda wincing on his behalf. He took time to greet colleagues at tables as he made his way around the bar, but when he arrived he still hadn't devised a retort witty enough to utter, not least because Rex's unobtrusively styled hair and elegant grey suit made him feel overdressed. "You look like a man after a drink. What'll it be?" Rex said.

"A Scotch will do me, thanks."

"Not even any water? Well, you know yourself best." Rex snapped his fingers once at the young barmaid. "Whenever you're ready, love. The same for the lady, and another of these on the rocks, and a plain Scotch. Better make that a double."

Jack thought Lucinda found Rex's tone as unappealing as the barmaid did. He thanked the young woman for his drink and topped it up with water from a jug on the bar, then nearly spilled it as Rex's glass collided with his. "Here's to the industry," Rex declared. "May it continue to prosper."

"And us," Lucinda said.

"And as many of us as it can support, Lucy, of course. When you've finished that cocktail I'm buying you both dinner in the restaurant."

"I thought we were thinking of going out, Lucy."

"What, and see miles of entertainments closed down for the winter? You want something better than that, don't you, Lucy? Maybe that's more your style, Jack."

Lucinda laid her free hand over Jack's. "It does look a bit bitter for walking."

"There's cabs outside."

"I wouldn't dig too deep into your pocket until you see how things are developing," Rex advised him. "Besides, I always think three in a cab is one too many."

"We can come in here for a drink after dinner, Jack."

There was that, and the way Lucinda had only now removed her hand from his, but Jack wasn't sure if these were meant as more than consolations. He lingered over his Scotch, in case he had reason later not to want to be too drunk, until Rex said, "Better get in there before there's no room."

The chandeliered oak-paneled dining room was indeed already almost full. Rex told the head waiter "Smythe party" and cleared his blank look by slipping him a fiver, not quite surreptitiously enough for Rex's guests not to notice. At the table by a fountain in the middle of an indoor flower-bed, Jack ordered the most expensive dishes on the menu and felt as though Rex was retaliating by insisting on the best wine. Two glasses of that made Jack take advantage of the first lull in the conversation about last year's films. "Who am I like?"

"Are we playing games now?" Rex asked, aligning his fish-knife and fork alongside the bones of his first course. "I wouldn't like to guess. Who are you?"

"You were saying in the bar you'd been talking about someone I was like."

"Ask Lucy. She brought him up."

"He wasn't much like you, Jack," Lucinda said, dabbing at her lips with a capacious linen napkin as if she wished she could use it to hide her face. "It was only... He wasn't really much like you at all."

"Except Lucy and our friend were like you and me, Jack, her with ten screens and him on the other side of town from her with just a triple."

"So what happened to him?"

"He hadn't been in the business anything like as long as you have."

Lucinda obviously hoped that answer would do, but Rex fell on the question. "Exactly what you'd expect from last year's takings is what happened. No room for two sites in one town. The company closed the triple and left Lucy with her multiplex."

"If he'd had more experience they said they'd have sent him to me." Lucinda found her wineglass and proposed a hasty toast. "Here's to how it used to be when I came into the business, when what we did for films meant something to the company. To showmanship."

Rex barely touched her glass with his. "To how things have to be," he said, and rang Jack's almost empty glass.

"Nostalgia isn't what it was," Jack said.

While Lucinda looked sympathetic, Rex emitted a grunt with which Jack could imagine he greeted any fault in his cinemas or in his staff. The arrival of the main course relieved an awkward silence, and Jack attacked his lobster until Lucinda coaxed him into joining her in reminiscing about favorite films. They'd agreed on *Casablanca* when Rex said, "I prefer to concentrate on current product," in the tone of a future director of the company and Lucinda interested herself in his opinions as though she'd been reminded that he was buying the meal. Jack thought it advisable just to listen or at least to give the appearance of listening while he ate and, particularly, drank, but eventually found himself saying a good deal about the way the company treated its staff and the cinemas it had bought a few years ago, his included, and how all the films he'd had to show since then seemed to consist of excesses of one sort or another. Diners were glancing at him, and he could see that some of those who were managers felt he was speaking for them. Perhaps he might persuade them to own up to that in the bar. He drained his coffee cup and brandished it for a refill, and considered pointing out that he'd been given a child's cup by mistake. Then Rex was standing up and saying, "Are you sure you'll be all right while I have a word with the big boss?"

"You bet your ding-dong," Jack told him, "and thanks." But Rex wasn't talking to him; nor, presumably, when he said, "Join us if you like."

Jack succeeded in staying beside Lucinda as far as the lobby, but when Rex strode into the bar she restrained Jack from following. "I should think about having an early night. If you'll excuse me, I'm going too."

"I'll see you up, shall I?"

"That's the idea."

By the sound of it she was only praising him for seeing sense. Once the doors of the lift off the lobby had closed she said, "Do you mind if I say something?"

"My pleasure."

"If I were you I'd try and keep on the right side of Rex."

"You aren't me, and it wouldn't be much of a world if you were." He was doing his best to recall if he'd insulted Rex, but couldn't remember anything he'd said. "Never mind Rex. I've had a bellyful of him."

Lucinda glanced down Jack's body, then up at his face. "Well, here I am."

The lift doors opened, and he stumbled towards her, though he realized she had only been announcing her floor. She put one hand on his chest and poked the eighth-floor button, and gave him a kiss so quick he didn't even see it coming. "You get up to bed and sleep it off," she said as the doors intervened between them.

He couldn't believe he'd wasted his chance on thinking about Rex. When the lift opened he stalked along the eighth-floor corridor, muttering. He'd struggled through the last pair of fire doors when he heard sounds besides his own—a soft thud on metal, and then an outburst of thumping and mumbling. Perhaps the attendant had just wakened and was groping to his feet, and Jack had the disconcerting impression that he was fumbling about in total darkness. Why shouldn't he have turned off the light in his box while he snatched a nap? All Jack cared about just now was not coming face to face with him.

Jack had slammed his door behind him, and was feeling about on the furry wall for the light-switch, when he heard the lift creak open. The attendant must have thought he'd just emerged from his room. Jack's thumb scraped against the plastic switch, and the room lit up, empty as ever. At least there had to be other guests on this floor, since the lift must have brought someone up in order to be where it was, or could the attendant have been waiting to hear when Jack returned to his room? One inadvertent step rushed Jack towards a confrontation with him, but he wasn't quite that drunk. His compensatory lurch took him into the bedroom to grimace at himself while he brushed his teeth, then he hung up his clothes and managed to aim at the toilet again before sprawling into bed.

His morning call wakened him. Darkness had gathered and grown stale behind his eyes and in his mouth. He held onto the wall, though its pelt made his fingertips twitch, all the way to the bathroom, where the shower attacked him with various extremes of temperature as he flinched against and away from the tiled wall. He took fifteen minutes to dress himself, hoping that would let him feel more able to face breakfast, and then he guided himself into the corridor, easing the door shut and muffling the key on its tag with one hand. He'd scarcely turned along the corridor when the lift doors wavered open. "Just us, is it?" the attendant said with a kind of morose triumph. "Hobble in then, Mr. Lamplighter."

"Latimer," Jack said, and had already had enough. The attendant would hardly have spent the entire night in there, though he looked as though he hadn't seen daylight for considerably too long. When Jack faltered into the lift, the man sagged against the handle to send the lift down, then turned his head with an audible creak to peer at Jack. "What's that on your finger?"

Jack had been trying to withdraw inside himself in order to ignore the mustiness, presumably composed of the smells of old carpet and of the book which appeared not to have moved from the stool, and the way the muffled light seemed to have caused the attendant's face to add to its pudginess, but the question made him unsure of himself. "Which?"

"Looks like it should be a ring."

Again Jack had the sensation of being singled out, this time to be accused of pretending not to be married. He held up the shaky finger that retained a band of paler skin. "I got engaged once, but that was as far as it went."

"Far enough if you ask me. Let it drop now, there's a dear. We don't want to look at that all the way down."

Jack found the other possibilities even less attractive, particularly the sight of the crowd of his own discolored faces, which looked as poisoned as he was trying not to feel. Nor was he anxious to see the attendant's face wobbling as he inquired, "Will we be a busy boy today?"

"I should think they've plenty in store for us. How about you? Busy, I mean?"

"Don't you know who that's up to?"

"Who?" Jack demanded, though the attendant was gazing up at him so hard that his lower lids seemed in danger of peeling away from the eyeballs. Jack closed his eyes and leaned against the back wall, feeling the lift quiver each time it passed a floor, smelling a staleness which seemed increasingly to be of flesh. "If you ask me," the attendant said, "you want something."

Jack kept his mouth shut, but opening his eyes was apparently sufficient encouragement. "Get a good fat breakfast down you," the attendant told him. "That was always my cure when I'd had one of those nights."

Jack managed not to rush for the doors until the lift reached the ground floor, and then he weaved his way along the corridor to the lobby and reeled out through the revolving doors. Far down the tram-lines beneath the ice-colored sky he could see a roller coaster and a Ferris wheel, so shrunken and immobile that they and the rest of the fairground resembled cheap toys. He thought the slaps of cold wind in his face were doing him some good, but when he returned to the lobby he found the hotel now felt unbearably hot. As he fled to the lifts, the nearest of them emitted several of his colleagues, Lucinda among them. She left the others and came to Jack. "Feeling better?"

"For seeing you, yes."

"What a gentleman. Are you on your way to breakfast?"

Her perfume—sweet but not cloying—tempted him. "If I can join you."

"That was the idea."

Jack dared to take her arm as they entered the dining-room, where he received a faceful of heat laden with the smells of bacon and sausage and fried bread. "Actually, I won't," he babbled, hoping that she didn't think he had recoiled from touching her. "I'd better just—I'll see you at the screening."

He was already sprinting for the lift she'd emerged from. It took him minutes to reach his floor and his room and the toilet. Some time later he lowered himself gingerly onto the bed, and made himself stand up again not much later than he was supposed to, and picked his way into the corridor. He heard the lift gape behind him, but kept on through the fire doors and down the emergency stairs to the ballroom where the conference was taking place.

He hadn't realized that the door off the staircase would open with such a loud clank, nor that it would admit him beside the podium from which the chairman of the company was holding forth. "As I was saying," Mr. Begin said while Jack made apologetic faces at him and raised his hands as if someone had stuck a gun in his back, "the future of our industry depends on teamwork. We all need to set examples to our staff..." Even when Jack located an empty seat and made himself small on it, the chairman took some time to finish looking at him, and much longer to repeat most of last year's address.

At last Mr. Begin gave way to previews of forthcoming films, and the darkness let Jack close his eyes whenever the spectacle proved too much for him. Explosions that felt like colossal migraines blew up people and buildings and spaceships and planets, men encased in latex demonstrated unlikely ways to walk and unpleasant things to do to people, young couples swamped in golden light and blanketed with music explored each other, actors found objects to fall over or into or through and roared jokes at one another as though to ensure that the audience made as much noise or couldn't hear itself think.... After more than an hour the lights went up, and it was time for lunch. Jack was on his way to standing, having found that sitting still had done him some unexpected good, when he saw Mr. Begin heading straight for him. "Jack Latimer, isn't it," the chairman said, towering over him even now Jack was on his feet. "Used to be the Grand."

"That's my place."

"Well, Jack, you missed me saying it's been a good year for us overall," Mr. Begin said, and at once Jack was hearing him beyond a hollow sound that filled his ears. The chairman had never called him by his first name before, and Jack knew why he was doing so now. He stared at Mr. Begin's several ruddy chins that looked gift-wrapped with a bow tie, and scarcely heard the chairman's words for hearing what lay behind them. He heard himself say he got on well with Rex Smythe and call himself a liar, this last after he closed his mouth. "That's the spirit. Teamwork, Jack, keep telling yourself teamwork," Mr. Begin said, clapping him on the arm.

Jack rubbed it as he stumbled out of the hotel, into the vicious wind. He caught a tram whose wheels kept up a screech like a circular saw as they followed the lines along the promenade, past miles of stalls boarded up for the winter. Even if the company retained him, what would happen to his assistants? If he could have afforded to take early retirement he would have made way for at least one of them. The fifth fish-and-chip shop he passed convinced him he was hungry, and eating felt like the first real thing that had happened to him all day. He walked back to the hotel, shivering from having left his coat there, felt steadily less present. In the ballroom he gripped his temples and stared at the floor throughout the afternoon's pep talk on management, and hadn't moved from that position when the room emptied and Lucinda came over to him. "Still nursing your head?"

"Just thinking."

"Nothing too bad, I hope."

"Looks like the Grand won't be seeing me for much longer."

"Oh, Jack." She squatted in the aisle beside him, the skirt of her dark suit inching above her smooth knees. "Is that what Mr. Big told you?"

"Not in so many words."

Lucinda rested a hand on his shoulder before she stood up. "We haven't had that drink yet."

"You've seen me when I've had a few."

"Let's make it just a couple."

"And dinner as well?"

"All right, dinner. I'm going up for a shower and then I'll see you in the bar, say at seven."

The notion of her in the shower revived Jack as much as anything could at the moment. The promise which it and her tone seemed to extend to him brought him to his feet, and he escorted her as far as the main lifts, only to see Rex Smythe and Mr. Begin waiting. "I'll use my own lift," he said in her ear.

As soon as he thumbed the button on the wall of the deserted corridor the lift doors jerked open, and the attendant stepped back further into the grey light, his unhealthy white faces burgeoning on both sides of him. "I thought it'd have to be you, Mr. Hatimer."

Jack was too exhausted to argue. "Almost," he said.

"Nearly got you now, have we? Scuttle in then, before I have to do a disappearing trick."

"I'm glad to hear I'm not your only customer," Jack said, stepping into the gray light and seeing it coat face after face until he turned away from himself.

The attendant fell against the lever, then poked his face over his shoulder at Jack as the lift swayed upwards. "Why's that, old thing?"

"I wouldn't like to think you were going up and down just for me. By the way, you're never telling me they still haven't sent anyone to take over."

"Aren't I? Well, I won't, then."

"Would you like me to see if I can get someone for you?"

"Too late for that."

The attendant rested his chin on his shoulder as though his neck had locked, a position which appeared not to bother him but which Jack found so painful to observe that he had to struggle not to close his eyes. "So how's your day in the big wide world been?" the attendant asked.

He was beginning to put Jack in mind of a ventriloquist's dummy which had twisted itself into a dismaying posture while continuing to talk. "Could have been worse," Jack mumbled so as not to be drawn.

"Not over yet, or is it? Did I feel the sun go down?"

"It's dark, yes."

"Time to play then, eh?"

The attendant winked, turning that side of his face into a mass of wrinkles that looked about to crack like the makeup it increasingly resembled, and shoved the lever up. "Here we are again, happy as can be. We'll neither of us get any higher."

His rearing up to move the lever had made Jack think of a body being yanked by a rope around its broken neck. "Are you sure you're all right?" he stammered.

"As sure as you are."

Once Jack had blundered out of the lift he didn't glance across the corridor until he was in his room. The attendant was turning slowly back and forth and yet keeping his face towards Jack. "I'll be waiting," he said, and levered the doors shut.

Jack slammed his door and leaned his forehead against it and groped for the chain, which he fumbled into the socket. He stood there for a while, unable to think what he was trying to do, and then he remembered his date with Lucinda. He laid his grey suit out on the bed, where it appeared to be making him a promise of company in his room, before taking a bath. As long as he lay in the water he found it possible not to think about the day or how he might sneak past the lift attendant. A few minutes before seven he dried himself and got dressed, and was combing his hair a third time when the phone rang.

Whoever it was, they wouldn't make him late for Lucinda. As he snatched the receiver he had to remind himself not to say he was the Grand. "Yes, who's this?"

"Jack?"

"Lucy! I'm just on my way down."

"Actually, Jack, forgive me, but I'm going to have to cancel dinner."

"Who's the problem?"

"Who else could it be? I told the boss I was meeting you, but he didn't offer to treat you as well."

"Shall we have our drink afterwards instead?"

"Mr. Begin seems to want my whole evening. Lots to discuss, he says. Never mind, Jack, there's always next year."

"Always has been," Jack muttered, and let the phone drop. He grabbed it again on the only impulse that seemed left to him and dialed Reception. "I've a complaint. Let me speak to the manager."

"You're Mr..." After a pause the receptionist said "Mr. Latimer, is it?"

"Last time I looked it was."

"I'm sorry, Mr. Latimer. We've been trying to contact you. There's been a slight mistake on the computer, and there was a new girl on the desk when you checked in. You weren't supposed to have that room."

"Where do you want me to be?"

"That wing wasn't meant to be in use this weekend, you see. Someone should have noticed you were there, but the chambermaid didn't mention it till she came off duty. So if we can just move you over to where the rest of your party is staying..."

"I like it where I am. That isn't what I rang about, it's a member of your staff."

"If we could just deal with your room first, and then I'll get you the manager."

"This has waited long enough. I called about the fellow in the lift outside my room."

"I'm afraid I don't understand, sir. If you'd like me to send someone up to help you move—"

"The lift attendant, whatever his name is. He's been in there ever since I got here yesterday, and if you're saying he's been just for me, that's even more ridiculous."

"You must be mistaken, sir. None of our lifts have been manned for years."

"You're as sure of that as you were of which room you put me in, is that right? Tell you what, you speak to the manager and tell him I've been buggered about enough for one weekend or the rest of my life, come to that, and while you're at it tell him nobody knows you've a man in your lift and it's past time someone did something about him, and then one of you call me back."

He had barely replaced the receiver when the phone shrilled at him. If it was the receptionist again, renewing her attempt to persuade him to change rooms—"Yes?"

"Jack?"

"No need to sound as if you don't know."

"Rex Smythe. I thought it might be an idea for us to have a chinwag."

"Whose idea?"

"Mine and the company's. Shall we meet in the bar for a dram? I gather you're free."

For a few seconds Jack was speechless with rage, and then he saw the chance he'd almost missed. "No, come up to my room. There's something I want you to see."

"Is it important?"

"Very." At the moment Jack could think of nothing more important than ensuring Rex saw the attendant too. "Don't use the main lifts. Walk all the way to my end of the hotel, and there's one that brings you right to me."

"I hope this is going to be worth it," Smythe grumbled, which made Jack certain that it was. He hung up the receiver and opening the door, shot the bolt so as to keep it from closing while he crossed the corridor. He thumped on the metal door and shouted, "I've reminded the hotel you're in there. They don't seem to know either of us are here."

The doors staggered open, and the attendant peered up at him. He was clinging to the handle as though for support, and his face, whose color and texture put Jack in mind of mold on an apple, was turned more or less towards the corridor, yet Jack had the decidedly unwelcome impression that he'd twisted his head even further around than before. Nevertheless he spoke, keeping his chin fixed while the rest of his head wobbled up and down. "Mr. Hatton."

Jack didn't feel disposed to argue with anyone who looked like that. "Better put it on, then," he said as lightly as he could.

"That's rich. That's good enough for end of pier." The attendant appeared to be laughing silently, his face quaking like a mask about to work itself loose. "Seeing as how you wanted to do me a favor, can I ask you one?"

"What have you in mind?"

"Can I use your...?"

It wasn't the pause which made Jack falter, it was the way the attendant jerked his head to indicate the hotel room, stretching his deeply ridged white neck until Jack had to look away. "God bless us, can't you even use the toilet?" Jack muttered, and raised his voice. "Go ahead."

He saw the attendant bobbing up at the edge of his vision as though someone had hauled on an invisible rope; then the man rushed across the corridor so fast that Jack hadn't time to look at him. He had the briefest glimpse of a figure on which the grey of the uniform and the white of flesh had somehow become less clearly separated, before the bathroom door slammed and the bolt clicked home like the hammer of a gun. "Keep an eye on the cage, there's a dear," the attendant must have said in transit, because the words were itching in Jack's ears. "Actually—" Jack called, remembering Smythe, and started back into his room just as the lift began to emit a waspish buzz.

He was afraid it was malfunctioning until he grasped that someone was trying to summon it—Rex. "Excuse me, but—" he recommenced, and then several observations silenced him. By the sound of it the attendant was using the shower rather than the toilet, and whatever he was doing in there, Jack could see from the gap beneath the door and the position of the light-switch outside the bathroom that he was doing it in total darkness. When Jack heard the noise the plughole of the bath was making, a prolonged choked gurgle that suggested some not entirely solid mass was being washed into the plumbing, he retreated into the corridor, almost falling over backwards in his haste. The lift was buzzing irritably, and it occurred to him that his nearest ally was Rex. The thought was enough to send him into the lift. He shoved the handle down, and the doors shut off the corridor at once.

He could have done without quite so much movement around him: the strip of indicator lights flickering one by one like candles that wouldn't stay lit, the shifting of his pack of faces leading into nothingness at both edges of his vision, the stool wobbling from his having bumped into it as he'd taken refuge in the lift, and now folding its unsteady legs and throwing the book on the worn-out carpet. As the book fell open Jack saw it was a biography of Tony Hancock, but it was the word written in faded ink on the title page that caught his attention. It must be the owner's name—Hatton.

"Don't you even know your own name?" Jack demanded, and then another possibility occurred to him. As he raised his head he glimpsed all his reflections shifting. He hadn't time to glance at them, because the lift was almost at the fourth floor, where he heard Rex grousing—but as he shoved the lever up to halt the lift, then exerted the extra pressure which opened the doors, he couldn't avoid noticing that his suit looked grey as a uniform in the dim light, which had also rendered the mark of his engagement ring invisible. None of this need matter, because the doors were opening, and Rex's surprise at the sight of him would restore Jack to himself.

Rex took one step towards the lift, staring directly into Jack's face, then he grimaced and recoiled, waving a hand in front of his nose. "Forget it. I'll phone him," he said.

"Rex, wait. It's me."

Smythe gave no more sign of hearing him than he had of recognizing him. Jack heard him shoulder the nearest pair of fire doors out of his way, and tried to follow. The light from the corridor felt like fire on his whitening skin. The doors in the deserted corridor bumped shut, and he flinched back into the lift. His reflections met him like two packs of cards collapsing towards him, vanishing as they came. He heaved at the lever, which took more of his energy to move now, and sent the lift reeling upwards. If he could just lure the attendant back into it—but he didn't like to think what he might have to change places with if there was anything left that could be called out of his room.

destination unknown
ANGEL OF THE HATE WIND
by Storm Constantine

My friend Jericho was taken by the Angel of the Hate Wind. At least that's what I think, and though people might not like to share my view of the world, or of the angels, I know it's a deep-seated fear within everyone. Taken by the wind.

We were rolling down the Fear Coast road in a land-dinghy when the seeds of the Taking were sown and took root. It was one of those hot, red evenings when you just feel it in your gut that anything is possible. We had stopped for the night and lit a fire within the skeletal shelter of a petrified spinney. Branches clacked like bones, bleached white in daylight, but black against the sun, sinking lovewards. The road plaited to each horizon. Mountains smudged the fear sky. We looked for spirit lights, but there were none, only wisps of cloud.

Jericho said, "I have to do something before we get there. Do something now."

We were on our way to Jasper's Fayre, on the hate coast. By profession, Jericho and I were tregetours, did a few juggling sketches with plasma spheres and firefly bhajis. The fayre meant income to us, but more than that for Jericho. He was sure he had tripped into a passion. I wasn't so sure, but he got hot and angry when I tried to reason with him, so it was easier to humor him. The object of his affection was Dendria, and she was a variant, not even completely human. What grew on her head was like feathers or ferns; her eyes were yellow, with vertical pupils, like a cat's; her skin a strange, blue-white color, which showed disturbing hints of bone and internal organs if the light caught her right. I suppose she was beautiful, in an aesthetic sense, but I would not have wanted to touch her, and I deplored the fact that Jericho had spent the last sennight mooning around, undoubtedly composing bad poetry in his head to the beloved. She was a cidaris, a created species wrought for pleasure in the nutrient vats of hatish Amalgamators. Some had bred. There were hybrids. Nowadays, with everything boiling over as it is, there are no regulations to control the incubi and succubi of our wildest dreams. Some learned to be tumblers; Dendria was one of those. She belonged to a troupe called Excoriasts, who as well as flipping and flapping in all manner of contortions, could insert sharpened rods through their skin and hang from hooks, recreating all the fakir stuff from an earlier time. Dendria was the only cidaris with the troupe, although some of her colleagues represented other sub-species: admerveyelles, with their spangled eyes and multiple breasts; erminee boys, softly furred; spine-haired errinies, with their vestigial facial features and muscular limbs. I enjoyed looking at the variants, with their unexpected surprises, but no way could I desire one. Like called to like, I thought. Jericho was mad.

True, he sucked too many stalks of the erigeron and saw visions I could not see. Sometimes, I had caught him inserting guidon thorns beneath his flesh, invoking a hallucinatory experience which would hover on the edge of his perception, but which would last for sennights. My disapproval of his habits provoked only outrage. I had hardened my heart. As long as he could pilot the dinghy, service its capricious sails and wheels, I could put up with his behavior. If it eventually killed him, or sent him plummeting down a psychological abyss I could not fathom, then I would find a new partner. Perhaps even a variant. No doubt they could juggle too.

So, I was squatting in the dust, reconstituting a protein slab, listening to Jericho rave. "It is the future," he said, "for us all to become one, all the differences and specialization's to meld into one unique template."

By that, I realized his fascination for Dendria had escalated into the desire to breed with her. This was too much. I said nothing, stirred my pot. Jericho's face was demonic in the jumping light of our fire, but he still seemed wild and stunning to me. I thought, sadly, that our association must eventually end, and sooner rather than later. At first, I'd imagined our friendship would develop into something physical. But it

seemed, being merely human, I was too common to ignite his libido, or perhaps he just regarded me as a sister. I rarely thought to primp and preen, and I knew I should pay more attention to personal hygiene, even though there is little point when traveling the roads between the fayres.

The end of the millennium approached. Humanity had grown careless and torpid, too lazy to make war, too idle to invent. Our technology fed and governed us; we had little to do but play. Anyone with any fire, zeal or curiosity about the universe had moved off-world to the spiraling colonies. I had often suspected we had out-lived our purpose, but because our knowledge protected us from extinction, we were doomed to linger on, wraiths of what once was, without particular promise. Perhaps Jericho was right. For the variants, life was new and exciting. They lacked seriousness of mind, but that might come eventually. Then what? Would they want to own land, claim territory, even fight for it? Would they turn their attention to the skies, covet the silent leviathans that circled our world, fly to make war with the remnants of humanity? I wondered about it, even though it seemed unlikely. Variants were frivolous; they had learned this from us. All that Jericho thought of was indulging his desires.

We had met the Excoriasts only four sennights back at Cackerel Festival. It had been prestigious to earn a stage there, as the most superlative of performers had shoaled to the area. I suppose it was my fault Jericho got to meet Dendria, as I became friendly with Intempera, the troupe-leader. She was a tall, weighty woman, who oozed sex appeal and had the best sense of humor I'd ever come across. Also, I envied her collection of wigs. My hair, forever unwashed, I hid beneath a caul of metal feathers whenever I performed. Intempera had glorious hanks of hair hanging up in her caravan; scalps of azure, viridian, cyclamen, daffodil, the longest of which trailed behind her on the ground as she stalked across the festival ground. Intempera taught me to drink Lizard's Tail liqueur, which is best imbibed without breathing. She had a lover/son, Loadstar, who was seven feet tall, with a beautiful sad face and plaits to his waist. She said he was an angel hybrid, because she had got pregnant during the

Rites of Ecstasy sixteen years before, and Loadstar had been born as a miniature adult, rather than a baby. I wondered how many of her recollections were colored by Lizard's Tail, but the story was fascinating, and I wanted to believe it.

I took Jericho with me to Intempera's caravan one night, to play livers, and the cidaris was there. It was obvious the game bored her, because she wouldn't join in, but neither would she let the rest of us get on with it. Personally, I found Dendria's behavior very irritating. She insisted on leaping around us, upsetting the liver-stones whenever anyone was near to winning, and giggling, extending her head fronds and widening her pupils in Jericho's face. I expected he'd find her a nuisance as well, but men's reactions can never be predicted. Intempera occasionally picked up a rug-beater and smacked Dendria with it, which elicited raucous cries, but it didn't stop her gadding about us.

"What a simpo!" I confided to Jericho later, on the short walk back to our wickyup.

He sighed. "I have seen a creature of aether, a denizen of love." His hands described cidaris-shaped outlines in the air before him. "Made flesh, but of a less common substance."

True, he had been quaffing Lizard's Tail, but I hardly expected such a sodden response. "Are you all right, Jericho?"

"She is divine," he answered, blinking.

I presumed the condition would evaporate by day, but it didn't. Dendria, I think, was aware immediately of Jericho's sudden and intense obsession. She flirted cruelly, forever wafting by the stage when we were performing, or else just standing to one side, in prominent view, biting into hunks of barbecued meat that dripped with spiced grease, or else sucking long fruits. Me, she ignored, all her attention being riveted on wretched Jericho. To his credit my partner never fouled the act, even when the paramour was present. I know that, at least on one occasion, she let him have sex with her because I happened to stumble across them while they were doing it. Perhaps that was intentional. I believe Dendria knew all about the way I felt for Jericho, and enjoyed pricking my feelings as much as tweaking Jericho's strings. I remember finding them in the wickyup, she on all fours, he taking her from behind. She was making a sound like a donkey, some kind of bray, which I supposed was of pleasure. Her buttocks were turquoise, as if bruised. When Jericho saw me, he could not stop, merely closed his eyes. Out of pique, I went in and made myself a sandwich while they finished. She cleaned herself up without modesty afterwards, even using some of my tissues, which I employed for removing stage makeup. I couldn't help but sneak glances. Her genitals were swollen, and dark blue, nothing like mine in shape or size. As if for my benefit, she spread her legs and twitched her muscles, and the lips of her vulva moved like a mouth. No wonder cidarises are so popular with men. Still, she had very little breast.

Poor Jericho. His torment lasted a mere four days. One morning the Excoriasts had left the site with no message from Dendria left behind. At first I was glad but, when it became obvious that Jericho wasn't going to get over his obsession, I relented and gave him what comfort I could. Intempera had told me we would be able to get together again at Jasper's Fayre. Jericho's joy at this news made me miserable: it was feverish, a cacoethes of passion. I felt it could kill him.

Now, he sat in the dust before me, shredding a dried grass stalk, his eyes watering with anticipation and longing. "I won't be denied, Saralan," he said, not really seeing me. "At Jasper's, I will have her." He paused then, as if becoming aware of my existence and the fact that I could hear and make deductions for myself. "Of course, this will not affect our partnership. Maybe we could work Dendria into the routine."

I smiled thinly, hoping he could see it was thin but knowing he would see only the upward curve of a mouth and read it as approbation.

"What can you do?" I asked perfunctorily. "A cidaris is a flighty creature. What if she does not want to come with us?"

Jericho was clearly annoyed with these remarks. "I will make her my wife," he said. As if that solved everything.

Part of me hoped he would make a fool of himself, but then I remembered I'd have to deal with the emotional debris. "What if she doesn't want to be a wife?"

Jericho shook his head abruptly, as if assailed by insects. "I know, I know," he said. "I've thought of that." His body language did not align with his words.

"So what are you going to do?"

He rested his chin on his clenched fists, staring at the flames. 'Obstacles will have to be removed. Namely, her ignorance. With clear sight, she will know for herself that we are meant to be as a pair.' He fixed me with a frightening glare. "I shall call upon the powers of hate to aid me."

I couldn't help sniggering a little. "So, you are a worker of magic now!"

He bridled. "You know hardly anything about me."

Something snapped inside me and let a feeling of defeat slide in. Jericho and I had never argued before, or sniped at one another. How things had changed. How cruel the powers of passion, ruled by the lords of love. I glanced at the sky in their direction, where still the sinking sun stained the threads of clouds, and thought how pitiless they were. As some were moved to deeper feeling, others were swamped and drowned.

While some might call upon the lords of ecstasy, with their weapons of fire to charge the will, and others invoke the mighty lords of fear to subdue the object of desire with their shrouds of midnight darkness, and yet more still would obviously, and dreamily, petition the lords of love, with their flowing vases of desire and harmony, Jericho went for hate. He had a very logical mind most of the time, which might explain his choice. Hate for clear sight, for sharp things, the sky of the rising sun, the morning, potential there but unfulfilled. He would call upon Amaritude, the Angel of Hate, Lord of the Swords, Prince of the Morning, White Eagle of the Dawn, Rider of the Hate Wind. Still, as we all know, Hate has its other side, that of the blooded weapon, of breakings and endings, of discord and cruelty. I would not have made that choice.

θ θ θ

There was a ridge on the other side of the road. During the day it looked yellow, at night it was black. It was here that Jericho decided his ritual would be performed. I had no wish to participate, but Jericho asked stiffly for my assistance; he needed someone to operate the perfume-squeezers. "I have to speak my mind," I told him. "This is folly." I wished I hadn't mentioned that the Excoriasts would be present at Jasper's Fayre. It had been a moment of weakness to reveal that. Now what would happen?

"I know what you think," he answered. "But I'm asking you, as a friend, to help me." Behind his words, but in his eyes, were the unspoken reminders of times when he'd given me support over emotional dilemmas.

"Oh all right," I said. "But don't blame me if things go wrong."

The sun was merely a slit-eyed sliver of red on the hateward horizon as we built a spiral fire of skinned sticks. The sky above us was black, unpricked by stars, yet it looked so clear, so translucent. There were greedy fogs around us, unseen, but sucking up the light.

Jericho's long toes gripped the dirt as he wove the shape of the fire. His hands shook. Occasionally, he cursed as a fumbling movement spoiled the pattern. The twig spiral wove outwards, deosil. I hid within it some shells I had picked up from the gape of a vanished sea, back lovewards. This I did for tenderness, as a protection. The Lords of Love drank salt liquors from shells, the tears of the infatuated. Their faint influence might temper the passions of the Angel of Hate.

Then it was time, and I was squatting outside the circle that Jericho had marked with small white stones. He walked deosil within it, sprinkling self-igniting Grains of Cloud upon the unlit fire, a powder we had bought from another fayre, far distant in time and space, when there had been a clear road between us, and no fog. I held a perfume squeezer in my hand, my toes ready on the foot-pump. Amaritude, as with all angels, was a cantankerous, capricious spirit. His requirements were precise. If I squeezed too much, he would not come, if I squeezed too little, he would not come, or worse, he might decide to put in an appearance anyway, and then do something dreadful. He might crack our bones and suck the marrow, or make us die of desire. I'd heard it could happen.

The Grains of Cloud began to smoke, exuding their own aroma of seas and rain and wet grass. Presently, the fire was crackling, and I risked a hesitant puff on the perfume squeezer. The essence vapoured forth in a couple of restrained coughs, little puffs upon the night air, round and friendly. Jericho stood with legs apart, his arms thrown high, his head thrown back, long, tangled hair fell down his back. My heart ached, and tears blurred my eyes. It was the fumes. Perhaps the squeezer was leaking. Jericho faced the direction of hate, his back to me. He began an invocation, a heart-felt plea to Amaritude's brethren, who preened and guarded him. "Brothers of Hate, of the Blue Morning, bring forth to me, your Father and Lover, Amaritude!"

A breeze stole furtively past me, shivering across the circle, influencing the flames, so that they leaned in the direction of hate. I applied my feet and fingers to the squeezing of perfume; careful exudations. The scent slapped my head before it flowed towards the circle; the smell of dawn, of fresh light and grass, but with the suggestion burning faint within it of the embers of someone's home.

It is the fumes that bring the visions to us. We are familiar with the archetypal forms of the angels because we have lived with them since we were children, when we were told about such things. We know what they should look like so, when we invoke them, we see what we expect to see. That is what I believe. I know there is power in the universe, and that it can be wrought into forms. Intention fashions our desires into shapes that we can see, and will-power charges them with intelligence. We can control these forms if we can control our desires, but hectic passion engenders hectic forms, and that can be troublesome. That night, as I sat hunched upon the dry dirt outside Jericho's circle, I pushed with all my will, some kind of temperance towards my friend. If he was frenzied, I would be tranquil. I was not afraid for myself, but for him.

They came, the shivering reeds of radiance, seven of them. The Lesser Angels of Hate. They twisted like smoke, made of smoke, some feet above the lunging tongues of the fire. My eyes were stinging. I could see the smudge of their faces, the smoking blue luminance of their eyes. Jericho was a black silhouette before them, frozen in position, his arms thrown up. Sparks swirled around him in a circling, dervish dance. "Bring forth to me, Amaritude!"

Slowly, the forms drew apart and there was a stair of light leading up to the infinite dark of our imagination, the sky. Amaritude came down this stair, robed in ferocious rays of blue-white effulgence. His hair was a smolder of stars. I wondered if he had captured them all that night, to wear. Was that why the sky was so black? I squeezed out some more perfume, trembling. I had seen angels before, naturally, everyone had. But in the past, they had been invoked, in my presence, for gentler purposes; a healing, a plea for security, a lessening of anguish. Never had I witnessed an invocation of this Lord of Hate to bend the will of another. It was frowned upon and, for that reason, I believed the essence of Amaritude, a creature formed from the dreams and desires of generations of people, would hunger for it.

Jericho looked so small and fragile, with the immense shape of the angel hanging over him. His words seemed like tiny, dry leaves falling to the ground. "Mighty Lord of the Morning, I entreat thee to hear my petition. Ignite the passion of the cidaris, Dendria, that she might adore me. Open her eyes to me, open her heart, open her mind to me, open her body."

The angel-form seemed to listen. Jericho versed his request in several different ways, over several minutes, presumably so that Amaritude would be in no doubt as to what he required. When Jericho had finished speaking, the angel raised his hands, each the size of a small tree, and shook his fingers so that grains of light fell down. Something occurred to me as I performed another discrete squeeze on the perfume. What was Jericho offering to the angel? Angels disliked doing things for nothing, and some small sacrifice was required, if only a pinch of incense. Surely Jericho could not have forgotten this important obligation? As I thought this, it seemed to me that Amaritude's giant hands swooped down and cupped Jericho in their blinding radiance. Jericho uttered a distressing sound, as if he were being crushed. His back arched. I heard him gasp, "I thank you Lord of the Hate Wind, for your presence, for your benevolence. Please accept my humble gratitude."

Would that be enough? I laid off the perfume-squeezing, thinking it was about time that Amaritude took objection to the taste of the air and departed. He had deigned to take notice of Jericho's invocation, so I had to believe my friend's petition would be granted. The giant hands lifted, the burning countenance grew dimmer, and Amaritude retreated swiftly up his heavenly stair. As he diminished, his brethren closed ranks until the smoke of their essence expanded into a roiling cloud and abruptly evaporated with a sound like someone opening a hundred airtight lids all at once.

Jericho sank to the ground. Half kneeling, half squatting, his head hung forward.

I kicked aside the white stones and went to him, took him in my arms. His skin was cold, crackling with frost. The fire burned blue, an effect of the Grains of Cloud. Hurriedly, I dragged Jericho from the circle and took him back to our homely fire down the ridge, on the other side of the road. Here, I wrapped him in a blanket, and gave him a tin cup of liquor, from which he sipped in silence, staring at the flames. There were spots of blue on his face. I feared frost-bite. "It is done," he said.

I shuddered. Above us, stars had begun to blink on and off, a binary language. Amaritude had released them.

It took us another two days to reach Jasper's Fayre. Poor Jericho. He was so ill, yet fired by a manic fever of emotion. I myself found it hard to keep warm. I dreamed of the Angel of Hate, the enormity of him hanging over me, his grains of burning cold light raining down on my face,

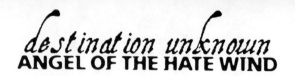

freezing out my eyes, scorching my tongue. What had we done? I asked myself that question many times each day, hoping that as my memory of that night receded, so would my unease. I thought that the impact of the Lord of Hate upon my mind was too great, too surreal, and that was what caused the nightmares and the physical discomfort. Jericho and I were doing these things to ourselves, because we believed we had seen something beyond belief.

We could see the flimsy pagodas of Jasper's Fayre several clicks down the road, as we approached at sundown. The tiers of the pagodas were spangled with winking lights; green and gold and white. Jericho seemed preoccupied, which did not surprise me, and we spoke little as the dinghy coasted easily towards the sinking sun. Soon, we heard music; a sad melancholy sound, as thin as the memories of childhood. The only other noise was the creak of the dinghy and then the hum of a dirigible hanging overhead, its gondola packed, no doubt, with the children of the rich, high on the rites of ecstasy performed in clear air. A pale silk ribbon came twisting down and landed on our mast, a trophy from someone's hair. I looked at it clinging there, so limply, and felt the spider hands of anguish flex within me, squeezing my guts.

Jericho left me securing the dinghy with hexes while he went in search of the Excoriasts, or more precisely, of Dendria. Furiously, I beat back the desire to follow him. I adored him as he walked away from me; the pain was total, almost as though Amaritude had inflicted me with the cankers of baleful desire. I refused to think about Dendria, about how she might be waiting with fluttering heart and eyes, her blue-palmed hands scored with persistent itches to wrap themselves around Jericho. If he succeeded in his advances, I would leave him. There was no way I could stand putting up with Dendria's sly eyes sliding off me all day, every day. I knew she would be lazy and cruel, and that I would never like her.

To ease my heart, I wandered off alone among the stalls and carousels, the houses of death, the tunnels of enchantment, in search of

liquor or philtres of forgetfulness. Every time I caught sight of someone vaguely cidarissy, I flung myself into the hectic crowds, drawing
bodies around me like a cloak of invisibility. At an apothecary's booth
I bought a small, dark fruit that tasted of carrion meat: I was assured by
the vendor that swift oblivion would follow its ingestion. Shortly, staggering from blaring sound to blaring sound, I bumped into a man I
knew vaguely and elected to spend the night with him. We found a Folly
of Dreams, built from stick-like bones of spun sugar and polymers,
paid our entrance to the masked admerveyelle at the portal and threw
ourselves into the marshmallow clouds of the dreams. When I woke up
the folly had evaporated into the dawn mist, and had apparently taken
my transient lover with it. I did not care. Today I must taste the most
bitter of reality's liquors.

Jericho was sitting on the edge of the dinghy, with his back to me, as
I approached through the mist. All around me, unseen, the entertainers
of Jasper's Fayre, and the sodden revelers who had fallen asleep or unconscious in the muddy sawdust between the booths, were making faint
noises of wakefulness. Sounds were muted but forlorn. I stepped over a
slim, discarded arm which lay, half-submerged in the mud. The fingers
were curled, beckoning. I hoped it had come from an automaton or a
doll, and did not look too closely at its ragged stump. As the dinghy
loomed nearer, my heart began to panic. The silk ribbon still hung,
damp, from it's mast. Jericho's posture was unreadable, but it did not
speak to me in loud tone of success and euphoria. He has failed, I thought,
emotions of different types swelling within me. He forgot to make sacrifice to Amaritude, and the petition failed. Jericho's grief would be terrible, but I felt I could cope with it. Eventually, his sad obsession must
fade and we could coast on to new roads until his grief became melancholy, and finally a wistful memory to be discussed over camp-fires and
liquor, late at night. Already, optimism was blooming within me, and I
increased my pace. I said, "Jericho," expecting him to ignore me, but he
turned at once.

I stopped walking, almost falling, as the huge headache carried in my brain sluggishly failed to respond to the change in pace. His face! Even now, I cannot find words to describe his expression. It was as though the history of the world, with all its atrocities and tragedies, had been etched into his features. His skin was colorless, all the muscles beneath it dragged downwards. Was this the face of loss, of passion unrequited?

"Saralan," he said, in a flat tone. "I wondered where you were."

I laughed uneasily, pressing with numb fingers the throbbing node of pain in my left temple. "Oh, I've been around... How did your night go?"

He grimaced. "I wish I could say it was indescribable, but it wasn't."

At that, I hastened forward, arms outstretched to embrace. "Oh Jericho, I'm so sorry! Still, we should have known! What sacrifice did you give to Amaritude? None! And now he has spurned your petition!"

Jericho flinched away from me, forcing me to clutch the painted sides of the dinghy instead. "Sacrifice? Oh, the sacrifice was taken, and the petition was granted."

"I don't understand." After climbing up over the slick boards, I sat down beside him. Now, I was shaking, and my teeth had begun to chatter.

"How foolish we are!" said Jericho, staring darkly into the mists. "We can't understand their ways, no matter how we delude ourselves into thinking otherwise!"

I presumed, wrongly, that he meant the ways of the variants. In a suitably hushed voice, I inquired, "What did she do?"

Jericho jerked his head around to stare at me. His eyes appeared unfamiliar and I had to glance away. I did not look at him directly once during the time he told me what had happened and his voice was painful to my ears, ringing with a new harsh note.

So, he had found the caravans of the Excoriasts, his heart full of dreams and scared hope. Dendria had been sitting on the steps of Intempera's wagon, playing cat's cradle with a red string, almost as though she'd been waiting for someone. Jericho described his approach to her, the dreadful nervousness and anticipation that had flowered in his heart.

She had caught sight of him and, for a moment, seemed surprised and afraid. Then she had leapt nimbly to her feet and had come towards him, her sharp face filled with welcome. Jericho had known then that his petition had been granted and that the fires of passion roared brightly in Dendria's body and mind.

It was at this moment, I think, that Amaritude, with a certain mordant humor, had taken his sacrifice. Even as Dendria had reached for Jericho with her long-fingered hands, his heart had turned to a muscle of stone. Her face, alight with desire, had filled him with repugnance. The scent of her body, reaching out to him in yearning, had made him gag. He no longer cared for her. She had become an object of disgust and embarrassment. Dendria, however, had clearly never felt more drawn to Jericho. Her obsession was evidently unique and total, which was only to be expected if Amaritude had infected her heart. Jericho, alarmed and sickened, had attempted to flee the scene. He talked incoherently of how he'd thought of running back to me for my support, but Dendria, since the object of her desire had manifested before her, intended not to be denied. Her lamentations had been loud, her finger-nails sharp. An awkward scuffle had taken place, quelled only when Intempera herself, roused from a snooze by the din, had come billowing out of the caravan to separate them.

"I had to hide from her all night," Jericho said, adding accusingly, "Where were you?"

I swallowed the sharp retort that came like bile to my lips. Inside, my spirits were singing like a heavenly choir. This was triumph, but I sensed that the smoke of battle hid vile carnage, and when it cleared the victory might not be as sweet. "If I had known, Jericho, I would have been here for you, but how could I know? The purpose of our being here was your pursuit of the cidaris, after all."

Jericho made a harrumping sound. "We must leave at once," he said.

θ θ θ

destination unknown
ANGEL OF THE HATE WIND

Dendria trailed us for several sennights. She was a sick wraith at our heels, and the strength of her obsession was as painful to Jericho as her indifference and aloofness had been before. I realized very soon that he feared her to the point of phobia. He dreaded her touch as much as some dread the touch of spiders or snakes. Of course, his dreams were full of her. The most regular nightmare involved Dendria creeping up over the sides of the dinghy and stealing to Jericho's cabin, where she smothered him with her body. In this dream, he could neither call out or move. Eventually, to assuage his night terrors, I began to keep watch until dawn, and sleep during the day, while he piloted the dinghy alone.

The end was horrible.

I was awoken at mid-day, by a hair-raising, womanly scream from Jericho. Pulling on my jacket, I threw myself from the cabin, still half asleep as I stumbled up the deck. The road was long and straight, running between dead, yellow fields, where nothing grew. A thin drizzle hazed down from a gray-green sky. It looked as though the land was in mourning.

Dendria must have overtaken us somehow, perhaps hitching a ride in a dirigible or hanging onto the runners of a train. Now, she ran towards us down the road; a hag, Jericho's nemesis. In her disarray and wretchedness, it seemed she had become more alien: she was stick-thing, gnarled and knobbled, that might have squeezed out from a child's worst dream into the waking world. Her color was dreadful, dark and contused, and her head fronds were torn and ragged. For a moment, I felt pity. Jericho had made her into this.

I hurled myself forward, shouting out at Jericho to trigger the anchors, for Dendria was directly in our path. My voice was blown away from me, gathered up by the cold, cruel hands of the winds of hate, sweeping like blades across the empty fields. I do not know whether he meant to run her down or whether, in his panic, he simply lost control, but before I could reach him, she had disappeared beneath our runners and wheels, with a thin scream like that of a tortured bird and some other, more stomach-churning noises of breaking flesh and bone.

Cursing, slipping, I smacked Jericho away from the controls and brought the dinghy to a shuddering, bumpy halt. There was a sound of liquids spattering onto the road and I jumped quickly over the side of the dinghy, worried our fuel-lines had been damaged. But the sounds came from what was entangled in the undercarriage: cidaris remains which jetted dark ichors like fluids that might come from a squid. I stood for a while, hands on hips, staring at the repulsive mess. Her head, mostly intact, was wedged between two moving parts and stared at me with expressionless eyes. Then, I became angry and yelled up at Jericho. I would not clean the bits of Dendria from the dinghy: it was unfair! I'd put up with so much, but this!

Jericho moaned and whimpered above me, hunched down, rocking to and fro. He seemed not to hear me, although I heard him say clearly, "Now, she has won. Now, she will haunt me forever."

Eventually, I poked what I could away from the dinghy with a long stick and later coasted it through a shallow stream. This seemed to do the trick.

Jericho was inconsolable, and I was forced to give him an overdose of erigeron to shut him up and stop him seeing things. I reckoned that if we sailed swiftly enough, I would reach the settlement of Migalissin within a day. Perhaps there, therapists might be able to do something with him.

The Winds of Hate worked against me, tugging at the dinghy with unseasonable rage, their shrieking whistles turning to laughter in my head. Jericho's ravings annoyed me to the point where it seemed Amaritude's mean trick had affected me too. My passion was dying, or mutating into despising. "Fool!" I told Jericho as he twitched in a rug at my feet while I piloted the dinghy through the dry storm. "What did you hope to achieve?" I had to stop myself from kicking him.

Migalissin was in sight ahead when, without any warning, Jericho leapt up, threw himself from the side of the dinghy and ran like a rat up a lovewards hill, bleating fragmented invocations and scattering dry incense around him. He was gone before I could trigger the anchors.

I jumped down and stood in the road for while, feeling tired. Abruptly, the winds dropped. I was not surprised. I waited, straining my ears for a scream or a cry, but there was only silence. The branches of the petrified forest which blanketed the hill were unnaturally without creak or whisper. Occasionally, a feeling would eddy up inside me, and I nearly ran after Jericho, but the urges were fleet, purling away from me before I could act on them. I knew that I had lost him, and even should I find the body that had his name, the persona I cared for had long fled from it.

Evening came in a gentle blaze and I climbed back up onto the dinghy. It felt empty and strange to be there alone. I wanted to be sad or sickened, but could only be numb. Drizzle began to fall in a veil around me, making the deck greasy. Wide-winged black birds came out of the wood, uttering mad cries. I could only leave the area, go on. Jericho had gone to the angels, of this I was convinced. I hoped Amaritude would be kind to him, now that he had Jericho's sanity trapped in his shining fist.

In Migalissin, I paid for lodgings in a shack of a bar with the story of what I had experienced. An oily fire sputtered and hissed, offering the only light in the low-ceilinged saloon. I described Jericho as a fool, and felt angry about it. Only later, would I find the strength to weep.

When I had finished the story, I sat back to sip a mug of wine in the apparently awed silence of my audience. Then an old woman in a red kimono spoke up. "That is an astounding tale, although I have heard both worse and stranger in my time. Still, if I were you, I'd seek Amaritude's favor quickly in case any residue of his displeasure of your partner's stupidity lingers around your vessel."

I shuddered: the thought of addressing the Angel of Hate, for any reason, made me feel ill.

However, after two days of thinking about it, I performed a small, respectful ritual on and around the dinghy, even though I felt no liking for the Lord of the Hate Wind, and resented having to petition him myself. He made no appearance as I squeezed his favored perfumes into the air, for which I was thankful. Hopefully, he has forgotten me now.

In the winter-time, I met Intempera at a festival. I had a new partner by then; a young girl with a great talent and a greater amount of impertinence, but her rather abrasive presence served to keep any lingering ghosts of Jericho at bay. I felt an unpleasant wrench in my heart when I recognized the voluptuous, statuesque shape strutting through the booths towards me, Loadstar in tow, but Intempera seemed delighted to see me. She told me she had disbanded the Excoriasts, in favor of a new troupe, comprising only sets of identical twins. "The variants were too unpredictable," she confided, grimacing. "Also, they would persist in contracting strange illnesses that I couldn't treat. Often, they even died."

Later, over the familiar, lethal cocktails in Intempera's wagon, I told her what had happened to Jericho. She expressed surprise, clearly having no idea that he had harbored a passion for the cidaris.

"Well," she said, wrinkling up her nose and flapping a hand at me, "I should not be amazed! It is a pity you did not speak to me at Jasper's about this."

I sensed a profound meaning behind her words. "Why? Would it have made any difference?"

She shrugged. "It is hard to say, of course, and I'm even wary of telling you..."

"Telling me what."

"They are famed for it!" Intempera declared. "Variants, and the cidaris strain in particular, flirt and frolic around us human folk, and pretend arrogance, but it is known that having once shared a human bed, they are entrapped! They do not show it, of course, because they don't see the need. But I have seen before what happens when a man—and it is generally men—falls for one of these creatures. Men cannot understand the ways of variants, and always feel rebuffed and used. Some even take sick on it. Whenever I come across a wretch in this condition,

I always tell him that all he has to do is turn away from the object of his passion. Then, in almost all cases, the variant will develop a peculiar obsession and throw themselves at the feet of what they perceive to be a cold heart. If I had known about Jericho, I could have told you this. Your poor friend didn't need to go invoking the Cruel and Shining Ones. He paid so dearly! What a waste."

I don't know how I felt after I'd heard her words. Perhaps my system was too shocked to organize itself to feel things. Instead, I took a sip of the evil liqueur, smiled and shrugged. "No matter. I could not have won, either way."

Intempera raised her glass to me. "True. I hope you are now recovered from the incident."

I nodded. "Yes, but I will never forget him," I said adding, "as he was at the beginning."

And it is true.

destination unknown
THE FIVE O'CLOCK WHISTLE
by Ian McDonald

Two things told Pirandao that the old man had not died in the night up on the catwalk on Pillar 39. The first was that he had not rolled over the Big Front Step in the night to take the three kilometer dive into the Lermontov Sea, rags and coat-tails fluttering bravely behind him in the wind of terminal velocity. The second was that the old man still clutched the beautiful silver trombone under the brown coat stained with piss and Belladonna brandy. The night things that prowled the high steel that held up the glass roof of the world could not have resisted such silver sheen, such cunning curvature, such tubing and valve work, but they had not the courage to pluck from warm fingers. It was the silver trombone that had drawn Pirandao's attention to the old man the night before on the way to his cleaning job at The Food's, and made him look, hopefully, for him when Pirandao went back to his nest tucked under girder 66. He had played the trombone. He had made the Sound. He had been the Sound, but he had fallen. Like Pirandao.

It is no less to fall from the music as from the sky, Pirandao thought. They are the same woman, in the end. But the music had been faithful to Pirandao. After the bad thing, the perfect lilt of woodwinds over horns had been the only friend prepared to climb down the two hundred and something steps to the cubby under the deepest cellar in subterranean Belladonna that had been the furthest place Pirandao could hide himself from the sky. And because he had been true to it, when the rest of the world had moved to musical climes happier and cooler, it had led him back up those two hundred and something steps to the ground, and up the many hundreds and hundreds more steps to the top of Pillar 39, to show him the sky and ask him if he would ever be brave enough to tempt its fortune again.

And then it brought this old man in his coat so foul, clutching his trombone, his eyes glittering behind their wire framed glasses with whatever it is that old man up on the catwalks on Pillar 39 three kilometers above Grand Valley remember.

If he is still there at noon when I go down to the shift in the Sputnik Lounge I will talk to him, Pirandao promised himself.

He was still there at noon when Pirandao went down to his shift at the Sputnik Lounge.

"Fine day," said Pirandao.

"Every day is a fine day, when the clouds are below you," said the aged aged man, looking up at the glass roof above him. Up in the high steel, where the pillar splayed out into a hundred buttresses that held up the Lermontov Sea section of the Grand Valley roof, one of the night things shat. It hit and splattered close to the old man's foot, centimeters from the edge.

"Considered lucky in China," the old man said. "But it has to be a bird."

Pirandao thought about that all shift at the Sputnik Bar. It was an insane thing to say. The old man could only have meant China Mountain, the headquarters where ROTECH had built the world, but there were no birds in it. There were tunnels, and caves, and cities and machines and what ROTECH had left from the manforming, but no birds. Perhaps he had meant on China, but that was not a superstition Pirandao had ever heard of, and he had grown up in the steep, well-watered valleys that perforated the lower slopes of the ancient shield volcano. But no one there had ever called it China, but always by its full and proper name (for they were a full and proper people, except Pirandao, who had fallen from grace with the sky), though Great Uncle Savvas, who claimed he was descended by direct line from St. Catherine herself, always insisted on calling it by its original name, Pavonis Mons.

When Ricky Sputnik let Pirandao go for a few hours of sweaty, vertiginous sleep before his night hours in The Food's, he took with him a pocketful of scraps. The old man was still there, with the evening sun shining on the side of his face and glittering from the bell of his trombone. He ate the food greedily, with his fingers. His fingertips, Pirandao noticed, were splayed out, like little fleshy spades. It was a sure sign that the trombone was not merely a precious thing he had brought to take the Big Step with him, as many did, who could not face having to take the step alone, but a living thing. A loved thing. This was a musician from the great days when the music was golden. A Big Band player, perhaps. He might even have met him, jammed with him, trombonists together.

"You play that thing?" Pirandao invited.

"A little," the old man smiled, recognizing the invitation. His blowin' lips were greasy with The Food's food.

I used to, way back," Pirandao said awkwardly. "That's how I knew you did. The fingers." He held out his own. They were gently splayed at the tips. "I liked the classics, you know. The Big Band tunes. Back when I was a kid on China Mountain, I used to wake up when the rest of the farm had gone to sleep and tune in to All Swing Radio and turn it up just loud enough for me to hear and no one else. But whatever way it was they built the farmhouse, back when the world was being invented, the music would slip out from under the covers and run around the inside of the dome and get into the other kids' bedrooms and they would come tappin' at my door and creepin' into my room and sittin' on the foot of my bed listenin' to the greatest damn music you over heard. You just had to dance to music like that—couldn't not—but Da would whop the daylights out of you if he caught you because you couldn't do no work the next day. So we worked out this kind of clever quiet dancin' you could do with your fingers, like this." He wiggled and jiggled and tiggled his forefingers but in the clear and the bright and the cold of Pillar 39 they did not look much like any kind of dancin' at all. "Best damn music you ever heard. Buddy Mercx, Hamilton Bohannon and his Rhythm Aces; we listened to them all, but greatest was the Glenn Miller Big Band. Maybe it was he had more soul, more jazz, I dunno, but the others, they could never match him. Sheer class. All gone now. This stuff they listen to these days, Child'a'grace, now that's not what I call music. If they could just hear the Sound, the Glenn Miller Big Band Sound, they would hear music."

"I remember it well," said the old man. "So tell me, what did it sound like, this Glenn Miller Sound?"

"Like an angel breathing in your ear telling you she was hot for it, and a devil weeping for the good things he could never know, and a warm summer night with the most beautiful woman in the world and cool ice in brandy," said Pirandao, knowing that words could not say what the Sound had been, unless the words were just streams of vowels and consonants and syllables that sounded like clarinets and saxes over horns and the gentle stroll of double bass arm in arm with the slush of brushes on skins.

"Was it anything like this?" asked the old man and he unbuttoned his stained coat and lifted out his trombone like it was a baby sucking from his withered old man's tits and brought it up to his lips. He let out his puffed cheeks and the breath that lived within him went down the tube and around the slide and through the valves and somewhere in all the plumbing it was changed and blew out the bell end as a tune; an old tune, one of the first tunes Pirandao had ever heard stealing out of the wireless grille as he listened by valve glow in the warm China Mountain night. The Five O'clock Whistle: that was the name of the tune.

The old man played it sweet on his silver horn. He played it like a man who had been married to the music so long that he knows every crotchet and twitch of it and can please it long and gentle and slow and tickle it just right to make it laugh and croon in its throat, like the way old people make love, that may not have the invention and excitement and passion of the young, but is maybe wiser and kinder and more loving. He played it the way Pirandao had always dreamed he might, in the control cabin of the dirigible jamming along to the radio with no one but a thousand kays of red desert to wince at the bum notes. He played it so that the sound that came out of the silver horn was more than just an old tune, but suggested subtle harmonies and chimed cunning echoes off the ironwork that held up the glass roof of Grand Valley so that if you listened, really listened, which is not a thing you do with the ear, but the heart, you could make out sounds like the plod of the bass and the whaup-whau-whaup of brass, layer upon layer, spinning up a whole band out of the echoes and resonances so that Pirandao could smell the brilliantine and see the gleam of the patent leather and the glint of the spangles on the frontals as the light from the glitterball caught them and suddenly there they were, the saxes, alto and tenor, and above them the soft, mellow glow of the clarinets and he knew then that what he was hearing was indubitably the Sound, and who it was that was making it.

The old man put down his tube and wiped his lips.

"The Five O'clock Whistle," said the dethroned King of Swing. "Do you know what that's about?"

"Quitting time," said Pirandao, too filled with wonder to pluck any of the who? why? where? how? questions roosting in the high steel above him.

"Exactly," said the old man. He saw Pirandao looking at the cold blue ripples of the Lermontov Sea three kilometers below that were like the grooves in worn blue needlecord and shook his head. "That's not what I mean, boy. That's not what the music is about, throwing yourself off because you have lost everything else."

"Then what is it about?" Pirandao asked. "What other reason is there to come here?"

"To take the Sound to the only place left in the world where someone might remember it, might still care about it."

"Me?" Pirandao felt as if he had been asked to foster an orphan angel.

The aged aged man studied him with his little square glasses.

"And then, when it's safe, go back to the place where it came from."

"Where is that?"

The old man pointed, along the three thousand kilometer canyon of the Grand Valley, to the place where the hexagonal tiles of the glass roof touched the world's short horizon.

"Out there, boy. In the place where everything that is lost is found again. And when I've taken the music back, it'll live again. But I can't do it unless you help me."

"I'll take you," Pirandao said, surprising himself with his own decisiveness. "Wherever you need to take the Sound, I'll help you get there."

"It is no easy road," warmed the old man.

"It never is," said Pirandao.

It is not the falling that kills, Pirandao had learned, but the ground at the end of the final fraction of the final millimeter. If you could somehow contrive to miss the ground entirely, you could go on happily falling forever. And no one falls all at once. That was another thing Pirandao had learned. The Big Front Step is not the start of the fall, but the last part of it. When you come up the elevator that climbs the side of the roof pillar, you are falling. When you get up out of your comfortable chair one evening in the middle of the Daddy Cool Show and walk out of your house leaving your family open-mouthed around the wireless and make your way by rail and road and dirigible under the glass roof of Grand Valley, you are falling. You are falling the moment the little grit of discontent gets into your eye and before you can blink it away it tunnels up your optic nerve into your brain and germinates, sending roots and shoots of discomfort and dissatisfaction into every part of you.

Pirandao's fall from grace with the sky had begun when he let himself be seduced by the blue semiquavers of the Sound from his other love, the sky. She is a jealous bitch, the sky; she specializes in mighty falls. Gravity and altitude are her bulging-jacketed henchpersons. He had chosen far away places: the Great Desert, the Argyre Sea, the lonely, frosted wastes of the poles, in which to take out his trombone and try out a note or a slide of the Sound, but she heard, for hers was the body through which he slid, and she set about his fall.

It was a desperate mission. A mercy dash. The plague of sarcasm had struck the isolated town, and the quartersphere government, mindful of the terrible time when half of a hundred thousand people had gone down with the plague, had moved quickly to prevent the infection from spreading. Trains were diverted along rickety single tracks to by-pass the town. Vigilantes from Silent Orders of Cathrinists turned back trucks and buses with placards bearing the grim warning: QUARANTINE AREA: SARCASM INFECTION ZONE. The robot spy planes that daily flitted up and down the streets reported that no one had left their houses in five days for fear of attracting a sarcastic barb from their neighbors. What might be happening within those adobe walls; all those people, locked up together, able only to communicate by biting sardonicisms, could only be surmised. If they did not get an antidote soon, there would be no one left alive. In the advanced stages of the sickness, the sarcasm caused burns and long bloody lacerations on its victims' bodies.

The jokes on the pamphlets had been certified by a board of clinical psychologists and the North West Quartersphere Guild of Comedians to be medicinal grade; guaranteed to break the plague. But it would take a desperate, skillful pilot to get low enough, long enough, to make the drop. One stray sarcasm, biting home, and all could be lost. A desperate, skillful, broke pilot. Like Pirandao.

A desperate, skillful, broke, mad pilot, like Pirandao. It was the shortest route. They had said time was of the essence. So he had pointed the rounded nose of his transport dirigible Tuxedo Junction straight toward the White Heart of the Great Desert, where the pure white stone boiled back the heat and light of the sun into a dizziness of heat-haze and, in fighter-pilot's lore, storms were born that reached beyond the edges of mere meteorology and angelic creatures from long before the world was invented and long after it had ended dwelled in the eternal shimmering, where visions of St. Catherine in the company of strange, green, time-travelling persons could be had. Dark legends, but any other way Pirandao drew the lines on the tracker-globe in his control cabin it meant a dead town, so he tuned the radio to the last Swing station still beaming out of Meridian and picked up his trombone and let the autopilot do the flying while he played along with the King of Swing. Engrossed with his new love, he did not see the old one creep up outside his cabin window and gather into a tight knot of jealousy and anger: a black eye in the white heart. He did not see the storm until it broke around Tuxedo Junction and then it was too late to go under or over or round or behind it; anything but go right through it.

Pirandao knew the nature of his sin the moment that the winds caught his 'lighter and swung it like a farm-girl in a ring-dance around the spiral of black cloud, and against whom he had committed it. As the gas canopy ripped like an umbrella in a typhoon and he was flung at the center of the White Heart in a storming flock of flapping fabric and psychologically approved jokes he saw a face form around the eye of the hurricane. The last thing he remembered was being exceedingly surprised because it was not the face he had been expecting, which was the cool disdain of a scorned woman, but something more grand and complex, that sometimes seemed like a face and then again seemed like a machine and then again like a city, caught up in the clouds.

Pirandao fell, and the sky would not have him. But he kept the trombone, even after the last Swing stations everywhere went bust and the great music died, because in the middle of the storm, when he saw the vision, he had heard something too, that was like the Sound, but moreso: the original Sound, the perfect Sound that only God ever hears and wraps around his cochlea and keeps to Himself, tapping his Panarchic foot.

And now three kilometers up on the ledge outside the lighterpersons' hostel on Pillar 39, Pirandao said yes to the old man who had once set the world dancing and realized that he was being given that impossible chance: to fall, and miss the ground, and keep falling, keep flying, forever, around the curve of the world. His two lovers were giving him another chance, another permutation. If neither could win him, then perhaps they could live together, coiled into a comfortable, intimate troilism; the Sky, the Sound, and Pirandao.

This was the charter. Pirandao would fly the thing, and the old man would teach him the music. Being who he was, the aged aged bandleader had money—sewn in thousand dollar bank of Syrtis bills into the lining of his pissy coat, kept for this purpose. They smelled a bit, but not so unpleasantly as to be refused as tender for an off-the-peg dirigible from the catalogue at Hussein's High-Hat Hotel, where the broken and the busted and the burned sold their liabilities cheap. Those that still had liabilities to sell. What was left the old man offered Pirandao for passage, but Pirandao would touch not one centavo of it. The music was all the payment he desired, and a second chance with the sky. Everyone knows that in the art of seduction the thing is over forever the moment you offer money for love.

The 'lighter, the Taasmin Mandella, registered out of Bleriot, was a wretched bucket with flotation cells like the sad breasts of aged aged Deuteronomy woman, and a very bad attitude problem. On the old man's instructions, Pirandao rolled the tracking globe in its gimbals, yellow plains and green land-locked seas turning beneath his fingers until the red oval of the Great Desert came up with its white center of it where there were no names and no elevations and no populations and every road and rail line ended. He had always known, perched up on Pillar 39 with the old broken fliers and maimed singers, that his answers would only be found back in the hidden White Heart. He spun the brass-bound wheel, the antique fans grouched in their housings as Taasmin Mandella cast off from the main pylon and immediately dropped a pant-soiling fifty meters. Thereafter it made its journey listing eight degrees to port. By the time it swooped under the edge of the glass roof and headed out over the green plateau lands of Chryse, its passengers had psychologically realigned so that their decks were horizontal and it was the remainder of the universe that sloped gently to the right.

The long hours up in the gaseous reaches of the atmosphere with the colored cantons scrolling beneath the ventral docking ports were passed in the learning of the Sound, and, when Pirandao would set down his trombone, sore-lipped, in the old man's telling of his tale.

"You see," he said, "it was like I had been given not just a whole new life, but a whole new world, a billion pairs of ears listening out for something, never knowing it was the Sound, because they had never imagined there could be anything like the Sound. Not every man can say he conquered a whole planet."

It was marvelous, the way the world worked, he said. How one little note blown in the meanest corner of the darkest alley in the lowest level could make a stir in the air that drew others to it and swell it into a little breeze of tune, and into a howling wind blowing all before it and at last a twister of jive and jitterbug that raged across the plains and the wastelands and the valleys and deserts blowing every up into a tornado and good times and swing.

"There was always the talent, down in the under-tunnels. All it took was one person with the vision, the knowledge that it could be done, to bring them together and plant the seeds of the Sound in them. From there it was inevitable. If a thing was great once—doesn't matter how long ago, and I suspect it may be thousands of years—it will be great again.

"See friend, it has to be from here." The old man banged the side of his fist against his heart. "But it has to be from here too." He clutched the sagging crotch of his appalling pants. "That's the only way to play it, boy. Heart and hurdies. Not one, not the other; both. That's why the folk I met down on Bottom Alley could play it: down there, you've nothing else left. Now, that triple-tonguing exercise again."

Military beacon balloons were up around Becquerel so they detoured half a morning around the target area and watched from the cabin window the violet beams of the orbital partacs sign their names across the landscape in ideographs of glowing obsidian. The old man talked of the glory days, which are always the first days, when it can still surprise and delight people because it still surprises and delights you; the days before

you become product and fill sports stadiums and imagine that the source
of your stellar success is still the same magic it was back them, never realizing that it has stolen away and is riding some other poor, visionary kid
in the heat and sweat of the night.

"All it took was one," the old man said. "That's all it ever takes,
one. But to find that one, we had to blow our way through every bar
and dance-hall on Tombolova Street and when Tombolova Street said
leave your name and number we'll get back to you, we took it to Sorrowful Street and when Sorrowful Street shook its head and pursed its
lips and went back to polishing the glasses we took it down to Bread
Street below which there was no where else to take it, but we knew that
if we could make the old grays and goondahs dance in the downdraughts
from the air-conditioning ducts on Bottom Alley, we could make the
world do the same. It was the last bar on the last alley off Bread Street
that looked up from cooking the books and said, Okay, we'll give you a
try-out; one night a week.

"One; that's all it takes, friend.

"You should have seen us. We were major contenders. Major contenders. It was best then, you see, it was all new, all fresh born and
sticky and noisy and demanding. The girls would hitch up their skirts
and flash their sweet little cotton gussets at the boys on sax and the
clarinets would kick in eight over four and it was never that good again
because it was all just the same thing, but bigger, which is not better,
believe me in this, friend. When it's young and dangerous, that's when
it lives. I can't go back there again, I can't re-invent it. But maybe you
could take it back and blow it sweet down those alleys and tunnels miles
under Belladonna and see who looks up and follows it and gather the
lost and the lonely and the ones who will try it because they have absolutely nothing to lose."

Tilted at eight degrees to the world, they flew over villages and towns
that grew sparser and smaller as they entered the edgelands of the Great
Desert. The world turned its face from the sun and the musicians sat on

the flight bridge playing Elmer's Tune in two parts by the wan glow of the rising moons.

"I always wondered who was the Man in the Moon?" Pirandao asked. "I can get the rest, but what man, which moon?"

"I miss the moon," the old man said. "We had a proper moon, back then, back there, with a silvery light by which you could dance and sing and walk and spoon and turn into a wolf and do all those things that are supposed to be better by moonlight. And there was a man on it, folk thought, a big face looking down at us all, though it was just a pattern of light and dark rocks. Can't do anything by the light of those two chunks of stone up there, let alone have a man smiling in them."

"We have the moonring," Pirandao said as the heaven-bridge of orbiting construction material caught the light of the eclipsed sun and glittered with ten thousand thousand stars.

"Doesn't work if folk put it there," the old man said.

After a silent time, Pirandao commented, "I always reckoned something so great as the Sound had to come from another world than this."

"Come from a place a lot further than the place you call Motherworld," the old man answered. "A lot further away." He said nothing more on that or any other subject until morning, when Pirandao rolled out of his sleeping bag and pulled up the bamboo blinds and found that Taasmin Mandella had brought them in the night deep into the big red. They passed over a line of wind-weathered bluffs where once upon another story a town called Desolation Road had been born, lived, achieved world prominence and been carried off into legend. The 'lighter hung a moment in the air, then locked onto the parallel steel rails of the Bethlehem Ares Railroads trans-desert track that led straight and undeviating as an ambition into the heat haze where sky and Great Desert met and shook.

They followed that rail through the desert of red stone and the desert of red grit and the desert of red sand. They followed it through the desert of yellow sand and blue sand and green sand and black sand. They followed it through the desert of salt and the desert of soda and the desert of acid. The followed it through the desert of silence and the desert of stillness and the desert of fear and the desert of enlightenment. And as the shining steel rail drew them deeper and deeper into the Great Desert they sat in their wicker chairs and drank mint tea and played jumpin' jive and jizzy jitterbug and the old man talked about how one night a week had become two nights and then five nights and one club had become two clubs and five clubs and one band had become two bands and five bands playing the hot and sweaty and smoky jungle hop, that mad bad music that did such terrible things to responsible youth, like make them feel young, and happy, and horny, and like they could do anything they wanted, including change the world, and the music gone free to become popular, acceptable, and in the end, compulsory.

"That was the start of the end of it," the old man said. "When every household on the planet had a copy of your Moonlight Serenade album; that's the time you should be hanging up your horn. Because when it gets to that state, it's mighty easy to have it all up here," he touched his forehead, "but nothing here," he grasped the crotch of his gray pants, "and less than zero here." He gently pressed he palm of his hand to his heart. "That's why I'm taking it back now, so it can die, like a seed falling into the ground, and grow again, and people will be dancing to it forever, boy, forever."

And the automatic navigator gave it's little clockwork ting! and the engines stopped in their swivel mountings and Taasmin Mandella had come to the white heart of the big red, and the railroad line ended in a half-kilometer wide hemispherical crater of cracked green glass. "Toka-mak explosion," the old man said knowingly. Cabin radiation monitors flickered nervously off their rest positions as Pirandao followed the old man's directions in to land the 'lighter. Spring-loaded legs unfolded and curtseyed gracefully as the airship settled.

After adjusting to a world tilted at eight degrees, a steady horizon was disconcerting. It took many minutes for Pirandao's sense of balance to pull the land straight around him and dust itself neatly down. Beneath his boots the white land was as gritty as spilled salt. Wave upon wave of heat reflected onto him, adding their wave-fronts into a blast of sweat that instantly dried to a crust of salts and urea on his skin. The insides of his nostrils burned. Whichever way he turned the distance hid itself behind liquid curtains of heat-haze.

The old musician headed determinedly off into the haze and waved for Pirandao to follow. Pirandao walked after him until the dark shape of the grounded 'lighter folded up in curtains of mirage and he was alone with the silhouette of the old man waiting with the trombone under his arm.

"We thought we had all died and gone to heaven or hell, when in fact we were caught someplace in between, like the souls of those poor bastard aircrews who went up and got killed and never came down, who are still up there, trying to find the ground," the bandleader said. "We didn't understand, you see. It's the simplest thing in the world, really. When things get big, and I mean really big, they become something else. They go someplace else. They become too heavy for reality, it's not strong enough to hold them and they tear through, and a lot of things fall through with them, into that place underneath where all the big heavy things come to rest. "

The old man stopped and raised his hand, as if calling for silence. Surrounded by a trembling circle of white heat, he seemed to be listening. He walked a few paces more, cocked his head again. Listening. He closed his eyes and furrowed his forehead in concentration. His free hand unconsciously beat time to a secret rhythm only granted to his ears. The old man smiled, eyes still closed, and flicked up a definitive forefinger

"This is the place."

He lifted the trombone and, oblivious to the blisters the scalding mouthpiece raised on his lips, he threw back his head and ripped a triumphant, bluesy, comical flourish into the sky.

"Fanfare from 'The Boys from Syracuse'," he said, smiling a smile of private wisdom. "Before your time, boy. Before everyone's time, but mine."

He shuffled his feet ninety degrees to the left, raised his horn and blew another fanfare at the burning sky. Another ninety degrees, another trombone blast, another turn and a final clarion into the eye of the sun. It seemed to Pirandao that the notes hovered in the air, trapped in a state of harmonic resonance by the waves of reflected heat. He reckoned that if he stared long enough and thought hard enough about them he should be able to see them as half visible stave-lines formed out of the infinite regress between heaven and the white earth, in the same way that he had imagined as a kid that if he stared long enough at and thought hard enough about the sky, the floaters in the backs of his eyes would become the sheets and wings of Praesidium Sailships orbiting inconceivably high above him and the green glens of China Mountain.

The old man saw his frowning as he tried to read the sheet music at the heart of the things.

"You're not making them up," he said. "They're the truest things there are: it's the tune reality sings to itself, that I heard once, so clear, so long ago, and worlds away, and tried to make everyone else hear it too, through the Sound. But I could only capture an echo of it, I don't think anyone can play it like it really is."

"You made folk dance to it," Pirandao said.

"Hell, maybe the music I heard all that time ago was the Sound, the sound I made, that got so big that it broke through and now the whole damn universe is jiving to the tunes we made. Maybe what I heard was the echo going outward in time from the great music we would make." The old man looked into the sky in a direction that was not any combination of up or down or left or right or forward or backward, but inward. "The Sound always was and always will be. Here, in the center, where the big things break through and everyone exists together all at once, underneath time, they'll hear that fanfare I played and they'll come back for me." He laughed in a way that was more a spit, but gentle, as if spitting out the unused crotchets and quavers inside him. "Might as well sit. They'll be a while coming. They've a distance to go. Millions of years. Sit, take your ease and while I've the time I'll tell you the true story, the story at the very heart of it all, and then you'll understand."

The white stone was hot underneath Pirandao's bony ass. Like sitting down at the feasting table of the Hell of the Faithless, which is hot and the promised food never comes and the music is just awful.

"There was a war, you see," the old man said, laying his trombone across his folded legs and looking again into the clear sky. "It was a stupid war, but it wasn't us that made it stupid. But it was an important war, because the stupidity we were fighting was strong, and very cruel and tried to dress itself up as the ultimate wisdom. It was a big war. In those days, when they gave a war, everyone got invited whether they wanted to or not. So the music got a ticket like everything else, and the Sound too. It was slap-bang in the middle of the great days of the Big Bands—maybe that had something to do with it all too, the bigness of the Big Bands. Benny Goodman. Tommy Dorsey. Jack Teagarden. But the biggest and the greatest was the Glenn Miller Orchestra. Or Major Glenn Miller's Army Airforce Overseas Orchestra, which was what the war called us. 'I Sustain the Wings': the whole damn European theater, on both sides, used to tune into those radio shows we would do. More listeners than goddamn Churchill. 'I Sustain the Wings,' heh, that's an irony."

He took off his wire framed glasses, wiped the sweat from the lenses with a corner of his shirt and replaced them. As he did so Pirandao became aware of a dirty smudge on the twentypast-five corner of the sky, as if the smear had been transferred from the old band-leader's eyeglasses onto reality. The dark stain grew: it seemed to Pirandao to be not so much approaching as enlarging, as if pouring through from another place and spilling out like ink in water.

"Yep, it's coming," the old man said as if it were the most natural thing in the world, like a train or a country bus running a little late. "I'll have to be quick. England in December. Worst goddamn place in the world: fog and drizzle and gray clouds and the wet cold that gets into your bones and rusts the music in your marrow. But they'd liberated Paris, and the boys wanted a show. Demanded a show. I was quaint and simple back then: I was a true-blue Born-on-the-Fourth-of-July patriot. If the boys wanted the Sound, the boys would have the Sound—they deserved it, they'd fought their way across Normandy for it. Anyway, the band had gone on ahead; the AAF had laid on a DC3 just for me and a couple of colonels or something."

The darkness spilling out of the place beyond was now the size of Pirandao's hand held out before him against the burning sky. A wind from nowhere tugged at his flight jacket lapels and teased his dreadlocks.

"The fog!" the old man said. "I'd never seen anything like. If you can say that you can see fog. Closed in around us, couldn't get over the top of it, couldn't get under it either, it went all the way down to zero. And it wasn't like airships, my friend, we couldn't just shut down the engines, anchor and stick out warning beacons until it cleared. The kind of thing the AAF flew had to keep moving or it would fall out of the sky."

The darkness had now expanded to cover a third of the sky, and had swirled into a vortex at the center of which was a dead, white dot like the pupil of an eye seen in negative.

"I still don't know what it was brought us down; maybe a stray Focke-Wulf nightfighter on patrol over the Channel—they were still running them down from Belgium to harass Allied air transport; maybe we got hit by a flak ship—could even have been one of our own side—but all of a sudden there was a tremendous bang and we were going down and I was trying to find things to hold on to—damn fool thing, I know, but you do—and all I could hear was the pilot up front saying shit, shit, shit, shit, shit, shit, like the word was a propeller and if he got it fast enough it would pull us up and out, and the wind screaming over the metal and all the time I was trying to keep my glasses on because I had to see what the end looked like."

There was no sky now, only dark, boiling cloud. Pirandao knew what it was now, and where he had seen it before, and what the face was he had seen inside it, when he had been thrown from grace with the sky. The white eye at the cloud's center winked at him, and a speck of dirt tumbled out.

"It's coming," the old man said, standing up. "They heard me."

The hot wind had risen to a howl, driving eddies of white grit across the polished stone of the White Heart. The thing that had fallen out of the cloud drew close and passed over the two men. It was no small speck of dirt at all: that had only been a trick of distances. It was a big, sky-filling thing that outraged even the grand architecture of the desert. It was a thing made up of many things, a congregation-thing, a congruence of the flotsam and jetsam of whatever currents flowed beneath reality, glued together with the pathetic gravitation of the lost. There were pieces of ROTECH orbital manforming machinery and the kilometers-wide mechanical Angels of the Panarch. There were balloons and dirigibles and abandoned space stations and what looked like continent-sized sheets of light-sail all crumpled up. There were clockwork albatrosses and Flying Dutchmen in it; the inconceivable mass of it glittered with a hundred orbital mirrors and was gritty with dislocated skyscrapers and pyramids and temples: it was an airborne cosmopolis, a flying city made up of all the things that got too big for the mundane world.

"The Sound got too big, boy!" the old man shouted over the hot wind that roared across the desert." The Sound, the War, everything, and we fell through, into that!"

A small bright object detached itself from the underside of the hovering shadow and glided toward earth. It looked like a bird whose wings had been splinted straight and unmoving. It made a sad droning noise, as such a maimed bird would.

"I knew they'd come," the old man said. "I knew they'd come back for me, at quitting time. I should have died in that crash, back then, all those thousands of years ago, but I fell through and missed death. The five o'clock whistle, don't you see? I've been given time that wasn't mine, and I've spent it, and now it's time to quit. Time to go back again."

The flying thing passed over their heads, a droning cylinder of drab green metal balanced on those ludicrous stiff wings. Small wonder it had been so dangerous to fly, thought Pirandao, watching it tilt to one side into a descending circle.

"But it's death," he shouted as the machine lowered wheels from the bulges on its wings and thumped down onto the wind-scoured stone. "You're going back to die, to your grave."

"Back, forward, what's the difference?" the old man said. "It's knowing when the time is right. I always knew I'd been let out of the tomb on the condition that I return to it of my own free will, when the time was right. And at least I've done right by the Sound. I have to go back now; the thing that made me too heavy, I've passed on, and I shall rise back through the place underneath to my right place and time." The flying machine came to a halt a hundred and something meters away, nose tilted to the hovering dark mass of the lost things. A hatch opened in the air machine's side. A man in a peaked cap and a coat too heavy by far for the Great Desert leaned out and beckoned with his hand. He frowned, as if he were seeing something he had not expected. "I tell you something, Pirandao. I'm glad to be going back. It was good while it lasted, but in the end, the Sound grew too heavy for me. I was too old, too tired, too sick. You're young, you're wild enough to let it run where it will and lead you on into Sound like no one ever dreamed of before. Me, well, the five o'clock whistle's blowin'."

And the old man swung his trombone up under his arm and shuffled toward the open hatch in the hobbling, painful half-run of aged aged men, but it seemed to Pirandao that with every step he took his legs became firmer and his gait surer and his posture stronger as if the wind from beyond was blowing all his tired years from him. At the hatch he turned and waved and he was a gentle-faced middle-aged man with wire-framed glasses and a cherub's smile. The door closed. The air machine turned on its fat wheels, made a little, droning run into the wind blowing across the white stone pavement and, to Pirandao' vast surprise, heaved itself into the sky. He watched it climb toward the flying city of heavy things and disappear into the mass of buildings and spaceships and miracles. He watched the flying city pass over him, kilometer after kilometer of it, for many many minutes, and recede back into the eye of the storm, and the eye wink once more at him and close. He watched the clouds boil and moil and coil back until they covered half the sky, then the size of his outstretched hand, then the tip of his upheld thumb, then disappear and the sun shone unchallenged and brutal on the Great Desert. At the White Heart of it, Pirandao noticed shadows in the shivering veils of heat-haze: the faithful Taasmin Mandella. Quitting time.

As he walked toward the dirigible, kicking at the little drifts of loose white grit, a tune came into his head in a place where he had never heard a tune before. Neither was it any tune he had ever heard before, but it reminded him a thousand things while being not precisely any of them. It was grand tune, a hummable tune, a danceable tune that put a little jump is your step so . And so. It might even be a great tune, with a bit of work. Once he got airborne, he would have to get the horn out and give it a try.

destination unknown
LULLABY OF BIRDLAND

by Kathleen Ann Goonan

It was cold in Boston and getting colder by the second. The wind was blowing a hundred miles an hour and spitting pure ice. As Sarah huddled inside her thin windbreaker and strode down the street, she felt as if her nose was about ready to fall off her face. Or maybe it already had. But she couldn't go home, not just yet. She'd about slammed the door to pieces when she'd left. No, she might never go back.

But she was freezing. It had been balmy when she'd left, several hours ago, but while she'd fumed in the coffee shop, newspapers began to skitter by on the sidewalk, people started to button their coats, and dark clouds massed. No, it wasn't spring yet.

Dekeiper's Books. Must be a new place. *And Coffeeshop,* continued the sign.

Great. Maybe she could find some odd book she could use to append her student's reading list. She was a philosophy professor at a small college. No phone call from the big guys begging her to come on-line yet. Or ever, now, she was afraid. She went down the narrow flight of stairs and ducked inside.

Her glasses misted over instantly. She took them off and saw only a blur of vertical, colorful lines, but the aroma of coffee was sharp and strong.

"Hello," said a man's voice. "Can I help you?"

She wiped her glasses and put them on, but they misted again in patches. He perched behind a counter on a tall stool. Wild, straight hair stuck up in a uniform burr around his head, pitch black, like he'd studied every avant garde layout he could find, then slicked himself into the image. Sarah contrasted him with Dan, a rapidly aging jazz musician and composer with a few odd jobs—very few, since he had a reputation for undependability—and some royalty checks coming in. Dan's hair was light brown and straggled into olive green eyes she knew as both kind and obtuse. He'd been looking more and more gaunt and disheveled in the past few months. Looking like an old man.

As her glasses cleared, she saw that the clerk's black hair was speckled with gray. He looked up from his hunched position on the stool and put his book face down on the counter. *Para-Info Realities*. Suddenly Sarah felt as if she was probably drooling.

"Where did you get that?" she asked.

"Aisle four," he said. "I think there are three more copies." Then he looked at her more closely. "Don't I know you from somewhere?" She could feel his eyes touch each freckle, trace her cheekbones. She looked down for a moment, feeling her cheeks grow hot. She found it odd that he would examine her so carefully. Her face had become completely transformed into one which Dan claimed "had character." She looked younger than forty-three, but not much.

"Hmm," he said. "I don't know."

And, as she looked at him, she felt that she didn't quite know, either. He had looked young from a few feet away, but close up his face showed signs of weathering—wrinkles fanned out from the eyes, behind black wire-rim glasses. His brown eyes held a hint of gold. He smiled.

"Well, we'll see," he said, and abruptly raised his book once more. "Aisle four, remember?"

As Sarah turned and walked into the interior of the store, enveloped by classical music, she felt annoyed but couldn't quite figure why.

She was even more annoyed when she had to use a credit card for her books, including one she special ordered by filling out a card which included her address and phone number. Her charm bracelet clinked as she wrote. "That's nice," the man said. "I didn't think anyone wore them any more."

"It was my mother's," she said, and tried to relax her scowl. She hated credit cards. She hated owing money. This just reminded her of the overdrawn bank statement, which was why she had stormed out of the apartment. Dan had completely wiped them out, and she hadn't even known it until the mail came. It wasn't the first time.

"I don't know what kind of drugs you're doing," she raged, "but I'm sick and tired of it. Look at you! You're a skeleton. You should be on the phone every single day about your royalty checks. Have you sent a single certified letter? There's a world, Dan. Things move in the world. The squeaky wheel gets the grease. I guess I'm stuck with you for the rest of my life." And then she'd said the most cruel thing—"You're just a has-been. Why don't you face it and get a real job instead of hanging out with those low-life friends of yours. `Musicians.' Hah!"

He'd been crying when she left. Bitch, she thought. You're really going to have to think of a more constructive way to deal with this. Then she sighed. So much work. So hard.

The man startled her by saying, "Sarah Tyne? The philosopher?"

"What?" she asked, dumbfounded.

"Look," he said. "I have your book here. I know it's ten years old, but I read it every so often. Usually right before spring, for some reason. I'm reading it now. I thought I'd seen you somewhere. You don't look much older than your picture." He reached under the counter and pulled it out. "Will you sign it for me?"

"Good God," she said, as she scribbled inside the cover. "What's your name?" He put a card next to her pen. "Michael? Dekeiper. Your store. It's a good one. I think there were only about 300 copies of this. I'm always afraid one of my students might run across it and use it to ridicule me."

"I think it's wonderful," he said. "You were really onto something."

"Well, I'm not any more," she said. "Something happens to your brain when you get old."

"You're not old," he said.

"Don't make me laugh," she said.

θ θ θ

Sarah, heavy laden with books, clumped up the dark stairs of the old apartment. The two bags had a coating of snow.

"Dan," she called, after unlocking the door. "Hey, honey, I'm sorry. Come and see what I found."

The high ceilings were dark with twilight shadows. He must be in the bedroom. She passed the table in the window alcove which served as a dining room and the kitchen, floored with peeling green linoleum, and glanced around the bedroom.

He wasn't there.

For a moment, she felt strangely empty.

She became aware of a periodic hiss/click, hiss/click; went back to the living room and saw that on what she called the sound wall, stuffed with electronic equipment, his grandfather's trusty old Victrola was on. Only used during times of extreme duress. The wooden lid was up; he'd left a 78 playing. The armlift mechanism had been broken for years.

She reached inside and put the needle to the beginning. It was Jerry Mulligan covering Shearing's Lullaby of Birdland. She hung up her coat and sang along with the saxophone:

Lullaby of Birdland
Kiss me sweet
Then we'll go
Flying off to Birdland,
High
In the sky
Up above.
We're in love.

Yes. That's what her old sweetheart had always wanted. To go flying off to Birdland via music, love, or drugs. Leaving her to do the work. But he was pure, she had to admit. He had beauty and depth, damn him all the more for not honoring it.

LULLABY OF BIRDLAND

She shivered and looked around. The window by the table was open and frigid air rushed in, scattering some papers. She had left the window open, she remembered, because when she left it had been so warm. Dan must have left soon afterwards in a maudlin mood, probably fueled by a few shots of whisky or, she was afraid, a shot of heroin. Maudlin, because they had first danced together to Lullaby. How long ago? Ten, fifteen years?

She went over and closed the window, turned on the little table light, and paused while the music spun out and the clicking began once more.

The paper she had been working on, periodically, for the past five years, was scattered in the pool of light on the green oilcloth. A red pen lay there too, its top off, and she pushed it back on, exasperated. Dan ruined every pen he got hold of.

She'd been trying to smooth the thoughts in her paper lately, make it cohere. She had to publish something. She wasn't just worried about tenure at this point. She was worried about keeping her job, crummy as it was trying to stuff The History Of Philosophy down the throats of engineering students.

Hadn't she left her paper on the nightstand? Surely Dan wouldn't have read it, but how else did it get out here? She shuffled the papers together and put the salt shaker on top of them.

A small brown bird lit on the feeder stuck to the window, but it was empty. "Can't do anything, can you?" she asked Dan. That was supposed to be his job. He loved birds. The movement of flocks was as beautiful to him as music. She'd often watched him observe them. She loved the rapt look on his face. There were so many sweet things about him, and so many crummy things, she reminded herself.

She bent and grabbed a handful of seeds from the bag of feed from the floor, loosed it into the feeder, and shut the window. She watched snow swirl. After a few minutes the bird came back, cocked his head, and perched on the feeder. Before he ate, he stared at her as if wondering what she was. She shivered and didn't know why—an unbirdlike look, to be sure.

She turned her back on the bird, went to the living room, and lit the gas fire. The orange-and-ash-painted logs hissed and flamed blue. She turned off the Victrola, switched on the lamp by the threadbare couch, and dumped out her haul. Dan wouldn't like these anyway.

Even *Para-Info Realities?* she wondered, as she opened it. It looked like something she could work into her curriculum. She was always trying to find new things to help with her teaching, get her students excited. In a good year she might manage to subvert one potential engineer, but it was slim pickings in more ways than one. It was time, way past time, to make a move. Dan's crazy life, which drained her as much as it drained him, could no longer serve as an excuse for being so stalled. She remembered the early days of her teaching, when she'd done a few semesters at good schools, where the graduate seminars seemed to glow with the light of thought. Then they'd moved to Boston because it looked like Dan's jazz career was going to take off. Her competition here was pretty damned stiff. And his career never had taken off.

As she stared at the fire, her right hand went to her charm bracelet. Absently, her fingers told them off, a soothing rosary, over fifty of them, double-layered: the ivory elephant, the silver lightning bolt, the Japanese geisha—friends since childhood, when she'd found it in the attic. Her fingers paused on a shape they did not recognize, and she raised her wrist, unhooked the bracelet.

She held the unfamiliar charm to the light.

It was a bird.

Suddenly she felt guilty. Dan must have added it to her bracelet as a present for last week's birthday and she'd never even noticed it. What a jerk she was. Maybe that was where the money had gone. Typical of Dan. He was so impulsive.

It was silver, beautifully detailed, wings spread in flight. It even had some sort of green jewels for eyes. Real emeralds? Probably. The more expensive the better. She sighed, but wished he'd hurry home so she could apologize. That, though, was an unlikely prospect. When he went

on a binge sometimes he didn't come home for days. When they first met, she religiously searched smoky bars, tiny jazz dives, the places where the Sunday afternoon jams took place; she knew them all. She'd call his friends, track him down, bring him home, take care of him. She hadn't realized then that he would never change, that he couldn't. He'd been on the high road to success, then—even played at Newport one summer. But somehow it had never jelled. Two albums sank like stones.

She looked at the bird again and thought, how wonderful it would be to fly. To an entirely new horizon. Sure, Sarah. Well, to an entirely new event horizon, anyway.

An odd thump woke her from her reverie. She glanced around, but couldn't tell where it had come from. Probably the elephants who lived upstairs.

She went into the kitchen and put the red kettle with white roosters on the stove to boil water for tea. Dan had picked the kettle up at a garage sale. The lid had patches of rust on it, but he seemed to like things like that, and she'd learned to put up with them. Gray winter twilight spilled in the window and merged with the grayness of Spike, their cat.

"Get off the table!" she said, and Spike glared at her from next to the salt shaker before he stood, arched his back, and jumped to the floor.

She switched on the light over the porcelain sink and poured boiling water into the cup, went back to the living room, and started to read.

The words entered her mind, seemed so direct and intense that when she looked up she was amazed to see that three hours had passed as if they had been minutes. That was the way it was with her and philosophy. She looked down at the page again; the typeface was fine and sleek, maybe that was it, that was what moved her mind down the page, on and on into... what?

She felt dizzy, stood, stretched, and saw that there were several more inches of snow on the sill. She looked closer, and saw fresh claw footprints in the snow. Was that the bird, that shadow huddled next to the rough bricks? Was it dead? She remembered the thump. Hours ago.

She yanked the window open and grasped the feathered bundle, careful not to crush its frail bones. She thought she could feel a faint heartbeat, and set it on the table while she turned to slam the window. She shivered in the cold blast. According to the thermometer it was five degrees and the wind must be blowing at least ten miles an hour.

When she turned back, she saw Spike's gray head. He laid his white front paws one at a time on the table while standing on the chair. He stared at the bird with huge golden eyes.

"No!" she said, and he whirled and ran.

She picked up the bird and held it in both hands.

After a moment it stirred and opened its eyes.

They were round and small, and the color of Dan's. Odd. She didn't know birds had green eyes, but then she didn't really know much about birds.

It staggered on the table and flapped its wings once, weakly. Then it hunkered down and closed its eyes.

She wasn't sure what to do. She couldn't leave it out with Spike around, but she didn't have a cage.

Finally she decided she could leave it in the huge, old-fashioned bathroom. She set him on the floor, closed the toilet, then closed the door. She'd have to leave a note telling Dan to make sure to keep the door shut.

What time was it, anyway? Midnight, and Dan wasn't home yet. No big surprise there.

She looked out into the courtyard, lit by a single street-light. A few bare trees stood dim and spidery in the dense swirl of snow. Six inches at least already.

Sarah went into the bathroom again. The bird was standing on the floor and she wondered if perhaps it had a broken wing. It was hard to tell. She didn't know anything about birds. Maybe it had just been stunned by hitting the window. She should probably let it go but it was so cold and horrible out. She messed a towel into a kind of nest on the floor and set him on it. The beat of his heart seemed slow, for a bird.

Moving carefully so as not to startle it, she put her book down on the floor next to the claws of the bathtub and turned on the water. It steamed and she switched on the space heater. Everything began to look a little different, oddly proportioned, from another world; it always did when she was tired.

She must have dozed in the bathtub, for when she woke the room was dark, yet a light blazed in the window.

She sat forward, and the water glimmered softly around her legs and where it dripped from her hands.

She rose swiftly and looked out the window.

The light was dim, and indeterminate in shape. Then it coalesced into Dan though she did not know how, and vanished.

The light over the sink came back on. The wiring in this old apartment was fire hazard stuff, but the landlord had the fire marshall in his pocket.

Sarah stepped out of the tub, grabbed a towel, and ran to the phone.

"Jerry," said Sarah, when Dan's friend answered the phone. "Is Dan with you?"

"Jeez, Sare, what time is it?" he asked.

She looked at the clock. "Three?"

"No, he's not here. Haven't seen him." Jerry hung up.

θ θ θ

YOU NEED TO CALL ME WHEN YOU GET IN, Sarah printed with a large black Magic Marker. WHY CAN'T YOU HAVE THE COURTESY TO LET ME KNOW WHERE YOU ARE? I WORRY. AND THERE'S A BIRD IN THE BATHROOM—DON'T LET IT OUT. She capped the pen, took a step, turned, uncapped it and added, I LOVE YOU. She checked the seeds and water she had put in the bathroom, left the note on the kitchen table, and slammed the door behind her.

The streets were slick, shiny black under patches of ice. The sky was still heavy and snow spat; swirled from roofs. She walked to the end of the block and went down the steps to the train.

It was snowing so much that afternoon classes were canceled. It was the last day before Spring Break, so she had ten days off. Good. Maybe she could wrest at least one paper out of that god-awful monster of a manuscript.

She had just unwrapped her ice-encrusted scarf and put her gloves on the steam radiator when someone knocked at the door.

She opened it and looked out through the chain.

It was the man from the bookstore.

"Ms. Tyne?" he said.

She felt flustered. "What are you doing here?" she asked.

"I'm sorry," he said. "I didn't mean to—bother you. I guess I just should have called. But I found that book you wanted in the back, and you said something about wanting it for a class—"

"Did I?" she asked. She didn't remember saying anything.

But he looked cold, and she was long past the age when she listened to the little voice in her head—her mother's—regarding strangers. This guy seemed all right.

"Why don't you come in for a minute?" she said.

"Well—" he grinned—"I was hoping you'd ask."

She unhooked the chain and he came in.

When he took off his coat and she looped it over the coat tree, she saw that he was a larger, more rangy man than she would have thought after seeing him hunched over on the stool at the bookstore. He was wearing jeans and heavy workboots, and a black turtleneck sweater.

"Do you want some tea?" she asked. "I was just getting ready to make some. Sit down."

She went into the kitchen and added another few spoons of Earl Grey to the pot and poured boiling water over it. When she came back into the living room, which was simply furnished with just a comfortable

couch facing the fireplace, a hand-woven rug, and two chairs, he was over at the sound wall.

"Are these records all yours?" he asked. He'd slid one out. "Do you mind?" he asked.

"Just be careful," she said. "They're my husband's." She watched him closely, but he didn't seem to have any reaction to her mention of a husband. She relaxed.

"*Sing, Sing, Sing.* Do you know how much this is *worth*?"

"Vaguely," she said dryly. Dan had spent a fortune on his collection.

He slid it back in. He peered into the Victrola. "*Birdland*, eh? Ever been to the Yardbird's place?"

"I'm not *that* old," she laughed. "I was just a kid."

"No, I mean, walk by the place where it used to be. I did once, on a real dreary day. What does your husband do?"

Drugs, she almost said, but then she said, "He's a jazz musician. Dan Hurleson. Ever heard of him?"

"As a matter of fact, yes. Didn't he write 'Sunman?' He plays in local clubs, doesn't he?"

Sarah set the tray down on the table by the couch. "Sometimes," she said. "What there are of them." When he can. "I'm surprised you've heard of him."

"I keep up," he said. "I like jazz. I'd like to meet him. What a couple. A philosopher and a musician."

"Yes," she said. "What a couple." She ignored his look, questioning in the face of her obvious sarcasm which she immediately regretted—he was a stranger, after all—and poured two cups of tea. "Here," she said. "Sit down for a minute." She didn't really want him staying too long. She had work to do.

He leaned forward, put his elbows on his knees, and blew on his tea. "But really, I wanted to talk to you a bit. I hope you don't think I'm too forward or anything, but I have a small—a very small—line of books. Just things that really interest me. I have a pretty strong clientele, and I can usually get them interested too. I was wondering if I could print a collection of your papers."

Sarah wondered why she'd never run across his store before. She thought she knew them all. But Boston was a big city, and she'd been so angry, she recalled yesterday, that she'd just jumped on a bus and ridden at random to a part of town she hadn't been to often.

"I don't have much of anything new," she said. Only about a thousand pages' worth of nonsense. Nonsense written at two or three in the morning, when it seemed like a white fire was rushing through her, and Dan was either sleeping or away, and solitude coaxed and solidified ideas out of the very air. That kind of nonsense.

"Do you mind if I use your bathroom?" he asked.

"No. It's right down the hall."

He got up and walked past the kitchen.

"Oh, be careful," she said. "There's a bird in there. I don't want the cat to get it."

"I saw the note," he said.

He came out in a moment holding the bird. "I think it might have a broken wing. Do you have a popsicle stick or something? I can splint it."

He took it over to the table and she rummaged through drawers to find the things he wanted.

"Is it a sparrow?" she asked over her shoulder.

"I'm not sure," he said. "I really don't know much about birds, to tell you the truth. What's this?" he asked, as he pushed her manuscript aside to make room for the bird.

"Oh, nothing," she said. She spied a white plastic carryout knife and pulled it out of the drawer. She held it out to him but he was staring at the papers.

"Something you wrote."

"Yes, but—"

"Do you mind if I read it?"

She shrugged. "I guess not. I can print you off another copy. That one's kind of messed up."

"I'm sure it will do," he said.

"Get away, Spike," she said, and stomped her foot. He disappeared into the bedroom.

Michael's hands, as he spread out the wing, were gentle and steady. Not like Dan's shaking hands, steady now only when he was playing the saxophone. She glanced over in the corner and saw that it was gone, breathed a sigh of relief. Maybe he was playing somewhere. He hadn't just gone out to score, or drink, or make sure that some Emergency Room nurse called her at two in the morning. The last time had been so horrible. They'd had to put a tube in his stomach and when she got there he was mumbling and shaking his head from side to side on the white paper-covered pillow, which crunched each time he turned his head. She'd tried to help, she'd tried, really she had, but there was only so much a person could do....

"Hmm," he said. "Maybe it's not broken after all. But I wonder why he didn't fly?" He looked at her. "Are you all right?"

She looked up into his brown eyes, which were genuinely kind. She looked back at the bird and wondered why she felt like crying. It was just a bird.

"I'm just tired. You know." She tried to laugh and it came out shaky.

For an instant he looked straight into her eyes and what she saw was weird. Distance, intensity, beneath the seeming warmth. An almost... she searched for a word... alien angle to what might be called his thoughts, or his being, mirrored there in his eyes. Alien simply in the sense of his point of view being quite unique, different from the way most people saw things.

"I'm sorry," he said. "Is there anything I can do?"

She shook her head.

He picked up the bird. Don't drop him, she thought. He put it back in the bathroom, shut the door. He looked at his watch. "I'd better get back," he said. "Janet gets off at five, and then it's just me and the books. Not that I think many people will be in tonight."

"Thanks," she said, as he put his coat on and buttoned it. He picked up the manuscript and put it in one enormous pocket.

"Oh," he said, and smiled. "I almost forgot." He pulled out a book. "The one you ordered."

She took it. "Thanks," she called, as he went downstairs.

She laid it absently on the table and sat down next to the phone. She practically had the numbers memorized. The usual list. Police, hospitals, friends.

No Dan.

The weather was so bad. He could have passed out in an alley somewhere; who would notice. If only she hadn't yelled at him yesterday. She began to toy with the charm bracelet, then froze.

There was a new charm on it. A tiny book.

She brushed her thumb across it. The cover felt like leather. The best charms were so realistic. The ones which had been her mother's were wonderful, precise. An old-fashioned three-wheeled bike on which the pedals and wheels moved. A typewriter with five keys which brought letters to the platen. Marvels of intricacy.

Where had *this* come from? she thought, I've been thinking the past month about a book, a book, a book, gotta get that book together and now this very strange man, and this tiny charm-bracelet book. Could it have been here all along, one of these fifty antique charms which crowded the chain?

Suddenly it seemed like her life had changed, crossed some threshold. Before it had been as solid, as unchanging as an oil painting. Now its edges wavered like a delicate watercolor, spreading into an odd space which she didn't understand.

Some more lines from *Lullaby of Birdland* ran through her head as she stood up and pulled on her boots:

Then there's a weepy old willow
He really knows how to cry

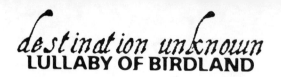

That's how I'll cry on my pillow
If you should tell me farewell and good-bye.

That's what she'd been getting ready to tell Dan, wasn't it? Of course he knew. No wonder he was off to Birdland again. Maybe he'd just stay away forever, like he'd threatened so many times.

Her hand was on the doorknob when she went back and checked on the bird.

He was there, huddled in the corner. You've already got a pet, Sarah. You don't need another one. This is a wild bird. You're going to let it go when the weather turns.

She closed the door firmly and left.

ø ø ø

That night it was hard to sleep. She'd been everywhere Dan might have been and discovered new networks of friends and acquaintances. Some of which she'd rather not have been aware. People who were more than shady: mean and hard. Why did Dan have to deal with them? What had she done to force him into this life? She examined herself and was appalled to find an enormous storehouse of things she had done. Guilt, woman, guilt. Don't let guilt get you. He's a difficult man. He's got addict-genes. You can't do everything. She tramped through the icy city until well after dark and came home exhausted. Dan had been gone for far longer before, but something was different this time. She could feel it. The world felt odd and hollow; the night, spitting snow, was the night of a strange netherworld, not her familiar Boston.

Before she went to bed she printed off her paper again, to give her mind some surcease. What was she trying to say in this paper? Something about thought and matter and perception, something cool, grand, rational, and fundamental. Something about reality. Something about how thought controlled reality, about how matter must be more fluid than it seemed. She absently braided back her long dark hair, with its recent streaks of gray, as the thoughts in the paper peaked and ebbed, peaked and ebbed. She kept the bracelet in her left hand, her rosary, and rubbed the little book between thumb and forefinger: Success, or at the very least, something new. She sat in her robe on the couch a long time, scribbling in the margins, with a cup of peppermint tea cooling on the table next to her, before she fell asleep with the light on, the bracelet clenched in her hand.

θ θ θ

The next day she ran the messages on the phone tape back, hoping for a clue. There was one, three days ago.

"Mr. Hurleson, please call the lab. Your test results are in."

Sarah called the number. "Hello?" she said. "This is Sarah Tyne. Dan Hurleson's wife. My husband had a message to call you."

There was a pause. "I'm not allowed to give out information."

"You've already given out information. It's on my answering machine. I need to know what kind of test he had."

There was a longer pause. "Sorry, ma'm, but I'm not allowed to give you that information."

"I'm his wife," she said. "Not only that, but he's missing. Is this an AIDS test? What is it? It might have something to do with him being missing. I need to know."

"I'm sorry," she said with all the inflection of an automaton. "That's the law."

Sarah wrangled with her and with her supervisor for fifteen minutes before she finally hung up. Her imprecations had been mighty but the information hoarders had been unmoved in the face of The Law. "Shitheads!" she finally yelled, and slammed down the phone.

She slid down the doorjamb until she was sitting on the floor. Then she curled up tight and began to sob—harsh, strong sobs which shook her body.

"Dan," she whispered. "Oh, Dan."

0 0 0

She was still on her robe, lying on the couch, when the knock on the door came later. She rushed to the door and opened it.

It was Michael.

He looked at her. "I'm sorry. Is this too early for you?" He held a sheaf of papers.

"Yes," she said. "No. I don't know."

He looked at her more closely. "You've been crying," he said. "What's wrong?"

She opened her mouth, then burst into tears again.

He held her for a long time while she cried. He didn't say anything. Finally he walked her inside, shut the door, led her to the couch, and made her sit.

Outside, the sky was gray and gloomy. Snow was starting to fall again. He looked at her for a moment, then asked, "Have you eaten anything today?"

"I'm not hungry."

"Tea," he said.

Spike followed him into the kitchen, tail undulating. She heard him rummaging in the cabinets. "It's on the counter," she said. "Next to the sugar."

Michael stood in front of her. The cup he gave her warmed her hand. He looked very apologetic. He sat across from her.

"I'm sorry to bother you. I seem to just barge in. It's just that something very strange happened to me last night when I was reading your paper. This is very intense stuff that you've written. But we can talk about that later. What's wrong?"

She took a sip of tea. She took another. "Dan's gone," she finally said. She took a deep breath. "Not only is he gone, but I'm afraid... I think he had an AIDS test. Well, it didn't have to be that. But it was some sort of medical test. I came across a message a few days old from a lab.

They wouldn't tell me."

"Sarah!" he said, and the depth of the concern in his voice surprised her.

"Oh," she said. "I have nothing to worry about. It's rather... sad, but Dan and I haven't had sex for—what is it now? Three years?" She shrugged. "An odd marriage, I suppose. I don't think that he's gay, but who knows. More likely it would be the needles."

"Needles?"

"He's been looking very bad lately, but I thought that was mainly because he's a drug addict." She pulled her legs up on the couch and folded her arms tightly. "I've tried to get him to stop, but you don't know how hard it is...."

He continued to look straight at her. "My mother was an alcoholic. I have some sort of an idea. You must feel terrible, though. Maybe I should leave you alone."

"No," she said. "I'm hungry. Why don't I get dressed and we can go out and get something to eat."

"Have you called the police or anything?"

"Of course," she said as she walked down the hall to the bedroom. "It's nothing new for the police, ho hum, Dan Hurleson isn't home again? Is he ever? It's nothing new for him. For us. Do you mind waiting? I think I need a bath." Hot water on skin. An automatic soother.

She flicked on the bathroom light; it was a very gloomy day. The bird hopped around while she cleaned up clots of birdshit with toilet paper and ran the water. He opened his mouth and cheeped. She felt relief; the room glowed for a second. Maybe he'd be okay.

In the hot bath, she wondered. Where was Dan? Did he think she wouldn't want to take care of him? She couldn't blame him. There were some relatives in Upper State New York she could call; perhaps he'd headed there.

She watched the small brown bird break seeds with its beak, twist its neck and look at her quizzically. She wondered how long it would take for the wing to heal, or for it to fly. Didn't Michael think the wing was okay? She wondered what she was going to do. And really, what was this character in her living room up to, anyway? For all his niceness, she felt a bit uneasy about him. Did he really publish books? What did he want with her? Her thin, pale body floated in the water until it was lukewarm, then she got out and dressed.

"Feel better?" he asked, when she came out.

She shrugged. "A little. Listen, maybe you'd better—"

"You've reconsidered. You want me to leave," he said. "I don't blame you. You don't even know me. But I hate to leave you alone. Why don't we just go ahead and eat and then I'll leave. Besides, I have something I want to talk to you about."

At a little Thai restaurant down the block relaxation finally hit as she drank her second glass of cheap white wine. "I'm just so terribly tired of my job," she admitted, when he asked. "I'd had—oh, bigger plans. Like everybody, I guess. Now I'm forty-three and it seems like I haven't done what I wanted to do. You know, change the world. Deflect the relentless march of embryo illuminating engineers into the joyous world of abstract thought. As if I knew what was best for them. The usual."

"I know," he said. "It shows in your philosophy."

"How could it?" she asked.

He smiled. "I know what you mean. It is terribly abstract. In fact, Sarah," his face became more serious, "it's like an exquisite landscape with no *people* in it. But *something* comes through. Quite a lot, I'd say." He'd said people like it was the most important word ever, with great gravity and reverence.

"But it's almost like the intensity of what you're thinking could change the world," he continued. "Could change matter. That's part of it, isn't it—that matter and consciousness are connected in a very fundamental way? That will and intent actually do interface directly with matter? It's all in that little book, the core of something absolutely new. I read it again last night. It's almost like religion." He said *religion* like it was something good.

"I know," she said. "It's embarrassing. You want to be objective, and look what happens." She made a face. "I guess that's why I've never published much. I can't change the way I think. What I think is why I went into philosophy. But no matter how logically I approach it, what I think doesn't make sense."

"I disagree. It's just very obscure and unexpected. And I think in this case something very strange happened. What was that quote from Derrida that opens the book? 'Within the horizon of the true,' is that it? What is the horizon of the true?" His eyes were very intense.

A feeling. But more than a feeling. Something concrete, palpable. *Visible.*

She grinned briefly. "Read on. But I think you'll find that even within the horizon of the true, what I'm trying to say is something rather twisted." She brushed her hair back and her charm bracelet clinked. "I guess I'll never really get anywhere. Just like Dan."

"But you love him."

She raised her eyes to his. "Yes. I do."

They ate in silence for a moment then he said, hesitantly, "This is the odd thing I wanted to talk to you about. I found something at the store this morning, next to the cash register." He reached into his shirt pocket and brought it out.

"It's a charm," she said, and put down her fork. She took it from his hand. "It looks like a St. Christopher. I think it is. He's the one that carries the Christ Child across the river on his back." It was gold, and beautifully detailed. As detailed as her new bird.

"That's who I think it is," he said. "I remembered your bracelet and I thought you might want it," he said. "I don't know. Maybe somebody lost it in the store, or something. But I closed last night and it wasn't there, and no one was in the shop last night. Of course, someone must have been, and dropped it there, or maybe it was there before and I

didn't notice it. But it was such an odd coincidence. Last night after I read your paper for several hours, I felt... well, I felt that somehow all my hopes and dreams, all my innermost desires, whatever they may be—that's certainly not very clear to me—were on the verge of becoming reality. I'm telling you, it made me feel a little crazy. Oh, it's not your paper's fault, I'm sure. Maybe I've just become a little unhinged lately. Kind of like you. I have this store, I have this press and where is it going...? Anyway, I picked up one of those old Catholic philosophers—I guess it was St. Augustine, to kind of settle my mind, and while I read St. Christopher came to mind, the image of a dangerous river, and a new shore. He was so real. But then, I had one of those horrific Catholic childhoods that happen to randomly selected children, and he always appealed to me. He seemed like such a nice guy."

She didn't say anything about the silver bird or the tiny book. She just looked at St. Christopher. "Thanks," she said finally, and put it in a little zipper pocket in her purse. St. Christopher, eh? He probably bought it, and cooked up this sweet little tale. But, she wondered, how would one represent, with just an image, a new and wondrous shore? How would she choose to do it? St. Christopher was perfect.

Oh, well. No more wine for you tonight, girl.

Michael kept looking at her. Finally he said, "Sometimes you have to trust other people, you know?"

"This curry is very hot," she said, and drank her whole glass of water at once.

θ θ θ

Evening was a hail of iceballs rattling the window. Spike meowed plaintively in front of the bathroom door, shaping his request carefully and persistently. "The bird," he meowed. "The bird. Give me the bird. I want the bird."

"Be quiet, Bozo," she finally told him.

She had changed into her nightgown and tossed on a robe on. She was wrapped in a blanket on the couch, but she couldn't concentrate on the book she had in her hand.

She called all the hospitals in the area again, but it was no use. Even the two unidentified men bore no resemblance to Dan. He seemed to have dropped off the face of the earth.

"We're going to sleep in the bed tonight," she told Spike. "I don't know about your neck, but mine is still stiff."

Michael came into her mind briefly before she slept. She dreamed of raging rivers all night long.

θ θ θ

She was awakened the next morning by the phone. Dully, she picked it up.

"This is Lorenzo."

"Lorenzo?"

"Yeah. You know. The pawn shop."

"Oh. Yes."

"Well, Dan left his saxophone here again a few days ago."

"He did?" Pawning his saxophone was something Dan had done since before she'd met him, but her comforting picture of him playing somewhere vanished.

"Yeah, well, this time somebody's here and wants to buy it. It's like they gotta have it, it's the Great Wonder Of The Jazz World Silver Saxophone or something. Is Dan there?"

"No," she said.

"I hate to sell it. I can hang onto it for awhile if you want."

"I'll pick it up," she said. "It was his father's."

"Yeah, I know," he said, sounding relieved. "I guess he's not doing too good now, right? I mean, it probably won't be long."

"Won't be long until what?" she asked sharply.

"Sorry," he said. "Sorry. But my uncle died of lung cancer, and it just don't take long. I know how you feel. I know how stingy the docs

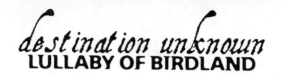

can be with the morphine too." His laugh was short and sharp. "You know—don't want to turn anyone into an addict. I don't blame him for wanting a little extra now at the end. He's a good guy, Sarah. I'm going to miss him."

He hung up.

She felt like she'd been punched in the stomach.

Why hadn't he told her? She hugged her knees to her chest, tightly, gasping for breath even though she couldn't cry. She wanted to, desperately.

But she had never been so angry in her life.

θ θ θ

Michael knocked on her door at three in the afternoon. Sleet had been falling all day. He was dripping wet.

"What are *you* doing here?" she asked.

He had a leather bag flung over his shoulder. "Can I come in?" he asked.

He set the bag down and hung up his coat.

"Well?" she said. "I am not in a good mood."

She was amazed when he seemed unfazed. Dan would be sulking in the corner by now. This guy just smiled slightly. "That I can see. But I wanted to talk to you about your paper."

"I think you just want to get into bed with me."

"That's not a bad idea," he said. "Maybe we should do that first."

"Oh, be quiet," she said. "I'm pretty rattled about Dan, is all. Apparently he has lung cancer, and he's out there somewhere, and it's cold and rainy and he didn't even tell me. You're all wet," she said.

"I'll survive," he said, and sat in the chair with the canvas bag. "What's this about Dan?"

She told him about the saxophone. "Well, who knows. It could be AIDS and he just told Lorenzo lung cancer. Who knows. But I'm sure he's terribly sick. The last thing I did was yell at him and call him a has-been. I should have known. I should have. I just blamed his appearance on the drugs. I'm a horrible person."

"He should have told you," said Michael, "Don't you think?" She didn't reply. "He should have," said Michael.

"Maybe he was meaning to. I think he bought me this charm as a going-away present." She heard her voice, a monotone, as the words spilled out. The tears which gathered in her eyes seemed automatic, not connected to anything. "He might have killed himself, somewhere. Who knows. I found his wallet in the bedroom. He left without any I.D. He's had two suicide attempts, anyway. Besides some other close calls that might have been, that is. You know, two genuine, real ones, with notes and all, and ambulances..."

He sat beside her on the couch and held her again.

"You really come in handy," she said after a minute, when she could breathe normally. "Thanks. Sorry. I feel better now." She went into the kitchen and washed off her face, came back. "Now what was this you were talking about?" She felt cleansed and calm.

He didn't say anything for a moment. "It's not important," he said. "Well, it is, but it doesn't seem like the right time to talk about this. You're upset."

"I've done all that I can," she said. "It might be a good idea to try and think about something else for a change."

Look," he said, "this is really kind of odd, this idea that I've had. I don't know..."

He pulled out the manuscript she'd given him. "You know," he said, "I'd only read about the first fifty pages the other night. It's very dense. Hard going. Hard *thinking*—yet extremely precise. And then," he said. He stopped.

"Something happened," he continued. "Inside. I wasn't sure—it all seemed so odd."

"What seemed so odd?" she asked. "What happened?"

"You've been doing this for quite some time, haven't you?"

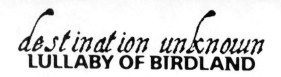

LULLABY OF BIRDLAND

"Doing what?"

"Writing philosophy."

"Oh. Yes. Of course. It's constant. It's just unpublishable, that's all. Apparently. It's so damned inaccessible, and yet the language, the exact, precise language is *it*. That exact grammar. Those exact words. I mean, I work them over and work them over until I get them right."

"Hmmm."

"But what is it? What are you trying to get at?"

"You're changing the world," he said.

"What?"

"Changing the world. I read this. The world changed. It's simple. I found the St. Christopher. Just little things, you know. Like concepts are concentrated into symbols, except they're not symbols, they're real things; events, objects. Didn't Breton call language the road to the absolute?"

"No," she said. "Surrealism was."

He looked a bit disconcerted, then continued. "Well, anyway, how much more absolute can you get than the interface between thought and matter?"

"You're crazy," she said.

He got up. "Yeah. How's your bird?"

The bird. Who arrived the same time as the charm.

Don't be ridiculous, Ms. Sarah Tyne.

"Oh, I almost forgot. What's this?" he asked, paging through the manuscript until he came to a page quite near the end.

The print ended a few lines from the top of the page. Below it, written in Dan's strange, spiky handwriting, was a poem.

Michael read it aloud.

309

woman
so strong
in the deep
house of autumn

I see you
from above.

you sit in an upstairs room, thinking.
a light shines from you.
you are foreign, and pure.

my eye circles like the falcon
but my brain is all my own.

at first I feel great pity looking on
for the greatness of your illusion

then the light glows brighter
and I see you as you really are:

woman of the light
free of time.

She looked out the window as Michael read. His voice had an odd, sweet timbre. "It's very old. Dan wrote that almost fifteen years ago. We used to have arguments about philosophy and music. He saw philosophy as so abstract. Not immediate, not like music. Not like drugs. But we got over that, I think. He wrote this poem for me about it. It was kind of like a capitulation. Or a truce. Or a little bunch of flowers. And he always had this flying fantasy." She smiled briefly, privately, her face turned away from him, remembering. So goddamned long ago.

"How did it get into this paper?"

She looked over Michael's shoulder. The poem was written in red ink, and she remembered the uncapped red pen Dan had left on the table.

"I guess he actually read this paper," she said. "He didn't read a lot of my stuff, but this was out on the table for a week. Maybe he was trying to tell me that he liked it. I'm surprised he got this far. It looks like he finished it."

"Why did he date the poem four days ago?"

She looked at the paper. He had, down at the bottom. The last day she had seen him.

"Mind if I have some tea?" he asked. "I'm very cold."

He looked it, pale, and the hand which held the paper shook.

"The bird, to answer your former question, is the same," she said. She felt cold just looking at Michael, as he shivered in his wet clothes.

"Why don't you take a bath? That will warm you up. There are some clean towels in a basket next to the tub. I'll get you a robe to wear."

She surprised herself by walking into the bathroom with the robe. What's the big deal, she thought, we're both grownups.

"Here," she said, then couldn't stop looking at him. She'd never paid much attention to men's bodies, not the way men seemed to pay attention to women. But he was so attractive, so perfectly put together, like a classical statue come to life.

"You're embarrassing me," he said.

"But you look so—*wonderful!* I mean, I had no idea."

He laughed, rippling the water in the bathtub. "Well. It's been a long time since anyone has called the way I look wonderful. Forever, I'm afraid. Thank you."

The bird startled them by flying up to the mirror frame.

"He's better, Sarah," said Michael. "Maybe you should let him go." He got out of the tub and grabbed a towel. "Want me to open the window?"

"No!" she said.

He wrapped the towel around himself, and they looked at each other a long time. Finally he said, "Why not?"

"It's still too cold out," she said. "I don't think he belongs here. Not at this time of year. He didn't migrate, or something, when he should have."

"It's supposed to warm up tonight," he said. "Maybe tomorrow."

The bird charm flashed into her mind. The brown bird looked at her and warbled a few sweet notes of song.

"Here's the robe," she said, and shut the door behind her.

This is really getting to you, she thought. Your husband is out in the cold somewhere probably dying and you're getting all excited about a strange man who says your ideas change things. Literally. He's nuttier than you are.

She was quite weary, and lay down on the couch for a moment. to think.

She must have fallen asleep, because when she woke it was dark and she could see him, sitting across from her on the chair, watching her by the light in the kitchen.

"I'm sorry I'm still here," he said.

"I'm not," she said, and reached for him.

θ θ θ

Suddenly, she woke. Michael was gone. Yes, he had been here, in bed with her. It took her a second to adjust.

She rose from the soft swath of blankets and sheets. A fan of light came from the half-opened bathroom door.

"Spike!" she yelled. "*Michael!* I *told* you not to leave the door open! Don't let Dan go!" She was sure he had the window open and was ready to heave the bird out of it.

She burst in the door as he flushed the toilet. The bird was still on the mirror frame. The window was still closed. Spike was nowhere to be seen. "I'm sorry," she said, after he looked at her a second. He seemed amused. "I thought you were letting him go."

He just looked at her as if he was expecting her to say more. So she did.

"I can't let him go," she said. "He's—" she stopped.

The bird looked down at them from the mirror frame.

"Winter's over, Sarah," said Michael. "I just woke up and it was like he was calling me." His face took on an expression of infinite kindness. "You *do* think he's Dan, don't you?" he asked, and the gentleness of his voice made her chest ache.

"It sounds silly, doesn't it?" she said, and sat on the white three-legged stool.

"No," said Michael. "Who knows? You may be right." With a quick motion he reached up and scooped the bird into his hand, opened it so the bird stood on his palm. "Look, Sarah," he said. "His wing is fine. He can fly now. What if he is Dan? What if Dan read your paper and it *changed* him, allowed him to be what he really wanted to be, in his sickness and pain. What was the shape of Dan's innermost desire?"

"I don't want him to be a bird," she said, and her voice was ragged. "I want him to be Dan. I want him to be my husband. I want him to be here. Did he think I wouldn't take care of him?"

"Is this the only strange thing that's happened in the last few days?"

"No," she admitted. "There was a little green book, then you came and wanted to publish a book. There was—"

"St. Christopher," he said. "And you came into my store."

"What does that have to do with it?"

"Not many people have read your book, Sarah, from what I gather," he said. "But I have. I never even dreamed of meeting you. But I fell in love with you. With your thoughts, anyway." He ignored her short derisive laugh and continued. "Your book helped me every spring to kind of—keep going. It really solidified my life. There's a great force of cohesion within you, some understanding of life, of thought, of consciousness. Something very fundamental and powerful. And you're able to actually put that into words. Can thoughts change life? Of course. Usually there's an intermediary. A blueprint, first. Then the work. The change takes place slowly. But what if you're hooked in? What if you're part of it? What if your brainwaves just synch in?"

"Are you finished?" she asked.

"You're angry."

"No. I'm afraid."

She stood, backed several feet away from Michael, held out her hand. "If you're Dan," she said, "Fly into my hand."

There wasn't room enough for it to soar. The traverse of a few feet was just a short, awkward flutter as the bird landed on her hand. Its claws grasped her fingers tightly.

"Receptive language capabilities," Michael said. "Very interesting."

"That didn't happen," she said.

"Of course not," he said. "That's quite clear."

She climbed up on the toilet. The window screeched as she opened it. The air which came in was warm and smelled of damp earth. She heard melting snow drip. She stretched her arm upward until her hand was outside. "Go," she whispered.

There was an instant's tight, scratchy grip. Then he was gone.

"Don't talk," she said to Michael.

"Did I say anything?" he asked.

She closed the door behind them and they went back to bed.

"What do *you* want?" Michael whispered as he held her. "What do you think the shape of your innermost desire would be?"

She fell asleep on that thought.

Her dream was a dream of flight. She watched herself, from a bird's dizzying height, as she soared. But she was often in a room—sometimes large, and sometimes small. Sometimes the ceiling was low, sometimes the ceiling was high, and sometimes over the door was an old-fashioned window with a metal rod connecting it to a lever down below. It was always full of children.

She flew outside, and the colors stunned her; the wind lifted her, and forests billowed below, and then endless plains which changed to rocky desert. She hunched to streamline herself as she flew.

But always she found herself back in the room, looking down on the heads of the children there. Occasionally one would look up, smile, nudge her neighbor, and point.

5:30, blinked the clock, when she suddenly opened her eyes.

She walked past the bathroom without opening the door.

She went out to the kitchen and switched on the small light, put the kettle on to boil. She took a long time fooling around with making her tea, because she was afraid of what she would find when she went out to the table, where she'd left the bracelet yesterday. She didn't know how to even begin to think about the ethics of wanting. She would live the rest of her life in the shadow of Dan's desire, no matter what had really happened to him, no matter if he'd changed into a bird or if they found his body in a little hospital five hundred miles away, or if he was never found, and it hurt. She knew, with a certainty she had never felt about anything before, that she would never see him again.

Stop avoiding it, she told herself. You let him out the window last night. It *was* him. He only came back to tell you good-bye. And everything, *everything*, is different today. The world is a very new thing.

In the dim light she saw it, tiny on her charm bracelet: another bird next to the first, on the oilcloth covering the old wooden table. This one was gold.

Had Michael put it there? What if he had? Even he was part of the new truth of the world, its manifestation and agent, like every object she saw now. She could join Dan. She could fly. Her grief and that old tie of theirs pulled with the unexpected force of water going over a falls. She didn't know the limits of the newness yet. Why not find them out?

She stood and stared out the window, sipped her tea, watched the morning light grow, and felt as if she stood on the threshold of her own unknown desires.

One step at a time, Sarah. You can't know everything at once.

Yes, but what should that first step be? What shape did she desire of matter, of time, of life?

What, for instance, was the shape of a phone call from a really good university, one where she could teach, learn, grow?

Then the words of Dan's poem came into her head.

Woman of the light. Free of time. His vision of her from so long ago. What thought was *really* leading to—a fountain of light, freedom, release.

Yes.

She yanked open the window, as high as it would go, her eyes on the tiny golden bird which glimmered in the first ray of sunlight in a week; the first light of spring.

"I don't think *you* need to have the window open, Sarah," said Michael from the doorway.

She turned. He looked disheveled, but rested. His face was calm, and as familiar as if she'd known him a million years.

No matter. She knew each stage of thought to take, as if she could see through the veil of existence and seize the essence of its truth, and the path Dan had taken.

The path she would take. She turned toward the window and rested her hand on the sill. She had to follow him. They had been together so long.

She could *feel* the white, pure wings forming inside her, her legs turning to the long, graceful sticks which were the legs of a crane. There was a rush in her ears like the rush of wind beneath wings, a radiance which burst from her heart like light. Already her hand was white, pure white, changing in the brilliant morning sunlight, thinning to wingtip. She had only to let go, to surrender. It would be easy.

But she was able to pause, as if poised on the edge of a cliff. That was *Dan's* dream for her, after all. Maybe hers was different.

She closed her eyes tightly, turned from the light, and whirled into the enormous absence of Dan, the absence of all light, all center, for what seemed a black infinity. Then she was lifted by sure hands.

She was riding on someone's back. His face was hidden from her, but she knew who it was. The river raged around them, deafening, covering her legs, his shoulders, as he slipped, recovered himself—

Then they were across.

"Why not?" she asked, turning. "Why the hell shouldn't I leave the window open?"

"Because," he said. "That's not the way *you* fly."

She was astounded. How could he know her so well? How could he have become so dear to her so quickly?

Sadness for Dan echoed through her body, but she silently accepted his choice, and let her anger go.

Then she turned and studied the newly blue sky, clear and innocent as a baby's eyes.

It looked so open, so inviting, but there were many kinds of skies she could explore.

Many.

She smiled, and realized that she still gripped the chipped white sill quite tightly. Perhaps she was not as ready as Dan to go.

She left the window open, pulled up a chair, and sat down at the table. Warm sunlight brushed her bare arms. She took a deep breath and looked at Michael.

"So you say you can publish my book?"

FEATURES STORIES BY

BRIAN W. ALDISS

STORM CONSTANTINE

ED GORMAN

URSULA K. LE GUIN

MICHAEL MOORCOCK

EDITED BY

PETER CROWTHER

Also Edited by Peter Crowther
BLUE MOTEL

Check into the Blue Motel for a sleepless night you won't forget.

Eighteen intriguing tales of mysticism and murder, hauntings and hor-rors, hypnotize and chill the reader.

Meet some bizarre guests with even more bizarre stories: a medieval, shape-shifting pope, futuristic light beings, and a hitman, to name a few. Travel through landscapes vaguely familiar, yet vividly unsettling. This captivating and thought-provoking anthology will lead you into the darkest corners of the night. And you never know what you might bump in to...

Horror
Paperback anthology
ISBN 1-56504-922-5
Stock#: 13301
Retail Price $5.99 US/$7.99 CAN

For easy ordering call 1-800-454-WOLF.
Visa/Mastercard/Discover accepted

DANTE'S DISCIPLES

An original anthology of contemporary tales which travel beyond our present scope of existence — and straight into Hell.

Dante's Disciples travels with lost souls through demonic gateways to the Netherworld.

This original anthology contains stories by best-selling authors Harlan Ellison, Storm Constantine, Brian Lumley, Michael Bishop, Gene Wolfe, Ian McDonald, Douglas Clegg, James Lovegrove, Brian Aldiss and many others!
Edited by Peter Crowther
and Edward E. Kramer

Horror
Trade Paperback
ISBN 1-56504-907-1
WW 13007
Retail Price $14.99 US/$20.99 CAN

For easy ordering call
1-800-454-WOLF.
Visa/Mastercard and
Discover accepted